I0761404

FROM THE IMAGINATION OF

TOM DELONGE

TIME RIDER

WITH *NEW YORK TIMES* BESTSELLING AUTHOR

A.J. HARTLEY

FROM THE IMAGINATION OF

TOM DELONGE

TIME RIDER

WITH *NEW YORK TIMES* BESTSELLING AUTHOR

A.J. HARTLEY

Based on the *Sinister Forces Trilogy* by Peter Levenda

To The Stars Media Inc.
1150 Garden View Road, Box #230393, Encinitas, CA 92024
ToTheStars.Media

To The Stars® is a trademark of *To The Stars, Inc.*

Cover Design by Joe Brisbois
Cover Art by Jay Beard

Interior Art by Dan Milligan, Gavin O'Donnell, and Jay Beard
Art Direction by Joe Brisbois

Book Design by Lamp Post
Managing Editor: Kari DeLonge

Manufactured in the United States of America

978-1-943272-49-5 (Hardcover)
978-1-943272-50-1 (eBook)
978-1-943272-51-8 (Hardcover Limited Edition)

Distributed worldwide by Simon & Schuster

DEDICATION

To my family, and to all who refuse to accept the inevitability of what will, one day, be called history.

ACKNOWLEDGMENTS

Thanks to Peter Levenda, Lou Aronica, Candace Shaffer, Joe Brisbois, David Wilk, Kari DeLonge, Brett Burner, and the whole To The Stars team, and—to the perfect creative partner—Tom DeLonge.

TIME RIDER

CHAPTER ONE

Dallas, Texas. November 19, 1963

The name on the identity card he had been issued was Abraham Washington. It had quickly become clear to him that that had been a mistake. He'd had to show it twice so far, once at a traffic stop at his last way point when he had misunderstood a road sign and then again here when he had checked in to the Adolphus Hotel, and both the cop and the hotel clerk had made jokes about past presidents which he didn't understand. The cop had called him "Mister Washington," but when the clerk introduced him to one of his colleagues so she could share in his amusement, he had called him "Honest Abe." The colleague—a younger woman who the receptionist watched with an almost predatory appetite clearly visible beneath his casual manner—said something about how he must have had real patriotic parents.

He had done his best to smile and say something noncommittal but had privately resolved to choose a less conspicuous name for daily interaction. Given his mission, it wasn't good to stand out. It was annoying and, if he was honest, worrying. If even his name marked him out as different, odd in some way, what else had his handlers gotten wrong? Even prior to this stage of his incursion he had been conscious of the thinness of the preparatory file, of its lack of detail and tendency to lump distinct periods and places together, but he had still been unprepared for just how alien this place felt. The previous decade hadn't been anything this bad, though that probably had as much to do with the sparsely populated environment as it did the period. Still, making that short detour to pick up a selection of newspapers prior to reaching his final destination had, he decided, been a good decision.

He spread them on the table of the corner booth where he was sitting now and returned to his study. The newspapers were called *The New York Times*, but much of their coverage seemed to be national and international, so "Abe" didn't think that would matter too much. The pages were broad and thin, all the print but the headlines small and cramped so he had to hold them close to read. That was all right though. It meant he either had his head down or had the excuse of holding the paper in front of his face. He didn't like the way people stared at him.

Another miscalculation by his handlers.

Compared to the locals, "Abraham Washington" was short and pale. His eyes were pale too, a blue so milky it was almost white. He considered buying some of the darkened glasses he had seen some locals wearing. He was less sure of what to do about his hairless head. He had been given a wig to make him less conspicuous, and it had seemed satisfactory to him when he had tried it before departure, but here it seemed more likely to attract attention. Compared to the people around him his hair seemed coarse, artificial.

Perhaps he could purchase a hat, though he would have to stow it when he wore his motorcycle helmet. He frowned at the thought. The bike, too, was just wrong enough to draw stares. He had parked it in the hotel garage, draped in a ragged tarpaulin he had found covering pallets of building supplies in a neighboring alley, but he doubted it would go unnoticed for long.

In his previous incursions he had been able to operate in isolated areas populated by few locals. Being in the center of a city surrounded by hundreds of thousands of them and in plain sight, was an entirely different experience.

Nothing felt safe. The barbarism of the place came as no surprise, but he had assumed that he would feel mere disdain for the people, volatile and mentally clumsy as they were. And he did. His pale skin crawled at the sight of the venal hotel clerk as he stared at his female coworker, his animal urges barely even disguised by the veneer of his professionalism. He was little more than an ape. Washington had seen others singing and dancing in the street the night he had arrived, drunk—he assumed—on alcohol, but also on something else, a stinking, bestial decadence in which he barely recognized his own species. He had expected as much. It was, in a roundabout way, why he was here. What he hadn't predicted was the unnerving sense of being somehow at their mercy, the feeling that—despite his superior intellect, enlightenment, and considerable skills at self-defense—if he made a mistake, he might quickly lose control of the situation in ways putting himself in real danger. It was a curious sensation. He was used to being one of the elite, untouchable, and utterly self-assured, but here he felt badly out of place, and all the things that had always signaled his safety, his power, now seemed to do the opposite. What had marked him as a figure of influence who you challenged at your considerable peril, now made him a target of beings which, though clearly inferior, didn't understand that they were.

Staying unobtrusive and reading the environment—distasteful though it was—was essential. Washington considered one of the newspaper headlines.

SAIGON'S CONTROL IN TWO
PROVINCES PERILED BY REDS

Saigon was, apparently, a place. What color had to do with it was not immediately apparent, but another headline (RED CHINA PLEDGES TO BACK CAMBODIA) suggested some kind of affiliation, possibly racial. Washington considered this, revising his instinct when he read another piece about Soviet diplomats being beaten in Gambia. It seemed "red" was some kind of political marker. He wasn't sure where Gambia was and felt another prickle of irritation which made him look up and take in the hotel bar. He found himself assessing the possibility of imminent assault. There were just so many of those awful people around.

He had observed a man and a woman at the next booth when he came in, each perhaps in their mid-twenties and wearing what he took to be business attire. He had an unpleasant mustache and wore spectacles. She had long, dark hair. They seemed entirely caught up in each other and were talking animatedly. No threat there. The rest were similarly all white, mostly men, some in suits and ties, some in shirt sleeves. A woman in a red dress, her hair carefully arranged and wearing some kind of facial cosmetic, was the center of a group of what Washington took from their attire to be businessmen at a table in the middle of the room, but there was another group of men at the bar eyeing her overtly. If there was a threat, it was them.

They looked rougher than the others. Two who wore their hair slicked back could not have been more than twenty, but others in the group were older, and the oldest was a barrel-chested man whose severe crew cut was silver with age. They were drinking beer from bottles and their laughter was loud and raucous.

Degenerates, Washington thought.

He found himself longing for those isolated places in the woods and the desert he had visited before, where he had been able to deal with a few individuals and keep the rest of the populace far off. Being in the city was like stepping on an ant hill. The loathsome things were everywhere.

"Get you a drink, sir?"

Washington realized too late that his looking around had inadvertently attracted the attention of the young woman he had met briefly when he checked in. She was blond haired and pink faced and wore an apron over her uniform as well as a professional smile. He hunted for the word in his head and came up with "waitress": a kind of servant. Her eyes slid to his artificial hair and away again. He wondered briefly why she thought he might want a drink rather than, say, food, or another newspaper, but decided not to ask.

"No," he said, remembering at the last moment to mute his natural hauteur. "I am not thirsty."

The female hesitated, as if he was in violation of some local ordinance by not drinking.

"You from out of town?" she asked.

"Why do you ask?"

"Just curious," she said. "You don't seem local somehow. I heard you speak when you checked in. You British or something?"

"No," he replied, his irritation mounting. It had not occurred to him—or, apparently, his handlers—that the way he spoke would further underscore the extent to which he didn't belong. Where he came from, everyone in his class sounded the same.

"OK," she said, refusing to take the hint. "So, where you from?"

He gave an expansive sweep of his gaze which took in both her and the hotel bar and said shortly, "Somewhere better."

Her smile stalled, shrunk, and froze as if something inside her had switched off.

"OK," she said, frosty now. "Only you can't sit here unless you are going to eat or drink something. House rules."

So there *was* a local ordinance, albeit an absurd one.

"Then bring me something," he snapped.

"Such as? Beer, coffee . . . ?"

"Since I will not be consuming it, I don't care," he said. "Just fetch whatever satisfies your ludicrous regulation and leave me to my reading."

The woman's mouth got thin, and her eyes moved to the tabletop where they lingered on the newspapers.

"New Yorker, huh?" she remarked, turning on her heel. "Figures."

Only when she had left did Washington realize with a surge of relief that the newspaper on the top contained little to arouse the waitress's suspicion. He had not anticipated her invasion of his privacy and would need to be more careful. If she had seen the paper below it, the one with the history-making headline, he would have found himself in serious trouble. He felt for the weapon in his coat pocket, scanning the bar's occupants and calculating how many times he would have to reload to ensure there were no survivors.

Satisfied that he had enough ammunition, he returned to the newspaper, meticulously adjusting the front page a fraction of an inch to read a column entitled AIR FORCE IS GIVEN WIDER SPACE ROLE IN PENTAGON SHIFT and then a related piece called SENATE APPROVES HOUSE SPACE CUTS. Those complete, he moved onto the bafflingly titled US COURT DISBARS HOFFA ATTORNEY which turned out to be a legal proceeding involving someone described as the "teamster union president." More minor local politics which was, like so much of what the newspaper presented with such self-important earnestness, beneath his interest. He turned the page. WRECKAGE OF U-2 PLANE FOUND IN GULF OF MEXICO. Several of the stories referred to people in the context of their familial relations: brothers, sisters, fathers, mothers, grandparents, sons and daughters. It was strange and faintly distasteful.

"Beer," said the waitress, setting down a bottle and a glass. She had shelved her welcoming smile but still hesitated, expectant of a response.

"And?" said Washington.

"I guess, nothing," she snapped, affronted, and stalked away.

Washington turned back to the paper. There was a story about the stock market barring two brokerage firms, whatever they were, and one about a failed investment by Las Vegas gamblers. He sighed. Just another few days and he could see the completion of the mission and go home, could shower off this entire era in the elegant, regulated peace of his own home, and never think of it again.

The Design lives on, he thought, smiling faintly to himself. *Praise to the Design.*

"So, who's the Yankee weirdo?"

It was one of the slick-haired men from the bar who had sauntered over unnoticed. Washington folded the papers over and gave him a level look, his lip curling, but he said nothing.

"Heard you were impolite to Rosie there," said the young man, nodding toward the waitress. He was wearing a short-waisted leather jacket covered in straps and buckles which he seemed to think made him tough looking. "We don't take kindly to that round here."

"What you got on your head, boy?" called the other young man. "Looks like some kind of daggum nest!"

Two of the others hooted with laughter and clinked their bottles. Still Washington said nothing, but his hand slipped silently to the handgun in his coat.

"See, this is our place," said the young man, shoving the newspaper aside with performative contempt. "What might you be doing here?"

Washington studied the man's sunburned face, smelled the greasy stuff in his hair, and his loathing and contempt for these people and their world spiked. His grip tightened on the butt of the automatic. Though he knew it would endanger his mission, a part of him wanted the excuse to shoot the man and his friends and walk out into the Texas night without a care in the world.

"So?" said the older man with an authority that silenced the laughter around him. "The boy asked you a question." He got off his stool slowly and took a swaggering stride to the booth where Washington sat. "You here to cheer on your clan-hating Catholic president?"

Washington didn't know what that meant, and simply stared back, smiling to himself as if watching from miles away. Six of them. He could handle six.

"Now folks," said the mustached man in the next booth, the one talking to the dark-haired woman, "no need for this to get ugly." He turned to Washington, his eyes heavy with meaning and his voice low. "You might want to move on out, friend."

Funnily enough, it was that last word that got the better of Washington.

"I am not your friend," he said.

The man with the mustache looked affronted but caught himself and shrugged as his female companion put a steadying hand on his arm.

"Hey," he remarked. "I was just trying to help you out."

"Do not trouble yourself," said Washington dryly. "I need no help from the likes of you. Thanks to the Originator, I need nothing from any of you."

"Why's that, boy?" said the older man, completing his slow walk over from the bar. "You think you're too good for the likes of us?"

Washington's smile finally blossomed.

"I would have thought that was self-evident," he said.

He watched their stupid faces as they processed the insult, and in the same instant he realized what the man had said; not "clan" but "Klan." That changed things a little. Depressing though it was, these people were his allies, whether they knew it or not. He cocked his head slightly, wondering how to walk the situation back, but it was too late.

The younger man was already in mid-swing, a great curling blow which he wound up like a clock and hurled like a boulder. Washington rolled out of his booth as he dodged the punch with an easy dexterity, then rose in an instant, his gun unveiled and whipping across the man's face. Allies or not, he despised them all. The boy went down hard, but the bigger man with steel gray hair dove at him, his arms spread, and fingers splayed. He hit Washington hard, pinning him against the table edge and thrusting the pistol wildly back as, behind him, the brute's compatriots came surging toward them, bellowing like bulls. The steel-haired man punched him with a fist like the head of a mallet, but Washington snapped his head back in perfect time, taking the worst of the force out of the blow.

Washington was stronger than he looked, and his resistance clearly surprised his assailant, whose eyes went wide with shock, then fear, as he felt the muzzle of the gun being forced back toward him. The older man fought back, but he was clumsy and unimaginative. Washington butted him sharply in the face, losing the wig in the process, and grinned as the man's nose snapped, blood flecks spraying in all directions. Washington shook himself free as his assailant backed off head down, his hands flying to his shattered nose, but by then the others were piling on.

Someone hurled a bottle from close range, and it caught Washington above the right eye. It didn't break, but the impact threw his head back. The momentary loss of focus cost him. A punch—he wasn't sure where it came from—caught him squarely on the cheek, and his knees buckled. Rage replaced the contempt he had been feeling. Outrage.

How dare they? These debased baboons!

He pulled the automatic up, not caring which of them he killed first, but he was badly outnumbered and a kick caught him in the gut, doubling him up and driving the air from his body. His gun hand slackened, and then someone was seizing his wrist and prying the weapon from his grasp. The moment of weakness was maddening. He was alert enough to know the pistol was gone, and quick enough to seize the beer glass from the table in its place and bring it sweeping through the air, catching the nearest of them across the face. The glass exploded but he had released it a fraction before the impact and his hand came out unscathed. His victim cried out in pain and horror as the sharp-edged fragments opened him up, but now Washington had the beer bottle and was coming to finish the job.

A man in a check shirt charged him, a bar stool raised over his head, but Washington leaned onto his right foot and lashed his left up high, catching the man under the chin with a scything kick that crumpled him on the spot. As the stool fell, the sixth leaped on him from behind, but Washington jabbed his elbow back with precise and ruthless force, striking him on the left temple. The man staggered back, dazed, and Washington turned into him, twisting his arm precisely so that it broke at the elbow. He shrieked at the jolt of pain, and Washington laid him out with a clean upper cut to the jaw.

Too easy, he thought, admiring the groaning, fearful carnage. There was a bustle behind the bar as the hotel staff scrambled to get help. Other patrons were bolting for the doors. The couple at the next booth were staring in stunned terror.

He heard the deafening crack of the pistol before he knew he was hit. For a moment he was simply stunned, less by the concussive effect of the gun blast than he was by the staggering shock of being bested by these degenerates. The anger flared before the pain, before he felt the hot wetness dripping from him, before the room spun and sent him sprawling. He turned to see the young man with the slick hair and leather jacket lying prone at his feet, the pistol still aimed and smoking. The dark-haired woman in the next booth had a hand frozen over her gaping mouth.

Her companion was using his body to shield her from the horror of what was happening, but she was staring over his shoulder, aghast.

He thought of his mission, the newspaper headlines. Were they already changing?

Apes, Washington thought, his vision swimming as he rolled over and the world turned dark. *Baboons* . . .

It was chaos in the Adolphus bar. Customers stampeded. The wounded drinkers who had begun the fight struggled to their feet and tried to get out before the police arrived, but the bartender had taken the pistol from the young man who had pulled the trigger and forced him into a chair. The killer—for the strange, pale man in the wig who had so nearly beaten them all was clearly dead—just stared around him, as if unsure how he had gotten there. His companions had abandoned him to a man as soon as they realized what had happened. Moments before, the man, whose name was Davy, had been all surly confidence and devil-may-care attitude; now he looked too young to be in a bar at all. Less than two minutes earlier he had been discussing the Cowboys' victory over the Philadelphia Eagles the previous Sunday, and privately planning when he could next see Cindy, who he thought might soon be his girl, and in two more minutes he would be arrested and looking at a lifetime behind bars, if he didn't get the chair. When the cops demanded why he had killed the stranger he would fumble, mutter that he just "got all riled up" because the other man "was so rude."

But that was all to come. Right now there was only the unnatural stillness of the Adolphus bar, the eyes of the corpse still open and staring sightlessly as the blood pool beneath him spread and thickened. The bartender stood a couple of yards away, the gun pointed idly, his face drained and his eyes somehow sad.

"I didn't mean to do it," said Davy vaguely, but the bartender just nodded with mute sympathy. In the corner, Rosie the waitress was crying showily, and the receptionist was taking the opportunity to comfort her. Neither admitted that if she had not complained about the stranger to the drunks at the bar, he would still be alive.

All the other customers were gone now, but the couple from the next booth had agreed to stay and share their testimony as witnesses when the cops arrived.

"We're reporters," said the man, whose name was Jimmy Spear. "So we have an eye for detail."

As soon as he had said it, he looked embarrassed by the remark. Again the bartender just nodded. Tragedy and drama did weird things to people. The female journalist had perched on the edge of the table and was gazing blankly at the newspapers the stranger had been reading.

Her face tightened as she made sense of what she was seeing.

"Jimmy," she said. Her tone was vague, dreamy. "Take a look at this."

Her companion gave her a bewildered look which sharpened into irritation when he saw what had caught her attention.

"News?" he said, exasperated. "Now, Sandra?"

"The date!" she said, confused but intent. "Look at the date."

"We just watched a man die," exclaimed Spear.

"Look!" she insisted before he could continue.

And then she slid the top newspaper aside to consider the one beneath it, the one Washington had been at pains to hide, and her face fell. Before she had even checked the date, she took in the headline, and she actually staggered as if caught by some invisible punch from the fight which had ended moments before.

"No," she gasped, unable to lift her gaze from the page. "This can't be. It just can't be."

CHAPTER TWO

It was 2157, and Bowie was late.

He hunched his shoulders as he moved through the throng. He was a head taller and two shades darker than 90 percent of the Alphas, so even though he lived like them, dressed like them, talked like them, he still stood out in all the wrong ways. They were pale, mostly hairless, effete people, slim and elegant as herons, their muscles kept toned but unobtrusive as if drawing attention to their bodies would be in poor taste.

By comparison Bowie was a hulking brute of a man, a throwback to less enlightened times, a man built on some outmoded and outsized scale who shone not for his intellect, his capacity for nuanced reasoning and cool, level-headed decision-making, but for the constant, groaning presence of bone, sinew, and muscle. He felt the Alphas' eyes on him everywhere he went, noted their momentary hesitation as they saw him coming, the way they suddenly remembered something that made them turn quickly aside, the flash of something in their eyes:

not fear—they were too secure in themselves for that. Distaste.

And those were the polite ones.

He was bigger, stronger than they were, but had learned as a child that if a few of them got him alone, his bulk alone wouldn't save him. They didn't need a reason, but if they wanted one, they were easy to find. His very presence, they said, was a threat to civilized society, and that enabled all manner of preventive retribution. As a boy in the orphanage, there had been times—despite his brother's assurances to the contrary—when living into adulthood had seemed improbable, and he carried the scars to prove it. By the time he was ten he had had more broken bones than whole Alpha families over several generations. He had been easy meat in those days. But as he got bigger, as his very presence communicated less outcast to be bullied and more of a looming threat, the violence had actually worsened. The security patrols were the worst since they saw his very existence as a crime, albeit one committed long ago, a crime which trailed others after it, even if he hadn't committed them yet.

And he didn't intend to. Miserable though aspects of his life had been, he lived in comfort now in the palatial Cloud City District which had once been the vast grain fields of what had been called (in the tribal tongue adopted from ancient times) Ohio. Back in those barbaric days the major population centers of the continent had largely clung to the coasts, but that was before the Awakening, before the Necessary Rise of the Design to save a decaying world, and before the Great Conflagration that had threatened to destroy it all. And now he was part of that Design, despite his birth, despite his childhood in the orphanages and work camps with his brother. He had risen above all hardship to a place, if not of respect, then of safety for himself and value to the society he served, and he was well paid for his efforts.

It was a monumental achievement, hard won on the battlefield over a decade before, and grudgingly acknowledged to this day, even as the fog of the war blew away.

But now it was 2157, and Bowie was late. He consulted his wristwatch and the action of raising his hand brought the glowing digits to life. He frowned and picked up the pace, though he knew that moving faster would only attract more attention. He had already had to show his ID twice since leaving home. Of the thousands permitted to be in this sector, only a handful were Betas like him, men and women who handled the minimal but necessary transition points between the residential districts and the Wastes. That was where the Gammas lived. Most of the Alphas around here had never seen them in the flesh—the Gammas or the Wastes—and they hoped to keep it that way. To an Alpha, all Gammas were degenerates. Some were recalcitrant. A few were dangerous.

One of them was Bowie's brother, but he couldn't think about him right now.

Like the other Betas in this sector, Bowie had dealings with both groups, serving as liaison and messenger between the intelligence sector (Alphas) and the labor depots (Gammas). Someone had to do it, and though it was lowly work—resented by the Gammas and disdained by the Alphas—and he was always one false step or inappropriate word away from dismissal, he was paid well for it. Humble though it was, it gave Bowie a function, a place in the larger world, and when he was reclining in his sleek and elegant sky mansion in Cloud City, looking down from the vast height over clean white stone and polished glass to the world beneath, he was more than glad of it. He was proud.

That feeling was harder to hold onto at street level, harder still when sent out to handle some issue with the endlessly squabbling and chaotic Gammas, or when sent to investigate an act of sabotage or terrorism. The Gammas out there didn't like him, because even though he himself wasn't an Alpha he still worked for them, and he carried the threat of their violence with him. It was another reason people of all classes gave him a wide berth.

He was all right with that. After his hardscrabble childhood on the margins of society with the other illicitly generated children, and his combat service in the war, Bowie had grown comfortable with solitude. He had few friends, none close, and he spent his off hours alone with his camera, shooting images of the city and the Wastes beyond it, or editing the images on his computer tablet, pushing color saturation and contrast until he had vast, stark images of his world. A few of them he had blown up and framed, but most he kept to himself, biometrically protected on a storage drive only he ever looked at. None of his pictures ever contained people.

In the evenings he watched the news feed and played soothing, ambient music consisting of evenly spaced, synthesized tones repeating in an endless loop. His daily sustenance allowance—almost flavorless but elegantly shaped gelatinous protein blocks infused with vitamins and minerals—arrived with pristine white linen napkins and chilled, slightly sparkling water. It was laid out for him by a Beta servant he never spoke to and barely ever saw, and he consumed it in a stuff-backed chair with the slow purpose of ritual. If it wasn't for his size, his hair, and the brownness of his skin, his posture and habits would mark him as an Alpha.

He took pride in that. He had attained what his world considered close to impossible: elevation beyond his biological class.

Today was Patriot Day—what had been called Thursday before the Awakening—and that normally meant that he took the shuttle to Westport to collect the data from the solar energy plants and check the security perimeter. Once, long ago, much of this would have been done by networked computers transmitting radiotronically via dedicated servers, but that had also changed since the Awakening. All such technology was now formally sequestered, all connections—cable and radio wave—severed, all units preserved in isolation to prevent the sharing of information. Now, people—Bowie, in this case—had to physically go to the site in question, detach the data chips and load them into a handheld unit which he would then take back to the control office for examination. Between the energy plants and the Westport shuttle station, he would have to travel some forty miles through arid desert lined by the great glass hydroponic farms where most of the Gammas worked, and for the last few miles he would pass through one of the desolate battlefields left over from before the Awakening. There was no dedicated rail line, so he would have to drive a personal vehicle along one of the ancient highways which predated even the war, maneuvering a utility cruiser through the rock and sand and blasted, rusting hulks of antique battle tech. While the Design was safer than at any point in Earth's history, its resources weren't infinite and there were occasional attacks by terrorist separatists and other Gamma anti-socials. Mostly they happened out here, in the near wilderness beyond the city.

Even so, and though Bowie would never admit it to anyone, he liked the journey, the isolation, the sense of being disconnected from the world in which he worked, alone under the vast, relentless sky, feeling the sun make his brown skin glow with warmth when he turned off the reflector shades. His pleasure at the sensation embarrassed him a little, as did the hint of disappointment he felt when he returned to the concrete and chrome of civilization, but alone in the cab of his cruiser, smelling the arid air and the metallic tang of the old-world tech, he felt a rare contentment that elevated the mundane nature of his work. From time to time, he took his camera and tried to capture it all, the emptiness, the broad, blank sky, the baking desert and the rusted remnants of the war.

He remembered the last time he had been out this way, and—against his better judgment—he found himself thinking of his brother again. That day he had been ahead of schedule and had taken his vehicle a few miles away from his designated route to visit the Paradise Valley work camp, home to some four hundred Gammas. It would appear on his daily report sheet as a drop-in inspection. He had taken his docupad and showed his badge to the gate security.

"I need to see whoever represents Sector Three," he said. "Got to have some data clarified."

The guards—Betas like himself, but lower in the grand chain of command—didn't question the order, rolling back the sliding gate with its coils of razor wire, and motioning him through to the visitation room, their weapons holstered. They crossed the last open-air section of the yard, hugging the shade cast by the slow slung prefabricated huts, walking along the deep drainage ditches dug for when the area got its rare but devastating storms and the whole area ran with clay-colored water for days. Bowie slowed suddenly, his head tipped up, mind a thousand miles away.

"What's that smell?" he asked.

The guards rolled their eyes.

"Gamma food," said the taller of the two contemptuously with an amused shake of his head. "No idea where they find their spices and such. Noxious stuff."

It seemed like he was talking about more than flavor.

"Yes," said Bowie, "but what is it?"

The guards exchanged confused looks.

"Gamma food," shrugged the shorter, his forehead wrinkling with confusion.

"Right," said Bowie.

They brought him the best root tea the place could manage, and he made a point of not drinking it. Five minutes after that they brought the sector rep, a tall, dark-skinned Gamma made darker by the sun. His hair was long, black and pulled into a ragged ponytail bun with an ancient leather thong. His face was hard, not so much tanned and windblown as blasted by the elements. He stood to attention on the other side of the table where Bowie sat. The guards lingered, one of them with his energy weapon unslung and ready. Bowie gave them a look which was almost as contemptuous as the one with which he had appraised the Gamma and nodded for them to leave.

He waited for them to go and the door to latch behind them before softening his haughty stare.

"Hello Sefton," he said.

It had been a month since he had seen his brother. Sefton's mouth wrinkled into a half smile.

"Bowie," he said. They knew they couldn't show any familiarity physically. The room wasn't wired for sound, but windows ran along all sides. Not that Betas were given to shows of physical familiarity. "How's life in your great glass city?"

Bowie heard the pointed pronoun but ignored it. Their lives had diverged long ago. So had their views.

"Great," he said.

"Yeah?" his brother replied dryly. "Well, ain't that grand."

"Why do you speak like that?" Bowie replied, irritated. "Nobody talks like that."

"No one you know, maybe."

"No one anywhere," Bowie replied. Sefton just shrugged and grinned, and Bowie glanced away, unsure how to respond.

"Seriously though," said Sefton. "You doing all right?"

Bowie took a breath and nodded.

"Mostly," he said. "You know how it is."

"Not really. Not out here. Most of the guys out here would kill to live like you do."

"Not you," said Bowie quickly.

Sefton smiled and it was his turn to look away.

"Not me," he agreed.

"You never wish for something more than this?" Bowie asked, glancing beyond the windows of the visitor room to the arid land and the primitive tents of the labor camp beyond.

Sefton shook his head.

"I could be bounded in a nutshell," he replied, "and count myself a king of infinite space."

"What's that? A quote?"

"Something Mrs. Dunn used to say. You remember Mrs. Dunn?"

Bowie frowned as the recollection came back to him across miles of space and time. A plump, pale woman in severe spectacles sitting in a rocking chair under high windows, a book in her lap and kids at her feet.

"I think so," he said vaguely, wary of the memory. "She used to read to us or something when we lived on Park Street."

"That's right, she did," said Sefton, smiling so broadly that his eyes sparkled. "Animal stories and adventures from those old books with the red covers."

"I don't remember that line though."

"She said it to me when I asked if she liked working at the orphanage. Stuck in my head."

"I don't remember," said Bowie, stiffer this time. He was a couple of years younger than Sefton and recalled little from their early years, almost nothing until he was conscripted first as a message runner, then as a soldier. The war had wiped away so much, including most of his own childhood. Somehow the thought broke down his habitual irritation with his stubborn brother and made him honest.

"You asked about the city," he said. "Things are strange."

"Stranger than usual?" asked Sefton.

"Perhaps. There have been . . . discrepancies. Little things: trains not running on time. Secret meetings among staffers. Diversion of resources. News alerts about suspected terrorist activity."

"Sounds fairly normal," his brother replied. "Why are you telling me?"

The question was loaded, wary, as if he thought Bowie had been sent to interrogate him.

"I'm not," Bowie replied. "I mean, I am, but that's not why I came."

"All right," said Sefton, still hard, unblinking. "So why did you come, little brother?"

The phrase made Bowie wince. Alphas didn't have brothers, sisters, parents, or children. Betas didn't either. Even the officially designated Gammas were raised in isolation with no form of biological family.

Little brother.

From anyone else it would have been a bitter insult. It wasn't that in Sefton's mouth, but it was hard not to be embarrassed by it. Bowie looked down, remembered the windows, and looked up again, giving his brother a level stare.

"I suppose I just wanted to see you," he said. "I feel like I may not get much opportunity for a while." His brother's face wrinkled with doubt, but Bowie cut off the question, "No reason. Just a feeling." He hesitated, awkward then—as if to fill the silence—said, "These recent rumors of terrorism, sabotage . . ."

"Don't ask."

Bowie paused, then nodded.

"You think if we'd been raised in, you know," he said, embarrassed by the question, "the usual way, our lives would be different?"

"Well, we wouldn't know each other for one thing," said Sefton, "so that would be different. But no. We couldn't have been raised in, as you call it, *the usual way*—which, for the record, has only been usual for a few decades, which is nothing in the great stream of human history—"

"All right," said Bowie, cutting him off before the rant could get up to steam. "I was just wondering."

"Come on, man," said Sefton, using that old-fashioned drawling slang of his again. "Look at us. Nothing was going to change who we were allowed to be."

"I changed," said Bowie, defiance spiking. "I proved myself in battle and have been rewarded. I don't understand why you don't do the same. You could change these camps. Prove yourself not just to the men under you but to the elite. Your life could be so much better if you'd just—"

"What?" Sefton demanded, his eyes hard now. "Roll over? Play nice? Be a good little pet Gamma? Get the camp to start the day by singing the Anthem of the Design? So that I can live like you, an outcast in my own home, rich but despised, a tool of an oppressive regime that has banished its own people to squalor and destitution in service of some bogus notion of racial purity and—"

"All right," Bowie cut in again. "Forget I mentioned it."

"You ever hear of Stockholm syndrome?" asked Sefton.

"No," said Bowie, keen to leave now.

"Old name for what happens when the victim of abuse or kidnapping or something starts to think like their abuser."

"So?" said Bowie. "I don't see the relevance."

"You should."

Bowie made an exasperated gesture.

"I'm going to leave now," he said.

"I could be bounded in a nutshell," Sefton intoned again, holding up his index finger and touching it to his temple, "and count myself a king of infinite space."

"All right," Bowie said again. "Great. Good for you."

"It's who I am," said Sefton.

Bowie gave him a long look, then nodded slowly.

"You know they hate you, right?" Sefton added. "The Alphas. They'll never trust you. They pay you and they use you, but they still hate you as much as they hate me."

Bowie said nothing for a long moment, then managed a half smile and a gesture with both hands that said he didn't concede the point but wasn't going to argue any further.

"I've slipped a credit voucher under the tea glass," he said. "Wait till I leave before you take it."

"I don't need your money."

"And I don't need your resentment," said Bowie, "but here we are."

The two men considered each other for a moment, then Sefton gave a crooked smile and Bowie got up and headed for the door. He hesitated before opening it however and spoke without turning around.

"As I was coming in, there was a smell outside . . ." he said.

"Mol Taury's pig foot curry!" Sefton exclaimed. "Not as good as Mrs. Alsace used to make, but not bad. You remember Mrs. Alsace? Looked like a hundred-year-old vulture, but when she showed up with her little bags of spices and whatever she'd been able to get from the food dispenser, we all went nuts!"

He laughed with a delight Bowie hadn't heard from anyone in a very long time, including himself, and he knew without turning round what he would see in his brother's face, the unselfconscious joy, the way he would throw his head back when he laughed . . .

"Man," Sefton exclaimed, "that woman could cook. You remember Mrs. Alsace's old-world curries?"

Bowie stood where he was, his hand on the door, feeling the glow of the sun on the other side warm in the metal. He shook his head.

"No," he said. "Long time ago."

His brother stopped laughing abruptly and for a brief, silent moment, Bowie could feel his brother's eyes on his back.

"Guess so," said Sefton.

Bowie still didn't open the door. Confused feelings ran through him.

"Sefton," he said.

"What?"

Again Bowie hesitated, unsure of what to say, feeling his mind crowding with big, complicated, unspeakable things. "Stay safe," he concluded, and, without looking back, he finally opened the door and left the room.

He thought about that visit now, this Patriot Day a month later. He had been right about the little irregularities. They had intensified since. Twice he had gone out with his camera only to be turned away from public places by security guards who offered no explanation, and on one occasion he had lost an entire afternoon at the railway station waiting for trains that never came. It was unheard of. There was a new tension at the office, as if the people in charge knew something was coming and everyone else in the building was picking up their anxiety like it was some low wattage radio signal. There had been no public statements. No changes to curfew. No restricting movement in certain regions. No large scale deploying of security forces. But something was going on. Something no one wanted to talk about.

There had been power outages, transportation disruptions, fires and explosions at several factories and storage facilities. At one of them, a pair of guards had been killed. The official news system declared such events weather related, but they had been vague on details about the dead guards. Bowie wondered what wasn't being said, and whether his brother knew things that he didn't. The thought gnawed at him as if it were alive in his gut.

Bowie hadn't seen his brother since that day and wasn't sure why their last meeting had come back to him in such detail now. At the Courage Street hyperlink station, he moved to the end of the platform and waited, pointedly looking at no one, checking the display board as it ticked off the seconds until the train's arrival, then boarding the car marked with the amber warning sign reading "Betas." It was overly warm inside, the climate control just that little bit less efficient than in the front carriages, but there was no one else in there with him so he was able to stretch out. The seats were a little too small. He wondered if that was deliberate. There was, of course, no coach for Gammas.

Sefton would have something to say about that, he thought, but the wry amusement turned to anxiety again and he squeezed his eyes shut, as if opening them again would release him from a dream.

He rode the train all the way to the Bastion, and it arrived—as the trains almost always did—exactly when it was scheduled to, which meant that he was still late. Even so, being unfamiliar with the district, he moved a little slower as he rode the escalator up to street level and located the carrier tube to the vaulted hall of the Domestic Security building, a cavernous structure of white marble emblazoned with the symbol of the Design. The logo was an intersection of circles along a line, with a hook on one side, an emblem which had emerged from the ruins of the Great Conflagration when what had been their military flag had become the motif of victory and the society which came about as a result. The hooked line and circles probably meant something, or had once, but Bowie didn't know what. Still, its familiar authority comforted him.

The security building was a blank faced, imposing structure decorated with faceless, heroic figures in uniform, fists raised in victory or defiance. Bowie wasn't sure. Under the great translucent environmental canopy, the area glowed with a cool, white light. By the entrance was a single, eye-catching anomaly, a hulking but battered and ugly metal box on tracked wheels that seemed to have sprouted guns and antennae: a cybertank from the war, now both monument and trophy. There was a scorched gash down one side and a blackened puncture wound in the front, the mark of the shell or rocket which had knocked out the machine. It was a terrifying thing and served as a reminder of the world as it had almost been. Bowie had seen it before, but he felt the heavy menace of the thing—lifeless though it was—like dread.

And he felt a prickle of something else: a thrill, perhaps, of pride which finally pushed his brother from his mind. The cybertank was, after all, why he was here, as opposed to grunting and sweating under the solar collectors out in the desert. He took the elevator and passed through a series of checkpoints before being left in a kind of anteroom by a secretary who kept an eye on him as she waited for her desk display to buzz him in. At last, Bowie saw the discreet console light illuminate and heard the snap of the security lock on the steel paneled doors.

"The director will see you now," she said flatly, her eyes not bothering to meet his.

Bowie got to his feet and tried not to loom as she directed him inside and closed the doors behind him. A guard inside the door snapped to attention and took a step toward him.

The room was unnecessarily large, elegantly if spartanly furnished, and surrounded by tinted windows which gave breathtaking views of the government center buildings and the Victory Ridge railway bridge.

"Mr. Bowie," said Merrick, the Counterintelligence Director, waving the guard on the door back. "Have a seat."

"It's just Bowie," said Bowie, sitting. The chair was padded with black leather on a bare steel frame. Like everything else in the building, it had a simplicity to it that belied careful engineering. It was also slightly too small, and Bowie shifted uncomfortably.

The ghost of a smile flitted across Merrick's handsome, angular features. He was tall for an Alpha, but slender as a reed, his arms and legs sinewy and smooth as cable. His eyes were a watery blue but bright and tightly focused, and his pale, bald head looked sculpted from marble. His name tag was adorned with the circles and hooked line of the Design crest. He barely moved in place, hands resting motionless on the glass desktop in front of him, only his eyes and mouth acknowledging Bowie's presence. He did not stand or offer a hand to shake, but Bowie had expected no less.

"Your name came to me from my predecessor in this position," said Merrick, opening a cream-colored cardboard folder full of paper and what looked like an identity package, Bowie's picture printed in the top left corner. "I see you have been of some small use to us in the past."

"I try to do my part," said Bowie.

"Most commendable, I'm sure," said Merrick. "And you have perused the parameters of your task as outlined to you in the file you were given at your last meeting with my predecessor."

"Not that there was much to read, yes," said Bowie. He smiled slightly but Merrick did not return it.

"Protocols must be followed," he replied icily. "These are matters of significant consequence. If you do not feel able to adhere to the necessary procedures associated with mission information transfer—"

"It's fine," said Bowie quickly. "I apologize for my frivolous remark."

Merrick's pale eyes flicked over Bowie's face, as if processing the sincerity of the comment then, apparently satisfied, he said, "Let us proceed."

He closed the folder and sat back.

"You have been tasked to act on behalf of the state to disrupt a terrorist action aimed at the destabilization of our society," he said, "in return for which your other employment will be temporarily terminated and your account will be credited at five times your current rate of remuneration."

"It doesn't sound like much if I am to put my life on the line," said Bowie. He was fishing rather than throwing up a real objection. The Designed world made much of its entrepreneurial spirit. They would expect him to negotiate.

"You have a brother in Sector Three, do you not?" said Merrick.

Bowie stiffened, all his conflicted feelings about his brother rushing up again. He glanced at the guard on the door, wishing he wasn't there to witness this. In all his dealings with the Alphas, Sefton's existence had never been referred to. Bowie had always assumed they didn't know. In fact, he had assumed that he would lose his Beta class status the moment they found out.

"Leave us," said Merrick to the guard who saluted and turned on his heel. Bowie, fractionally relieved by his departure, thought the man gave him the briefest sidelong glance as he closed the door behind him, a look loaded with curiosity and disdain.

"His name is Sefton," Merrick continued blandly. "He is involved—albeit peripherally—with a dissident group of Gammas who have raised calls for laborers in their sector to unionize, contrary to law, even to strike, an act which is specifically marked as direct and substantive subversion of the state."

"I was not aware of his involvement in illegal activity," said Bowie.

Not exactly *aware of it*, he thought. He had suspected something along those lines but made it clear to Sefton that he didn't want to know.

"But he is your brother?" said Merrick.

Bowie swallowed. It would be pointless to deny something they clearly already knew.

"He is."

Merrick looked at him, head cocked slightly to one side as if considering the model of some strange long-dead beast in a museum.

"A man with a sibling," he mused in mock wonder. "And working for the Design!"

"I am a loyal citizen," Bowie tried. "My military record and my work since then have surely demonstrated that—"

"Yes, yes," said Merrick with another casual wave of his elegant hand. "No doubt. But you should know that security forces are poised to arrest the dissidents for subversion of the state. I don't need to tell you what fate awaits them if they are found guilty."

When, *not* if, Bowie thought. The conviction rate for such arrests was as close to 100 percent as made no difference. Their crimes would be trumpeted on state media and their sentences would be televised as a sad reminder of the constant state of vigilance required to maintain the security of the Designed world which its citizens enjoyed. And that was just for pushing matters of workers' rights. If they were deemed guilty of more drastic action, the punishment was swifter and considerably more severe.

"Why are you telling me this?" Bowie asked, feeling pinned like an insect under a microscope.

"Come now, Mr. Bowie," said Merrick, all composed geniality, "you know the game. You played your card asking for more funding, and I have played mine."

"If I agree to the job, my brother won't be arrested?" said Bowie.

"So baldly put!" Merrick remarked with mock shock. "Such blunt instrument directness! I see why you were designated for this mission."

"Director . . ."

"He will not be arrested with the others," said Merrick, adding hastily and emphatically "at this time. Further such activity on his part will make such an agreement void, of course."

"Of course."

"As will word of their imminent arrest reaching the suspected Gammas," said Merrick warningly. "Their number can always be increased, by present company if necessary."

"Understood," said Bowie.

"So," said Merrick, smiling easily as if they had merely passed the time of day. "You agree to these terms?"

"I do."

"And you understand that while the state will compensate any injury sustained according to the guidelines laid out in the agency charter, a degree of risk is unavoidable in actions such as these."

"I do."

"And you further acknowledge that deviation from the letter of your instructions will result in the cancellation of your contract, any moneys owed, and a reassessment of your living conditions, including an alteration of your class status?"

Bowie knew this was coming, but he had to stare straight ahead not to register the alarm that clause raised in him. It was one thing to ride the train into the desert; it was another thing entirely to be forced to live out there with the Gammas in the camps, grunting and sweating his way through endless days of back-breaking labor.

"I understand," he said.

"Sign here," said Merrick, shunting a docusheet across the glass. "You can sign, I assume?"

There was that momentary flicker of amusement again. Bowie didn't rise to the implication. Some Betas couldn't read. Almost no Gammas could. Most people lived their entire lives in the class into which they had been born and that affected every aspect of those lives, including the forms of education they received. He took the docusheet and flicked his finger across the signing bar, tracing out his name with a deft, confident movement.

Merrick just nodded, unimpressed.

"Then we will proceed to your briefing," he said. "This is a counter terrorism action. The stakes are very high, as I am sure you will understand."

Bowie knew that he should probably just nod and look serious, but the question that had been on his mind since the meeting began forced its way out nonetheless.

"So why me?" he said.

"Are you saying you don't want or can't complete the assignment?"

"No," he cut in. "I'm just asking the question. You say the stakes are high, but I'm not trained as a counter-intelligence agent. I have worked for this office before, but my mandate has been low security data collection. This is something different entirely and I'm wondering why you aren't using one of your own people."

Merrick smiled again.

"Meaning an Alpha?" he said.

"Frankly, yes."

"As I said, there is some element of danger," said Merrick.

Bowie shook his head.

"There's always an element of danger when dealing with terrorists," he said. "You have security agents trained specifically for such missions. What makes this one different?"

Merrick seemed to consider his options for a moment, and for the first time he shifted in his chair, a minuscule movement but one which suggested a new level of discomfort with the way Bowie had forced the issue. At last, he pursed his thin lips and nodded.

"Very well," he said. "You would find out eventually. But understand that if I answer your question, I will take that as confirming your engagement in the mission."

"I thought we had already done that."

"No. There is a stage to come after your next round of data briefing when you would be permitted to withdraw from the assignment without penalty. Are you waiving that right to know the details of your task?"

Bowie blinked. If it had been any other issue, he would have stood down, agreed to go through the usual mission protocol and weigh the risks before committing, but Merrick had confirmed something he had already suspected: that he had been chosen for this mission not because of some general use function, but because he was somehow uniquely qualified for the job.

For the first time in his life he wasn't being offered a role grudgingly, thrown scraps despite his class status and all the other things that made him different from the Alphas he served. They wanted him—maybe even needed him—*because* of who and what he was.

It was both thrilling, and baffling. What could make him, of all people, special?

"Yes," he said, without another thought. "I waive that right. So. Why me?"

Even as he said it, a terrible possibility occurred to him.

It would be some undercover placement in a Gamma camp where he would serve as an informer, blending in with the rest of the throwbacks and misfits, a glorified courier whose task would be to stay alive and report back. Perhaps it would involve infiltrating a terrorist cell, posing as someone sympathetic to their dreams of rebuilding the world and destabilizing the regime.

It might involve Sefton.

The thing which had been squirming in his gut re-awoke and writhed, though he fought to keep any sign of the sensation from his face. What if that was it, what if he had to choose between the Design, and—the word bubbled up from a rank and toxic place in his subconscious—family?

Family. The Design acknowledged no such thing. Admitting to having one made you an outsider, a degenerate. Alphas were bred apart, their genetic makeup engineered for optimal purity and performance, then incubated in a central lab which was the crowning glory of the Design. The Design was all the family its citizens needed.

Bowie felt a bead of sweat run down his neck. Merrick saw it and his expression curdled slightly with distaste.

Family or the Design?

The world Bowie lived in had been good to him, and for all its faults, it was a thousand times better than the faction-riven chaos of former ages when humanity had been mired in greed, violence, and misery. The Design was the phoenix risen from the ashes of that world, and whatever the likes of Sefton said to the contrary, it had brought peace and reason, organization and a clear sense of what was right . . .

"Where do you need me to go?" Bowie asked.

Merrick frowned.

"Well, that's the thing," he said, and for the briefest of moments Bowie thought the agent's air of smug efficiency wavered. Something uncertain, uneasy flashed across his face, though he quickly suppressed it and recovered his former officious equanimity. "It's less *where*," he said, "than *when*."

Bowie stared at him.

CHAPTER THREE

Two weeks had passed since that first briefing, time spent in intensive exercise and study of the past, but Bowie had not managed to get his mind around the core idea.

Time travel? It was impossible. Literally impossible. It defied everything he understood about the world. Yet somehow, even harder to comprehend was the idea that of all the people who might do this impossible thing, the Design had chosen him.

Bowie was to be a time traveler! He was to journey into history to do he knew not what. A lowly Beta, born outside all the Design's codes of legitimacy and raised with other outcasts, who had grown to be menial functionary and low-grade investigator was about to venture into something beyond all human experience.

He had never heard of anything even close to this in all his time working with the security services and knew of nothing to suggest it was even possible. When he asked how what seemed to him to be the basic laws of the universe could be bent or broken in so dramatic a way, or how long they had had the ability to do this, he was told to focus on his studies and leave the esoteric questions to people with considerably higher clearance and expertise than him.

Which made sense, he supposed, but still: time travel? It was madness, the stuff of the kind of fiction which had vanished before the foundation of the Design, before people had realized that the indulgence of the imagination, the wallowing in make-believe was just a decadent avoidance of reality. But if it was real, if it could really be done, if they could send a person back in time, and if that person was to be him . . . It was staggering.

Bowie was not a fanciful man. If such tendencies existed in him, he kept them firmly in check for the sake of his position, which was why he kept his interest in photography private. It would be considered at best pointless, at worst suspect, confirming other misgivings about this dark-skinned, hulking throwback. So, he wondered now if his excitement at the prospect of traveling in time was also decadence, and resolved to conceal it, though he lay awake every night, imagining what it would be like to step back into another world, to carry the secret knowledge that of all the people there, he alone did not truly belong.

That, at least, was a feeling he knew something about, but he didn't want to think along those lines. The Design had elevated him, trusted him, and now he was to be given the kind of gift most people could not imagine, a gift no one knew existed. He thought back to when he had sat in the director's office mulling whether to take the assignment!

He had come so close to turning it down, to missing this most astounding of opportunities.

So, he focused on his studies, though it was quickly clear that he was being expected to learn far too much for the time allotted. He asked if his departure date could be reset, but that idea was quickly shut down.

"Our operatives suggest that an incursion into the past is imminent," said Merrick. "We are, of course, doing what we can to ensure it does not happen, but if it does, its effects on our present will be immediate and absolute. We cannot risk the fracturing of the timeline. The terrorists are still in their preparatory stages, and we expect to have as much as another month before they are ready to make their attempt, but we cannot be certain. Prepare, but be ready to go if we are unable to prevent the inciting incursion."

So Bowie studied the history of twentieth-century America, using not just The Teleology of the Awakening, the official state history book taught to every student in grade school, but also a series of classified pamphlets that added detail to the sweeping generalities of the text book—and sometimes added troubling wrinkles to its triumphant overview of the circumstances of the Great Conflagration war, the Awakening itself, and the rise of the great social structure known as the Design.

"Too long," said the Teleology,

> had human culture evolved at random, pushed by the impulses of the few and the tendencies of barbarism. The Great Conflagration wiped the slate clean, leaving a blank space on which a new world, one built on

> the columns of might, right, and natural ability, could be imagined and realized. This was the Design, and its architects were an elite subset of society known as the Alphas, an apt name given their standing as the world's naturally gifted leaders, thinkers, and organizers. They would be the apex of the new world, and with the lower orders united in love and service beneath them, they would lead humanity into a brighter, safer, and stronger future . . .

Every schoolboy knew this much.

Bowie was now initiated into a few of the specifics which had made this grand vision workable. When he wasn't doing tactical training, he studied these materials until he could barely keep his eyes open, and first thing each new day he faced a barrage of questions on the period he was to enter, the mechanics of his mission, and the workings of the tech he was to employ.

The Separation, when computer intelligences had been irrevocably severed from each other after the Great Conflagration, had severely contained the previous era's rampant digitization and the expansion of the vast communication networks that had made society so vulnerable to hacking and digital manipulation, so Bowie had grown up with little of what the late twentieth and early twenty-first centuries took for granted: there were no Wi-Fi-linked computer systems, no cell phones or other telecommunication systems. The world of the Design had such things, of course, and—in terms of pure technological capacity—much more, but they remained carefully sequestered, monitored like viruses to prevent pestilential spread. Home systems were checked by dedicated maintenance experts periodically, and since all such tech was property of the state and rented out to the citizenry, those experts were all disciplined government employees. In practical terms, Bowie—like everyone else in his world—knew which buttons to push to summon his meals or request entry into trains, secure facilities and so forth, but the tools required to modify or repair those systems were a closed book. Even the attempt to replace a frayed wire in what was little more than a doorbell was subject to criminal prosecution, and all but the most prioritized of government facilities were under perpetual surveillance.

So, Bowie learned about screwdrivers and simple circuitry, as well as antique American currency and firearms. He studied museum collections, much of it stowed out of sight in basements far below the shining halls that were the face of the Design, a society that had never had much interest in the past except as proof of why the present needed to have taken the shape it had. And, perhaps as a result, though the amount Bowie didn't know seemed insurmountable, it was also clear to him that the state archive's records were patchy at best. What they had were lists of facts, but they didn't add up to a complete picture of the world he was about to enter and didn't come close to making the people who lived there feel real to him. When he asked questions, he got stonewalled, so he suspected that his instructors knew little more than he did, if that.

"I don't understand these telephone switchboards," he remarked to one of his instructors. "Why did they work this way?"

"Because the humans of that period were unsophisticated," said the tech without looking up. "Much of what they did defies reason."

"OK, I suppose," said Bowie, dissatisfied, "but when did those switchboards go out of service? There are references here to cell phone networks in the twenty-first century, but I don't understand how they went from limited telephone exchange systems to wireless networks, and when that happened."

"That information is unnecessary," said the blank-faced technician.

"How do you know that? How can you possibly know what I will need when I'm there?"

"We retained what was useful from that period. The rest was discarded as corrupting, decadent."

He said this evenly but with a stern look that suggested that to even ask the question Bowie had raised aligned him with similar decadence.

Bowie shook his head.

"I guess I'll find out and improvise," he said by way of conciliation.

"I expect you will," said the tech. It was not a compliment and went some way to explain why Bowie had been the one chosen to venture into the barbaric past. They thought he would fit in.

He decided not to be offended by such assumptions. He had proved his usefulness before—defying their expectations and bettering his lot in life when he returned—and he could do it again.

Bowie quickly decided that his time was best spent studying what the Design could tell him that was both essential and incontrovertibly accurate, and that came down to the mechanics of time travel as presented to him. On this, it was clear, there was no room for error.

"A changed event in the past cannot be changed again," said his instructor, a scholarly type with skin so pale it looked translucent and blueish. He had a sickly look Bowie had seen in many of the Alphas who rarely left the confines of their artificially lit offices. This one had been introduced to Bowie as a Professor Reissen, though Bowie knew little about him, never learned his specific area of study, or even if he held an actual academic position to justify his title. "I repeat, a changed event in the past cannot be changed again. Interference in history must therefore be prevented decisively since you will not be able to return to the same moment without damaging the fabric of space-time, thereby causing reality to fold in on itself and collapse. Any alteration of the past will create ripple effects through time, altering all possible futures."

"So what am I doing there if I am not changing time?" Bowie demanded.

"The opposite," said the professor. "You are charged with ensuring the maintenance of the current timeline as we understand it, protecting it from temporal terrorists who seek to destabilize the future in the buildup to the Great Conflagration."

"The terrorists want to derail the Design? Why?"

"They are delusional fanatics and are beyond reason."

"That doesn't sound like an explanation," said Bowie.

"Then when you go back there," said Professor Reissen coolly, "and are wallowing in the pre-civilizational slime of the twentieth century, maybe you can ask them. But I would suggest you focus on the *how* of things rather than the *why*. Let me bring you back to the bedrock of all moral and effective action: the rules. The device via which you can move in time can be programmed to enter different periods in space and time but can only move backward in time."

"Wait, so how do I get back here?"

"As I was about to say," remarked the professor with a show of superhuman patience, "the exception is the preset home button which will move you back to the terminal, here in 2157."

"So, what if I want to go forward in time but not back here?"

"Is that not self-evident? You return here, then go backward to your desired destination. But that should be avoided where possible. The device requires immense power to make the jump, and each attempt is potentially dangerous."

"But it can be done? So, if I fail to achieve what I went back in time to do, I can return here and go back again."

"Only by going back to a moment before the point of your last entry and living in that period until the moment naturally comes around."

Bowie frowned.

"How much before? Seconds? Minutes?"

"It depends on the scale of the event you might alter. The larger the impact of that event, the farther back you have to go in order to avoid creating a temporal paradox. You cannot exist in more than one version of yourself in the same space at the same moment. If you do, the multiplicity creates a contradiction that will eliminate you—all versions of you—from the past and restore the initial timeline."

"So on any first attempt I should get as close to the event I am attempting to maintain, so that if I have to go back and try again, I have a broader window of opportunity."

"Correct. But, again, I would suggest getting it right the first time."

"No doubt," said Bowie, who found the man's abstract pronouncements on what he would have to do in an entirely unfamiliar world annoying. "But if I do have to go back, how far in advance of the event is safe . . ."

Reissen made an irritated noise.

"As I said, it varies by the scale of the event. You could be in the same moment as another version of yourself so long as you do not interact, but since interaction could be as simple as seeing yourself, or picking up something the other version of you set down, it is safer to ensure you are never in the same location as another version of yourself. The farther back you go, the greater the distance in time and space seems to need to be. Returning to the present—our present, the moment from which you first departed—seems unaffected by the requirement."

Bowie noted his use of the word 'seems.'

"So if I return here several times, there could be multiple versions of me walking around but that doesn't trigger this paradox thing?"

"The closer we are to the present the less contradiction can be caused by the consequences of a person's actions, even if that person exists in multiple forms, so long as the multiple versions are not literally present in the same moment. In the present, a matter of even a few seconds of discrepancy seems enough to prevent temporal paradox."

All this abstraction and protocol was making Bowie's head spin.

"All right, but what about in the past?" he pressed. "How much of a gap between incursions are we talking? Minutes? Hours?"

"Perhaps," said the professor, and for the first time he looked slightly flustered. "Days. Weeks. Months, maybe, for history-altering events where the consequences of an act cause greater ripples in reality."

Bowie put this answer together with the 'seems' of the previous one and came to a conclusion.

"You don't know," he said flatly.

The professor was momentarily silent, affronted but without a comeback.

"Just how many times have we done this?"

"We?" echoed Reissen, with a contemptuous curl of his lip.

"The Design or its agents," Bowie clarified, his jaw set. "How many times have we sent agents back in time?"

"This is comparatively new technology," the professor blustered. "We are responding to an imminent terrorist threat, using the means forced upon us by deviant action . . ."

"How many times?" Bowie demanded.

For a long moment the professor held his eyes with mute defiance, then glanced down. At last he spoke.

"That information is classified," he said.

Bowie nodded thoughtfully, reassessed the situation, then tried one more approach.

"Then why me?" he said. He thought he already knew but wanted to hear it. "There have to be a thousand better qualified candidates, men who understand the tech or the history, agents with years of tactical training and military discipline, citizens of higher rank or clearance. Why turn to a low-level intermediary like me?"

The professor gave him an appraising look.

"I would have thought that was self-evident," he remarked coolly. "The security forces are comprised entirely of Alphas. In the twentieth century their superior physical evolutionary features will make them conspicuous."

"While I'm a throwback?" said Bowie with bitter amusement. "More likely to blend into a pre-Awakening world?"

"Correct. Darker, larger, less refined. Many of the people in the twentieth-century exhibit similarly un-evolved features."

"So, the things that keep me permanently fixed in Beta class and threatened with relegation now make me useful?" Bowie mused aloud. "And they also, I assume, make me disposable."

The professor merely smiled a flat, joyless smile that did not reach his eyes.

"I trust we can count on your patriotism," he said.

"Of course," said Bowie.

So there it was, the condensed version of what they thought of him: useful enough to be an implement, but not so useful that he couldn't be lost, defined in both cases by his birth, his genetic makeup. He had guessed as much, so why was he surprised to hear it laid bluntly out for him? What other reason for his selection could he have realistically hoped for?

"Then it is time to introduce you to the means of your temporal transit," said Reissen.

Despite all his misgivings and frustrations, Bowie felt his heart skip a beat.

"Now?" he asked.

The professor shrugged.

"Is there a reason you wish to wait?"

Bowie frowned and looked down.

The means of your temporal transit . . .

They were going to show him a time machine! Again, Bowie fought to bury his curiosity and excitement deep.

"No," he said, managing a shrug that mirrored the professor's from moments before. "Now is fine, I suppose."

"Very well."

Bowie resolved to contain his emotions as the professor made his secure calls initiating the next stage of this surreal adventure, then walked beside him through the Intel Center's white, dustless halls, under constant surveillance of uniformed security Alphas. Inside, however, his mind raced. He wondered what had thus far only been referred to as 'the device' would look like. A craft of some sort, fitted with some type of cloaking technology, probably: something as sleek and shiny as the city itself. It would be crisp and precise, reflecting the values of the Awakening and the Design: a monument to the present he was enlisted to save.

His identification band was scanned three more times before they reached the hangar gate, where he was subjected to haptic and retinal scans, then told to stand aside as two larger guards with compact directional charge weapons searched him. Their faces were carefully blank and—since they were Betas like him and taller than most Alphas—on a level with his. When they were satisfied, they simply nodded to the professor and stood to attention on either side of the hangar door.

Professor Reissen tapped a numerical sequence into a pad and the door, which was marked simply with the hooked line and circles insignia of the Design, slid aside. Bowie managed not to crane his neck to look in and waited patiently until Reissen and the guards motioned him through.

Half a dozen Alpha techs paused and turned to look at him, their frank gazes unabashed and unimpressed. The professor smirked and nodded for them to get back to work, and they did so, ignoring Bowie like he was the janitor, not the man assigned to use everything they had built.

It was unlike anything Bowie had ever seen. There were banks of tech on all sides of the long room, illuminated displays flashed with scrolling data. At one end of the room was what appeared to be a closed circular door, also marked with the Design's emblem. It looked like it might cover a tunnel mouth, and for all its nondescript efficiency it oozed potential, so that Bowie again felt his heart rate increase.

That was surely where he would be going: through that door and—somehow—through time.

It was cool in the hangar, the ambient light low so that the various console lights winked in rafts of color around him. In the center of the roof, flanking what seemed to be a gantried walkway, slightly elevated, and running directly toward that close-mouthed tunnel, were towering stacks of unfamiliar mechanical components, humming with energy, blinking with computer displays and read out meters. There was a vast exhaust hood, curved like the funnel of an ancient steamship Bowie saw once in an illustration, and a bewildering number of interlaced cables and hydraulic tubes tying everything together, and leading, like the strands of a spider web, to an object which sat at the center.

Bowie's gaze followed them, and this time he could not prevent the gasp of amazement as he found what sat in the heart of the building. It was the device, and it was unlike anything Bowie's fevered imagination had been able to conjure. He gazed at it, torn between bafflement and hunger for the thing, even as his mind rebelled at the disconnect between what it was supposed to be able to do and what it appeared to actually be.

CHAPTER FOUR

It was, for want of a better term, a motorcycle. Bowie's world hadn't used anything like it for close to a hundred years, and even when they had, they were nothing quite like this. It was long, rangy as Bowie himself, and low slung, with the wheels and saddle creating the shallowest of triangles. The core frame was chrome, but the dull metal of the engine was exposed, and the trim—including a fairing which covered most of the front wheel and trailed back like a shield around the rider—was a chipped and scratched copper-bronze. The leather upholstery of the seat was stained and cracked. It smelled of oil and iron. The windshield, which swept up like a half bubble from the handlebars, was clouded and fissured with tiny cracks. Altogether, the thing looked barely of the same world that they were standing in, where everything was clean and sharp, elegant, and carefully formed to mask all inner workings. This was a relic, unabashedly—albeit clumsily—powerful, and seeming to hum with an energy that gave the impression of life.

Instinctively, Bowie put his hand on the scarred, angular fuel tank, as if feeling for a pulse. He found only cold steel, but still the sense of power was overwhelming.

"You expect me to ride this?" he said, not taking his eyes off the bike.

"A larger vehicle would be cumbersome and conspicuous," said Reissen. "This packs all the necessary technology into the smallest possible device, and it's fast." He moved toward it, but warily, as if afraid it might bite him, indicating a set of analog dials and electrical switches. "These controls here allow you to set the temporal immersion point. The ignition will respond to your home unit key."

"Just mine?"

"They are a standard design: any key from our time will start any bike."

Bowie looked up.

"There's more than one?"

The professor opened his mouth to say something then changed his mind.

"The controls are quite simple. This is the throttle, rotate it back to increase speed, forward to decrease. It can be used to slow your speed to a degree, but for more extreme changes, the lever here applies additional stopping power. This red button will always bring you back here," he said instead, "but don't hit it, or the other temporal insertion controls, until you've fired the boosters—here. You don't want the vortex open longer than is absolutely necessary, so don't fire the boosters prematurely. Once you do, get through quickly and the portal will close behind you. It may require a little mental fortitude."

"Mental fortitude?" Bowie echoed bitterly.

"You'll need to be prepared for the sudden acceleration," the professor replied. "The space-time anomaly will seem to project directly in front of you, so you'll need space. Sixty feet of open road should do it."

"That doesn't seem like much space at speed. How does that work?"

"You want the mathematical formulas?" said Professor Reissen smugly, knowing the science was beyond Bowie.

Bowie glowered, but let it go. No, he wouldn't understand it even if Reissen explained it. He wasn't sure why he had asked, except to get his mind off the prospect of being rocketed through a space-time vortex on the back of this thing.

"These instruments are where you set your coordinates in time and space, the latter will be accessed from map data from the period in question stored in our database. Always select a remote entry point."

"So people don't see me appear?"

"Among other concerns," said Reissen noncommittally. "For similar reasons, it's best to enter after dark, local time. Peter," he said, turning to one of the techs, a young man with eyes so blue and sharp that it was unnerving to look at him. "Show Mr. Bowie his operations equipment. Weapons first."

Bowie tore his eyes from the bike, curiosity piqued. He had been eyeing the guards' compact directional energy weapons, state of the art things the Gammas called "juicers." He had never fired one but had heard that a concentrated stream from one of those things could slice right through steel and concrete.

Peter ignored Bowie but moved briskly to a glass-fronted cabinet. He placed his palm against a reader which turned green. The heavy glass door opened with a pneumatic hiss, as a wisp of steam or smoke escaped.

"Antiques," said the professor. "They have to be stored in hermetic units to protect them from the effects of oxygen."

"Antiques?" said Bowie, disappointed. The mist inside the cabinet cleared, revealing three ancient looking handguns: two automatics and a revolver. Next to the juicers in the hands of the watchful guards, they looked clunky, primitive. The grip of the revolver looked like it was made of real wood. Nothing had been made of wood since before the Great Conflagration. Longer. The tech opened a drawer in which rounds of brass ammunition were nestled in foam rubber, a dozen or so per weapon. "Seriously?" said Bowie. "You have the ability to move me around in time, but I have to sling bits of metal at people when I get there."

"Our mission is to maintain the past as it is," said Reissen. "That means not disrupting the environmental culture of your destination any more than is absolutely necessary. Bringing future tech into the twentieth century could do as much harm as failing to stop the terrorists. If our current weapons were to fall into the hands of humanity two centuries before they should be invented, that would upend the entire timeline, which means that the world as we know it, you, me, this moment . . ." he made a little exploding gesture with his fingertips. "Gone."

"But if I'm the one who changes the past, how could I vanish from the future? I have to be in the future in order to go back and alter the past. It's a causal loop."

The professor's eyebrows raised.

"And I thought you were just the muscle," he remarked.

Bowie bridled at the condescension.

"So do I get an answer?"

Professor Reissen shrugged.

"Time is bound to perception, to consciousness," he said. "Alterations in a timeline necessarily alter the future or at least create alternate futures which run in parallel. Your perception would dictate your sense of the timeline, maintaining an internal logical coherence based around your own memory and perception, but for everyone else, it would change, shifting them into alternate futures. This moment would vanish. This world would vanish. All we have created in the face of the machines, the Design, the ordering of the chaos, the rise of the Alphas, everything we have built that is good and noble and strong, would be unmade and never permitted to come into being."

Bowie stared at him. In all the hours he had spent with the professor, he had never seen any emotion beyond mild amusement and thinly veiled contempt. Now his eyes burned with a patriotic intensity.

Bowie nodded once.

"Got it," he said. "Antique weapons it is."

"They are crude and require some practice, but are effective up close, especially given the limited medical capacity of the period."

Bowie hefted one of the automatics. It was surprisingly heavy.

"Where did you get these?" he asked.

It was a casual question, but Reissen's face froze, and he turned away, busying himself with a docupad. For a second he didn't speak, then he said, "They were recovered from a vault discovered while doing constructive work. They fit the period."

Something about the man's manner felt evasive.

"What period, exactly?" said Bowie. "The twentieth century is a big place."

"The specific details of your mission are classified and will be given to you immediately before departure," said the professor.

"You say I am supposed to be inconspicuous," said Bowie, raising the pistol as Exhibit A. "How am I supposed to blend in if I don't know when exactly . . ."

"It's the twentieth century," said Reissen, his habitually bored exasperation at Bowie's slow wittedness returning. "One year is very much like another. You have been furnished with the history."

Bowie frowned, unconvinced.

"It's thin on cultural detail," he said.

"It's a distasteful period," said the professor. "The value of the past is that it contributes to the present. That is all. Once you progress, what you were before ceases to matter."

"But history is complicated," Bowie began, "full of tensions, competing—"

"The twentieth century was a degenerate period," Reissen cut in. "Chaotic. You need to keep it out of your head as much as possible. You wouldn't want your exposure to barbarism to taint you more than is strictly necessary, would you?"

Taint you more than you already are, said Reissen's challenging stare.

"No, sir," said Bowie. "I just think that the period probably evolved some over the century . . ."

"Evolved?" scoffed Reissen with unbridled scorn. "Nothing matters before the Awakening. Everything before it is prehistory: decadence and barbarism. That's all you need to know. It's your job to make sure we don't slide back into it."

Bowie considered that, but wasn't ready to let it go.

"Understood, but a hundred years is a long time," he observed. "Are you suggesting I think of the 1920s and the 1990s as essentially the same?"

But the professor had had enough. His pale face was flushed with indignation.

"Enough!" he barked. "You were not hired to think. You were hired to point that gun and pull the trigger. Think you can manage that, for the good of our society?"

Bowie hesitated only a second.

"Yes, sir," he said, adding with the merest trace of surliness, "So what is the next stage of my training?"

"Training?"

"Learning to use these guns," said Bowie. "Tactics. Covert operations."

"You served in the military, did you not?"

"Forty-Second Motorized Infantry," said Bowie.

"And attained some measure of distinction," said Reissen with grudging admiration. "Unless your file is in error?"

Bowie pursed his lips. The Gammas—those that had fought on their side, at least—had been the cannon fodder and the Alphas had given the orders. Not many Betas had served. Fewer still had become platoon commanders successfully completing a string of significant—even decisive—missions.

"It is not in error," said Bowie.

"And it is not overstating the case to say that it was your military record that brought you to the notice of your superiors and that—in more peaceful times—attained you the work and lifestyle you now enjoy."

Bowie understood what was being said, including the veiled threat of what might happen to his "lifestyle" if he stopped being useful. He took a breath.

"But my last military action," he said, "was twelve years ago."

"The end of the war," the professor shrugged, pretending not to get Bowie's point.

"And I have not handled a weapon since."

"Oh, I'm sure it will come back to you," said Reissen. "What do they call it? Oh yes: 'muscle memory.'" As he said the words there was that ripple of distaste in his eyes again, that half smile of disdainful amusement. He didn't wait for Bowie to respond. "Right. Peter? Helmet, leathers, and utility pack, if you don't mind."

The tech moved to another, taller cabinet, and produced a rack of clothing and assorted accessories.

"Put those on," said the professor.

"Now?" said Bowie.

"Need to make sure they fit."

"Is there a changing room or—"

"Now," said Reissen. "Here."

Bowie gave him a hard look, knowing he was being punished, albeit in some petty way aimed at humiliating him, then slipped out of his light jacket and pulled his undershirt over his head. He wasn't as thoroughly toned as the guards, who spent their off-duty hours with dedicated trainers ensuring that their sculpted muscles reflected the Design's model of physical perfection, but he had a brute solidity which came—if not from his less relegated genetic heritage—from the physical tasks he was constantly assigned as a Beta.

He stripped down to his underpants, saw that the pile of clothes presented to him by the tech included Y-fronts, and took his underwear off too. For a moment he felt their eyes on him, curious and a little repulsed by the sheer physicality of his presence, and in his mind he heard the old taunts which had been thrown at him since he was a kid: "throwback," "neanderthal," "mixer"—a shot at the multiple racial components in his genetic makeup—and "free range," a term used for those conceived outside of the lab.

For the briefest of moments he stood there, naked, forcing himself to hold the pose, determined to be unembarrassed, defying them and the voices in his head, before dressing.

The heavily padded canvas trousers smelled musty, so did the tall, rigid boots. Whatever atmospheric stasis they had been stored in, they oozed an alien pastness that wasn't about other people's bodies exactly, but clearly didn't belong in the pristine world of the Design. There was a light tunic and a leather jacket, also padded at the elbows and covered in utility pockets, and a helmet with a tinted, metallic visor. A heavy belt of some coarse khaki fabric was holstered for sidearms. Altogether they seemed to bulk him out still farther, outgrowing even the guards, and dwarfing the Alpha techs and the professor. They regarded him with a show of amusement, as if there was something clownish about him, but he thought this was partly a blind to mask their growing trepidation—fear, even—at his transformation.

As he dressed, Professor Reissen had made a call using a communication pad by the door. He had spoken softly but earnestly, his eyes on Bowie, who had not been able to make out what he was saying or who he was talking to. As Bowie put the helmet on, the professor stepped toward him.

"Your helmet is your primary information system," he said. "It is fitted with retinal and other bio sensors so that it will only activate for you. It is voice activated and contains geospatial data for guidance purposes and a digital compendium of relevant historical data. As a computer it is rudimentary, but it also maintains a mission tracker which will confirm from temporal consequences when your task is complete."

"It tells me when I've done what I set out to do?"

"Quite so. The breast pocket of your jacket contains a wallet with facsimile identity card and the paper money used in the period."

"Paper money?" Bowie said. He had read about dollars and cents, but what form they took or what things actually cost, the history books hadn't said. Indeed, his reading material had had surprisingly little to say about the day-to-day details of life in the past, their agenda always being on showing in macro terms why that past was inferior to the present which had grown from it. The omission suddenly struck him as significant. What else didn't he know that might prove crucial to blending in?

"You won't be there long," said Reissen, dismissing his concern before he could voice it.

The mystery of who the professor had been speaking to on the comm was solved as the hangar door opened, and Counterintelligence Director Merrick entered walking briskly, a pair of guards at his elbows, pulse strafers held across their bodies, ready for action.

Reissen took this in stride, greeting him and handing over a docusheet, but the other techs looked surprised. They exchanged wary glances, eyeing Merrick and the guards with something just this side of alarm. At last, Merrick turned to Bowie.

"Your orders," he said, handing over a folder of paper. "Commit the materials to memory and be ready to depart in ten minutes."

The techs' unease rippled around the hangar bay like a groan of anxiety.

"Wait, what?" Bowie demanded. "Today? I'm not even close to being ready. I've only just laid eyes on this thing," he said, nodding to the bike. "I need training in these museum weapons and still have no clue where I am going or what I am going to do."

"Which is why you have ten minutes," said Merrick, unmoved. "That's more than we can spare."

"I don't understand," Bowie replied, taking the folder but not opening it. "If I'm going back in time, what difference does it make when I go."

"Your job is to counter the actions of terrorist operatives, and is therefore dependent on their movements," said Merrick evenly. He had clearly expected Bowie's reaction. "Intelligence reports that operatives have already made the time jump. The consequences of their actions could reach us at any moment, completely resetting our reality. The indicator light in your helmet's mission console will illuminate when your task is complete and the timeline is set. Do not return until that happens. Study the parameters of your machine and go before it is too late."

"Ten minutes?" Bowie protested. "I can't possibly—"

"You can and you will," said Merrick with finality, "or we will revisit the terms of your agreement in all its aspects. If I were you, I would waste no more time debating what cannot be changed."

CHAPTER FIVE

The roar of the bike was deafening in the confined space of the hangar. The Alpha techs shrunk away from it, hands over their ears as the tunnel mouth opened. Sirens wailed and warning lights flashed. Bowie had already punched in the geospatial and temporal coordinates provided to him, and as the engine came up to temperature he could feel its untapped potential growing ever greater. He gripped the handlebars, turned them slightly left and right, leaning a bit as he did to get a feel for the weight of the machine, then twisted the throttle on the right until the bike bellowed like a chained beast straining to get free. He shoved his visor down and focused on the shimmering path ahead, the flat runway and the curved steel of the tunnel walls. He was like the bullet in one of those antique pistols, about to be shot from a steel tube and into God alone knew what.

It was madness, making the jump with so little preparation, hurling himself through time and space into a period he couldn't possibly know to complete a mission he didn't begin to understand. But he felt their eyes on him, and the pressure to prove himself throbbed within him, loud and potent as the bike. He didn't look at Merrick or the professor, the techs or the guards all of whom, though they wanted him to succeed, would take his failure as something to have been expected. He revved the engine again as if charging his own will, teeth bared inside the helmet, a long snarl of furious determination streaming unheard from his lips. He eased the bike into gear, and felt it change: a living thing straining at the leash, eager to be free. Finally—his breath held and his jaws clamped shut—he released the brake.

The bike rolled forward, unsteady at first, so Bowie had to fight to control its weight and direction, settling only as he gave it more fuel. The hangar seemed to slide behind him, the watchful faces and blinking lights forgotten before they were even out of sight. Bowie got low in the saddle, eyes front, feeling the speed of the thing build like a thunderhead, loaded with unshed lightning.

Then he was in the tunnel and rocketing forward, faster and faster each dizzying, breathless second. He felt his body stiffening with fear as he concentrated on keeping the bike going straight and true.

He didn't notice the speedometer hit a hundred but moved his right forefinger over the bike's booster button, not daring to look down. He pushed it.

The bike's fairing seemed to envelope him as the bike itself stretched longer, the rear wheel extending out behind him, making the whole thing sleeker, more arrow-like. There was a bang which he felt deep in his core as much as in his ears, and the force of the bike's sudden leap forward almost threw him backward from the saddle. He felt the breath leave his body and for a moment he lost all sense of what he was doing and who he was.

Now, he thought, seizing the idea and holding on fiercely with what was left of his mind. *Now or never.*

He punched the temporal launch button, and the air in front of the bike rippled like a troubled pool. A beam of energy seemed to project forward from a point under the bike's headlight, expanding funnel-like until it became an opening in space, roiling with uncanny blue-white light. It was there for a fraction of a second, and then the bike was shooting through it.

For a moment he thought he had lost consciousness. His head lolled and his hands, which had been clamped for dear life on the handlebars, loosened their grip. There was a second or two of dreamy imprecision, of an out of body vagueness as if he was nothing more than breath or spirit, and then he was yanked back into himself with a deafening roar of sound, of blackness all around and two hard, round lights coming at him fast.

He felt the bike sway and drift dangerously beneath him, and fought to get it under control, as his barely awake brain tried to make sense of the blaring noise and the rapidly approaching lights. Directly ahead, the source of the light and noise loomed suddenly out of the night, and Bowie's sleepy brain finally put a name to it:

Truck.

Panic leaped in him. The 18-wheeler's horn blasted its warning again, its headlights filling his vision with the promise of imminent death. Instinct took over.

He yanked the handlebars to the right and the bike turned hard, so hard that he felt it kick and slide. He leaned into the turn, realizing too late that beyond the truck's glare he could see nothing in the dark. The wheels jumped and skittered as the massive articulated vehicle blew past, its horn still shouting its fury.

Still blind, Bowie threw his weight left, dragging the bike back upright with all his strength. He had to remind himself to use the brake and finally brought the machine to a skidding halt.

He slumped forward, tore the helmet from his head and sucked in the night air with a series of gasping pants. His heart was racing so hard he could barely breathe, and he hugged the gas tank as he caught his breath, knowing how close he had come to ignominious death.

"First," he said aloud to the night, "let's figure out how to turn this thing's lights on."

He considered the bike's dials and buttons, made a few experimental adjustments and found the headlight. It lit the world ahead with a faintly amber radiance, and what it showed was mostly a green emptiness: a long straight highway stretched through a flat belt of coarse grass and low trees, quite unlike the deserts of 2157 where the solar farms sat. He took a long, steadying breath, felt it flutter in his throat, but held it, half closing his eyes, before slowly blowing it out.

All right, he thought. *I'm here and I'm alive.*

First hurdle passed. But he was starting to see why time travel was inherently dangerous. There was no way to know what would be awaiting him at the end of each jump, and being spotted making the leap now looked like the least of his problems. The professor had said nothing about materializing in the path of an oncoming truck.

The road was quiet now, but Bowie was taking no chances. He got off the bike and wheeled it onto the dusty hard shoulder, getting as far from the road as he could, then positioning the kickstand. By the light of the bike's headlight, he chose a pale, yellow boulder under a clump of small trees and settled on it, feeling its wind-softened edges through the thick fabric of his gloves, listening to the sound of the truck fading away to nothing. On impulse he tugged one glove off and put his bare hand down into the grass. It felt cool to the touch and very slightly damp. He scrunched the blades and smelled the slight sweetness of their sap on his fingers. He marveled at the life of it. The air vibrated with a strange, pulsing hum which did not sound mechanical.

Insects? He had never heard the like. It was also cooler than he had expected, being used to the scorching, relentless heat of the world he came from, and he breathed the chill air in with something surprisingly close to pleasure.

Even as he did so, however, Bowie realized that he was nauseous. Whether that was the time leap, or the traumatic nature of his arrival, he couldn't say, but he sat quite still, breathing in the night and the strangely vibrant silence as he waited for the feeling to pass. He stared at the ground, which was bright in the glare of the bike's headlight. There was a thick weaving of weeds and grass in the seemingly untended earth, and as he watched he saw a line of flame-colored ants march purposely by his left boot. He adjusted slightly to give them room, marveling at their ordered focus. Two of them were carrying a piece of bright-green leaf between them. Two others were carrying one of their own dead. Bowie, who had never seen ants before, stared like a man hypnotized. Something called overhead, and he looked up to see the silhouette of a great bird—an owl of some kind maybe—angling shrewdly as it scoured the earth for prey. Bowie gazed at it, his mouth open. For someone who lived in the carefully maintained artificial environments of a blasted desert world, all this life was overwhelming.

I am in the past, he thought, marveling.

"I am in the past," he said aloud, as if the sound of the words would make it easier to grasp. It would have been unbelievable, but there was no doubt about it, and as he gazed into the night, breathing it all in, he began to chuckle softly to himself.

In a couple of minutes, the motion/time sickness—if that was what it was—seemed to pass, and he got up, returning to the bike with a careful stride which left the ants undisturbed. With one last deep breath Bowie replaced the helmet, noting that as he put it on the visor flickered with a soft glow, followed by a series of data points: date and time (orange)—the seconds advancing as he watched—a map indicating his position just outside Baird, Callahan County, Texas, with a directional pointer (green), and—in square red letters—the simple message "Mission Incomplete," beside which was another counter, this one also red and ticking down from thirty-six hours.

Bowie frowned. Professor Reissen hadn't said anything about that. What happened when the counter reached zero? Presumably that was the end of the window he had to complete his task.

So, he had a day and a half. The professor had said the helmet was voice activated. Bowie cleared his throat and, feeling awkward, said, "Access address from mission file."

The helmet's display flickered and added a new map over the upper right quadrant of the visor display.

"Plot directions to that address," he said.

The map indicating his current location, spun, zoomed out, fixed, then added a new directional arrow and a series of turn-by-turn directions in blue, heading east-northeast.

The display brought a degree of comfort, but he wondered how accurate it would be given the scant information in the official history. There was probably no network of communication satellites wherever and whenever he was, and if he were to go somewhere that there was such a system—*somewhen*, he supposed—the helmet would not connect with it. Like everything else from his home world—from what he had to start thinking of as the future—the bike and helmet would be rigorously air-gapped to prevent any possibility of machine infection. But he was used to that. His world, for all its advancement, had no need of the perilous fad which had been the internet, not that that would be a meaningful part of anyone's life here for another three decades.

He checked the date and time, and the distance he had to cover. It was almost one o'clock in the morning, on Thursday, November 21, 1963. He had gone back almost

200 years! The address of his target—1026 North Beckley Avenue in the Oak Cliff section of Dallas—was some two hours away.

All the time in the world.

Bowie turned the ignition and the engine coughed, then roared, a guttural purr like one of the jungle cats the kids in the Gamma camp used to imitate when they played lions and tigers, storied animals they'd never actually seen, but which had once lived on Earth.

Still do, Bowie thought with a ripple of surprise. In 1963 there would still be lions and tigers, not around here, perhaps, though there would be other long-dead beasts roaming the desolate places of the continental United States. The idea pleased him. He leaned forward over the bike's headlight and thought it was like a searching eye, and he was a warrior riding into battle on the back of one of those great hunting creatures.

Riding the motorcycle got easier too, as if it was adjusting to him as much as the other way round. He felt its power coursing through his body from loins to heart, and he was glad that the helmet hid the delight in his face. He felt like a child, all glee and savagery, and knew immediately how immense the disdain of his Alpha masters would be if they could see him now.

He wondered about that. The mission status light in his helmet suggested a tie back to his home world, but it was—fittingly—primitive, a binary indicator: incomplete/complete. There was no reason to believe they had more knowledge of him than that, or even that their sense of his task would unfold for them in anything like the real time he experienced. He was in the past. If his engagement created ripples through the timeline, however minor, they would experience them immediately, right? Or rather, their world would alter in ways preventing the knowledge of any prior state. But then how would they know to send him back in the first place? The temporal loop was a self-defeating paradox.

And yet here he was, astride a bike the size of a tank drone, rumbling through the night of a Texas which had long since ceased to exist. How had they done it? The Alphas were acting in response to Gamma terrorists using salvaged tech, but how could that be? Bowie had seen the Gammas, their primitive camps, the way they scratched their hand-to-mouth existence day-to-day until the work broke them. He knew what happened if they were caught with the most basic cyber device and had seen the brutal show trials of those accused of trying to create a network link between a few rudimentary computers. That they had the capacity to build and operate a device capable of time travel was inconceivable.

No wonder the Alphas are afraid, he thought.

They hadn't said so, of course. They would never concede such a thing even to themselves. But the urgency of the plan, the desperation of sending someone like him back to tackle the problem all smelled of fear. He grinned at that too, feeling a tremor of triumph, of pride, which immediately bothered him.

Still, he thought, he was from the future. He was a mystical traveler to a barbaric past, and in his head he carried knowledge of the world and the times to come that the people around him could not dream of. The idea renewed his sense of purpose, even superiority.

For a while he rode steadily, confidently, getting accustomed to the feel of the highway below him, building his awareness of the traffic, its rules and habits until he felt comfortable. But after a few minutes his concentration lapsed, and he strayed fractionally from his lane. A car screamed past, missing him by inches, its horn blaring angrily as it shot by. Bowie corrected, the bike wavering dangerously before it recovered its cruising position, and it took a good minute for his heart rate to return to normal. Another heavy truck barreled by him, and he felt the drag of the thing as it slid past, like there was a hungry vortex under the wheels that wanted to pull him in. In addition to monitoring the other vehicles on the road, he got used to scanning constantly for curves, dips, and other hazards of the unlit highway, measuring his position according to the scant road markings and scanter road signs. It was harder work than he had imagined, and after an hour he felt a stiffness coming into both mind and body. Though he appeared to be simply sitting, he was working with his arms and shoulders to guide the bike and keep it upright, and with his mind to stay one step ahead of the thousand possible disasters which suddenly seemed more than possible.

Not quite so superior then, he mused, recognizing the accumulating mental exhaustion.

He still had forty minutes or so to go, and the traffic was getting heavier as he got closer to the city, despite the antisocial hour. He saw what looked to be a fuel station set back from the road, gaudy white lights, a round sign with a star and red lettering proclaiming "Texaco." He pulled over, easing down and directing the bike under the stiff, narrow awning where the fuel pumps stood. Shutting the engine off, Bowie basked for a moment in the silence, then set the kickstand and swung his leg up and over, feeling his muscles creak like the leathers he was wearing. He straightened up and flexed, then removed his helmet.

"Fill her up?"

He turned to find a white man in his twenties, scrawny and with what Bowie recognized as a cigarette dangling from the corner of his mouth. Bowie stared at it, watching its smoke, like he was in a museum and confronted with something ancient and inexplicable. He realized the young man was eyeing him, waiting.

"What?" said Bowie.

"Fill her up?" said the man, though it took Bowie a second to make the words out, the accent was so unfamiliar. The attendant had a peaked cap with the name of the fuel company on it scrunched into one hand. "The bike," he added, as if Bowie might be mentally deficient. "You want gas, or what?"

"Right," said Bowie. "Yes. Fill her up."

The words sounded strange in his mouth, especially that "her." Another detail missed from the historical records?

"Nice hog," said the attendant as he stuck the fuel nozzle into the bike's tank.

Bowie stared at him.

"Hog?" he said.

"The bike," said the attendant, with a look that was both amused and puzzled. "Kind of weird looking. What make is it?"

Bowie's mind went blank. Feeling the other man's gaze on him he fished around in the scattering of historical details he had read about and said, "Ford."

"Ford?" scoffed the attendant. "Fine. Don't tell me. Custom job, huh?"

"That's right," said Bowie, feeling stupider and more out of his depth with each passing second.

The fuel pump cut out and the attendant shot him another dubious look.

"Tank was practically full," he said.

It wasn't a question exactly, but the man's look demanded a response.

"Didn't know where the next station would be. I have a way to go and don't know the region," he said.

"Not from around here, huh?" said the attendant. "I figured as much. That's sixty-five cents."

Bowie blinked.

"Right," he said, fumbling for the wallet in his jacket. "Money."

"They don't pay for gas where you come from?" said the attendant, that same teasing amusement in his manner under which was . . . what? Suspicion? Distrust?

Bowie pulled open his wallet and scanned the folded notes. He chose the smallest and handed it to the attendant.

"You want change from a twenty?" he sputtered. "What the hell, man? You just fly in from Monte Carlo or something? You got nothing smaller?"

"Sorry," said Bowie.

"Hold on," said the attendant, annoyed. "I'll have to go to the office."

He left and Bowie, uncertain whether to follow, decided to stay where he was, if only so that he wouldn't get dragged into further conversation. Basic communication was proving more of a challenge than he had anticipated. The less he said, the better.

The attendant came back, his cap now on his head but pushed back so the peak stuck up. He was counting out the change, some of which came in the form of coins. Bowie managed not to marvel at them, but only with an effort.

"Where you from, man?" asked the attendant, obviously picking up yet another oddity in the way Bowie handled the money.

"Ohio," he replied simply.

"Fine," said the attendant again. "Don't tell me. You drive safe."

He turned to walk away, and Bowie, unnerved by how difficult the interaction had been, remounted the bike, keen to be back on the road, whose undeniable perils made him feel less like a fish out of water.

This wasn't going to be nearly as easy as he had supposed.

The huddle of Gamma men and women who worked the great solar collectors in the desert stood in the shade of the toilet block and considered their leader with wary disbelief.

"That's crazy," said one of them, a hulking brute of a man with shoulders like boulders. "Impossible."

"I know," said Sefton. "But it's still true."

"And you know this how?" said a lithe, dark-skinned woman with a bandanna to keep the sweat out of her eyes.

Sefton hesitated. He hadn't wanted to say this part but knew it was unavoidable.

"My brother," he said.

"That Beta lackey!" the woman shot back with a curl of her lip.

"It's not that simple," said Sefton.

"It is if you want us to act on his instructions."

"They aren't instructions," said Sefton, holding up a hand. "Not for you, Greta. Not for any of you."

"But you intend to follow them?" said the woman called Greta.

Sefton considered his shadow on the hard, sun-baked ground, then nodded.

"I do," he said. "I think . . ." he paused then nodded again. "I think it's time."

There was a long, hot silence, then Greta looked slowly around the anxious faces before turning her gaze back to Sefton. Her eyes were big and they fixed him with a frank, level stare.

"What's the plan?" she asked.

CHAPTER SIX

The closer Bowie got to the center of the city, the more an uncomfortable truth began to insist itself into his brain; the navigation system he was following through the helmet interface wasn't always right. Twice he had tried to make turns onto streets that simply weren't there, and once he had followed directions almost into the side of a building. He brought the bike to a sudden juddering halt and looked around, double-checking street names from the little road signs and checking them against the map on the inside of his visor. The building—some sort of brick warehouse, seemingly abandoned, its dark windows smashed and some kind of bush growing out of its fractured roof—shouldn't be there at all. The map clearly fit the period in general terms, but it wasn't keyed to his present moment. The road indicated in reassuring lights inside his helmet probably hadn't been built yet, wouldn't materialize until the warehouse was pulled down. That would take time. The idea bothered Bowie. It meant that the maps—and maybe other pieces of the local information he had been given—might be months, even years off. The Alphas clearly knew less about this period than they had let on.

It made sense, he supposed, and not just because a lot of data had been lost during the battles of the Great Conflagration. The civilized world of the Design had little in common with or interest in this crude and barbarous period. As he rode into the city, the point was driven home in graphic terms: gray concrete high-rises sitting beside seedy little shops and dirty underpasses, the cars and trucks composed of every imaginable color and shape, all deafening and belching smog. The houses and shops were variously gaudy and drab, newly pristine and tumbling down. The architecture was a mishmash of styles and periods which shifted from block to block. There was no uniformity, none of the clean-lined elegance of form and function that he was used to in Cloud City or the imposing regularity of the Design's government buildings. The whole culture seemed to have been haphazardly bolted together, an act as violent as it was arbitrary. Bowie didn't like it, and the fact that the Alphas had chosen him because they thought he would blend in better than they would, made him like it even less. It was as if the twentieth century had taken all the things about himself which bothered him most and built a world out of the parts.

He kept his helmet on and his visor down at all times. The info system—despite being unreliable—comforted him, made him feel a little closer to home, less like a denizen of this chaotic, stinking, and unpredictable place. He kept his eyes forward and focused on the traffic signals. For all the varieties of vehicle on the roads, no one had a bike like Bowie's, and he could feel them watching him, reading from the motorcycle the very thing the Alphas had wanted to conceal:

You don't belong here.

"Absolutely right," he muttered to himself. "I don't. And the sooner I can get out of here, the better. If this is Dallas," he began, then corrected himself. "If this is the twentieth century, you can keep it."

But the bike was like the road maps. It indicated a lack of knowledge about the period which bothered him, even if it came in part from a deliberate lack of interest in this clumsy and primitive world. It might make his job harder.

The house, when he found it, was a low-slung brick affair with a porch with chairs facing the street, decorative wrought iron trimming, and an angled, vaulted roof in the center. Between the road and the house was a lawn and trees. At home, where conditions meant that keeping anything alive outdoors put huge demands on time and resources, they would have been signs of opulence, but here they seemed ordinary, normal, and the house itself was small and nondescript. Bowie hadn't known what to expect, but it hadn't been this.

Bowie pulled over on the opposite side of the street near a public phone booth and turned the engine and headlight off. The neighborhood seemed impossibly quiet after the deep thrum and growl of the bike, and for a moment he stayed in the saddle, considering the building and drinking in the night, the strangeness of this place. He had at least two more hours until sunrise and he wasn't sure of his next step.

"Personal details on target," he said.

The helmet visor flicked up a black-and-white picture of a nondescript looking white man alongside the address and a series of text boxes. They read:

> TARGET NAME: A. HIDELL, RESIDENT.
>
> MISSION: PROTECT AT ALL COSTS. DO NOT ENTRUST TO LOCAL LAW ENFORCEMENT.
>
> SECURE HIDELL'S SURVIVAL FOR THIRTY-SIX HOURS.

Bowie frowned.

"Other occupants of residence," he said.

> EARLENE ROBERTS, HOUSEKEEPER.
>
> OTHER TENANTS.

"Identify other tenants," said Bowie.

> UNKNOWN.

"Seriously?"

> REQUEST NOT RECOGNIZED. PLEASE RESTATE.

Bowie thought.

"Personal details on suspect."

> TERM 'SUSPECT' NOT RECOGNIZED.

"Hostile agent," Bowie tried.

YOU WISH TO SEE DETAILS ON TERRORIST ADVERSARY?
Y/N.

"Yes."

The screen flickered again and another picture replaced that of Hidell, also black and white. The man was white, with deep-set eyes with a neatly trimmed moustache. His mouth was crinkled at one corner, as if about to smirk.

Bowie hadn't known what to expect—maybe a dangerous-looking Gamma, all wild eyes and a mane of unruly hair, or a rogue Alpha, pale and effete but with a twinkle of madness in his stare—but this wasn't it. The terrorists had done a better job than the Alphas in sending back someone who would blend in.

The text box identified him as operating under the code name Jimmy Spear, twenty-eight, but said nothing further.

"More details on terrorist adversary," said Bowie.

NO FURTHER DETAILS AVAILABLE.

"All right. More details on mission," he said.

TERRORIST ADVERSARY EXPECTED TO ATTEMPT APPREHENSION OF TARGET BEFORE DAWN TODAY. THIS MUST NOT HAPPEN. TARGET MUST SURVIVE ENCOUNTER. TERRORIST ADVERSARY MUST NOT.

"What time is this supposed to happen?"

BEFORE DAWN.

"All right, but exactly what time?"

BEFORE DAWN.

There it was again, that lack of precision. Despite the aura of surety of the crisply lettered message lighting up in his visor, his commanders were clearly low on specifics. Or if they knew them, they weren't sharing them with him.

"More mission details," he said.

NO FURTHER DETAILS PERTINENT.

Bowie cursed his righteous exasperation, but the helmet had nothing further to offer.

"This is absurd," he remarked.

REQUEST NOT RECOGNIZED. PLEASE RESTATE.

"Forget it."

Bowie pulled off his helmet in frustration. You couldn't reason with a machine. He knew that of old.

The war had mostly been fought by machines: semi-autonomous drones of various kinds, remotely commanded but programmed to function independently. Both sides had used them, and in his mind, combat was inextricably bound to using heat scopes to spot weaknesses in armor, targeting servos, antennae, and power packs. In the years after the war there had been sporadic uprisings by rebels—mostly Gammas—as they attempted to disrupt the implantation of the Design, but armed confrontations had been few and mostly confined to the coasts. Bowie had destroyed his share of roamer tanks and C-bots, and he had helped contain riots and protests, but he had never knowingly fired a lethal weapon at a human being.

"The terrorists are no different from the machines," Merrick had remarked one day shortly after the broad terms of Bowie's mission had been laid out for him. "Their circuitry is bio-chemical rather than simply electronic, but their mission is the same: the total destruction of civilized society. All we built in the wake of the war, the shining, ordered society we raised out of the chaos and bloodshed of those years, they want to undo it all. Unmake it. That is all they know how to do: sabotage, unravel, erase."

Sefton would beg to disagree, Bowie had thought, but he had said nothing and let the director complete his speech.

"You cannot afford them an iota of humanity any more than you would a C-bot stomping through the wall of your home, leading with the barrel of its blaster and programmed to eliminate all detected life. If you hesitate, if you try to start a dialogue with them, if you even look for the humanity in their eyes, they will kill you. And then they will detonate our future. You know what that means."

Bowie did. He laid his hand against the cool steel of his primitive gun like a monk from some former age touching his prayer beads.

The street was quiet and dark, especially the yard of number 1026, which was heavily shaded by a tree bigger than anything Bowie had ever seen growing outdoors. Even so, he knew he would stand out to anyone who happened to look outside. He walked the bike into the deepest part of the tree's shade, propped it up, placed his helmet on the tank, and moved quietly across the lawn toward the hedge that ran along the front porch.

Walking on the grass felt strange, illicit, and again Bowie wondered at this world's casual attitude to the abundant life around him. It hummed in the darkness of the garden. He thought of the dead Wastes outside the city where he lived, the dust storms that plagued the Gamma camps, the relentless heat of the day and the frigid nights. By comparison, a November night in the Dallas of 1963 was positively balmy.

He slowed as he reached the veranda, stepping around a fallen branch thick as a C-bot's blaster barrel. His boots had been silent on the grass, but the steps and porch looked like solid flagstone. They would echo. He hesitated, unsure if he needed to be inside to protect his target, and in that instance, he heard the rising sound of an approaching vehicle. Instinctively he dropped into a half crouch and scuttled right and down the narrow strip separating the house from the neighbors, hugging the shadows and inching backward, away from the street. He could tell the car was slowing even before he saw it, and his apprehension spiked again as he saw the vehicle turn its lights off long before rolling to an inconspicuous halt halfway down the block.

Before dawn, the mission brief had said. This was it.

Bowie took up a position squeezed into the flank of a heavy shrub with thick waxy leaves, mostly screened by the low hedge. He dropped to one knee and made himself as small as he could, his right hand reaching for the pistol in its holster.

For maybe a minute the car—a burgundy thing with a white top and weird little fins on the back—sat in silence, then the driver's side door opened and a man got out. He stood up and looked over at the house, nudging the car door quietly shut: a man who didn't want people to know he was here. For a moment it felt that he was looking directly at Bowie, though it was unlikely that he could see him from there, and Bowie got a sudden clear view of the man's face, neat mustache and all.

Jimmy Spear.

A chill ran through Bowie at the realization that, while not perfect, the Design's information about the past was somewhat—somehow—accurate. He drew the pistol and held it close to his side, settling into the muscles of his haunches, poised to spring.

His heart rate had stepped up. It had probably begun the moment he heard the car, when all those forgotten impulses and instincts had woken up after twelve years of slumber. He blinked, and for the merest fragment of a second, he was in a bombed-out building on the edge of Dayton Sector battlefield, his shoulder-mounted striker raised and aimed as the C-bot came in on its great, tungsten legs, the metal toes spread like bird claws, the muzzle of the blaster which was the sole reason for its existence searching for him like a great black eye ready to spit fire and death . . .

Wait. Wait.

The man with the mustache was coming up the path. His hand moved under his jacket, reaching for a weapon.

Bowie leaped out in front of him, raising the pistol. He saw Spear's eyes widen, and the hand under his coat froze, but in the same instant there was another clunk and Bowie's eyes slid toward the sound.

Someone else had gotten out of the car. A woman. On the passenger side. She had long, dark hair, wore a pale blue, form-fitting jacket and skirt, and held an oversized shoulder bag by a strap. She stared at him, her eyes suddenly wide with surprise.

Bowie hesitated, and the man with the mustache charged him.

It was an unthought out attack, rough and improvised, but effective. Spear slammed into Bowie's chest with a lunging dive which brought his head into Bowie's shoulder. They went down together hard, Bowie landing on his back, his head catching the corner of the veranda so that for a moment he couldn't see for pain. The world swam, and though it was only for a second, it gave his adversary the opportunity to seize Bowie's gun hand by the wrist and bash it hard against the ground.

Bowie's old combat training had kicked in enough to keep his finger outside the trigger guard, so the gun didn't go off as he clenched and fought to retake control of the weapon. He squirmed under the weight of the man, then jerked his knee up into his groin. Spear grunted, but didn't let go, then drew back his left arm and crashed a fist into Bowie's face, one, two, three times.

Bowie rolled hard to the side so the worst of the blows fell on the side of his face, trying not to lose himself in the rage and terror of the moment. Spear was right-handed, and his grip on Bowie's gun hand was strong, but the punches with his left were clumsy, inaccurate. Bowie kicked again, then rolled first left—a feint—then right, a hard, determined surge of energy that threw Spear off him and sent him sprawling into the hedge. Bowie rolled into a crouch, training the gun on where the man had fallen, but he was already moving toward the dark passage between the houses. Bowie stood up, shaking off the disorientation of the struggle as he leveled the pistol and sighted down its barrel at Spear's retreating back.

Just another machine . . .

The blow to the back of Bowie's head didn't knock him out, but it did crumple him. He had just enough presence to turn and see the woman with the long hair, eyes wider than ever, the fallen branch she had hit him with held up in front of her like a talisman. He spun clumsily to face her, raising the gun once more, and her defiance evaporated in panic. She dropped to the ground, hands over her head, whimpering.

Not a threat.

He ignored her, stepping around the porch after Spear.

The sound of the gunshot was flat but echoed between the houses, and the muzzle flash lit the early morning with flame and specks of burning powder. Bowie shrunk away from it, and the air fizzed as the bullet shot past his head. He returned fire instinctively, two quick shots that made his hand kick so badly that he knew they had gone wide. Another shot from Spear, barely visible now at the back of the house, this one wild and blowing fragments from the brick.

Bowie went after him, no hesitation now: a series of pounding, determined, strides and a vaulting of a low hedge as he chased Spear into the area behind the house. A light went on inside, throwing an unearthly amber glow into the yard, bringing color to the greenery. Spear saw it too, and he used the distraction to chance a quick turn and fired another shot. It may not have been blind, but it was more a warning than a serious attempt to bring him down, and Bowie barely broke stride.

And then there was the snap of a latch and the back-door opened. A man was silhouetted in the doorway: slim, nondescript, wearing a baggy white shirt.

Hidell.

The man Bowie was charged to protect.

Bowie saw him. Spear saw him. And then Spear glanced back at Bowie as if making a decision, before stepping suddenly into the light from the doorway, his gun raised and leveled at Hidell.

Bowie fired twice. He knew right away that he had hit Spear, who dropped before he could get his own shot off. He might have been dead before he hit the ground.

The woman's wail of dismay spun him around.

"No!" she was crying. "What have you done? What have you done?"

It was horror and grief and confusion, all rolled into one accusatory lament. Even after the gunfire it sounded unnaturally loud. Bowie stared at her, his gun still raised, though he felt no threat from her. Around him, the predawn stillness of the respectable neighborhood was starting to fracture. Lights were coming on. A screen door popped and a window opened. Across the street a man's voice shouted something about calling the cops.

Bowie couldn't take his eyes off the woman in the blue suit who was still moaning and staring at him. Some of it was shock, but there was something else in her eyes which he didn't understand, something which got under his skin, threatening infection. He took a breath as if to clear his head.

He had done what he came for, he reminded himself. He was following his orders and serving the greater good. The police could come but he would be gone, back to a world far beyond their grasp . . .

So why does this feel wrong?

And then the woman's face shifted. Her eyes focused and she was looking past him.

"Where is he?" she demanded. "Where did he go?" Bowie turned back to the rear door of the house but the man in the white shirt, the man Spear had been poised to shoot, was nowhere to be seen. "You let him get away!" she gasped. "My God."

She looked wildly around, scanning the empty street, and again Bowie felt that touch of wrongness. He had assumed she was grieving for Spear, her dead colleague, friend, even lover. But she wasn't looking at the fallen man at all, and now that he thought about it, she never had.

"You have to find that man!" she exclaimed to the world in general.

Another window opened and a woman called out.

"The police are on their way! I saw the whole thing! They'll take him in."

The woman just shook her head in defiant exasperation as if she was the only sane person in the world.

"Not *him*!" she shouted back with a glare at Bowie. "The one who ran."

"Hidell," said Bowie. "Why do you care?"

"His name isn't Hidell, you idiot," she shot back. "It's Oswald. Lee Harvey Oswald. He's about to kill the president."

CHAPTER SEVEN

Bowie didn't wait. The woman who had been shouting from the window ordered him to stop but he ran back to the bike and kicked it into life. As he peeled away, the headlight off and with no clear sense of purpose or direction, he saw the female terrorist scurry back to the car Spear had parked. He took the first right onto North Zang Boulevard, then the next onto North Crawford, which brought him along the dark, tree-shaded edge of a park. He did the same at the junction of East Fifth Street, finally completing the loop back onto North Beckley. He slowed the bike, wishing for something a little less conspicuous, and paused. Spear's car was gone but as he looked frantically around, it passed him going south: that distinctive burgundy body and white roof. The driver was sitting forward and clutching the steering wheel with both hands, eyes directly ahead. He was as sure as he could be that she hadn't seen him.

He gave her a few seconds, then—just as he picked up the distant sound of sirens—he gave the bike a little gas and eased out into the junction. The road was still quiet, and even from a couple of hundred yards behind he had a clear view of her. He settled back, registering the display inside his helmet visor which still showed the "Mission Incomplete" sign. He had to assume she was still a threat, so the logical thing was to track her. It wasn't like he knew where Hidell—or Oswald, as she had called him—had gone.

He kept his distance, staying at least one car behind where possible, and as he rode, the helmet visor up so he could take in his surroundings, he thought about what the woman had said.

"*He's about to kill the president.*"

Presumably, she meant the president of the United States, but that couldn't be right. Bowie was pretty sure the president didn't live in Dallas, and even if he was around why would terrorists from his own time be trying to stop an assassin? Why would Bowie have been charged to do the opposite, to ensure that a major political figure from almost two centuries ago got murdered? It made no sense.

He had been charged with protecting someone and he had done it. He had shot someone to do it, but he had saved a life, one which was—presumably—more important.

"*He's about to kill the president.*"

It couldn't be true.

It was getting light now. The streets were busier with both pedestrians and vehicles. Store front shutters were being rolled up, and when Bowie paused at a traffic signal, he thought he could smell something evocative and pungent coming from a corner establishment with large windows through which he could see people sitting in booths. The sign over the door proclaimed it JOLENE'S COFFEE AND DOUGHNUTS!

Maybe that was the smell.

Bowie felt his mouth begin to water with anticipation, though what the stuff would taste like, he had no idea. Where he came from—outside the Gamma camps, at least—food was mostly protein blocks and nutritional supplements, taupe-colored gelatinous cubes that tasted—as near as made no difference—of nothing. There were restaurant services but eating for flavor rather than nutrition was considered decadent, a moral failing to be kept carefully in check. He thought of his brother enthusing about Mrs. Alsace's curry, and Bowie saying he didn't remember it.

That hadn't been true, though a tortured part of Bowie wished it was. He couldn't really remember what those meals had tasted like, but he recalled the kids' enthusiasm for them. Still, years of proving himself to the Alphas had convinced him that sensory indulgence was weakness, a sign of a lower, less intellectual nature. The image of those kids at the orphanage clamoring for Mrs. Alsace's curry like pigs fighting to get to the trough—himself among them—made him wince with shame.

The light changed and he pulled through the junction, increasing his speed to make up the ground to the car he was following, and glad to get the scent out of his nose. As soon as it was gone he closed the visor on his helmet with something like relief.

She hadn't gotten far. In fact, she'd pulled over, and Bowie had to do the same to keep his distance. It was a good thing the car was so distinctive. In the dark he had barely noticed, but now with the sun up, he could track that red-and-white combo with the odd little lighted fins in the back from a couple of hundred yards away, no problem. The driver was still sitting inside, and as he watched he thought she slammed her hands against the steering wheel with fury or, he supposed, desolation.

Either way, for a trained agent it was a strangely personal response.

Again, he felt that ripple of confusion and unease, but he didn't have time to think it through, because in the next moment the woman had sent the car lurching back into traffic. She made a hard left turn, forcing the nose of the vehicle into the next lane so that there was a fanfare of horns and a screech of brakes. Bowie lowered his head, but she wouldn't have seen him anyway. The car sped up, making a series of right turns, moving with a new urgency as if she had only just decided where to go.

Bowie gave her a few seconds head start, then followed.

But going where? he wondered.

They were back on North Beckley and heading north, skirting the trees of what seemed to be a river to the right. She took the ramp onto Interstate 30 heading west, accelerating hard. Bowie gave chase, but he felt obvious. The bike was huge, low slung and, with its aggressive fairings, unlike anything else on the road. He tried to stay well back, to nestle behind trucks out of sight, but she must have seen him by now. For all he knew she was leading him straight into the arms of her allies or even local law enforcement.

But if that was her plan, she was taking a long way around. She stayed on the highway for more than three miles, then went north. The road signs pointed to Irving.

"What's in Irving, Texas?" Bowie demanded of the computer interface in his helmet.

The text on the visor said:

RESTATE REQUEST.

"Irving, Texas. Details."

IRVING, TEXAS, WAS A TOWN IN TEXAS.

Bowie cursed.

"Significance of Irving, Texas, for mission."

IRVING, TEXAS, HAS NO SIGNIFICANCE FOR THIS MISSION.

Maybe she wasn't heading for Irving.

"Extrapolate from current trajectory a location relevant to this mission."

The visor blinked up its response.

THERE IS NO RELEVANT LOCATION ON THIS TRAJECTORY.
RETURN TO DALLAS.

He was surprised by the command, and a little unsettled. He knew the computer couldn't be in contact with his superiors in 2157, but he didn't like the idea that they would have access to records of his apparent deviation from the mission on his return. And he *was* still on mission, even if the computer didn't understand why. It made sense to pursue the would-be assassin. The alternative was driving around a city of almost two million people looking for Hidell.

"Connection between Irving, Texas, and Hidell," he tried.

NO CONNECTION FOUND.

Bowie stared at the road ahead. The burgundy-and-white car continued to eat up the road, cutting around slower vehicles with palpable impatience.

"Connection between Irving, Texas, and Lee Harvey Oswald," said Bowie.

He expected the computer to give the same baffled "restate request" prompt, but this time he got something else entirely.

It said:

THAT INFORMATION IS RESTRICTED.

"What does that mean?"

RESTATE REQUEST.

"Details, Lee Harvey Oswald," Bowie tried.

THAT INFORMATION IS RESTRICTED.

"But you know who he is," said Bowie. "If you know who he is, and he's clearly central to my mission, why won't you tell me about him? How am I supposed to complete the task if I don't have all relevant information?"

RESTATE REQUEST.

"All known information on Lee Harvey Oswald, mission critical request."

THAT INFORMATION IS RESTRICTED.

"Details of the current president of the United States.

THE CURRENT PRESIDENT OF THE UNITED STATES IS JOHN F. KENNEDY."

"I said *details*, not name."

JOHN F. KENNEDY WAS BORN IN 1917 AND BECAME PRESIDENT OF THE UNITED STATES ON JANUARY 20, 1961.

"Death date of John F. Kennedy."

THAT INFORMATION IS NOT AVAILABLE.

"Dates of Kennedy's presidency."

THAT INFORMATION IS NOT AVAILABLE.

"Computer off."

> MISSION PROTOCOL RECOMMENDS MAINTAINING COMPUTER ACCESS AT ALL TIMES. ARE YOU SURE YOU WANT TO POWER DOWN INFORMATION SYSTEM?

"Yes."

The lights winked out.

Bowie rode on in silence, his mind humming.

The car he was following left the highway and entered south Irving, eventually stopping outside a modest looking single-story house on West Fifth Street. Bowie hung back, killing the engine before the woman made it out of the car. Once they had come off the interstate the traffic had been light, and it seemed unlikely that she hadn't seen him tailing her. Maybe she just didn't care. That impression was confirmed when, on getting out of the car, she threw an accusatory glance down the street toward him, before flying up the driveway of the white, ranch-style building and pounding on the door.

A house? Definitely not a law enforcement station.

Bowie got off the bike, checked his sidearm and hurried after her. His cover was already blown; what did he have to lose? He pulled the helmet from his head as he broke into a run, and once more was taken aback by the aroma of trees and grass, the life of the place. He passed the parked car but had barely made it up the drive when the front door opened and another woman appeared. She was slightly built with thick, bobbed hair, heavy glasses, and a long face, whose expression was hard as she considered the clearly agitated woman on her doorstep.

"Where is he?" she demanded.

"Who?" the woman in the door replied, "and who are you?"

"Oswald!" shrieked the woman. "Where is he?"

"I don't see what business that is of yours," said the other woman coolly. "And you still haven't identified yourself."

The woman took a ragged breath, forcing herself to slow down, then said, "My name is Sandra Rossi and I'm a journalist with *The Dallas Morning News*. It is vital that I speak to Mr. Oswald right now."

"Mr. Oswald is at work. He lives in town during the week and only comes here on weekends."

Bowie had moved quickly and quietly but at last the woman who had called herself Rossi heard him. She snapped her head around, her long hair flying out with the motion, and her eyes got big with terror and something of the desperation and grief he had seen in her earlier. She returned her attention to the woman in the doorway, pleading now.

"Let me in," she begged. "And call the police. This man is a killer!"

"I'm sorry," said the woman, taking a step back and pushing the door closed, "I'm going to have to ask you to leave."

"No!" yelled the journalist. "Please! Call the police!"

"Everything is fine," said Bowie to the closing door, taking Rossi firmly by one elbow, and almost lifting her backward. "The lady is just upset."

"Let go of me!" she protested, but Bowie tightened his grip and kept her positioned to ensure that she couldn't reach for his weapon with her other hand. He spun her around and propelled her back along the driveway toward the street. She fought him every step of the way, but it was a child's resistance—furious but ineffective. She showed no tactical knowledge or experience. He braced himself for a precise jab of her elbow into his gut, a stamp of her heel onto his toe, or a deft spin which might bring her knee into his groin, but she just squirmed uselessly.

And that's odd too . . .

"Get in the car," he said, bundling her to the curbside.

"So you can shoot me like you did Jimmy?" she sputtered. She was crying now, desperate, angry tears whose appearance seemed to increase her fury.

"He was about to kill a man I was charged to protect," Bowie replied. "He gave me no choice. Now get in the car."

"Oswald is an assassin!" she protested. "Jimmy was trying to stop him."

"Who did Oswald kill?" Bowie demanded.

"No one yet," Rossi shot back. "But he will. Tomorrow."

"The president of the United States."

"Yes."

"That's not possible."

"It will happen. Tomorrow."

"So the two of you came back in time to prevent him," Bowie concluded, letting the assassination story go for the moment. "I know that part. I just want to know why."

She stared at him then, her face momentarily quite blank. She went quite still, staring at him, then her face registered first confusion then scornful disbelief.

"You think this is funny?" she gasped. "You kill my partner right in front of me and then make jokes about it?"

It was Bowie's turn to be bewildered.

"Jokes?" he replied. "What? No. Just get in the car before the police get here."

The journalist shot a dark look at the house.

"She won't call them," she said. "You're quite safe."

"Last time," said Bowie. "Get in the car."

He nodded at the vehicle. It said "Chrysler" across the front in square, chrome letters. At the passenger door he quickly studied the latch and then pushed it. The door opened.

Rossi gave him a defiant look, then shook her head and shrugged.

"Fine," she said.

She stalked around the front, opened the driver's side door, and climbed roughly in. Bowie timed his move to coincide with hers, dropping into the passenger seat before she got behind the wheel, so she didn't have a second to reach for a concealed weapon inside. That was what he would have done in her position. She made no such move. He closed his door and waited for her to do the same.

It smelled synthetic inside, but there was another scent, floral and pleasantly sweet. It was her, Bowie felt sure. She was wearing some kind of aromatic. He had a vague idea that this was something women had once done, but it was a detail that unsettled him, and not merely because it was a strangely precise thing for a time agent to have copied. For a moment there was no sound but the journalist's quavering breath, and he opted to sit there still while she calmed a little. He took out the pistol and laid it on the inside of his thigh idly, his palm flat over it.

"If you are going to kill me," she said in a softer tone, "just get on with it."

Bowie grinned.

"You're good," he said.

She turned to him then, and there it was again, the blankness and confusion.

"What," she demanded, "are you talking about?"

"The blending into the local period thing you are doing," Bowie explained. "The look. The voice. Even the words you use. It's good. Way better than me. But then I assume you had more mission prep. What sector are you from? Are you a Beta? I thought this was a Gamma operation, but you don't look like a Gamma."

"What are you talking about? Gamma? Sector? I'm a junior reporter for *The Dallas Morning News.*"

"Right," said Bowie. "Sticking to your story. I get that. But it's over. I don't see what you hope to achieve by lying about it."

"Lying about what? Who are you and what the fuck do you want with me?"

Bowie gave her that indulgent smile again and nodded. If she wanted to play this game, that was fine by him.

"Who was that woman?" he asked, nodding toward the house.

"You don't know?"

"If I did, I wouldn't ask."

"Not sure. Probably Ruth Paine. I thought it would be Oswald's wife, Marina, but it wasn't."

"Ruth Paine owns the house?"

"Yes," the woman snapped. "Look, I don't know who you are or who you are working for, so I'm no threat to you, right? Just . . . let me go and I'll say nothing."

"We both know that isn't true," said Bowie.

He sounded calm, collected, but the woman's manner was bothering him. She was either extraordinarily good at this or something was off. Neither possibility filled him with confidence.

"What can I tell anyone? I don't know who you are or where you come from. Killing me won't make any difference to anything."

"I'm not going to kill you," he said. "Unless you go after Hidell."

"Oswald," she corrected reflexively.

Bowie shrugged.

"I don't care what you call him," he said, "but I won't let you kill him."

"Because you are part of it," she said darkly, staring sightlessly ahead through the windshield. "You are with him. With them."

"Who is *them*?"

"You tell me. CIA? FBI? The Soviets? Pro-Castro government forces? Anti-Castro militants? The mob? You're their hit man. If you're gonna kill me anyway, at least let me know who is pulling your strings."

"I don't know what those things are," said Bowie simply. "I'm here to protect a target. That's all."

She turned to look at him then, leaning forward slightly and peering at him intensely. Her gray eyes were bright and focused and for three or four seconds she just stared into his, before sitting back, eyes narrow and mouth slightly agape.

"How is that possible?" she said musingly.

Bowie felt suddenly embarrassed about his own ignorance. He didn't know the people or organizations she had listed, but someone *was* pulling his strings, and he didn't like to be reminded of it.

"I don't want to play this game," he said. "I wasn't ordered to gather information on specific terrorists, so as far as I am concerned, you can walk away. But if you go after Hidell—Oswald," he added before she could correct him, "we'll meet again, and it will not go well for you. I should probably kill you now to prevent the possibility. I'm sure that's what my superiors would have me do, but they aren't here. So, as long as Oswald stays alive, so do you. Try to change that outcome in the next twenty-four hours, and I will drop you where you stand."

He said it simply, without menace, as if he was simply stating a fact. Rossi gave him a long, blank look, then nodded once. She was afraid of him, but something about the reason for her fear felt wrong, though he couldn't put his finger on what.

"Do you have a weapon?" he demanded.

She shook her head quickly.

"I can search you and the car," he said. "It will be better if you just tell me. Easier for me. A lot easier for you."

Again, something like panic flickered through her eyes and then was gone.

"There's a small automatic in the glove box," she said. "It's not mine but . . ."

Bowie looked into the back seat.

"Where?" he asked.

She gave him another puzzled, wary look.

"There," she said, nodding to the dashboard in front of him. "The glove box. I said. In there."

"How many of you are there?" he asked.

"What?

"Don't be tiresome, Miss."

"Rossi. Sandra Rossi."

Bowie noted the way she volunteered her first name: trying to put him at his ease, perhaps. Show him she wasn't hiding anything.

Like he said, she was good.

"All right Miss Rossi," he said. "How many of you are there?"

"How many what?" she said.

"I told you, I don't want to play games."

"Then don't ask riddles!" she blurted. "How many what? Women in Texas? Reporters in Dallas? Human beings on the planet? What?"

"Agents," Bowie inserted. "On this mission."

"I'm not an agent. I have no mission."

"You just went to Oswald's house this morning by chance? Armed and ready to kill? What was that if it wasn't a mission?"

"I wasn't armed," she shot back. "I hate guns. I certainly wasn't ready to kill."

"Your friend was."

"That was on you," she snapped, looking away. "It wasn't supposed to go that way. We just wanted to talk. See how he responded to questions. Then we could go back to the police, which is what we should be doing right now, by the way. While there's still time. Just let me go and I'll do that. I swear I'll keep you out of it . . ."

"You weren't intending to kill him?"

Rossi hung her head, looking suddenly distraught. For a long moment she said nothing, then she shook her head fiercely and a tear flew from her chin and landed on Bowie's hand. She opened her mouth to speak but couldn't manage it without sobbing. At last she gasped out, "I didn't even know Jimmy was armed. He wasn't supposed to . . . We were just there to talk. Then *you* came." She gave him a savage look, and her bloodshot eyes were hard with accusation. "And now he's gone, and Oswald has . . ." she made an explosive gesture with her fingers that reminded Bowie strangely of the professor: vanished. "And tomorrow . . . This is all your fault."

"Tell me about tomorrow."

She sagged then, all her defiance draining away.

"I don't know," she shrugged. "Oswald will kill the president. Right here in Dallas. I know where and when but if I told you how I knew . . . It made more sense when Jimmy was here. I know it sounds crazy but it's true." She gazed out of the window, then turned back to him with new urgency. "I need to call the hospital. See if he's OK."

"The president?"

"Jimmy!"

Bowie winced.

"I don't think that's a good idea," he said.

"I have to know if he's still alive," she said.

Bowie thought the man was probably dead, and that learning that would only make her more difficult, but then he also felt like he needed her on his side. Though it seemed she was an expert undercover operative, he felt no threat from her.

"First, answer my question," he said. "How many of you are there involved in this thing you say isn't a mission?"

"Two of us! Me and Jimmy. That's it. The whole enchilada. We got a kind of tip. A weird one. Not the kind we could take to our editors. They'd say we were crazy or that it was a hoax. But we knew it was worth pursuing, so we did, and here we are. That's the story. We weren't planning the D-Day landings."

Bowie didn't know what they were, but he thought she was probably telling the truth.

Probably?

It was enough for now.

"OK," he said, using her slang. "Call the hospital."

She frowned quizzically again.

"From where?" she asked.

"You don't have some kind of mobile communication device?" he asked.

Once more she gave him that slow considering look, as if trying to decide whether he was joking, playing her for the fool, or just very stupid.

"Like a walkie-talkie?" she said like he had gone mad. "Who am I, James Bond? No, I don't have a *mobile communication device*."

"OK," said Bowie, stalling.

"I could go back to the house," she said, inclining her chin toward the building where the woman she had called Ruth Paine continued to watch them discreetly from a window. "Ask to use her phone."

"No chance," said Bowie.

"Then we should drive till we see a pay phone. Or a cop."

"Pay phone," said Bowie.

"Whatever," she said, taking a ring of keys from her leather shoulder bag and inserting one into the ignition. "Back in Dallas. There's no point being here."

"Wait," said Bowie. "You sure you have no . . ." He looked for a phrase other than mobile communication device and concluded simply "telephone?"

"What am I gonna do, spool the wire out behind me as I drive?" she spat. "Of course I don't have a fucking phone! What the hell is wrong with you?"

"OK," he replied quickly. "Then I'll follow on the bike. Use your turn signals and stay five miles under the speed limit. You see a pay phone, you stop immediately. Got it?"

"Or you'll drop me where I stand," she said bleakly. "Yeah, I got it."

Bowie gave her a long look, trying to decide whether she was being serious. He found her manner, her way of speaking—especially the flippancy and hyperbole—very hard to read. Eventually he got out, closed the door behind him and returned to the bike. She waited to pull away before he was on, the engine revving, and when she moved off, she did so slowly, indicating with her turn signal. If she was going to try and lose him, she was being subtle about it.

He pulled out into the street, his eyes locked on the burgundy Chrysler.

Some two hundred yards behind where Bowie had been parked, a tall, slender man emerged from behind a tree, lowering the strange looking binoculars he had been using, then closing the visor of his motorcycle helmet. His face was pale, handsome in the angular way of someone whose features might have been chiseled from marble. His nostrils flared and a sour look curled his lip and half closed his hard eyes. He watched Bowie ride away before returning to his own bike which—though different from Bowie's—had the same long body, the same aura of power, and the same impression that it had been designed by someone with only a passing familiarity with the vehicles of the twentieth century.

CHAPTER EIGHT

Merrick studied the air-gapped computer terminal, then checked his time band. Bowie had been gone from 2157 for almost six hours. He picked up the comm on his desk and called Professor Reissen.

"How close are we?" he said, without preamble.

"Seven minutes to maximum charge," said the professor.

"We need to act now."

"I think we should wait a few more hours. There is no reason to suspect a problem with the mission thus far."

"We won't know till it's too late. As we have already learned . . . to our cost."

"That problem was rectified by Bowie's deployment," said Reissen.

"It was countered, not rectified. We need an update on his status."

"Again, respectfully, I think we should wait."

"No," said Merrick. "This needs to happen now. I'll meet you in the hangar in ten minutes."

"I have some tests to run in the stasis lab," Reissen began. "I can have one of my assistants join you—"

"No, Reissen," Merrick snapped. "You. Ten minutes."

He hung up.

Merrick was two months shy of his sixtieth birthday, but he wore his years lightly and moved with a decisive economy that was unusual for an Alpha. He exercised religiously, patiently sculpting his muscles until he resembled one of the statues outside the Design Assembly. It made some of his coworkers uneasy, this embrace of his physical dimension, a habit better suited to Betas, even Gammas, as if paying attention to the body itself was necessarily in poor taste, but it gave him an edge in confrontations, made him intimidating, and few Alphas would dare to contradict him. Merrick walked down the center line of every hallway and the middle of doorways, forcing people to step out of his way with a look. He enjoyed their wrong-footed hesitation, the instant certainty of who was the dominant in every micro altercation. He was the *Alpha* Alpha. He didn't swagger, exactly, that would be too much, but then he didn't need to. He projected a physical confidence borne of his authority, and an authority borne of his confidence. In another age he might have been a general or an emperor, a prime minister or a president, or—more likely—a dictator. One day, if things worked out as he intended, he still might be.

He took the beltway hover train, sitting up front in his designated seat, ignoring the furtive glances, the apologetic head bobs when they were caught staring, the wheedling smiles from subordinates. He kept his face blank, his eyes hard, and his smile buried deep inside as he scanned the security bulletins for updates on the isolated incidents of unrest he had been monitoring for weeks. There had been a series of power failures impacting transit systems west of the city, their root cause, not yet, unexplained.

The public had no reason to believe that the outages were related, but Merrick knew otherwise. How long he could keep them in the dark, he did not know. He made a call and gave a series of orders. They were becoming routine which, even for a man of Merrick's iron certainty, was worrying.

Not for much longer, he thought with a flicker of pride: one bold, decisive strike—an action few would have even been able to imagine—and total victory would be theirs.

At the lab Merrick barely acknowledged the guards who snapped to attention as they saw him coming, saying simply, "With me," as he walked between them. They turned hurriedly to escort him, speaking into their lapel communicators to require replacement sentries on the door to the facility, marching double time to keep up with him.

One of them sped up to clear the lab door for him, entering with his directional charge weapon swung around to show he meant business. There was a flurry of hand-prints and security card readings and then the heavy red hazard doors split aside with a pneumatic hiss. Merrick was pleased to note that he had just crossed the thresh-old as Professor Maximillian Reissen came stumbling in behind him, red faced and—in so far as was possible for an Alpha—sweaty.

Merrick checked his watch pointedly.

"Director," said the professor by way of acknowledgment.

"Reissen. So glad you could make it. It's an auspicious day."

"Indeed," said Reissen. "Successful so far."

"You know that?"

Reissen's face flushed still further.

"Not officially," he said. "But we see no alteration in the temporal monitors—"

"Not good enough," snapped Merrick. "You have a secondary agent in place?"

"Yes, sir, but we usually wait at least twenty-four hours before . . ."

"Which one?"

The professor made a show of consulting a file as if he didn't know for sure, but the attempt at a level stare and noncommittal tone when he looked up again did not convince.

"Jäger Zero Four Nine," he said.

Merrick had guessed as much so he was prepared, and his face gave nothing away.

"Recall him," he said.

Reissen got a hunted look.

"With respect, sir," he cautioned, "that could seriously compromise his operation. We have no way of knowing exactly what he is engaged in at this moment, and he can't tell us without returning, after which—as you know—he will not be able to return to the same temporal coordinates without generating a paradox."

"I am aware of how the system works," said Merrick coolly.

"So to bring him back before he has completed his mission could jeopardize . . ."

"We need to know what Bowie is doing. I have reservations about his capacity to stay on task."

"As do I," said Reissen, finding a little more backbone, "as I said at the time. Trusting a Beta with such a sensitive task always seemed to me too great a risk for someone of his standing. Indeed, I remain unconvinced that any of this was necessary or wise. We meddle with the past at our considerable peril, as I've repeatedly told the board. When we learned of Washington's death, we should have abandoned the mission."

"Bowie is a better fit for the environment than Washington," Merrick replied curtly. "He'll blend in."

"But why are we even attempting this?" Reissen exclaimed, his composure evaporating. "Altering the past to refine the future? Our present? It's madness! I've said so every step of the way—"

"I recall your reservations," said Merrick, cutting him off, "as I recall your rank and status."

Reissen took a breath and held it. There was nothing to say to that. Even so, Merrick felt that it might help to say more, not because the professor had earned it, but because he needed him to be utterly invested in the project.

"The Design is vulnerable," said Merrick, almost under his breath. "People don't know it, but it's true. The insurgents we thought we had wiped out in the war have found new toeholds on the edges of society and they are organizing, getting bolder. The recent power outages, the fire at the western supply depot . . ."

Reissen looked aghast.

"I'd heard those were degradation caused by intense solar activity!" he remarked.

Merrick gave him a confiding shrug so small it stayed in the lines around his eyes and mouth. Reissen gasped.

"Insurgents?" he whispered.

"Their successes have been limited so far, but they are increasing in boldness and ambition."

"Can't something be done?"

Merrick made a calming gesture and spoke soothingly.

"We are doing it," he said. "You and me, right now." Reissen looked blank, unsure, so Merrick went on. "We fight the threats to the Design in the present, naturally, gathering intelligence and cracking down on the insurgents, but we also tailor our history to erase the problem. If by adjusting the past we can eliminate those threats, make it so their seed never takes root, and thus ensure that the Design becomes the totalizing and harmonious entity we always dreamed it would be, is that not a cleaner, more elegant solution?"

Reissen stared for a second and then, when Merrick continued to fix him with a beady stare, offered the required agreement.

"Yes, sir. Of course. I regret doubting your wisdom."

"Very well," said the director, satisfied, though he still detected a smoldering coal of doubt and defiance in the professor. That would need watching. "So, how long does it take to recall an agent?"

"No time at all to send the signal device through the portal," said Reissen, clearly glad of the opportunity to discuss something where his knowledge of the mechanics of the system gave him the advantage. "It's a standard homing beacon which his helmet sensors should detect quickly, but we have no precise fix on his location. If he has moved out of the device's communication range, or if it takes damage at the entry point, he won't know we want him back. The range is only about twenty miles, so if he has moved a long way from where it lands . . ."

"Only twenty miles?"

"Depending on local conditions and interference," Reissen replied. "It's a very small device, a disk only a centimeter or so across, fashioned to look like a low-value coin, so it will go unnoticed if found by anyone from the period. All part of the non-disclosure protocol, the parameters of which you laid out yourself, sir."

Merrick listened, unimpressed.

"Do it," he said. "And if he doesn't respond, do it again."

"To the same coordinates?"

"Unless he logs in with a new location."

"The beacon's power source will last at least a few days," the professor countered. "Maybe a week or more. So long as we are within that time span, there's no point in reissuing the recall until we get a new location from him."

Merrick scowled, irritated by the correction.

"Do I need to remind you that we have already lost one agent on this mission?" he said.

"No, sir, but I still feel that, for maximum efficiency . . ."

"Is there a reason why we are still discussing the clear and direct instruction I already gave you?" Merrick said softly.

"Some agents prefer to be given free rein to work," said Reissen in a still lower voice. "This particular one, as you know, has a tendency, or perhaps a temperament which leans toward . . ."

Merrick stared him down, and Reissen's voice tailed off, though whether that was because he saw the futility of the argument or was embarrassed to admit to his misgivings, Merrick couldn't say.

"My agents follow orders," he replied simply. "*All* my agents."

The professor bit his tongue again.

"Initiating firing of signal beacon now, sir," he said. He raised a hand and two of the techs who had been watching from a discreet (and safe) distance, began moving immediately. "Prepare to fire a signal beacon to the last reported coordinates of Jäger Zero Four Nine. On my mark."

There was a bustle of activity as the hangar leaped into purposeful life. A pair of orange warning lights began to rotate, strobing the hall, accompanied by the rising tones of a siren. A panel in the ceiling above the track where Bowie had first fired up the great bike opened and a platform mounting a piece of equipment resembling an anti-tank gun on legs was lowered until they locked into slots in the floor with a dull thunk. The gun's barrel was square and the muzzle was a narrow slot only a half inch across.

One of the techs retrieved a slim black box from a drawer beneath the platform and raised the lid. In it were six copper pennies. A slim plastic flange stuck out of a slot in the rim of each. The tech removed one, inserted it into the breach of the cannon, breaking off the flange which caused a discrete red flash from inside the disk. Once in place, the breach was sealed, a switch thrown, and the tech stood back, straightening a ten-foot cable with a remote control on one end.

"Cannon primed," he announced.

The other tech raised a series of dimmers and pushed a master button. The wall at the end of the runway buckled and flickered, its material fixity giving way to something stranger and more volatile.

"Portal open," he called, over the rising din.

Reissen shot Merrick one last inquiring look.

Still want to do this?

Merrick smiled so fractionally that no one saw it, then gave the professor a hard look and nodded once.

"Fire!" said Reissen.

The cannon tech squeezed the remote and the gun fired once, a deep booming sound which filled the hangar and made everyone but Merrick flinch away. A long streak of flame shot toward the portal, and the air was suddenly thick with the stench of gun powder.

"Such a primitive delivery system," Merrick observed.

"It has proved adequate to the task," said Reissen.

And right on cue the portal pulsed with a maelstrom of turquoise energy which seemed to collapse in on itself, the light sucked down to a pinpoint of black in the center, from which exploded a helmeted man on a huge, smoking motorcycle.

It came in fast, sliding and skidding as the rider tried to brake the machine's heart-stopping velocity. Again, the hangar crew shrank away, and the air seemed suddenly to lose its transparency in the haze of gasoline smoke and some nameless ether from the portal which seemed to trail the bike as it came to a noisy halt.

No one spoke. The rider seemed to satisfy himself that all was well, then slowly dismounted and—slower still—removed his helmet.

If Merrick's confidence inspired awe and deference among the Alphas, this man pushed such feelings past their limits and turned them to fear. This was the sculpted Aryan superman who had been watching Bowie in Texas moments before. He was at least a couple of inches taller even than Bowie, blond, blue eyed and powerfully built, though these were not the main source of the power that came off him like heat. That came primarily from the eyes. They were hard and cold as ice, and they swept the hangar with a haughty disdain as clinically appraising as any of the bots he had fought in the Great Conflagration. He radiated contempt, as if an artist from a former age had tried to carve the idea in stone, had sought for an image of what certainty and scorn would look like if it could manifest itself and walk the Earth, and had come up with this.

Having been bred and raised for this function, he had no other name. His designation, Merrick knew, as Jäger Zero Four Nine, was unique in the Design's classification of operatives, no other field agent having the fore-number "Zero." There had once been others, hence the "Four Nine," but they had all been lost, mostly in the Great Conflagration, some in the unrest which followed, and one more recently—code named Washington—in the failed operation which had necessitated the recruitment of a Beta, Bowie. No new "Zeros" had been commissioned for well over a decade. Four Nine was a throwback to the days when the Design had relied on its ability to deploy the Alpha equivalent of a surgical strike, a man with a single, destructive purpose coupled with the skills and heart-stopping ruthlessness required for total and deadly efficiency. That was the source of Zero Four Nine's power, and everyone in the hangar felt it now, their hairless skin shrinking and crawling instinctively as if, like in ancient tradition, someone had walked over their graves.

"For what reason was I recalled?" he demanded of the room as a whole.

His tone was clear, resonant without needing to shout, his articulation tight, clipped, the voice, almost, of a machine.

The techs looked at their shoes. Reissen pivoted pointedly to look at Merrick, and something like a smile appeared on his face.

You insisted on calling the shots, it seemed to say. *Be my guest.*

Merrick swallowed but his voice, when he spoke, was clear and unbroken.

"That was my decision," he said. "I need a full update on the actions of the agent, Bowie."

Four Nine's lip curled slightly, though it was unclear if his disdain was directed at Bowie or the director for recalling him on so paltry a concern.

"Bowie intercepted the agents bent on detaining Oswald," Four Nine replied, "leading the male to be taken to one of their hospitals, possibly dead."

"So he has operated as ordered," said Merrick.

"He has since attached himself to the female," said Four Nine.

"To what end?" asked Merrick.

"Unclear," said the agent. "I was tracking their movements when I was recalled." The statement held the whiff of disapproval but complaint was beneath Four Nine's dignity. He merely laid out the phrase as if the absurdity of his situation was self-evident. "They had just visited the Paine woman when I received the summons."

"He spoke to her?" said Merrick with new urgency.

"Yes. I was able to monitor their exchange."

"What did she tell him?" said Merrick. His skin had developed a waxy pallor even greater than was typical for an Alpha.

"Nothing of significance," said Four Nine. "But he continued to talk to the journalist—Rossi—in her vehicle and my sensors could not verify what they discussed. He proceeded to leave with her."

"In her vehicle?"

"No, on his time cycle."

"Why would he do that?" cut in Reissen.

"Had I been permitted to continue my mission," said Four Nine with crisp condescension, "this would have been ascertained. As it is, you will have to dispatch another agent to continue surveillance. Perhaps they may be able to answer that question."

The professor eyed Merrick with a touch of smugness.

"Who do you want to send? Our options in terms of suitable operatives are few and we have only two other motorcycles which are mission ready."

"Can't someone use this one?" Merrick replied with a nod at the still smoking bike Four Nine had come in on.

"No," said Four Nine abruptly.

Merrick gave Reissen an inquiring look.

"The vehicles are fine-tuned to the preferences of their primary riders . . ." he offered apologetically. Merrick's face twisted into an exaggerated version of Four Nine's contempt, but the agent spoke before he could give voice to his scorn.

"No one touches this vehicle but me. Any maintenance work done is only to be done under my direct supervision."

Merrick considered arguing the point, but let it go.

"If you were to return, how close to your previous incursion point could we get?"

"Safely," Reissen began, "at least a week earlier than his previous arrival point, which would put us around November 13, or thirty hours after the point he just came out, which would be . . . about 4:00 p.m. on November 22."

"Which is too late," said Four Nine.

"And less safely?" said Merrick with a steely glint in his eye.

Reissen hesitated, unable to keep his gaze from shifting apprehensively toward the agent.

"Professor?" Merrick demanded.

"Well," Reissen began, "maybe as early as November sixteenth, though he would have to be back within forty-eight hours to avoid a temporal paradox, or as late as . . ." he hesitated, "noon on the twenty-second. That would be just inside the mission parameters, but I'd have to advise against it."

"But we could do it," Merrick said.

"It would be disorienting for the agent and leaves no room for error, but yes, I suppose it is possible."

Reissen avoided looking at Four Nine.

"Very well," said Merrick. "Do it. And insert two more agents at the earlier entry point. Use the remaining time riders."

"Which agents?"

"Of those available," said Four Nine, "I recommend Vrubel. And Svenson."

Merrick considered this, then nodded his agreement.

"Is this really necessary?" said Reissen. "You don't know Bowie has gone rogue. He has completed his assignment thus far."

Merrick considered this and now he turned to face the time agent directly.

"Four Nine?" he said.

"Bowie is a Beta in fact," said the agent, "but a Gamma in his heart. It was a mistake to involve him in a mission of this seriousness."

"We had no choice," said Merrick, his indignation finally vanquishing his other feelings. "Washington's recklessness has forced our hand."

"Time riders take the steps you are too timid to enact," said Four Nine placidly. "Recklessness is part of the job description."

"And as a result, a Beta has the potential to jeopardize all that we have worked for," said Merrick coldly. Four Nine glared at him, but said nothing and, at length, Merrick shrugged off his fury. "Very well," he concluded to Reissen. "Prepare the incursion of all three agents. Secure Oswald and ensure completion of both strike missions."

"And Bowie?" asked Reissen. "Monitor and leave to the field agents' discretion?"

Merrick looked at Four Nine and read the man's wishes in his face.

"No," said the director. "Mark Bowie for termination."

Jäger Zero Four Nine did not smile, because he never smiled, but if he was a man given to such shows of emotion, he would have.

Forty miles away, where the solar energy plant sprawled in the barren Wastes devastated by the sun and bearing the battle scars of the Great Conflagration, two men in security overalls were checking the work rosters in response to Merrick's orders. One, whose designations name badge read Anders—tall, tanned and dark eyed, almost a Gamma in appearance—scrolled through the list and grunted.

"See?" he said. "Team four should have been moving ten minutes ago."

His colleague, technically his superior though not in ways that mattered beyond the work camp, was called Harvey. He was shorter and paler and, partly as a result, harbored delusional ambitions of being promoted to Alpha status one day.

"That's the second time this cycle," he remarked. "I'm putting their team leader on report."

Anders said nothing but he raised an eyebrow, grudgingly impressed. He didn't think Harvey had it in him. The team leader was a rugged, charismatic Gamma called Sefton who had a fiercely loyal following among the workers. Putting him on report would win Harvey no friends among the laborers. Of course, it could just be talk. Harvey did that sometimes: swaggering and boasting but never actually following through.

"No time like the present," he observed mildly.

Harvey gave him a hard look, recognizing the challenge for what it was.

"That's right," he agreed with an edge of defiance. "Come on."

Anders hesitated.

"Now?" he said. "You know how hot it is out there?"

Harvey glanced out the window at the acres of baked dirt and bright, barren stone which shimmered in the heat haze.

"Like you said," he replied. "No time like the present. And I need to report back to the director."

They were barely out the door when there was a distant boom. Both men ducked instinctively then glanced hurriedly around. A cloud of thick, oily smoke was rising from the eastern transit station. As they watched, one of the pylons which routed the cables from the collectors leaned, then buckled at the base and collapsed.

Harvey snatched the comm from his belt while barking instructions at Anders.

"Get an armed squad over there now and secure the area!" he ordered, then turning to his comm, "We have a pylon down in Zone Four East! Repeat, we have a pylon down!"

A siren began to wail, but before it could reach its full pitch, it died abruptly.

"What—?" Harvey began, but then there was another explosion, closer this time, and they caught the flash before the billowing smoke even started to rise, as another transit station went up.

"Attention all personnel!" Harvey shouted into his comm, "we have a major incident in process!"

Another bang, and a shower of debris which made the two men duck back into the office doorway for cover.

"Why is no one responding?" Harvey muttered, staring stupidly at his communication unit. "Where are the maintenance teams?"

Anders glanced around but offered nothing. All around the station the lights were going out as the transformer shut down. Within seconds the entire power array was offline, many of its core components reduced to black and twisted metal. Over on the north side of the collector array, something was burning. Anders savored the metallic hotness of it in his nostrils and, smiling faintly, drew his sidearm. He leveled it at his superior.

"Comm," he said simply.

Harvey stared open mouthed, stupefied. Anders raised the weapon just enough to make the point.

"You Gamma loving traitor," he sputtered.

"Your comm," said Anders, cocking the pistol.

"This is an outrage," huffed Harvey, but his indignation only made him look small and weak.

"No doubt," said Anders taking the device and flicking to a different channel. "This is Anders," he said into the comm. "All good at this end."

There was a moment of silence and then the comm finally came to life.

"Initiating phase two," said Sefton.

CHAPTER NINE

"Jimmy's alive," said Sandra Rossi, relief pouring off her as she walked away from the pay phone on Powhattan Street in Dallas. "In surgery, but alive." She caught herself, as if remembering who she was talking to, and her face closed up hard and tight. "No thanks to you."

Bowie wasn't sure how to respond. A part of him was glad to hear the man wasn't dead, but that was absurd. These people were terrorists. He had to keep reminding himself of that. How else could they be involved?

"If I wasn't here, what would you do now?" he asked.

She was clearly wrong footed by the question.

"Go to the hospital, maybe," she said, her confusion seemingly making her honest. The thought seemed to solidify in her mind and she opened the driver's side door of the Chrysler and climbed in. Bowie moved quickly to the passenger side and dropped into the seat beside her before she could put the keys in the ignition.

"What about your mission?" he demanded.

"It's not a mission," she snapped back. "I told you. I can't drive around Dallas looking for Oswald. I guess I could wait for him to go back to the rooming house tonight, but if he doesn't . . ." She shrugged. "I could go back to the cops, but that won't do any good."

"You went to the police?" asked Bowie, noting that she was making no move to start the car.

"Of course!" she exclaimed as if it was obvious. "First thing we did."

"When?"

"I don't know," she said vaguely with a waft of her hand. "What day is it? Thursday. So Tuesday night. God," she mused, "has it only been two days? Anyway, yeah. Tuesday night. The night of the shooting."

"What shooting?" Bowie demanded. "I thought you said Oswald hadn't killed anyone yet."

"Not him," Rossi responded brusquely as if that was obvious. "The weird guy at the Adolphus."

Bowie just stared at her. When she gave him a pointed look, he shook his head to say he didn't know what she was talking about.

"The Adolphus?" he prompted.

"Buy a fucking guidebook," she snapped.

Bowie's irritation crested. Everything about her manner was unfamiliar, off putting and infuriating. He leaned a few inches toward her but she didn't flinch, glaring at him, defying him to hit her. He took a breath.

"I'm just asking you a question," he said with superhuman self-control. "What is the Adolphus?"

She gritted her teeth, turned away, then shrugged, unsnapping her shoulder bag. Bowie tensed, hand drifting to the gun in his belt, but what she pulled out was a small cardboard carton from which she pulled a slim white tube which she popped into her mouth. He watched with revolted fascination as she then produced a device from which she snapped a flame that she touched to the end of the tube until it smoked.

Cigarette, said some forgotten archive in his brain. *A kind of nicotine delivery system.*

She sucked on it with something like relief or satisfaction, the tip glowing hot.

"It's an old hotel downtown," she said, like it was as unimportant as the smoke she was now blowing into the cramped car. "Jimmy and I go there sometimes after work. It's fairly close and classy—usually. Tuesday night there was a brawl. A guy got shot."

"Who?" asked Bowie. He knew none of this.

Another shrug.

"No clue," she said. "Some out-of-towner. Odd looking. Got into a fight with some local toughs."

"Including Oswald?"

"No, he wasn't there!" she exclaimed suddenly, as if maddened by the attempt to explain. "The fight had nothing to do with him. Why are you even talking to me?"

It wasn't a real question and Bowie ignored it.

"So what's the connection?" he demanded, wafting away the smoke. It was sickening, oppressive. He coughed and, as if it was a reflex, she wound her window halfway down and turned to blow the smoke through the crack.

She squeezed her eyes shut and, for a moment, did nothing but smoke and brood. When she opened them again it was with a sense of reluctant resolve.

"See for yourself," she said. And reaching into the back of the Chrysler, she retrieved a pair of folded newspapers that she slammed into his lap.

Bowie gave her a last appraising look. If she was lying or trying to trick him, he got no sense of it. He bent over the copies of *The New York Times*, his large frame seeming to fill the vehicle, and scanned the first one.

Nothing struck him as unusual or out of place.

"What?" he asked looking at her. Rossi was sitting quite still, one hand rested on the steering wheel, watching him. "I don't understand."

"The date," she said.

He looked back to the paper, located the date at the top and read it aloud.

"Thursday, November 21, 1963. Today. So?"

"So?" Rossi replied. "So the weird man who died at the Adolphus had it with him on Tuesday night. Two days *before* it was printed."

Bowie hesitated.

"So he was one of yours," he said.

"My what?" she demanded. "I've told you: I'm not an agent on a mission. I'm a junior reporter for *The Dallas Morning News*."

"From here."

"Of course from here," she shot back. "As opposed to what?"

"The future," he said. "The mid-twenty-second century."

A strange calm came over her then. She considered him with a new wariness that had nothing to do with his size and strength. For a moment she seemed to forget the cigarette and sat there with her mouth open, her head tipped slightly back.

"You're one of them," she said flatly. She thought, paused, then clarified the statement, laying out the words cautiously as if unsure of what they would do. "A time traveler."

Bowie thought then said simply, "And you aren't."

She shook her head slowly, and then suddenly laughed at the ridiculousness of the thing.

"I am not," she said.

And at last, he believed her. He wasn't certain why. He just felt it inside him. It wasn't a logical or otherwise intellectual conclusion, and he knew that it was little more than a hunch, but it felt unshakably right. The thought—and the vague, unsystematic way he had come by it—bothered him.

She reached over and put the second newspaper on the top. It was dated Saturday, November 23.

Two days from now.

The headline was bigger than anything in the other edition, big, bold italic type:

KENNEDY IS KILLED BY SNIPER
AS HE RIDES IN CAR IN DALLAS;
JOHNSON SWORN IN ON PLANE

Bowie's mind raced. This was the event he had been charged to ensure happened.

"Jimmy didn't think anything of it at first," said Rossi. "Thought it was faked, some kind of propaganda.

Or a prank. But then the details in today's paper started coming true."

"Details?" said Bowie. He felt like he had been considering a picture only to realize that it was nothing like what it had initially seemed. It was disorienting. Worrying. "Like what?"

Rossi took the paper from him, flipping through the pages of minuscule text, grainy black-and-white photographs, and stylized line drawings in boxes advertising sharp suits and Thanksgiving Day sales, stopping at the sports page. She stabbed her finger at the lead story and read the headline.

RANGERS TIE BREWERS AT GARDEN, 1-1,
AS VILLEMURE MAKES 32 SAVES.

The tie could have been an educated guess, but thirty-two saves? That game happened last night, twenty-four hours *after* I took this paper from the booth where the stranger died. We checked the wires before we went looking for Oswald. Every detail in the paper was right. So were all the other scores." She read more.

BLACK HAWKS BEAT THE RED WINGS 5-2.

76ERS CRUSH KNICKS 118-101 BUT LOSE GAMBEE
TO A SUSPECTED FRACTURE IN HIS LEFT FOOT.

You can't fake this stuff or guess it two days before the games are played."

"So you figured that if this paper was telling the future, then so was the one announcing the assassination."

"By Lee Harvey Oswald," said Rossi with grim finality. "Twenty-four-year-old, worked at the Texas School Book Depository, former resident of the Soviet Union, and supporter of a pro-Cuba activist group."

Bowie felt the world in his head spin, and he fumblingly reached for the handle to wind his window down. He needed air untainted by Rossi's smoke. This was all so unexpected, so strange. Why hadn't he been told? He stared at the headline.

"This man who died," he said, determined to make sense of it all, "the weird one with the newspapers," said Bowie, "tell me about him."

She seemed about to protest, to resist, but changed her mind, not—he thought—because she was interested in helping him, but because she was working through something nonsensical that had so far resisted any explanation. She was using him as a sounding board.

"The first cop to arrive checked his wallet. Said his name was Abraham Washington, which was clearly fake."

"Why?"

"Abraham Washington?" she replied with a sardonic look which triggered his annoyance again. "You people aren't big on history, huh?"

"History is decadence," Bowie replied reflexively. "The past is dead. We live for the future."

She gave him an odd look, as if he had spoken a foreign language.

"O . . . K . . ." she said.

"That's what we were taught," Bowie offered, though he wasn't sure why he felt the need to explain himself. "Interest in the past, where I come from, is considered self-indulgent, suspect."

"So you aren't taught history in school?"

It was the first time she had sounded interested in him, but it came out quickly, and immediately she looked as if it had slipped out against her better judgment.

"There is a limited module on the rise of the Design—what we call our society," he said, wondering why the admission embarrassed him, and thinking of the minimal and error-ridden briefing he had been given before coming here.

"Sounds very official," she said.

"It is," he agreed, realizing after he had said it that she didn't think it to be a good thing. "But it doesn't so much teach the past as explain why the present—*our present*—was necessary and better." He thought of the training he had received before the mission, the inconsistent strings of facts without context, the patchy data and simplistic logic he had been offered as insight into what was, in fact, a very real and complicated period of time. He changed the subject. "So, you were saying about this Washington person."

"He was staying at the hotel. He sounded a little like you, but he looked different. Pale. He wore this ridiculous wig. Bald as a billiard ball underneath. And he was . . ." she sought for the word. "I don't know. A prick, frankly. More than rude. It was like everything and everyone was beneath him."

Alpha, thought Bowie.

"Was he one of those terrorists?" she asked.

Again, he noted her interest. A journalist's curiosity, perhaps.

"I don't think so," he answered, "which is strange."

"Why?"

"Because I wasn't told about him. Perhaps I was his replacement," he said, but even as he said it he wondered why, if that were true, he had not been given the full story. And, he thought, the truth of the thing growing firmer, clearer in his head with each passing moment, this woman Rossi was no time rider. That might have been little more than a hunch at first, but now that he was used to the idea, it seemed more obviously true as he ran it through every test his brain could construct. She belonged here. The period was in every detail of her voice, her hair, her clothes, even the satisfaction with which she drew on the foul cigarette. It was not possible that she was a terrorist sent from 2157.

Maybe there were no terrorists. Not here at least, not crossing time from your present to disrupt the past.

The idea startled him, alarmed him because of what it implied about those who had given him his assignment, but immediately it felt true. But then why, if they'd already happened, send him back to preserve the timeline outlined by those headlines? He lay the newspapers down and stared straight ahead, seeing nothing.

"You OK?" said Rossi.

There it was again, and it was stronger this time, a question that implied more than merely being intrigued by a puzzle or mystery. He gave her a quick, suspicious look, but her concern seemed real, if momentary.

"No," he said. "I don't think I am." Her right hand moved an inch or two toward him, then stopped and pulled back. She looked away and drew hard on her cigarette, so that half of what remained shrank to ash. He blinked at the smoke and pulled himself together as he reached for the door latch and climbed out of the car. He hesitated, neither truly in nor out of the vehicle, and his stillness caught her attention.

"What are you doing?" she asked.

"I am not sure," he said. Again, the honesty wasn't really intended and it immediately felt unprofessional.

She looked down, thumbing her way through the car keys on the ring in her hand as if searching for a clue, for inspiration.

"So . . ." said Bowie, "if I were to let you go, what would you do now?"

Her head snapped up and she gave him a suspicious look.

"Attempt to stop Oswald?"

"Yes."

"Well, I know where he works and where he'll shoot from tomorrow," she said, thinking it out as she spoke. "I can call it in as a threat, say nothing about time travel. Tell them Oswald told people he was going to kill the president. They would have to at least take him into custody, right? Stake out the building? Better safe than sorry. And if none of that works, we go to the book depository ourselves and stop him."

Bowie did a momentary double take.

"We?" he said. "Did you forget what I told you? My mission is to protect Oswald."

"So he can kill John F. Kennedy?" She gave him a narrow-eyed look, then shook her head. "I don't think you'd let that happen."

It was such a strange thing to say that he was completely wrong footed.

"Why?" he asked.

She shrugged.

"You don't seem the type," she said. Once more it was a throw-away remark, impossible to read.

"I shot your friend," he said.

"You did," she said. "But he's going to pull through."

"That makes no sense," he said.

"Perhaps," she said. "But you didn't know what Oswald was going to do," she said, pointing squarely at him. "Now you do."

This was too much. Bowie straightened up and looked away down the street. She didn't know him, had no idea of what he had done or was capable of, and the idea that—based on a few minutes of conversation—she had real insights into him was absurd. But in one respect the maddening woman was right. No one had said anything to him about what they had really wanted him to do—save an assassin, kill a president—and that bothered him.

Why am I here?

Merrick and Reissen had said their society was in jeopardy, their whole way of life was being threatened by terrorists who were trying to rewrite history. There was an event in the past which had to take place to secure the future he knew. If terrorists disrupted that event everything would unravel. It was his job to secure the future and ensure that his present evolved as it should.

And is it a good future?

The question in his head startled him as much as the thunk of the driver's side door.

"Of course it is," he muttered aloud.

"What?" asked Rossi. She had gotten out of the car and was staring at him across the white roof.

"Nothing," said Bowie, rattled. "Just talking to myself."

He wondered why she had gotten out of the car. In his reverie she might have driven away . . .

"Someone lied to you," she said, pointing the car key at him and sighting along it like it was a gun. "Or they didn't give you the whole story."

"That's what happens when you're a soldier," said Bowie. "You get your orders because people who know more than you do have figured out the best course of action. They don't explain the big picture to you."

"Oh yeah," she replied dryly, "we know all about that here. A decade ago it was Korea. Now we're shipping boys to a place called Vietnam—which most folks couldn't find on a map—and I'm sure as hell those soldiers have no idea who they're fighting for or against."

Bowie didn't know what that meant, so he just shook his head again.

"Soldiers follow orders," he said, repeating the mantra like a drowning man holding onto a life raft.

"Theirs not to reason why, theirs but to do and die?" she said, clearly quoting from something. "Is that it?"

"When your society is under attack, you do as your superiors tell you," he said through barely parted lips.

"Into the valley of death, rode the six hundred."

"Will you stop doing that?" he demanded. "I don't know what you are talking about."

"Sorry," she said. "An old poem. But for the record, I can't think of a clearer example of your society being under assault than having your president assassinated."

"Your society, not mine."

"And yours is better?"

Her question, so close to the one he had just asked himself, caught him so off guard that he could think of nothing to say and just stared at her until she clarified. Her face was earnest, her dark eyes fixed. A wisp of her long hair had broken free and rippled in her face with the wind, but she didn't seem to notice it.

"I mean" she said, "this Washington character said that he came from somewhere *better*. I heard him say it. The guys in the bar thought he was from New York or somewhere. The waitress asked him where he was from and he said, 'Somewhere better.' It's part of what eventually got him killed. So. Is it?"

"Is it what?"

"Is it better?" she persisted. "The world you come from. God knows we have our problems here—war, poverty, racism, injustice, greed—but we are working to improve them, at least some of us are. But there is also joy and love, art, music, culture. And we make scientific breakthroughs daily. Kennedy says we are going to the moon . . ."

Her eyes flashed to the newspaper headline proclaiming the president's death and her momentary enthusiasm failed her like an engine that had run out of fuel. In her sudden desolation she seemed to forget the question with which she had begun, and Bowie was glad because he did not know how to answer it.

His world was cleaner and more orderly. In his portion of the world at least. The rules were clear and people followed them to the letter. Because the consequences of not doing so were best left undiscovered. Everyone—or mostly everyone—knew their place. There was none of this place's scrambling to reach the top of the heap. As to the other things she had listed, the decade since the Great Conflagration had been primarily peaceful, and greed had been somewhat curtailed by the restriction of what was realistically possible for individuals within a highly stratified society. But while poverty, racism and injustice were mostly hidden, glossed over, they were still there, as Sefton would have been quick to point out. Bowie's brother's entire life was dictated by the conditions of those things, and they were what drove him to resist where Bowie had chosen to assimilate. The thought pained him. It often did, but usually he could go back to Cloud City, to the comfort and minimalist elegance of his home, and put such unpleasantness from his mind by reminding himself that such injustices—however unpleasant—served order and the greater good. Already it was harder to think like that here. He wasn't sure what she meant by art and culture—more than the austere statues outside security headquarters or his spare monochrome photographs, and more, no doubt, of what the Design's official history called decadence. As to joy and love . . . ? Irrelevant. He wasn't even sure he knew what they were.

Still . . .

"Call the book depository," he said. "Find out if Oswald is there."

"You want to speak to him? He'll recognize you from this morning."

"Maybe," said Bowie, flustered by his own uncertainty. "I need to think."

"Which side are you on?" she pressed.

"Just make the call!" he shot back abruptly. Her knack for getting under his skin was undermining his habitual composure. He turned away from her, closing the conversation, so she shrugged and fished inside the car, pulling her shoulder bag out by its strap. On opening it, she removed a lined notebook full of minuscule scribbling, flipped through the pages until she found what she was looking for and returned to the pay phone.

He sidled after her, keeping his distance, but making sure she knew he would be able to hear what she said. She pushed a coin into the slot and dialed.

"Good morning," she said, professional, businesslike as soon as someone came on the line, "this is Marsha Stanfast from the Social Security Administration district office. I'm making some routine inquiries about one of your employees, a Lee Harvey Oswald. Is he at work today?"

Bowie couldn't hear what the muffled, tinny voice on the other end said, but he gathered from Rossi's manner that she had been told to wait while the office manager checked. Rossi avoided Bowie's eyes, listening intently. After some twenty seconds she spoke again. "Excellent. No, there's no problem. And can you tell me how long Mr. Oswald has been employed at your facility? . . . October 16 of this year? So, he's been working there for just over a month? . . . I see. And can you tell me how he came to be employed at the Texas School Book Depository? . . . Thank you. That's very helpful. No, there's no problem. One of my colleagues and I will be along to speak to him shortly . . . No, there's no need to let him know we are coming. Thanks again. Goodbye."

Bowie had to admit that she was good. Still not an agent, but smart and resourceful.

She hung up and for a moment her eyes narrowed in thought so intense that it was as if she had forgotten Bowie's presence until he spoke.

"Well?"

"He's there," she said. "Only been working there a month."

"I heard," Bowie replied. "Why did you ask?"

She put her notebook away but kept the car keys out. She had a way of sliding each key absently through her fingers as if the familiarity of the action helped her mind focus on other things.

"Well, the obvious question is why he wants to kill the president, right? Is it just an impulse, or has he been planning it? Is he alone, or part of some organization?"

"He's not a time rider, if that's what you mean."

"I know that," she said, dismissing the possibility with a vague wave of her hand. "His personal history is too long and complete for any of that. Less than a day after the event the papers already know a lot about him. And unlike your friend Washington, he clearly belonged here."

"Not my friend," Bowie inserted. She ignored the comment.

"But if he's only been there since mid-October, it's possible that he got the job specifically to be there when the president came to town."

"When was that announced?"

"Late September. My paper announced the dates of the visit."

"And the route the president would take?"

"That only came out a few days ago, but the book depository is right there on Dealey Plaza, just down Houston from my paper's headquarters. There was a good chance the motorcade would pass through that area."

"You asked how he got the job," Bowie prompted.

"Yes," she said, her thoughtfulness deepening into puzzlement. "Apparently his interview was set up by the woman we saw earlier: Ruth Paine."

"Is that significant?"

"I don't see how it could be," Rossi answered, "but it's odd."

"What is her relationship to Oswald?"

"Not sure. Not family. A friend of his wife's, I think. Marina. She's Russian."

"Paine?" Bowie asked.

"No, Marina. I don't know anything else about Ruth Paine. I don't suppose it matters. But we know where he is. I'm going to call the Secret Service." She delivered the line as a challenge, holding his eyes. "Are you going to stop me?"

Bowie hesitated. The question reminded him of how they had met, what he had been ordered to do, and it struck him again that the way they had just been talking—as if they were on the same side—was odd. Again, he avoided her question.

"Why does Oswald want to kill Kennedy?" he asked.

"How the hell should I know?" said Rossi. "Supposedly he's pro-Cuba and a former Soviet defector. Actually *lived* in Russia. But that actually makes him an odd person to hate the president. Most people who hate Kennedy think he's too soft on communism. Too liberal. Too progressive. Doesn't really want to be in Vietnam, wants to build bridges with the Russians. He's obsessed with space and has talked about some kind of partnership with the Soviets on that front. Maybe sharing resources to accelerate the process. Build a united humanity in the exploration of the one thing neither side can claim to own." She shrugged, but her face was sad, as if she sympathized with the idea but knew it couldn't happen, not with the man in the White House doomed to fall to a sniper's bullet. "He's also been tough on organized crime, so he's made no friends there either. And he's Catholic. And he's getting more and more liberal on racial issues. Such things don't make a man popular in a Southern Baptist town like Dallas, so who knows?"

Bowie looked off down the street, stalling, but also uncomfortable. There was a wounded fervor in her eyes, a weary despair which felt suddenly raw. He didn't know how to respond to it.

There was a sound drifting like smoke from an open window in one of the buildings which housed an electronics store on the ground floor, its wares advertised in rounded cursive letters, red and dotted with exclamation points. He focused on the sound. It was rhythmic, and melodic, and over the music a ragged voice was singing strange elliptical phrases. It was stirring, soulful, and unlike anything Bowie had ever heard. It sounded like Rossi looked, wistful and pained but also honest as the tip of a blade.

"What is that?" he asked without looking at her.

"The music?" Rossi replied. "Some kind of jazz. Maybe Billie Holiday. Why?"

Bowie shook his head, saying nothing. Again the question about his society which he had dodged earlier floated into his mind:

Is it better?

Then another sound tore through the music. It should have been an explosive bang, but it seemed to happen backward, and following it was a moment in which all the background noises of the morning—the distant traffic, the improbable birds chirping in the trees, the music from the window—all vanished for a split second as if sucked into some kind of vortex. The light in the middle of the street seemed to shimmer and contract, and then reality returned and there was a helmeted man astride a great motorcycle riding right at them.

It wobbled for the briefest of moments as if successfully concluding a jump, and then the rider took one hand from the handlebars and held it straight out in front of him.

Bowie recognized the weapon just as it fired its first shot.

Even as he dove, barreling into Rossi, who was staring at the bike in bewilderment, and pushed her down onto the hard road surface, he knew that his indecision and uncertainty were gone.

Which side are you on?

His handlers, the representatives of the world he had sworn to protect, had taken that choice away from him.

CHAPTER TEN

The gun shot sounded flat and hollow at this distance, but that made it no less lethal. The Chrysler's passenger side mirror exploded in a gleaming shower of glass and Rossi cried out as a fragment found her cheek. Bowie was on top of her, but rolled, drawing his pistol and firing twice at the oncoming bike.

It was different from his, shinier and sleeker than his primeval juggernaut, and the man in the saddle showed no alarm at the return of fire. The helmet—red with a mirrored visor—made the agent's face utterly unreadable, but he exuded a professional calm and efficiency that Bowie did not feel.

It was fewer than a hundred yards away and closing fast. The rider fired again, not a single round this time, but five or six in rapid succession.

Some kind of automatic weapon with a long barrel, thought Bowie, with a rueful look at his half-empty revolver.

"Get behind the front of the car!" he yelled at Rossi.

That automatic rifle would punch right through the doors and fenders as if they were cardboard, he thought, his mind flashing back to the Great Conflagration. Without armor, only the engine block was solid enough to offer protection. He shoved her up and forward, and she grunted, grazing her knee as she struggled into a ragged scramble. Bowie fired twice more, the revolver kicking so that the second shot went wide. He cursed himself and rolled through a squat and into an apelike bound which took him toward the rear of the car and right at the approaching bike. He fired his last round, then scrambled onto the sidewalk as bullets kicked off the road around him, throwing grit in his face. The rear window of the Chrysler took two rounds and burst like an egg.

There was a gray van parked between Bowie and his own bike. Wherever he went, Bowie thought, it was imperative that he took the bike with him or he would be stuck here. He knelt by the van's near-side tire and cast a look back to where Rossi was huddled against the side of the Chrysler, scrunched up small and staring at him, eyes wide and mouth clenched. He showed her the flat of his hand—*stay there*—then cocked his head to listen to the approaching bike. It was louder, not slowing down.

Which means he's going to drive by shooting, then circle back, Bowie thought. For a split second he was back in the ruins of old Detroit, calculating his move as the C-bots came through on their cleanup sweep. This was just a man on a bike, but Bowie was outgunned and trying to protect an unarmed civilian. He didn't pause to ask himself why he was doing that. Instead, he adjusted his position so that the van gave him maximum cover, drew the larger of the two semi-automatic pistols and aimed across its hood, waiting for the biker to ride into view.

But the bike never arrived. In its place he heard a strange whirring sound and looked up to see a sphere the size of his fist rising into the air behind the van. At the apex of its trajectory it radiated a sudden flash of brilliant, ultramarine light which was followed instantly by a high pitched keening sound as if the fabric of the world was being torn apart. The sonic shock wave that came with it blew through reality like wet tissue.

Even with the cover of the parked vehicles the explosion sent Bowie sprawling on the sidewalk. Hunks of steel and copper rained down around him, while the concussive force of the blast left him momentarily deaf.

The bike! Bowie realized with a rush of fury and despair, his only way to get back home . . .

The sonic grenade had shredded the parked cars and blasted a crater in the road. Bowie's befuddled mind knew just enough to stay down as the biker came on, his rifle spewing out another burst at the spot Bowie had been moments before. He slithered through the smoke and falling debris toward Rossi beside the ravaged Chrysler, mouthing "Get in!" over and over, though he couldn't hear his own voice.

The reporter's eyes widened still farther, but she reached blindly for the driver's side door latch, snapped it, and dragged the door wide. She still had the keys in her hand and—consciously or otherwise—had already selected the one for the ignition. Bowie nodded his agreement and reached for the backdoor as he thumbed the safety off the automatic. Bowie stood quickly, found the motorcyclist riding by and fired off three quick rounds. The first made the rider flinch and may have caught him in the shoulder. The second sparked off the arch of chrome pipe which was the saddle's lower back rest, and the third caught him just right of his spine.

The bike sped up to get clear, though Bowie had no idea how much protection the rider had on under his bulky leather coveralls.

"Go!" he roared, launching himself onto the glass covered back seat. This time he heard himself, though the sound was muffled and out of phase, so it seemed to cycle and distort.

"Where?" Rossi gasped as she snapped the engine into life.

"Away from him!" Bowie shouted.

The car lurched forward, but immediately she twisted the wheel hard to the right and sent it across the street and into the far curb. It jolted to a halt and she fought for reverse. Bowie looked up through the shattered rear window and saw the bike tracing a wide circle to come back for them. He squeezed off another shot, but the car surged backward as he fired. He aimed again as Rossi hit the brakes, put it in gear and sent it back the way they had come. As they passed the van, Bowie saw the smoking ruins of his bike. Two-thirds of it was just gone and the road was streaked with the blast lines from the sonic grenade the agent sent to kill him had used. It seemed that only he was limited to twentieth-century tech.

The agent sent to kill him . . .

That was a sobering thought.

Bowie's jaws clamped tight and he turned away from the wreckage. Even if he survived the hour it would only be the beginning of his time in 1963. He looked back as the Chrysler hit a good rolling speed and watched the bike complete its turn and begin to come after them. The rider leveled his rifle again and Bowie ducked as its muzzle flashed.

"Stay down!" he yelled, ducking as another bullet tore through the roof of the Chrysler.

"Trying to look where I'm going!" Rossi shouted back.

"Get off the main road!" Bowie replied, sitting up again and returning fire.

A gravelly, rumbling sound had started as soon as the car reached third gear, and now the whole vehicle began to shudder. Bowie could smell bitter, oily smoke quite unlike gunpowder or the sonic device which had destroyed his bike.

"The engine's hit," he said. "We're going to need to find a place to ditch it and run."

She turned to face him then, her face taut and pale, but she just nodded, and put her foot down, as if determined to get as much as she could out of the car before it died. The surge of speed heightened the noise of mechanical failure and smoke gushed from the dash, black and acrid. She made a hard right, then a left, then another right, all in quick succession as she tried to lose the bike. Bowie checked the magazine in his pistol and waited. At this distance there was no point wasting precious ammunition.

There had been little traffic so far, but as they made the last turn they merged with a steady stream of vehicles, and though they cut in efficiently, Rossi had to halve their speed almost immediately. There were cars, vans, and trucks of various sizes everywhere, most fewer than three feet apart. Bowie had never seen anything like it. He gazed wildly through the smoggy haze, marveling at the array of colors, the noise, the smell.

"Not good," Rossi muttered to herself, checking the rearview mirror which was, miraculously, intact. But even at their current crawl, the smoke from the engine seemed to be thickening around them until they were enveloped in a bitter cloud. Someone up ahead leaned on their horn and it was answered by a round of others, blaring their frustration as the traffic ground to a halt. Somewhere in the distance he could hear what sounded like sirens.

For them?

Bowie looked back. They had pulled clear of the bike which was now only just visible some two hundred yards behind them, but the cycle would be narrow enough to cut through some of that distance while they sat here in the car, trapped.

"Give it more gas!" he shouted.

"We're parked," she replied, "more gas just means more smoke."

"Exactly," he replied. "Do it."

She frowned, then pushed the accelerator. Immediately a choking cloud suffused the vehicle.

"Jesus!" she coughed, wafting the air in front of her face with her hand.

"Keep doing it." Bowie encouraged.

She revved the engine until it raced, shuddering and belching out its noxious plume. As the dark cloud thickened all around them, Bowie tapped her shoulder.

"Time to go," he said.

"But my car!" she shouted in protest.

"The car is dead. Do you want to join it? Slide out and stay low."

"And go where?"

Through the black smoke, she saw Bowie's face make an expressive shrug.

"I hate you," she said.

"Understandable," he replied. "Now go."

"No," she said. "I hear sirens. We should wait for the police."

"And tell them we are under attack from an agent sent from the future?"

She stared at him through the smoke.

Agent Carla Vrubel scanned the stalled column of vehicles. In her helmet the mission status bar which identified her target simply as Rogue Agent Bowie, still showed "Incomplete." It seemed there had been some kind of accident or emergency ahead—at least two junctions in front of her, if her binocular visor setting was accurate. She considered dismounting and approaching the target vehicle on foot, but she couldn't see it precisely from where she was: there was too much smoke. That meant their vehicle was crippled, which was all to the good.

She smiled at the thought and—better still—the memory of the devastated remnants of the enemy's time cycle.

They were trapped.

And in another few minutes, they would be dead, and she could leave this festering backwater and go home.

Another smile. Cold. Hard. A smile without pleasure, without joy. She would get a promotion for this. Maybe the Medal of Service. At the very least, a letter of commendation in her file.

She forced the bike between a pair of cars and in front of a third. As she maneuvered into the next lane the driver of a white open-topped car emblazoned with the word Lincoln, the driver—a tanned white man in large, reflective sunglasses—blew his horn and shunted the big vehicle forward warningly. Vrubel swung her M14 rifle around to point into the driver's face, letting the man's response dictate whether or not she fired.

The driver raised his arms in a swift, panicked movement that dislodged his shades, and he flung himself sideways into the empty passenger seat with a confused plea for mercy. Vrubel stared at him, unblinking, until the man had the presence of mind to cautiously pull his vehicle back a couple of feet, allowing the motorcycle to move in front and navigate its next move.

The smoke from the Chrysler had become a billowing wall, obscuring much of the highway. Vrubel thought that it was still moving, though that could have been the wind. The cars around seemed stationary, but the more she looked, the more she thought that the traffic in front of her target had started to move. As she watched, a blue truck behind it started nudging its way into the next lane to go around it, much to the exasperation of the nearby drivers.

So they were stuck. One of them may even be dead or dying. Maybe both. She had hit the car multiple times, and she knew that the man called Bowie—low-value operative that he was—had not been equipped with the body armor she was wearing. It was certainly possible that she had caught the driver who had finally succumbed.

She would need to check. It wasn't like she could reach the necessary speed to generate the heat envelope on this stretch of road anyway, even with boosters engaged, so she wouldn't be opening the temporal portal any time soon. She angled the bike into the lane which seemed to be moving quickest and stashed her rifle in the purpose-built pannier. No need to attract the attention of local law enforcement.

The Chrysler was only twenty yards ahead now, but she still couldn't see into it for the dense pall of oily smoke. Even through her helmet she could taste the bitter tang of it. It stank like the world it was part of: filthy, chaotic, and degenerate. She couldn't wait to get back to the cool, measured elegance of the Design . . .

She rolled another few feet forward, and suddenly a gust of wind parted the fumes spewing from the Chrysler and she saw it clearly, its burgundy-and-white shell bullet-pocked, its rear window gone.

There was no one inside.

Getting through the almost parked vehicles on the highway had been the easy part. Once over the concrete divider, Rossi and Bowie had had to weave and dodge, stagger and sprint their way across the free-flowing traffic going in the opposite direction. Then they had scrambled down a grassy embankment, across a smaller street, and into the narrowest alley they could find. It ran behind a pair of tower blocks, mostly square and unadorned but new looking: a stab at a version of the future which, from Bowie's point of view, managed to be both quaint and crass.

"Wait!" Rossi called out.

Bowie, a few yards ahead, stopped and turned.

She had one hand up and was doubled over, that shoulder bag she hung onto as if her life depended on it clutched to her stomach.

"Where are we going?" she breathed.

"We have to keep moving," he said.

"I'd like to see you run in these heels," she snapped. She was breathless with fear and exertion.

"So take them off."

"And run around like some wino saying 'buddy, can you spare a dime'?"

"I understood a third of the words in that sentence and none of its meaning," said Bowie.

"You sound like a robot."

"What?"

"A machine. You sound like a machine."

"I know what a robot is," Bowie replied, inexplicably irritated. "I am not one."

"I didn't say you were one . . . Oh, forget it."

"We have to keep moving," he said again.

"And again I ask, where to?"

Bowie checked that no one was following, but it was a stalling tactic. His mind had been galloping faster than his legs but he still had no plan, no way out of this mess. She inched closer, her face getting that shrewd look he already recognized as she studied him.

"You're lost," she said. "You have no idea where to go. You're dragging me along, but you have no more idea what to do than I do. Why don't you just leave?"

"Leave?"

"Back to your own time, or," she added, as if still embarrassed by the implications of what she had just said, "wherever the hell you come from?"

"Maybe you should just do as I say in the interest of staying alive."

He turned away, scowling, but she moved with him, that stare of hers unflinching, until her eyes widened with discovery.

"You can't!" she exclaimed. "Oh my God. You're stuck here. Right?" Bowie said nothing, so she continued. "What was it, the bike? That's how you came here but it got blown up so now you're stuck? Oh, that's terrific."

She gave a bleak laugh.

"What's funny?" Bowie demanded.

"This is not a laugh of amusement," she clarified darkly. "It is derision. You know, the kind of scorn you people direct at our world, the contempt that justifies you rewriting our world to safeguard yours. Only this time it's directed at *your world* and its Flash Gordon bullshit gadgetry."

"Flash . . . ?"

"Let me guess," she cut in, "you don't know what that is. You know, for people happy to rewrite your history, you sure don't know much about it."

"How much do you know about life two hundred years ago?" he shot back.

She considered that and shrugged.

"Bits," she conceded. "If I could research it. Still, would mostly be the big stuff. Not enough to live there. That's where you come from? Two hundred years in the future?"

Bowie nodded and she got a dreamy, dazzled look in her eyes, momentarily forgetting her irritation.

"We should get out of the street," Bowie said.

"And. Go. Where?"

The annoyance was back.

"If I could get that agent's bike from him, maybe it would work for me," he mused aloud. "The helmet would be bound to his biometrics, but I could still ride it, and the time vortex is controlled from the bike itself."

"That's insane," said Rossi. "The guy has the fire power of a battalion. And anyway, we have something to do here."

That brought his attention back to her.

"Like what?" he asked.

"An assassination to prevent," she said, leaning forward like she was addressing a young child.

"I didn't say I would do that."

"Because you're a good soldier following orders. As is the guy trying to put holes in us. So what is he? One of these time terrorists you were talking about?"

Bowie took a breath, then shook his head. Once more her eyes narrowed, then widened as another realization landed.

"He's on your side!" she exclaimed. "Oh, that's perfect!" Again she laughed, a bleak, mirthless laugh that turned her face skyward. "You hesitated, so they've come to kill you, and yet you're *still* trying to do what they told you to. You *are* a goddamned machine."

"I am not a machine!" he snapped, turning on her, fury flushing his face so that she stepped back and raised her hands.

"Easy there, champ," she said. "Touched a nerve there, did I? OK. You're not a machine."

"Can we please get out of the street?"

"Sure," she said. "We are close to Akard Street. There's a diner a block ahead. Good waffles."

"Waffles?"

"What?" she demanded, shrugging expansively. "Apparently, getting shot at makes me hungry."

"I mean, what are waffles?"

Rossi made a face.

"What kind of hellhole do you come from exactly?"

"Can we just go?"

She grinned at that, a brief, crinkled smile that was at least a third derisive smirk, but it was the closest thing to a smile he had seen from her since they met. It transformed her, lifting the anxiety and fear, making her look fresh, young, captivating in an ordinary sort of way. Bowie blushed, turning to study the backs of the buildings, their metal fire escapes and bright windows. Then she was walking briskly ahead, and he had to jog a little to catch up.

CHAPTER ELEVEN

The waffles were better than good. They were spectacular: rich, sweet, and warm. They were crisp on the outside, light and fluffy in the middle, and they came with a preserve loaded with chunks of fruit that Rossi said were strawberries, and a bowl of thick cream. He had never tasted anything like it.

"Still think your world is better than ours?" Rossi inquired after another of those long looks in which she seemed to deduce whatever was going through his head like his mind was an open book.

"How do you do that?" he asked, his guard knocked down by the festival kicked off by his taste buds.

"Do what?"

"Figure stuff out by looking at people."

She shrugged.

"My journalistic instincts," she said with mock seriousness. "Don't people in your line of work do the same?

Read people, I mean? Figure out when they are telling the truth?"

Bowie shook his head.

"I mostly kill things," he said simply.

"My mood included," she replied, laying down her fork, her face suddenly serious. "OK. You want to tell me what happens next?"

"Next?"

"Yeah, the post-waffle stage of your homicidal mission."

He smiled then, but when she didn't return it, he lowered his eyes to his plate.

"I don't know," he said with absolute honesty. "I seem to have been . . . stood down."

"With a view to being *put* down," she concluded, then, when his blank face said that he didn't get the joke, adding, "Sorry. Go on."

He thought, sampling more waffle for inspiration.

"I suppose I stay here," he said at last. "With you."

"With me?" she blurted, as if he had suggested something indecent. "Why?"

"Because you are going to try to prevent Oswald from assassinating the president and there is at least one time rider who has been sent to make sure that you are unsuccessful."

"So what, you're my guardian angel now? My knight in shining armor?"

"I think so, yes," he replied.

"No," she returned. "I don't need your help. Did you forget how we met? You did your best to kill my partner while protecting the man who is about to turn this country on its head! The only reason you now want to protect me instead is because your masters have punched your ticket, or tried to."

Bowie didn't understand that phrase, but he got the gist.

"It clarified things for me, yes," he agreed. He didn't add that while he had been charged to ensure that nothing he did should draw attention to himself for fear of altering the timeline, the agent sent to kill him seemed to have been given no such instructions.

She rolled her eyes at his sober manner.

"You're not even mad!" she exclaimed. "They tried to kill you and you're just reassessing your position like one of those computers they are trying to teach to play chess!"

"The situation is complicated," he said.

"How?" she almost shouted, so that the waitress by the counter looked over. Rossi lowered her voice with an effort, sliding into a rasping, staccato whisper. "They tried to kill you! You were working for them and they tried to wipe you off the map. Doesn't that outrage you?"

"My society, everything I have ever known, hinges on this event. I don't know how or why, but if it doesn't take place, if your president doesn't die tomorrow, my world will never exist."

"How is that possible? You are here. You came from the future," she said, lowering her voice still further so he had to read her lips to be sure what she was saying. "If that future goes away, you can't be here before the event which destroyed your present! It makes no sense."

He nodded.

"I know," he said, "unless reality is constrained by individual consciousness. We are real to each other, but the future

I know has already gone, been replaced by a million other alternate timelines, each one a different experiential universe."

"So your actions here just create different possibilities," said Rossi. "I don't see the problem. All those other realities are hypothetical. Abstract. I don't live in the abstract. I live in the real right now. This street is real. This diner. This table. These waffles. These people." She looked around. "The waitress who is saving up to go to college but is also supporting her mother who is elderly. That man over there who is going through a rough patch at work but is doing all he can to keep his family together."

"Wait, how do you know . . . ?"

"I'm speculating! I'm telling a story. It's what reporters do. My point is that everyone around us is one of those individual consciousnesses and they are each living their own reality. Good or bad, it's what they have, and it's what matters to them. Who are you, or anyone from some future that hasn't happened yet, to decide that your version of the world is more important than theirs?"

Bowie nodded slowly and toyed with the last of his waffle, pushing it idly around the plate on his fork, his face set. Without looking up he said,

"They have my brother."

Rossi's face blanched.

"What?" she said. "What do you mean?"

"Sefton," he said. "That's his name. I am Bowie, by the way."

"Like the knife?"

Bowie looked perplexed but she waved the question away as unimportant and he went on speaking.

"The Alphas—the ruling elite of my world—have identified him as a subversive. If I don't do what they want, they will take it out on him. So, even if they can't reach me here, I can't risk his life."

Rossi sat back then, all the fire draining out of her, but when he said "So you see . . ." she shook her head sadly but emphatically.

"They came to kill you, Bowie," she said. "You think they haven't already acted against him? I'm sorry. But you must see that. The future, your present, is past now. It's gone. All you can do is work to protect the world we are in. And, again, sorry, but even if your brother wasn't already dead, you can't ransom this and all subsequent worlds just to save him. I think you know that."

He stared at her for a long moment, rigid in his seat, fighting the impulse to shout her down or storm out. She was exasperating.

And right.

He hated it but he knew it was true. He thought of Sefton, talking about curry in the visitation room at the Gamma work camp and knew that his brother's instincts about their world had been right. While Sefton had resisted, Bowie had done the bidding of the Design for the sake of an easy life, and now his brother would pay for it.

"So what do I do?" he said softly.

"What you like," she said, getting to her feet and pulling money from a purse in her shoulder bag. "I am going to my office. I will tell the rest of the *Morning News* staff that there is a credible threat to the president from Oswald who was heard talking about it. That I heard him myself," she said, revising the story as she told it. "And that when my partner and I confronted him about it, he shot Jimmy. That ought to be enough to get him arrested, and in case it's not, I will notify the Secret Service, FBI, and CIA as well. I'll tell them where he lives, where he works, and where he intends to be to execute the assassination. They will handle it from there."

Bowie was surprised by how quickly she had refocused on the matter at hand. He had expected more . . . what? Sympathy for his plight? Compassion?

"They will stop you," Bowie said grimly. "My people."

"Then I will act quickly," she replied, businesslike now.

"They will keep looking for you, trying to find a way to rewrite history."

He could hear the barely suppressed anger in his voice, and knowing that some of that was about her attitude, felt even more conflicted.

"Then I will hide," she said. "I won't be intimidated by these people."

Bowie sat back and looked at the ceiling for a long second.

"I will help," he said at last.

It was a big decision; one he expected her to embrace with gratitude.

"No," she said. "I'm fine by myself."

"I already saved your life!" he exclaimed, his annoyance spiking again.

"It wouldn't have needed saving if you hadn't barged into my world all guns blazing!"

"I had my orders!"

"So you keep saying," she said, getting to her feet. "What would be great now is if you left me alone."

"You won't survive without my help," he replied, seizing her wrist.

She wrenched herself free, glaring at him.

"You can't do anything for me!" she hissed.

"I can," Bowie insisted. "I can hide you where they will never find you."

That stopped her.

"Where?" she demanded, her chin jutted out in defiance.

"I can hide you in time," he said.

"You need your bike," she reminded him. "Your time cycle, or whatever you call it. It's gone."

"I need *a* time cycle. The controls are standardized. The helmet won't work for me, but I don't need that. The bikes themselves will accept any standard key from my period."

"You are going to try and take the motorcycle out from under that guy with the machine gun? That's suicide."

"I owe you that," he said.

She stared at him then, her face full of doubt and uncertainty, then she shook her head.

"I can't have you do that," she said. "I understand why you feel responsible for me, but it's fine. I'll be OK. For what it's worth, I forgive you. Let's just . . . move on."

"Wait!" he gasped.

"Bowie . . ." she began, but he cut her off.

"It's not the only bike!" he said, his face brightening as the idea caught fire in his head.

"Huh?"

"The onc being used by the agent sent after me. It's not the only one!"

"Yours is trashed, remember?"

"The agent who called himself Washington!" Bowie pressed. "The one with the newspapers? He must have had one. You said he was staying at the hotel where he was killed."

"The Adolphus. A block north of here on Commerce."

"The bike might still be there!"

His ticket out: hers, too, if she wanted it. But a ticket to where? Into a past even more foreign and strange than 1963? He couldn't go forward in time without returning to the lab in 2157, back to Merrick and the professor with their guards and the Design's version of justice when confronted with a rogue operative.

He thought about that. He hadn't even really made the decision to rebel. His hesitancy, his curiosity, his mere *wondering* about his mission had been enough for Merrick to set the dogs on him. Which meant that though they had used him often enough, they had never really trusted him. His momentary questioning of his assignment had been all the proof they needed that he was not, had never been, one of them. It was no great surprise, Beta that he was, but still Bowie felt it like a knife between his ribs, and for a merest fraction of a second, it took his breath away. He could not go home. He had no home. All he had known was lost to him, his brother included. He may have helped to save that world, but he could never go back to it, even if he did find Washington's bike.

"*You know they hate you, right?*" Sefton had said, that day in the visitation room. "*The Alphas. They'll never trust you. They pay you and they use you, but they still hate you as much as they hate me.*"

Bowie hung his head, overwhelmed with emotions he was not used to feeling.

"OK," said Rossi, missing all his rumination. "Go to the hotel and see if the bike is there. I'll walk with you that far, then head to my office. If you find it, meet me outside *The Dallas Morning News* building on Houston and we'll decide what to do next. And Bowie?"

"What?"

"Try not to sound like a robot."

The Adolphus Hotel sat on the corner of Commerce and Field, a strange mix of red brick and ornately carved stone rising some fifteen or sixteen stories. It was topped with a steeply sloped roof and a turret on the corner that made it look like a fairytale castle. Bowie strode in, a few choice phrases gleaned from Rossi's description of local law enforcement procedures carefully memorized and ready to go. Inside, the hotel was imposing—all dark, polished wood, intricate moldings and marble statuary—and Bowie felt that shiver of unbelonging that he felt whenever he stepped into the Design command offices. He shrugged the feeling off and forced a smile that balanced between genial and purposeful.

At least physically he was no oddity. The city was full of people closer to his coloration than anyone in the Alpha realm at what he still thought of as home. Many here were darker than anyone he saw outside the Gamma camps, though he noted that it was the paler sort who occupied the public-facing jobs. Such was the case for the man at the reception desk: white, gray haired, perhaps fifty but trim and with an authoritative bearing which, to Bowie, looked ex-military.

He met Bowie's smile with something similar, practiced and efficient rather than warm.

"Good morning, sir," he said, "and welcome to the Adolphus. How can I help you?"

"Thank you," said Bowie, flashing his identity badge in a manner supposed to look casual but fast enough to evade close scrutiny.

"Sergeant Matthews," he said. "Dallas PD, vehicle impound. I'm here with regard to the shooting you had here Tuesday evening."

The receptionist—he may actually have been a manager—glanced over Bowie's shoulder, a furtive look in his eyes. He stooped a little, as if trying to become inconspicuous and his voice lowered.

"Terrible business," he muttered, "and quite out of keeping for an establishment of this quality. Perhaps we could discuss it in my office."

Sensing an advantage, Bowie stood his ground.

"No need," he said. "I believe the victim . . ."

"Mr. Washington," said the manager quickly.

"Right. I believe he was a guest at the hotel and that he had a rather unusual vehicle with him. A . . ."

"Motorcycle, yes. A strange machine and a stranger choice for a man of his type. It occasioned some comment among the staff."

"I'm here to collect it," said Bowie. "As evidence, pending the result of the trial, and subsequent matters of inheritance according to probate."

He had only a passing understanding of what those words meant, but they sounded impressive and his hunch was that that would be enough. He was right.

"Absolutely," said the manager. "Parking here is limited and we weren't sure what to do with it. You have an impound truck?"

"Parked outside," said Bowie without missing a beat. "If you could bring it around . . ."

"We already tried to move it, but the wheel is locked. I'm afraid you'll need to cut it free before you can move it. It's a large, heavy machine. Like nothing I've seen before, actually."

"Not a problem," said Bowie. "Just point the way."

How was that? Not too 'robotic'?

"I'll be glad to get it out of our hair," the manager confided. "All part of the service. A bad business which does nothing for our reputation. This is a fine old establishment. Half a century old and the last word in Dallas hospitality."

"I see that," said Bowie.

"They say that it was entering our hotel with his wife, pursued by a jeering mob, that got Senator Johnson elected!"

"Is that right?" said Bowie, keen to be gone.

"Class, you see. Elegance in the face of barbarism. Now a crowd of yahoos conducts a brawl in our cocktail lounge, and we have the likes of you wearing out our carpets, asking questions in front of our guests. No offense meant."

"Right," said Bowie, not sure he understood the nuance of what that "the likes of you" meant, but not liking it. "If you could just direct me to . . ."

"Yes, of course. Follow me."

Bowie did so, walking through the narrow hallways and stairwells which were the inner workings of the hotel. They were dim and battle scarred, quite at odds with the aging but dignified opulence of the public areas. The manager said nothing as they walked, as if this entire private episode was not really happening.

Washington's bike was the only motorcycle on this subterranean floor and it stood out, managing to be both futuristic and oddly retro next to the spacey, chrome bedecked cars with their aircraft fins and rocket-style taillights. Fixed to the frame where it extended over the rear wheel, a pair of suitcase-style panniers hung, one on each side.

"Quite the beast," said the manager, having presented the bike with a theatrical gesture and a scowl of fascinated disapproval. "If you could just sign here and show me your credentials one more time . . . ?"

Bowie removed the key from his own bike, slotted it into the ignition and turned it once to release the wheel locks. The manager gave him a puzzled look.

"You have the key?" he said.

"It was with the victim's personal effects," Bowie improvised.

"Ah," said the manager, apparently satisfied. He produced a form and a pen.

Bowie stooped to the nearest pannier and tried the key. The lock turned and a pair of catches popped open. He raised the lid, saw what was inside and closed it quickly.

"Everything in place?" asked the manager, craning to see.

"Looks like it," said Bowie quickly, snapping the lid shut.

He threw his right leg over the bike, took the paper from the hotelier's hands and scribbled on it, then, before the man could ask for his ID again, twisted the key again and filled the parking deck with the bike's low, animal rumble that resonated through bone and bowel. The manager stepped back with something like respect, even awe, but spoke over the noise as if to make his position clear.

"Oh my lord!" he exclaimed disapprovingly. "It must be like riding a bear."

"It suits the likes of us," said Bowie flatly, and twisting the throttle he drowned out anything the manager might say in response, easing the bike into motion.

Having left Bowie at the Adolphus it had taken Sandra Rossi twelve minutes to reach Houston Street. As she walked the long, straight, and busy route along Commerce, she rehearsed what she was going to say, the—slightly bogus—story that would ensure Oswald found his way onto the radar of law enforcement and journalists before it was too late. The reporters wouldn't run anything without hard evidence, but they would make pointed inquiries of the police, FBI, and Secret Service that would put pressure on them to apprehend and hold the would-be assassin before he could do anything. She went over what she had read from *The Times* piece, about his involvement with Cuban socialist, pro-Castro groups. That would not go down well in Republican Dallas and would be a good way to ensure the local cops—many of whom were no fans of JFK—took the matter seriously.

She smiled grimly at the thought, but her mind immediately began to worry at why a pro-Castro revolutionary would target Kennedy, of all people. What had that redneck in the Adolphus bar called him? A Klan-hating Catholic? It was strange, to say the least, that people who thought like that might find themselves in bed with a leftist revolutionary. Almost as strange as how quickly the shadowy details of the assassin's life had made the papers.

Strange . . .

And then there was Bowie and agents from the future. It was madness. Three days earlier she would have dismissed anyone who spoke of such things as a dangerous lunatic who needed a padded cell and the kind of coat that fastened up the back. But that bike with the gunman in the red helmet had appeared out of nowhere. She had seen that with her own eyes. One minute the road had been empty, then there had been that unearthly ripple in the air, a sound like the boom of a jet hitting the sound barrier, and he had been there, guns blazing. Maybe the newspapers could be faked. Maybe Bowie was delusional. But she had seen the bike, the time rider . . .

Strange didn't begin to cover it.

Or Bowie. He was unlike anyone she had ever met. He had a rugged shell and a commanding manner of the type she would normally run from, but then there would be a flash of something in his eyes that suggested an entirely different kind of person, a thoughtfulness, even a vulnerability. It was in no way soft, but when he talked about his brother he looked lost, childlike. Whatever world he had come from, and whatever skills he possessed, he was almost as out of his depth here as she was talking of time traveling assassins.

Strange indeed.

She imagined her sister Veronica rolling her eyes at that. Veronica, a real estate agent in Fort Worth, who had always accused Sandra of a tendency to over analyze, was more straight forward in her attitudes to men. But then the men in her sister's life probably weren't time traveling soldiers from the future, so what she might think wasn't exactly relevant.

At the familiar old sandstone courthouse, she turned left toward Union Station and the newspaper offices, and as she did so a part of her mind registered the uniformed policeman on the corner. He was simply standing, perhaps taking a break between depositions in court, perhaps serving as a security guard, though she had passed this spot a thousand times before and never noticed such a guard there. Perhaps it was the way he seemed to be so clearly doing nothing—not smoking, not using his radio or eating a sandwich—just standing, watching the passersby. She passed within thirty feet of him and kept walking but she felt his shaded eyes on her, and some primal instinct told her that if she turned, she would see him following.

She did not change course, but she looked sharply at the road ahead, scanning both sides for signs of the bike which had pursued them. She felt sure that if the rider had been dressed as a cop she would have noticed, but without that distinctive red helmet he could be anyone. If he knew who she was and had come here, intending to intercept her, all he would have to do was stash the bike on a side street, and he would immediately become impossible to spot. Her heels chafed the backs of her ankles, but she picked up her pace, walking now just short of a run and hunting for anyone who might help.

The street was mostly empty of pedestrians. A couple of hundred yards ahead she could see the steps leading to the railway station on the right and the little patch of greenery which was Ferris Plaza on the left. Her office was on the other side of Young Street. It felt like a million miles away.

Maybe she should go into the station, she thought, walking faster still. There would be people. Officials. Cops.

And which ones can you trust?

Even if they believed her, they weren't ready for the ruthlessness she had seen from the gunman on the bike. She glanced over her shoulder. The cop who had been loitering outside the courthouse was gone. She paused, a rush of relief flooding though her, and then she saw him, walking purposefully down the street toward her, the badge on his breast pocket flashing in the sunlight. She couldn't see his eyes behind his sunglasses, but she caught the hitch in his step as he turned suddenly aside. He knew she had seen him.

And there was something else: a thin hum in the air above her, fading in and out like the swooping exploration of a mosquito. She risked a glance skywards. It took a moment to home in on it, but something darted across the street, maybe twenty feet in the air and no larger than a hummingbird. It seemed to hover expectantly, then adjusted and came toward her, and there was something deliberate that she recognized instinctively as being mechanical. As it swept toward her the sun flashed on it.

Metal.

Some sort of surveillance device? Or a weapon?

Rossi made a strangled cry and launched into a clumsy run. Each step on those damned heels felt precarious, but she had no choice. Going into the railway station and taking her chances suddenly seemed a doomed option: no stranger would trust her if her pursuer was dressed as a cop. She considered hiding in the park, but other than the fountain there was no cover there. It was her office or nothing.

The Rock of Truth, she thought wildly, recalling the building's nickname, taken from the quotation carved into its facade. Truth was what she had. Truth was all she had.

With an infuriating little whimper, she kicked off her shoes and left them on the sidewalk without a second glance. She ran flat out, a long hard dash for the corner of Young Street and out into the street before she had paused to ensure it was clear. A taxi driver braked hard and blew his horn, but she kept going, weaving barefoot across the road, her eyes locked on the series of steps up to the Rock of Truth.

A jolt of pain sliced through the sole of her foot. With a yelp she pulled up and saw a curl of glass—the neck of a coke bottle—skitter and roll away. She lowered her foot gingerly but it gave another yelp of pain and she knew a shard was still in there. She limped over the curb and onto the sidewalk, risking a glance back at the cop who was coming after her. He was waiting for the traffic to clear before crossing, the hovering metal device balanced a few yards above him. One hand was drawing his gun, all pretense abandoned. He was ready to shoot her down.

Rossi made another stumbling hop, but even keeping her weight off her injured left foot felt like someone had driven a spike through it. She looked around wildly. A woman in her thirties, meaty and heavy jawed, was sitting on one of the steps up to the *Morning News* headquarters reading a paper, her short, cropped hair an almost white, unnatural blond.

"Help!" shouted Rossi, as she staggered onto the sidewalk. "There's a man after me! I'm hurt. If you can help me get inside . . ."

And then the blond woman lowered the paper, her face implacably hard and her eyes dead, and Rossi saw that the paper had covered some kind of control device, and that sitting next to her on the steps was a shiny red motorcycle helmet.

CHAPTER TWELVE

The blond woman, who Rossi could now see was dressed in the padded leathers of a biker, dropped the small controller she had been using to guide the hovering device, and pulled a handgun from her waistband. She raised it with an efficiency of movement that was terrifying. Her eyes took in everything but betrayed nothing. She had done this before, many times, and had lost not one night of sleep over it.

Rossi dropped into a half crouch which became a clumsy sideways roll as the biker squeezed off two quick shots. They sounded thin, unimpressive after the rifle fire, little more than snaps, but at this range the weapon would be just as deadly. The shooter was clearly surprised by the speed of Rossi's move, but there was no cover and nowhere to go. On the other side of the street the second agent, the one dressed as a cop, was crossing the road, his gun at the ready.

Rossi heard the guttural snarl of the bike at her back and recognized it as the kind of monstrous machine the murderous biker had been riding.

Three of them? She was dead.

She winced away from the sound of another pistol shot, but it didn't hit her and she looked up to see the blond assassin, ducking and training her pistol on the road. Rossi spun around just as the cop turned in surprise to face the source of the noise, the massive time cycle that was roaring around the corner, astride which sat . . .

Bowie!

She gasped as the bike mowed the cop down, sending his shades skittering across the asphalt, and then, before she fully even realized what she was doing, Rossi charged the blond woman, keeping low, ignoring the scream of pain from her bleeding foot. The woman half spun to face her, but Rossi hit her hard in the side and sent her crumpling down the steps, though she had no idea what to do next. She pulled away, instinctively, and looked wildly around for the gun, but the woman still had it and was already rolling doggedly into a shooting position. In her peripheral vision, she saw the cop gathering himself too. She had assumed he was dead or incapacitated.

Apparently not.

"Get on!" shouted Bowie over the roar of the bike.

Rossi didn't hesitate. She hated the idea, but there were no other options. Even this was a long shot.

She took three long, wincing strides, and leaped on behind him, wrapping her arms around his midsection. The bike lurched forward before she was secure, and for a dreadful moment she felt herself falling as the motorcycle lunged into the street so fast that it felt like the front wheel kicked up off the road. Bowie clamped one strong hand to her left forearm to steady her, and then a bullet was shrieking past her head.

With a yelping sob she huddled as small as she could, as if she was burrowing into his back, and they sped off through the Dallas morning.

"You hit?" Bowie shouted, half turning as he made a left and opened up the throttle.

"No," she called back, clinging hard as the time cycle leaned frighteningly.

"They will both have bikes. And more fire power than we can handle."

"Could there be more of them?"

"Maybe. No way of knowing."

"We should get out of town and hide," she shouted, not least because she wasn't sure how much of this ride she could take. He drove like a madman, gunning the bike through traffic, weaving in and out of cars, nipping down alleys barely wide enough to accommodate them, speeding through lights and stop signs like the devil was after them.

Which, she reminded herself, *may as well be true. Admittedly they were human devils, time travelers on motorcycles armed to the teeth . . .*

She held on and tried not to throw up.

The look in the hard-faced female assassin's eyes was lodged in her memory: a blank contempt, like she was sweeping up dead cockroaches.

Rossi didn't hear the first shot until after she saw the window of a car in front of them explode. Glass fragments rained down as they careened through and Bowie made another hard turn. Only then did she risk a glance back. Fifty yards behind them was the cop. He had a helmet on now but the visor was up and even at this distance she recognized his face. The bike he was riding was no police bike. It was broad as an ox, with a gas tank like a great barrel and handlebars like bull horns. In his left hand he was holding what looked like a shotgun which he jolted hard to reload, then leveled at them.

"Incoming!" Rossi bellowed.

Bowie twitched the steering and the bike kicked alarmingly to the right. He had to fight to keep it vertical, but the shotgun blast missed them, tearing away half the panel from a pickup truck ahead. They slid wildly as the driver tried to figure out what had happened, and the pickup clipped the convertible to its left, sliding into a chaos of shrieking brakes and blaring horns.

Bowie dodged the sudden pile up, then bowed his head and opened up the throttle. The bike spat its fury and surged forward like a spurred horse, driven by pain and the animal madness of a wide-eyed, teeth-bared sprint. Sixty . . . Seventy . . . Eighty miles an hour weaving through congested city streets.

More gunfire behind them, and Rossi thought she heard a cry.

People were getting hit.

Caught in the cross fire, she thought wildly. How many times had she read that phrase in her own paper? So many times it had lost the horror which should come with it. She understood that now, and the idea that she was in the middle of it all, was responsible for whatever might be happening to the people around them, stung more than the glass in her flesh.

"We have to get out of here!" she yelled.

It sounded like she was just thinking of her own safety, but that wasn't it at all. Their being here put other people's lives at risk, people who had nothing to do with them, people like the ones in the diner whose backstories she had invented to make a point. Some of them were going to die because of her.

"Where's the woman?" Bowie shouted back. "The one in the red helmet. Do you see her?"

Rossi looked back. The cop was still coming, shotgun raised like the flag of some old west cavalryman, but there was no sign of the woman. Remembering the surveillance device which had been tracking her outside the newspaper offices, she looked up and back.

At first she saw nothing, but then caught the glimmer of movement in the air some twenty yards behind them.

"I don't see her!" she called, "but she has some kind of airborne monitor behind us. We have to . . ."

"I know!" he replied. "Open the pannier on your right!" Bowie shouted.

"The what?"

"The luggage thing. Open it."

She gripped him harder with her left arm and reached blindly back and down with her right. Fumblingly, she found the catches. She didn't dare look away from the road, but her fingers found something cool and spherical about the size of a softball.

"This?" she shouted.

Bowie glanced over his shoulder just long enough to assess the device.

"Push the button and throw it behind us," he ordered. "Throw it high!"

"What? How high?"

"Just do it!"

She adjusted her grip on the sphere and studied it. There was a red button and a digital display: the numbers, which were dull as if offline, displayed 4:00. She hesitated, then pushed the button, but it didn't give and the display didn't alter.

"It's locked!" she shouted.

"There must be a safety catch," he roared back. "Try—"

But before he could say anything more she had reached around him, found her other hand and given the top and bottom halves of the sphere an instinctual twist. She felt the shape of the thing change as the two halves popped a half-inch open. She lifted it up to her face. The display was bright now, and the red button stood a little proud of the casing. She pushed it, and immediately the numbers flickered down. The four was already a three . . .

She tossed it up and back with something like panic. It seemed to levitate under its own power as the bike shot out from under it, and she had to turn to see it burst its dazzling halo of light before the sound and the shock wave hit. For a moment it was like nothing in the street behind them could have survived the blast, as if the sonic grenade would reduce all matter to nothingness. Then reality returned and they were speeding away.

Rossi risked a look back. The hovering device was gone—probably vaporized—and the cop was swerving away from the hole in the road, slow and cursing, his bike jerking and billowing smoke.

One down. But there was no sign of that psycho bitch in the red helmet.

And then she saw her, and not behind them. She was up ahead on the right, emerging from a side street. Somehow she had gambled and found a faster route, probably getting updates from her cop accomplice as to where they were.

Doesn't matter how she did it, she told herself. *The point is . . .*

The point is . . .

The point was that she was waiting for them, her automatic rifle at the ready. They were heading into an ambush and the gun would take them apart.

"There!" Rossi shouted, pointing at her.

There was no turn off between them and the time rider. They had left the traffic behind and there was no cover, only speed. Rossi looked over Bowie's shoulder at the speedometer, which was climbing past one hundred, then up again at the first flash of the rifle's muzzle.

"Hold on!" Bowie roared, and before she could ask what he meant he had hit a button, and the bike seemed to explode in a sudden, impossible burst of speed which maxed out the speedometer. They were pulled forward as if by some unstoppable force and Rossi tightened her grip, her eyes almost closing.

Bowie hit another button and a jet of energy shot into the road ahead from the bike's headlight, opening into a swirling maelstrom of sliding color and the expanding ripples of a refracted light. The energy spiraled and expanded into a circle like a tunnel and they shot into it with a thunderous clap of sound so loud that she almost lost her grip in her impulse to slam her hands over her ears. For a moment she was sure they had been hit, that the bike had been torn apart, and they had been thrown free, turning over and over in nauseating space before hitting the iron-hard roadway, and then they were through and somewhere else entirely.

The wide straight road was gone. So were the tall buildings which lined it, the billboards, the cars, and—most importantly—their attackers. In their place was a single narrow road flanked by tall trees which streaked by as their impossible speed carried them on.

Rossi cried out, or was still crying out, a long wail of terrified despair. She wasn't sure when that had started. It was all too much, the speed, the gunfire, the impossible strangeness . . . And then Bowie was braking hard, bringing the bike to a sliding halt at a tight bend in the road.

Before he had turned the engine off, Rossi slid from the saddle onto her knees and shaking, she vomited into the grass, though whether that was the journey or the aftereffects of the gunfight, she wasn't sure. When she had finished, she spat once, her head low, and rocked slowly back onto her ankles. She closed her eyes and focused on her breathing until the world returned to something like normality.

But what normality was this?

She looked up at the trees. They were tinted with the first blush of fall. She inhaled and thought she could taste something utterly unlike the smog of Dallas. It wasn't just that the air felt cleaner, there was an unfamiliar, salty taste which felt like . . .

The ocean!

But that wasn't possible.

"Where are we?" she demanded.

"Not sure," said Bowie.

"How fast were we going?"

"Pretty fast."

"We could have been killed!"

"Yes."

"They were shooting at us!"

"Yes."

She stared at him, aghast at his composure, and said it again, enunciating each word carefully this time.

"We. Could. Have. Been. Killed!"

He opened his mouth to agree again, then thought better of it, and gave her a single nod.

"Sit down," he said. "Breathe."

"What do you think I'm doing?" she snapped. "I'm alive aren't I? Of course I'm fucking breathing."

She hadn't meant it to come out that sharply, but this was all far too much. Her gaze fell on her right hand and saw that it was trembling. It annoyed her so she tucked it under her thighs to still it. She did breathe then, a deep intake which filled her lungs. She held it, closed her eyes, and then blew it out. She drew another until she felt a little better.

Finally, she swallowed, then asked the question that had been trying to fight its way through her panic and outrage:

"What did you do?"

"I made a time jump."

"A *time* jump?" Rossi gasped, some of the previous nausea swelling up in her guts again. "To where? Or when?"

"Not sure," said Bowie again.

"Are you kidding?"

"I didn't have time to program the bike's system," he replied, "so I used the last coordinates entered. The only thing I know for sure about where we are is that the agent who called himself Washington came here recently."

"But you don't know where or when?"

"That data would be relayed through the helmet interface, but I don't have that, and even if I did it wouldn't work for me. I suppose we'll just have to ask."

"Ask?"

"A local," Bowie clarified.

"You want us to walk up to some random guy and say what part of the world are we in and what year is it?"

"Oh," said Bowie turning the engine back on but keeping it to a low purr. "I'm sure you can find a less robotic way of doing it."

Rossi shook her head, but she moved back to the bike all the same now.

"What," she muttered, "you're doing jokes now?"

"All part of the service," said Bowie, trying a phrase the Adolphus manager had used.

"I think I liked you better as a robot," said Rossi. She caught herself smiling and looked around quickly, as if expecting to see the opposition's bikes bursting in on them.

"They don't know where we went," said Bowie, reading her look. "They will find us eventually, but we have a little time."

"To do what?"

"Find out where we are," said Bowie.

"And why Washington came here," said Rossi, her journalistic instincts spiking. Bowie gave her a thoughtful look.

"We can't go back," he said.

"To where?"

"To the moment we just left," he explained. "It would create a temporal paradox. We are caught up in a major event. That severely limits how close to it we can get, and we can't cross our own timelines. Not that it matters."

"What do you mean?"

"We can't go forward in time without returning to my world, which is impossible. They'd be waiting for us, and not to welcome us with open arms."

"So we've come back in time?" she asked.

And Veronica thought my life was weird before . . .

She had no idea why she thought of her sister again now, except that she was the only person Sandra Rossi had ever really confided in. As kids they had shared a room and gossiped into the night. Now, they chatted on the phone once or twice a week, when she wasn't working late, and Veronica wasn't out on a date. She wondered suddenly where her sister was now, in whatever version of the past they had entered, and when she would speak to her again.

"That's the only way it works," said Bowie.

"What?" she asked, momentarily lost.

"The time cycle," Bowie explained, "can only go backward in time. Not forward. We might be able to get back to the date we left Dallas just by waiting, by living through to it, but . . ."

"You have no idea how far back we have come," Rossi concluded.

"Right."

"Well," she said, looking around. "The road surface looks modern so we won't have to fend off dinosaurs or Apache raiders." Bowie gave her a blank look. "You don't know what dinosaurs are," she said in disbelief.

"History," he shrugged, as if the answer was both obvious and irrelevant.

"T. rexes and brontosauruses and triceratops?" she said. "Big, scary lizard things the size of a house that lived on Earth before there were people."

Bowie gave the bike some gas and they began to roll slowly along the road.

"Sounds made up," he said.

"Says the *Time Rider*."

Bowie grinned.

"So, what else do your finely honed journalistic talents tell you about this place?" he asked.

"Well, we're not in Kansas anymore, Toto," she said.

"We were in Kansas?" he replied, giving her a blank look.

"Sorry," she said, rolling her eyes. "Private joke. Or historical joke. Doesn't matter. No, we were in Texas and this ain't Texas. Those are oaks and beech trees," she said, nodding toward some of the tall and heavy trunks which grew a few yards from the road, "but that's old growth and thick forest. There's nothing like that close to Dallas. The temperature isn't much different than when we left but these trees are beginning to turn color, which suggests it's early fall, but probably somewhere farther north. And I think we're close to the ocean. I can smell it, but the trees are eastern. Nothing like California or anywhere like that. So, Delaware, maybe, or farther north. New Jersey? Connecticut? Massachusetts? Maine? I need more data, but I'd say northeast coast, perhaps September."

Bowie was impressed.

"You can tell that from seeing a few trees?" he remarked.

"It's not about seeing, my dear Watson," she said, knowing he wouldn't get the Sherlock Holmes reference and not caring, "it's about observing."

They pressed on, moving slowly and as quietly as the bike would go, alert to their isolation and feeling both the peace of the woods and a distinct sense that they weren't supposed to be there. This last was confirmed when they came to a fork in the road and saw a weathered sign, white letters on a blue background, elegant but emphatic "The entirety of Naushon Island is private property and open only to residents and their guests. Trespassers will be removed and prosecuted to the full extent of the law."

"OK," said Bowie, bringing the bike to a halt and killing the engine. "So we either leave or we try to figure out what Washington was doing here, and that probably means hiding the bike. It is too conspicuous, especially on these small byways, and given the sign we should expect private security patrols."

"Hold it," said Rossi, her face creased up in concentration. "Naushon Island rings a bell. Some rich family like the Vanderbilts live here. But they're in the south . . . The Rockefellers? No. The Forbes! Yes, I think so. I read something not long ago about them hosting all sorts of bigwigs on this private island. Naushon. It's a sort of enclave up near Martha's Vineyard and Nantucket." Her eyes got wide as another memory flashed into view like lightning. "Those high-profile visitors?" she exclaimed. "One of them was the president! One of them was JFK!"

Almost two hundred years in the future, Sefton watched the empty access road as his deputy, the slender black woman called Greta, her face clay-smeared, set the charge and removed her hands carefully, as if a shift in the air itself would set it off. In the early days they had relied on leftover munitions from the war, but that was an ever-diminishing supply and the resistance had quickly realized that it would need to go into the weapons production business. A network had been created between the maintenance engineers of the power stations and the farmers of the food production sectors. It was amazing what you could do with enough circuit boards and fertilizer. It was almost as amazing that they could do it under the Alphas' noses, but then that was one of the many failings of their carefully Designed society: when you farmed the real work out to the lower social orders, the people who police them don't actually understand that work. Change a few minds among the few who do, and a lot of possibilities present themselves.

"It's not working," muttered Greta. "I can't get a connection."

"Let me see," said Sefton, dropping to his belly and shimmying under the conduit and giving the deputy an urgent tap on the shoulder for her to get out of the way. They didn't have a lot of time.

He checked the main conduit, noted the streaked and tarnished join where the wire had been rubbed bright, then squirmed under the pipe and reached for the portable soldering kit. The sun felt almost hot enough to melt the solder by itself, and as soon as he got onto his back he could feel the sweat running down his face. He adjusted his bandanna to keep it out of his eyes, and pulled at the live wire from the solar array with a gloved hand. It came away instantly.

Figured.

Years ago he might have suspected rodents, but nothing lived out here now, so it was probably just elemental wear.

"Here's the problem," he muttered, as much to himself as to the deputy.

The soldering iron was still hot. He wiped its tip on the corner of his shirt, making it smoke, then dipped it in the can of flux until it smoked some more, and tinned it with the solder. He applied it to the broken wire.

"Try it now," he said.

"Contact," said Greta, satisfied.

"Good," said Sefton rolling out from under the conduit. "We need to get out of here."

The Alphas would know that the power station had suffered a systems failure, but they probably weren't sure what had caused it, and the full impact hadn't hit their electrical grid yet, because the moment the collectors went offline, the backup storage systems were programmed to take over. But now that was about to change.

This land had once been fields. Before that it had been forest. Now the energy relay station sat in a desert, the topsoil long blown away, revealing endless sun-roasted flats of stone and pockets of sand. Most days at the solar farm he worked in goggles, every inch of his body swathed in fabric like some shambling mummy, despite the heat, to keep out the sting of the grit and sand particles that blew around like shards of glass in a tornado. He checked his watch.

"What's taking B Team so long?" he muttered, picking up a battered pair of binoculars and looking through them. One lens was cracked but they did the job. He focused on the second servo station where two of his people were still working. The wiring was probably no better over there than it had been here. Even so . . .

"We gotta go," muttered Greta, putting Sefton's concern into words.

Sefton thought, then nodded.

"Go," he said. "Give me two minutes."

"And then?"

"Then blow it," Sefton remarked, as if it was obvious.

"Guards will be all over the area as soon as—"

"I know," Sefton cut in. "You have your orders."

The deputy set her jaw as if bracing for a punch, then nodded, checked over her shoulder and sprinted away.

Sefton refocused his binoculars on B Team, and as he did so, he saw a pair of security officers heading right for them. He swore under his breath and forced himself to watch for a moment longer, studying their body language. They were talking, and their pace was casual: a routine patrol rather than an investigation. Even so, as soon as they rounded the corner they'd see B Team setting their explosives. He had maybe twenty seconds.

He got up and walked with forced casualness out into the sun-blasted openness of the station. He raised both hands high above his head, waved, and called out to the guards.

"Hey! Over here!"

The two men exchanged glances then changed direction and began ambling toward him, their deliberate casualness designed to show how little urgency they felt. Sefton continued to wave and shout. He saw the confused faces of B Team poke out from the rear door of the servo station, but the guards were focused on him and strolled right past. Hopefully, this would buy the saboteurs time to finish up and leave when the guards were well past.

"Well?" snapped one of them.

Sefton checked his watch.

"You should take cover," he said with a grin.

"What?" sneered one of the guards.

"You know," said Sefton, still friendly, "like this."

And he dropped to the dusty ground, hands over his head. He glanced up at the two disdainful guards, and then there was a flash and a double roar, the explosions staggered less than a second apart. They shook the earth and tore the servo stations apart.

Sefton lay where he was until the dust cloud blew clear, then he got cautiously to his feet and wiped the gritty residue of the blast from his face and considered the wounded guards.

"Told you," he said.

CHAPTER THIRTEEN

"You think Washington came here to kill the president before," said Bowie, "failed, and tried again in Dallas?"

"I didn't till you said it," said Rossi. "But that makes a kind of sense. Except that he wasn't the one who killed JFK if what the papers said was true. He was probably just charged to do the same as you: keep Oswald alive so he could do it, right?"

"I suppose so."

"But if he wanted the president dead, why not do it himself?"

Bowie shook his head.

"Time agents taking decisive and conspicuous action invites all kinds of temporal paradox and attracts attention. If intervention in the past by a time traveler is to work, it has to look like a natural part of the timeline. Assassins who materialize and vanish, people who clearly aren't part of the current period or culture and commit history-altering acts foreground the act of intervention and risk disclosure."

Rossi gave him an odd look.

"You sound like a manual," she said.

"Part of my briefing," he said.

"So if Washington had been involved in a plot to kill the president here, he wouldn't have been the trigger man," Rossi concluded.

"Right," said Bowie. "He would be here to guide and protect an agent who was part of this world."

"We should look around: see if we can find out who is here, presidents included."

"How big is the island?" asked Bowie. "Can't be very large if it's owned by a single family, right?"

Rossi waggled her head uncertainly.

"You really don't know much about twentieth-century America, do you?" she said wryly.

"So you keep saying," said Bowie, his irritation showing. "I'm asking if we can hide the bike and walk. I'm assuming you don't want me to shoot anyone who tries to ask us what we are doing here."

"OK," said Rossi. "Yes. Sorry."

"It's fine," said Bowie, still a little stung. "But I don't see why you think it so amazing that I don't know anything about your period. You don't know anything about mine."

"Yours hasn't happened yet."

"And yours has been over for almost two hundred years," Bowie snapped.

"I said sorry," she observed.

"And I said it was fine," he replied, brittle as a frozen twig.

She grinned.

"Robot man has feelings," she cooed.

"Help me with the bike," he said, pushing it down a ditch and into the woods.

Together they threaded the motorcycle through the trees. It was hard going. The ground was soft and thick with leaves, some of which concealed shallow pools of cold standing water. Rossi winced and limped.

"Let me see your foot," said Bowie.

"It's fine," she said, but he didn't believe her. "Got some glass in it but it's out. It's just tender to cold and pressure."

"We need to keep the cut clean," he said, fishing in one of the pockets on his tactical jacket and pulling out a first aid kit which included sterile wipes. "Brace yourself against that tree," he ordered, lifting her foot as soon as she was in position. He dabbed at the wound, pausing when she flinched, then doing it all again. "I can bind it for now, but you need shoes. Try to keep it dry in the meantime."

"Aren't you the Boy Scout?" she said.

"Soldier," he replied.

"Right. You said. And you fought who?"

"Dissidents," he said simply. "Insurgents. People who wanted to prevent the Design from taking total control of all livable portions of the planet. Give me your arm and try to keep the weight off your foot," he said, businesslike as he finished wrapping the wound. "But if we don't find what we need soon, we'll have to risk the bike, no matter what. You don't want that getting infected."

"That's sweet of you," she said, giving him a smile that might have been ironic.

"Just don't want you slowing me down," he said.

"My hero."

He said nothing, busying himself with pushing the bike into a patch of tall ferns and carefully lowering it onto its side until it was barely visible. Before they left it, he ran his thumb along the bright crease in the steel where a bullet had grazed the fuel tank. It was long, almost elegant, as if carved by design. Had the angle of impact been a few degrees closer to the perpendicular, it would have gone straight through, and the resultant spark might have blown them apart.

"You'll be able to find this again?" she asked. "Woods have a tendency to all look about the same, and eventually the sun will go down."

Bowie looked up, oriented himself and nodded. He opened another pocket and produced what looked like a button and a device the size of a matchbox with a tiny screen on it. He pressed the button to the bike's gas tank, and it snapped into place with a magnetic click.

"Tracker," he said. "Very basic but should give us a directional line so long as we stay in range."

"Which is how far?"

"Ten, twelve miles, maybe," he said. "The trees might reduce that. But the island can't be that large, can it?"

"I hope not," said Rossi, glancing at her bandaged foot. "Which way?"

"Stay in the woods but follow the road. We assume Washington knew where he needed to be and materialized close by." He looked around and decided. "This way," he said.

"Why?"

"There's a slight incline. If the island is sparsely populated, the houses are likely to be on high ground."

"Better views," she agreed.

"I meant away from dangerous high tides," he said.

"That works too," she shrugged, taking a cigarette from the pack in her shoulder bag and lighting it. They began to walk, picking their slow way through the trees. "So your side won?"

"What do you mean?"

"The war you were fighting?"

"Mostly, yes," he replied, not wanting to talk about it. "There are still independent pockets on the edges of civilization, and there are people within the Design who don't support it, but they are confined to designated sectors."

"Like your brother."

He gave her a quick look, then nodded.

"And you and your brother fought on opposite sides?"

"Not exactly. Much of the actual fighting was conducted by machines."

"You mean tanks and such?"

"Kind of, but without people inside them."

"Like, remote control?"

"Not really. They were programmed to operate independently but shared information so they could coordinate. It's why the Design outlawed digital networks after the war."

"OK," she conceded, puffing on her cigarette. "But this was a political fight, yes? An ideological struggle?"

"Depends who you ask," said Bowie simply. "My bosses called it an existential war, a battle for order and stability from whose ashes emerged the Design, the society I live in."

"You sound like the manual again," said Rossi, and the look she gave him had no smile in it this time. "What would your brother call it?"

"This way," he said, ignoring the question and nodding to a path, probably worn by deer or other animals, which made the going easier. It was getting cooler, and the sun that had been high overhead when they arrived, was now beginning its slow dive toward the horizon. He had a small flashlight in his gear but wasn't keen on trying to navigate these woods in the dark. If they didn't find signs of life—and some kind of purpose for this blind investigation—they should leave before the other agents picked up their trail. The bikes couldn't log their trips automatically, but if Washington had been back here, he would have had to return to 2157 before going to November 1963 in Dallas.

Unless he just stayed, Bowie thought. If this was only a matter of weeks or months before the Kennedy assassination, it was conceivable that Washington just stayed, kept a low profile, rode his bike down to Dallas and waited for the day to come.

That's dedication, he thought. But he had picked up the newspapers from days *after* the assassination, so he must have time traveled forward and then back again at some point.

He thought of the newspapers. They suggested that the assassination happened even after Washington had been killed. That reinforced what he had been told, that he was here to secure a moment in history, make sure it occurred the way it was supposed to. But if there were not temporal terrorists to jeopardize that event, if that had been a lie, then why was he here? Why send agents back to secure something that has already happened?

It made no sense.

He felt Rossi's eyes on him and remembered he had dodged her question about Sefton.

"What?" he demanded.

"It must be hard to be so divided against yourself," she observed.

The comment irritated him.

"I am trying to figure out if Washington went from here back to my time before showing up in Dallas," he said, navigating a fallen tree and pointedly not offering a hand to help her over it.

"What difference does it make?"

"If he reported back before going to Dallas, my handlers will know he was here," said Bowie. "Once they know we have his bike they'll send agents to check his previous waypoints. But if this is only a few weeks before he died, he may have stayed in this period."

"Doing what?"

"Gathering intel. Setting up the specifics of the assassination."

Rossi shook her head.

"That would have meant being around people from this world—my world—for weeks, months even," she said.

"So?"

"So he would have learned how to blend in, to be more like us," she said. "Or he would have got himself into trouble way earlier. The guy I saw was clueless, and a contemptuous asshole. Didn't look like someone who had absorbed jack from the natives."

"Jack who?"

"Figure of speech. Means 'nothing.'"

"So," Bowie said, unraveling the double negative, "he looked like he had learned something . . . ?"

She gave him an exasperated look and blew out a plume of smoke.

"The opposite! He knew jack. Nothing. Holy shit. How can you not even follow the basics of how we talk?"

"Slang is decadent where I come from. It is not used in civilized society."

"Sounds terrific."

He gave her a sharp look.

"Ah," he said. "Sarcasm."

"Give the man a gold star."

He knew he looked baffled again, which annoyed him, but said nothing.

"Tell me more about your brother," said Rossi.

Bowie frowned.

"Why?"

"Just curious. Are you close?"

"We aren't."

"But you were once?"

Bowie shot her a quick hostile look.

"You said you grew up together," she said, hands raised in mock surrender.

Bowie shrugged.

"We did. Made a lot of trouble. Got separated. Sefton fell in with revolutionaries, dissidents. I tried to walk the line, be the man the Alphas wanted me to be. Thought I'd be rewarded. And I was, but it took serving in the war to get there."

"This was the war in which your brother was on the other side?"

"I didn't know that at the start," Bowie said distantly.

"And?"

"And what?"

"Jesus, what's the big secret? We're stuck here. We have no one else to talk to."

"I don't know why you care."

"Call it professional curiosity."

Bowie climbed over a branch that had fallen across the path and blew out a long breath.

"Fine," he said at last. "Sefton and I had lost touch before the war began. I thought he was pumping me for information to feed to his terrorist friends, so I cut him off. Then the war started and it was chaos. All usual communication lines broke down. I tried not to think about him and what he was doing. I figured there was a chance he was on the other side. That or he'd have been sent to the front lines by the Alphas. We weren't what you would call high-value assets. Six months into the fighting I heard he was dead. That was wrong, obviously, but I only found that out a year or so after the war, when I showed up at a solar energy work camp as a low-level Design functionary. And there he was, big as life. He was casually eating some kind of sandwich, staring off at nothing while one of the Alpha guards screamed at him about not doing his job properly. Sefton didn't care. Looked like he couldn't hear him."

He grinned at the memory.

"I couldn't believe it. Went running toward him like I was going to embrace him or something—something I hadn't done to anyone in years. When he saw me he looked like he would meet me half way, but then he registered my uniform and just kind of stopped. Tipped his head back and just looked at me, like . . . I don't know. Like he'd guessed as much but hoped for better. So. No big reunion. We talked some, but once he knew he'd see me every time I came to pick up the solar plant reports, he kept his distance. I respected that. And besides, he was a Gamma, and one with some unhealthy connections. Wouldn't be good for my career. Or his, I suppose. So that was that."

"Pretty sad."

Bowie considered the thought then made a face.

"It was fine," he said. "To be expected. We live in different worlds."

"And you're OK with that?"

"It's how things are."

"I would have thought that all this time travel business would make you see that nothing has to be as it is."

"My brother and I are very different people."

"Family, though," she said.

He wasn't sure what she meant by that, but the phrase lingered between them. Where he came from, family was a dirty word, a source of shame. Respectable citizens didn't have families. They were a sign of degeneracy, displayed only by those born outside the confines of the official labs. To have a family meant you were un-engineered, the fruit of a criminal carnal act, and the Design did everything it could to break down such ties. He and Sefton had been placed in the same orphanage only because nothing officially tied them together. By the time their genetic link was discovered, the world was fracturing under the strain of the war and they were sent out to fight. From then on, they had lived apart, on opposite sides of every meaningful line the Design had drawn.

Family, though . . .

He turned to ask what the word meant to Rossi but she held up a hand to stop him from speaking, then lowered herself behind a shrub.

"There's something up ahead," she whispered.

He dropped into a silent crouch, peering through the undergrowth to where a large and elegant stone house framed with timber sat beyond the tree line.

They stared. The house was massive, opulent. As they watched, they heard the rumble of tires on gravel.

Someone was coming.

Bowie put a hand on Rossi's shoulder, drawing her down deeper into the cover of the vegetation as a jeep-type utility vehicle crunched its way up to the house and parked. He opened a tubular pouch from his jacket and drew out a digital monocular lens, only three inches long, another of the twenty-second-century treasures he had found in the panniers of Washington's bike. He looked through it, adjusting the focus automatically using the hard lines of the car's bodywork as a guide. The jeep's door opened. The first man out was uniformed—perhaps a policeman or private security guard—and he immediately went to the back of the vehicle to help unload what turned out to be suitcases.

The sound of the vehicle's arrival had alerted someone within the house. The front door opened, and a couple emerged, smiling, expectant. The man was in his fifties, white, solid-looking, his thinning hair swept back and his skin deeply lined from the corners of his mouth to the sides of his nose. The woman beside him was about the same age, slim, vaguely aristocratic in bearing but smiling with welcome. Beside him, Bowie heard Rossi gasp. She reached across, taking the miniature telescope from him and pressing it to her own eye.

"That's Ruth Forbes Young!" she breathed without looking away. He smelled the tobacco smoke on her breath. "Doyen of the society pages, New England royalty, great-granddaughter of Ralph Waldo Emerson!"

Bowie registered her feeling, though he understood little of the specifics.

"And the man?" he asked in a low voice.

"Her husband, Arthur Young! Inventor of the Bell helicopter. But lately they have both been involved in some kind of new age consciousness and spirituality. All very strange. Made a lot of ripples in the usually still pond of the Boston Brahmin set."

"How do you know this?" asked Bowie, genuinely impressed, even though he didn't understand half of what she said.

"We do advance obits on people," she began but, realizing she was using language Bowie would not understand, stopped. "I'm a journalist" she explained, lowering the butt of her cigarette into the dirt and stubbing it out. "It's my job to know things."

Before Bowie could respond there was a distinctive, guttural thrum. He turned, horrified, to see the bike they had arrived on being ridden up the drive.

"They found it!" Rossi gasped. "We're stuck!"

Bowie took the telescope back and trained it on the bike.

"No," he said. "There's no bullet trace on the fuel tank."

"Are you sure? It looks just like ours."

"It is ours," said Bowie lowering the lens, anxiety puckering his features. "It just isn't ours yet."

"What do you mean?" Rossi asked, but before he had a chance to reply the rider of the bike removed his helmet and she recognized him, the haughty pale face, the odd looking wig. "Washington!"

"We've crossed into his timeline," said Bowie. "This is dangerous. We need to keep our distance. It's a good thing we left the bike back in the woods."

"Why?"

"We are on the very edge of a temporal paradox. Two versions of the same item in one place. It shouldn't happen. If we are not careful the whole episode could short circuit."

"You mean, we could cancel each other out? Leading to what?"

"I don't know. But I was told to avoid situations like this. I'm not sure even my handlers know what could result. What we can't do is derail the timeline. If Washington doesn't die in that Dallas hotel, I don't get sent here, and this entire timeline evaporates."

"But it has already happened!" Rossi protested. "It doesn't make sense that . . . wait, someone is getting out of the car."

She took the telescope back and looked through it. Bowie peered through the trees to where the agent called Washington stood respectfully aside, a bystander to the greetings taking place between the Youngs and the two women who had emerged from the car, one of whom was cradling a baby. One of the women went to embrace the one Rossi had called Ruth Forbes Young, and in turning to lay her head on the older woman's shoulder her face caught the late afternoon light. Beside him, Rossi drew in a sharp breath, then pressed the telescope back into Bowie's hand.

He took it, confused by her response, but as soon as he looked through it he understood why. He knew the woman from the car, that long, faintly austere face, the heavy glasses, the slightly severe cut of the hair.

"That's Ruth Paine!" Rossi gasped. "The woman we spoke to in Dallas this morning. And the one with the baby? That's Marina! Lee Harvey Oswald's wife! What are they doing here?"

CHAPTER FOURTEEN

"When are we?" Bowie asked, not expecting an answer.

"If that's the same baby, it can't be more than a few months younger than it was in the Dallas we just left," said Rossi.

It was a good observation, but he just nodded.

"We have to go," he muttered.

"What?" Rossi shot back at him. "Why? We need to know what's going on here."

"We can't risk being detected," he replied firmly. "If Washington sees us or our bike—*his* bike—it will alter his course of action and that will collapse the entire timeline."

"What would happen to us?"

"I don't know," Bowie admitted, "but if the events that brought us here change, then we never come here. Maybe we never meet. Maybe I never leave my home. Maybe that future never exists. I don't know. And I'm not ready to find out. We need to leave."

He didn't know why he had said the part about he and Rossi not meeting, or why he had quickly added to the list so that phrase wouldn't hang between them. He didn't look at her, keeping his attention on the group of people as they said their hellos and filed into the house, but then he took her wrist and tugged her back into the woods. She slapped his hand away and the sudden sound reached the time rider called Washington, whose head snapped around to face the tree line.

Bowie and Rossi became utterly still, not even daring to try and inch into better cover for fear of attracting attention.

Washington took a step toward them, his pale eyes narrow as he tried to make out details in the shade of the trees. As his eyes slowly swept the edge of the woods, his right hand strayed to his holstered pistol. Bowie and Rossi held their breaths and moved not one muscle.

A twig snap some thirty yards to their left made them turn, however involuntarily. A young white-tailed deer was standing stock still staring at the house, one forefoot raised as if caught mid-stride. It lowered the foot and moved cautiously to the right, stopped, and then, with a frantic swish of its tail, bounded out into the clearing and through, around the back of the house and off into the woods on the other side.

Washington watched it go, his hand still on his side-arm, as if contemplating shooting it for sport, but then the man on the porch steps who Rossi had called Arthur Young said something, and Washington turned back to the house. A moment later they were all inside and Bowie was, once more, pulling Rossi back into the forest.

"That slap nearly got us killed," he whispered as soon as they were safely out of earshot.

"Then stop pulling at me," she replied. "I can't believe we are walking away. We don't know what they are talking about!"

"True," said Bowie, following his tracker back to their version of Washington's bike through a thicket of beech trees. "But we also haven't caused reality to fold in on itself, eradicating ourselves from existence. So that's good."

She gave him a shrewd look.

"Was that supposed to be funny?" she demanded.

"Maybe a little," he said.

"OK," she conceded without smiling. "It was. A little."

They trudged on through the woods, the softening sun tinged greenish by the forest canopy.

"So, we can't go back to Dallas," said Rossi at last.

"Sure we can," Bowie replied. "Just not to a moment after this one."

"So we can't save the president."

"There may be other ways, other moments in time before the day of the assassination itself," said Bowie musingly. "But if Oswald is not simply a . . ."

"A lone wolf?"

"Exactly, then we have to assume that if we were to intercept him before the event . . ."

"Someone else would take his place," Rossi concluded. "Ruth Paine got him the job at the Texas School Book Depository. Now we see her meeting with some of the most powerful people in America. Arthur Young is one of the prime cogs of the military industrial complex, inventor, mystic, philosopher, and married to one of the wealthiest and most respectable women in the country. These people who have hosted every bigwig and luminary in the nation, including the president! Now they're hosting the family of the man who will kill that president? It's madness. What's the connection? Ruth Paine? Is she related to them? That would explain why they are visiting. They looked closely. But then why bring Oswald's wife here if he's just a hired hand?" She shook her head, abandoning the attempt to smooth out the details, and returned to the larger question. "You think Oswald is just the trigger man that Washington couldn't be, that other entities are involved?"

"Entities from the future working with powerful people in your present, yes."

It was a grim remark and for a moment it hung between them like a threat in the in the early evening stillness. At last Bowie confessed what had been festering in his mind since they saw the gathering at the house.

"I don't know what to do next."

He wasn't sure why he said it. Rossi had been looking to him to provide the direction behind what they did, but he suddenly found himself unclear on what he was trying to achieve, let alone how to do it. His mission had been taken away from him and upended. He had no sense of how he could ever get home safely, what would happen to him when he arrived, and what the consequences would be for his brother either way. He feared his hesitancy here with Rossi had already cost Sefton his liberty, maybe even his life. It was maddening. He hadn't even been the one to decide which side he was on. That choice had been made for him by his handlers, by Merrick, by Professor Reissen, and by their superiors, who had treated him as a tool, an inefficient, untrustworthy tool at that, prone to strain and breakage. He felt a sudden, violent urge to strike back at them, to break the things they cared about, maybe even bring the whole Design crashing down, but that was impossible. He was stuck in the woods of a private island in the mid-twentieth century with a woman he barely knew who looked to him not to be her savior but to save her nation. Even assuming that was the right thing to do, he had no idea how to do it.

"You still have those newspapers?" he asked.

Rossi shook her head.

"They were in the car."

"Do you remember what they said about Oswald? Anything on his recent activities?"

"Yes," she said, clearly glad to grab hold of something concrete, some area that might give them an avenue of activity. "There were a couple of pieces, including one by Peter Kihss—good reporter—on the oddity of Oswald's life, his time in the Soviet Union when he tried to defect, then came back, and his work for two rival Cuban political groups, one pro-Castro, one against. It was bizarre. There was some suggestion he might have been working for a US intelligence agency, trying to infiltrate the Cuban regime but it was all a mess, and none of the US agencies claimed him. But you have to remember, that paper came out *the day after the assassination*. The fact that they had gathered that much information on Oswald was pretty amazing, to be honest, but it was all still an emerging story. I expect it got clarified over the next few days or weeks, but we don't have those stories."

"But he went to Cuba?"

"I don't think so. I remember there was something about dealings with a Miami office, but I don't think he went there either." Rossi thought for a moment then exclaimed, "New Orleans! Oswald was born there and went back there this summer, assuming we are still in 1963. July, I think it said. He was working for something called Fair Play for Cuba, but it was based in New Orleans. I'm sure of it."

"Think you could help me figure out the geographical coordinates for New Orleans so I could program the bike?" asked Bowie.

"If we can find a map I can get you close. I need to get to a library or maybe a travel agency."

Bowie nodded, then frowned doubtfully.

"What?" she demanded.

"I assume that means getting off this island," he said.

"Can't we use the bike?"

"No, we can't risk anyone seeing it," said Bowie with absolute certainty. "Not while Washington is present in the same moment with the same bike. We need to find another way off the island."

"He can't see us back here. You can't just input new coordinates and take us to a nearby town?"

"I could if I had them but jumps through time and space with the bike are inherently risky. And loud. At least when we used Washington's presets we knew he had used those entry points successfully. I don't want to materialize in front of a truck again, and guessing at coordinates could put us anywhere: out at sea, inside a building, a few feet too high or too low and we are . . ."

Rossi shuddered.

"I get it," she said.

"I need longitude, latitude, and altitude, as precise as possible, and as current as we can possibly get. If a highway gets moved or an empty lot gets developed between the map being made and our arrival at a hundred miles an hour . . ."

"Yeah, as I said, I get it," said Rossi, holding a hand up as if asking for silence. Bowie gave it to her and a few seconds later she nodded. "I'll go," she said. "There's probably a ferry, but since Naushon is a private island, we won't be able to just get on board without attracting a lot of attention. Especially you, no offense."

Bowie could have been offended, given a lifetime suffered under similar Alpha remarks, but he saw her logic.

"You stay here, look after the bike," she continued. "I'll get what we need and come back."

"How? It's still a private island?"

"I'll wave my press credentials," she said, patting her shoulder bag, "say I'm doing a feature on the Forbes family or something. I don't need to get into their house, just onto a ferry."

"What if Washington sees you?"

"I don't see him as the library type. Besides, he doesn't know me."

"Not yet," Bowie cut in. "But if he sees you here, he'll remember you, and he'll react when he sees you again at the Adolphus bar a couple months from now! That could change everything, derail the timeline . . ."

"OK, OK," she said. "I'll make sure he doesn't."

"How?"

"I don't know: by not being a moron, all right?" she shot back, exasperated. "I don't see a better option. If he shows up, I'll improvise, figure something out. I've trusted you, despite you shooting my partner, and despite a whole bunch of things most people couldn't get their heads around, now I'm asking you to trust me. I can do this."

Bowie considered her, and knew she was telling the truth. He couldn't say for sure she would be all right, but he also couldn't say for sure that his being with her would better her chances. In a firefight, sure, he was useful, but wandering around the woods of an alien world like this? He could barely say more than a couple of words to a local person without giving away how badly he didn't belong, and that may as well put a target on her back. She was smart, resourceful. She'd be better off without him.

"OK," he said. "I trust you."

"Thank heaven for small mercies," she remarked.

"What?"

"Figure of speech."

"I wish you wouldn't use these period clichés," he replied. "They are hard to follow."

"Well, pardon me for breathing," she replied, then playfully rolled her eyes at him.

He smiled despite himself.

"Why do I get the feeling that wasn't very original either?" he remarked.

Rossi suddenly got a distant look.

"Original," she said vaguely. "What does that remind me of? It was something to do with . . ." She tailed off looking miles away, then something came into focus and she snapped back. "Washington! When I first saw him at the Adolphus the night he died. I had completely forgot."

"Forgot what?" Bowie pressed.

"It was something he said," she replied. "He was being all high and mighty with Jimmy, saying he didn't need help from the likes of us, then he said, 'Thanks to the Originator, I don't need anything from any of you.' I didn't know what he meant. But I expect you do."

Bowie grew very still.

"Are you sure that was what he said?"

"Certain," she replied. "Who is the Originator? Your name for God or something?"

"There is no God in the Design."

"Your president then, the person who runs or founded your society?"

Bowie shook his head, awash in confusion and something close to excitement which he was doing his best to mute.

"Our president is called the Designer. No official in our world has ever been called the Originator."

"So what does it mean?"

Bowie wondered.

What indeed?

"There was a rumor," he said at last. "A whisper among the Gammas and the subversives. That somewhere deep in the heart of the Design, there was a kind of vault, a place more secret, more heavily guarded, than anywhere else in all Designed society. And this vault, or whatever was inside of it, was sometimes called 'the Original.' Maybe this is what Washington meant by 'the Originator'?"

Rossi looked pleased.

"OK," she said. "So what does it mean?"

Bowie's excitement drained.

"Probably nothing," he said. Seeing immediately the way she deflated he added, "Or maybe, it confirms what other people suspected." She looked at him for more but he had to shrug. "But I don't know what that would be."

"Maybe you should ask your brother," she said.

It was a shrewd remark but he had nothing useful to respond to that either.

"I wish I could," he said.

Originator, he thought vaguely. *Not Designer. Originator. Something or someone that came before. But before what? Before the Design? Before everything?*

But it was more than that. Washington had thanked the Originator that he didn't need anything from the humans of 1963. So maybe it was about tech? He didn't need them because of something he had. Or something he *was*?

A shiver ran down Bowie's neck. He didn't know what Washington had meant, but it felt significant.

"I should get ready to go," said Rossi, looking up at the sky.

"Right," said Bowie, coming back to the moment with a start. "Can I help?"

"I don't think so," she said, then caught herself and gave him a searching look. "You OK?"

"Yeah," he said, more breezily than he felt. "If you are going, you should leave now. It will be dark in a couple of hours."

And while she's gone, you'll do what? he asked himself.

He thought about what he had felt earlier, that impossible urge to strike at the heart of the Design for what they had done to him, what they were probably doing to his brother, and what they were trying to do to this world.

You can't touch them from here, he thought. *Not directly.*

Which left two options. The first was to touch them indirectly here, by sabotaging their agents, perhaps, but that felt remote, like the pulling on a thread to unravel a sheet of fabric; it would take an age and he may never see the results. The second option was even riskier, too risky to share with Rossi. Indeed, the less she knew, the safer she was likely to be.

And you were right: she's better off without you . . .

"OK," he said, glad of the deepening shadows so she wouldn't see the anxiety in his eyes. "Take the tracker. That will help you locate me when you get back."

It took an effort to say "when" rather than "if."

It was 2157 and the city had been dark for over an hour. A disruption at one of the solar collection facilities, apparently, though why the backup storage units were not yet engaged he could not fathom. Merrick found the silence as unsettling as the eerie tint of the office building's backup lighting. At least the comms were still working.

"Why don't we have power yet?" he demanded. "There are generators and multiple redundancy batteries built for exactly this eventuality."

"A number of distribution lines seem to have failed," said the engineer.

There was a hesitancy about his voice that Merrick didn't like. He shifted forward as if the man were sitting in front of him.

"What does *seem to have* mean, exactly?"

There was a momentary silence. Either the man couldn't answer the question or he didn't want to.

"We lost the monitor signals just after three o'clock," said the engineer.

Merrick ran the numbers in his head.

"That's over an hour after the failure of the collector grid," he said.

"Yes, sir."

"They weren't caused by the same problem?"

"No, sir. The backup system came online as designed at the time of the original power failure, but it shut down an hour later."

"Caused by?"

"Undetermined as yet."

"Speculate," said Merrick with icy precision.

The engineer faltered.

"If I had to guess, I'd say the two failures had separate but related causes."

"And in plain speech you think we have experienced multiple separate but coordinated attacks on our power system and supply."

"That would seem the most logical explanation, sir, yes."

"And you did not inform the security forces immediately because . . . ?"

Merrick could practically hear the engineer squirming at the other end.

"We didn't think it possible, sir, to be frank. We didn't believe that they had the capacity or the . . ." He hunted for the word. "Audacity. Didn't think they would dare, sir, even if they could."

"They?"

"The terrorists. Those Gamma subversives. We didn't think . . ."

"Clearly," said Merrick. "But you will. I will see to it that you do."

He hung up. For a moment he sat in the uncanny stillness, staring at the graying dimness of the office, the way the brightness of the windows to the world outside seemed to make the interior somehow darker, as if color had been drained from the building. This was why the professor's temporal incursions had to succeed.

No one knew it, but the very fabric of the Design was fraying at the edges. The threat was minor at the moment, but it was building steadily, spreading not just in its violence but, he suspected, in its message. It was hard to comprehend but unavoidable: the insurgents simply couldn't do what they were doing without inside help. They had to be winning people over. That was why they had to nip the insurgency not just in the bud, as the old saying went, but before the seed could even germinate.

Change the past and the present will fall into line.

He made the first of several calls, speaking with a calm urgency that deliberately allowed his irritation to bleed through.

But not his anxiety. That he kept guarded in a place darker than any corner of the increasingly stricken city.

CHAPTER FIFTEEN

Sandra Rossi had no clear strategy for getting off Naushon Island, so she began by retracing her steps until she found the access road they had skirted through the woods. After walking away from Bowie and the house for about a mile, she came upon two women and a man heading in the same direction but at nowhere near her quickened pace. Locals, from their accents. One of the women was little more than a girl, while the others—a couple, she thought—were in their late fifties, their hands rough with work and their faces tanned and leathery from the sea air. She had intended to keep a distance, see where they went, but the older woman saw her and, more particularly, saw her feet.

"Good lord!" she exclaimed. "What on earth have you been doing?"

"Stepped in a puddle and took my shoes off to dry," she said, smiling bashfully, "then cut my foot on a stone."

"Where are your shoes now?" asked the woman, curious rather than accusatory, but Rossi blushed anyway.

"Left them to dry," she said.

"You can't walk to the ferry like that!" She turned to the man who might be her husband. "Ray, help the girl."

"How?" he demanded. "You think I carry a pair of women's sneakers around in my toolbox?"

"I wouldn't put it past you," the woman replied darkly. She had iron-gray hair and a face that could have been carved from limestone. "At least give her your arm till we get aboard. Men!" she added, rolling her eyes. "What are they good for?"

Rossi took the offered arm and muttered her thanks.

"You're new," said the woman, giving her a beady look. "You at the Big House?"

She said it like that was its name. Rossi made a quick assessment and nodded.

"First day," she said.

"And you're what? Secretary? Child minder?"

A wild literary impulse almost made Rossi say "governess" but she decided to stay close to what she knew.

"Secretary," she agreed.

"I'm Mattie," said the woman. "Mattie James. Housekeeper at number eight. This slip of a thing is Sarah, the au pair," she said, putting a flourish on the last two words and adding with a suggestive look, "From France, if you can believe it. And this useless lump is my Ray, gardener and odd-job man. Emphasis on *odd*."

Her husband, apparently used to this kind of treatment, grinned.

"Jean," said Rossi, picking the name out of the air.

"Pleased to meet you I'm sure," said Mattie matter-of-factly. "You're bound for the mainland?"

"That's right."

"Falmouth or farther in?"

"Falmouth," said Rossi. She'd heard of the town, which meant it was probably big enough for a library. "Need to pick up some books."

"Books, is it?" said Mattie with a kind of haughty suspicion. She checked her watch. "You'll need to be quick to catch the library. And then what? You're not staying in town."

"Have to get back here," said Rossi, fighting to conceal her flash of anxiety and annoyance with herself. She hadn't considered what the closing time of a rural library might be. "Work," she offered lamely by way of explanation. "After I have picked up the books."

"And some shoes," said Ray.

"Right," said Rossi.

"Well, I'm not sure how you'll get back tonight, unless you hitch a ride on a fishing boat."

"That was what I was hoping," Rossi improvised. "I have money."

Mattie scoffed as if nothing could be more absurd.

"I'll talk to Leila Derringer's boy," she announced. "He'll take you or feel the back of my hand."

And so, to Rossi's immense relief, it was arranged. The water was less than a half mile across and they made the trip quickly, watching what Rossi was told was the Nobska Lighthouse, beyond which lay Nantucket and the gray, open waters of the Atlantic. It was, in a stark sort of way, beautiful, and Rossi wished her sister could see it. Veronica had always had a thing for the ocean. As kids they had occasionally vacationed as a family down in Corpus Christi, and they had been without question the best moments of their childhood. Her father was different on holiday: less stressed, quicker to laugh and kinder to their mother. Rossi gazed out over the flat vastness of the water and felt a wash of conflicted emotions. She didn't speak to her father much anymore, They could barely get through Thanksgiving without him lapsing into a drunken rant about what she did, her liberal politics and "book smarts." It wasn't entirely his fault. He was a narrow-minded man, but he had also been scarred by the war—he had fought in Italy—and had come home only to be frustrated by his lack of success in business and confused by the changing nature of the world. And being honest, she goaded him. Even when he talked about fighting at Monte Cassino—which he always did when he railed about the problems with young people today—she'd roll her eyes and tell him to change the record. She winced at the memories. The pure insanity of the firefight she'd faced just a few hours before was putting her father's tales of all-out war in an entirely new perspective. Maybe the next time she saw him she would manage a little more patience.

Maybe, she thought, though she knew her father had a gift for undercutting her best intentions.

Mattie gathered a handful of men on the quayside and, in her sergeant major manner, presented her new friend, Jean, who needed to get back to the island an hour from now. She then directed her to the public library between Main Street and Mullen-Hall School, before—in a rush of generosity that brought tears to Rossi's tired eyes—gave her her shoes.

"I'm nearly home," Mattie pronounced, "and you can give them back to me when you see me next. I expect we'll be crossing paths a lot on that ferry."

Rossi, the various stresses of the day suddenly having time to settle on her now that she wasn't hiding or running from killers, found herself overwhelmed, and though the woman shrugged the matter off, it lingered in her mind as she explored the library, leaving her feeling guilty and regretful that she would never see her again.

The library was an elegant, turn of the century building, well maintained and spacious. Rossi felt more guilt as she squeezed a large format book entitled *Atlas of the USA* into her shoulder bag and slipped out.

It was dark now, and it took a moment for her to orient herself.

"Miss Jean?"

A young man in the cab of a rusty pickup truck parked with two wheels on the curb in front of the library was addressing her through the open passenger side window. Rossi took a second to still her spiking anxiety and managed a smile.

"You are—?"

"Craig," said the driver, adding with an embarrassed smile "Leila Derringer's boy. Mrs. James said you needed a lift to the island?"

Fifteen minutes later Rossi was nestled in the prow of a small wooden power boat called, apparently, a dragger as it chugged its way back to the Naushon wharf before heading out in search of cod and flounder. Craig, the young man who captained the boat was deferential, even shy, and barely spoke except to ask if she was sure she knew where she was going, "it being dark and all."

She assured him she was and, once ashore, set to retracing her steps, privately thanking Mattie James for the gift of her sturdy shoes, which allowed her to venture back into the darkness of the tree line, so as to stay off the road.

All she had to do then was to find Bowie.

But Bowie was not on the island. Moments after Rossi had left him, he had wheeled the bike as far from the house as he could manage before the thick brambles forced him out onto the road they had arrived on. Then, when he was as sure as he could be that there was no one around, he had fired up the engine and, seconds later, made the jump through time.

Professor Reissen was studying the monitors, though there was annoyingly little that could be learned from them at this temporal distance. The status display still read "Mission in progress," which told him nothing, but since the nature of time was that events in the past would register immediately in the future, he had no choice but to wait. If he went home to sleep, he could miss everything. But it would be over, soon, surely?

A light began to flash and an alarm sounded. He looked up, frowning, his brain still fogged by inaction.

"Incoming agent," called Peter.

"What?" snapped Reissen. "Were they recalled?"

"Sir, not that I can see."

"Who is it?"

"Trying to determine the vehicle's identification code through the vortex," said Peter, tapping a screen and adjusting a slider. "It seems to be . . ."

"Yes?"

"Sir, I think it's Washington's bike!"

Reissen stood abruptly.

"It can't be. Washington is dead."

"It's definitely his bike!"

"Security to launch bay!" barked Reissen into the intercom. "Intruder! Repeat, intruder!" The hangar exploded with panicked energy, but the doors of the portal were already opening. "Prepare to shut down power to the drive assembly as soon as he arrives! And take cover!"

Bowie! It had to be.

The fool had come back! They'd been chasing him through time and the idiot had returned to the one place he could not possibly escape! Survive the next thirty seconds and Reissen would be a hero, the man who caught the rogue agent single handedly . . .

The vortex flashed into swirling view, and Reissen turned away from the glare, shielding his eyes. There was a sidearm in his desk drawer and he reached for it, turning to the portal as the roar of the bike filled the hangar like liquid poured into a tub, filling every corner, overwhelming it with weight and pressure.

Reissen dropped to a crouch, readied the weapon and, as soon as the sound began to dissipate, came back up, pistol raised. Even as he sighted along the barrel, however, he knew something was wrong.

The sound for one thing. The bike engine hadn't simply shut down, leaving the room silent. It had faded in and then—after a familiar popping sound—had faded out again. Then there was the light. The vortex hadn't simply flickered shut as it should when an agent returned. It had started to dim but then had immediately flashed and reset in a swirl of color before closing.

And neither the bike nor its rider were parked on the pad in front of him.

"Where did he go?" Reissen demanded.

"Unclear," said Peter, hastily tapping at his screen. "He can't have returned to the past without commencing a whole new launch sequence."

"So he's here? In this moment?" Reissen demanded. "Somewhere in the city?"

"Possibly," the tech replied. "If it was Bowie, the present extends to the period around his initial departure. Weeks, perhaps even months before."

"It was him," said Reissen. "What would be the point of returning to a moment before he left? No. He's here, in the city, now. Alert the director! Engage maximum security protocols. Bowie, and that bike, must be found!"

But Bowie wasn't in the city. He wasn't even in what Reissen thought of as the present. Where he was, weeks before he first journeyed into the past, it was that Patriot Day when he had taken the shuttle to Westport to collect data from the solar energy plants and check the security perimeter, the day he had taken his vehicle a few miles away from his designated route to visit the Paradise Valley work camp, and the Gammas who were incarcerated there. He was here to see only one of them. The bike kicked up the dusty sand on the road between the great solar farms, and Bowie gripped the handlebars and braked hard, scrubbing off speed as a great tan-colored plume ballooned up behind him.

He checked the chronometer, assessed his proximity to the camp perimeter, and made some hasty calculations. His previous self had been here only moments before, but he was gone now and there was no danger of meeting him. Bowie brushed himself down. He didn't have the docupad which had got him in last time, but he didn't think he would need it. The Beta guards at the gate knew him. In fact, they had seen him no more than a minute or two before.

"Back again?" said one, smirking.

"Left my badge in the visitation room," Bowie remarked, managing to look annoyed and apologetic.

"Changed your jacket too," said the taller guard. "You have a fall or something?"

Bowie realized he had accumulated an assortment of cuts and bruises, apparently in a matter of minutes.

"Stumbled in one of the drainage trenches," he muttered, hoping the guard didn't examine his injuries too closely. "There should be warning signs."

"You need the first aid kit?" asked the other guard.

"No, just let me back in."

"I'll send someone," said one of the guards.

Bowie shook his head and sighed.

"I'd rather handle it myself," he said. "I need to speak to the Gamma that was in there."

One of the guards looked perplexed, even doubtful, but the other grinned.

"Got the drop on you, huh?" he said. "Grabbed your ID when you weren't looking."

Bowie gave him a shame-faced smile.

"My fault for flashing it in his face like I was the Designer himself," he said.

"You gotta watch these Gammas," said the other. "Especially that one. Want us to come teach him a lesson? He's still in the visitation room."

"I got it," said Bowie.

The guard looked momentarily confused by the phrase and Bowie quickly backtracked.

"Starting to talk like these low lifes," he remarked. "I can handle the Gamma."

"You know best," said the guard, rolling back the gate and nodding him through.

"Thanks," said Bowie, then, realizing that even gratitude to the guards was out of character, added, "Don't bother bringing me that nasty tea this time."

Sefton was exactly as he had been, his hair still pulled into a ponytail, his face hard, but thoughtful as he waited to be sent back to work. He half turned as the door opened and his eyes tightened when he saw not the armed escort returning him to the plant, but the brother who—in his timeline—had left him no more than a couple of minutes before.

Bowie closed the door carefully behind him.

"Missing me already?" Sefton said with a smirk.

Bowie smiled, wider, more candid than usual at seeing his brother again after all he had been through.

"What?" Sefton asked, alert to something strange in his visitor but unable to process it. "You seem . . . different."

"I am," said Bowie simply. "Seff, I don't have long, so you're going to need to listen very closely. I need you to come with me. Your life depends on it."

Sefton's face clouded with suspicion and amusement, as if this was some kind of practical joke.

"Now, Seff," Bowie pressed.

"What's this about? What's with you?"

Bowie had rehearsed a series of explanations and half truths as he walked the bike through the woods of Naushon Island, but as he met his brother's eyes they all seemed preposterous, disingenuous.

"You were right," he said, sitting opposite his brother.

"About what?"

"A lot of things," Bowie confessed, "but mostly about how they hate me. Hate us. How they'll use us but never trust us."

"All right," said Sefton, still cautious.

"I've been a fool," Bowie blurted, saying words he hadn't even admitted to himself. "Worse. I've been an implement of . . ."

"An unjust and oppressive system?" Sefton offered, when Bowie couldn't find the words.

Bowie nodded.

"But not anymore," he said. "I've turned against them. Or they turned on me and now I see . . . It doesn't matter. I've come to get you out of here."

"And take me where? It's a totalitarian state, Bowie. They have eyes everywhere."

"Not where we're going."

"Where's that?"

"1963."

Sefton frowned.

"What's that, a sector . . . ?"

"The year," said Bowie. "I can take you to a world before any of this came into being."

He gestured at the visitation room and everything beyond it. Sefton stared at him.

"I know," said Bowie. "It's crazy. But it's true. Listen."

And he told him. Everything. The mission, the time cycle, the assassination of a president, the agents sent after him, Rossi, all of it. And, as he talked, Sefton just sat there and listened, saying nothing. Bowie spoke quickly, unsure how long they had before the guards came back, and when he finished a breathless hush descended on the room. He looked at his brother and then leaned forward, elbow on the table, head in his hands.

"Like I said," he concluded. "It's crazy."

But Sefton shook his head slowly.

"Actually," he said, "it makes a kind of sense. Of you at least. I saw you leave, your usual self: stiff, delusional, still an officer of the Design with a purpose tied to theirs. Minutes later you come back in as a completely different person. Not the clothes, the cuts and bruises, *you*. There's a fire in you I haven't seen since we were kids. It's you, but it's not the you that walked out of this room a few minutes ago."

Relief swept over Bowie.

"OK," he said. "Good. Follow me."

He started to rise, but Sefton didn't move, and as Bowie met his eyes his brother just shook his head, slow and sad.

"Sorry, Bowie. I'm staying."

"But you said you believed me!"

"I do. That's why I can't leave."

"If I'm successful, this timeline might cease to exist!" Bowie protested. "*You* could cease to exist!"

"Might," said Sefton. "Could. We don't know for sure. What I do know is that I have good people who depend on me, people whose lives need improving not in the past but right now in the present. I respect what you're doing. And I'll support you any way I can, but I can't come with you."

"In a few week's time, the Design is going to send me back into the past. Soon after that, they're going to send agents into that same past to *kill me*. What do you think they'll do to you when I fight back?"

"That means I've got weeks. Time to plan."

"Sefton, you don't understand . . . !"

"Maybe not. But my place is here."

Bowie stared at him, mouth open.

"You said you wanted to strike at the heart of the Design," said Sefton. "So let's do it. Not little sabotage missions. Not minor disruptions and inconveniences. Let's take the fight to them, to the very heart of the Design."

"I can't. I have to go back," said Bowie, thinking of his new mission to unravel what Washington and the other time agents had been doing, and of Rossi whom he had left on the island. He had convinced himself she was safer without him, but now they were apart he found he didn't believe that anymore.

"I know," said Sefton. "But that doesn't mean we can't work together."

Bowie thought fast.

"A pincer attack," he said at last, "but instead of the two assaults being separated by space—by points on a map—they're separated by time. You work in the present. I work in the past."

"Right."

"There is a great rottenness at the heart of our world," said Bowie gravely. "I see it now, but I don't know where it comes from. *Came* from. I think it's buried deep in the past and I need to find where and pull it out."

"But you don't know what this *rottenness* is?" said Sefton, articulating the word warily, like a man circling a snarling dog.

Bowie shook his head.

"We'll figure it out together," he said.

"Yes," Sefton agreed. "But fact finding isn't enough. We need to blow things up. Literally."

Bowie checked his watch. He couldn't stay much longer.

"What are the cornerstones of the Design?" he mused. "Not concepts and principles. The actual physical building blocks of what makes this world work."

"It's a police state," said Sefton. "So, the security services."

"Agreed," said Bowie. "That will diminish them, but we need more. The injustice is deeper. It's built into who we are from birth."

"The incubation labs," said Sefton. "They breed the Alphas to rule, and the rest of us to . . . this."

"Exactly," said Bowie. "Strike at those two and we cut out their fist and their heart."

Sefton sat back and laughed. It was a bleak, hopeless sound.

"Attack the incubation facilities and the security services?" he said. "When you change sides, you really change sides, huh, little brother?"

"I know it's a lot," Bowie said. "But you won't be alone."

"I'm never alone," said Sefton.

"I know," said Bowie. "I see that now. But I meant . . ."

"You'll be back?"

"I will. One more thing. The agent called Washington, told some people in 1963, 'Thanks to the Originator, I don't need anything from any of you.'"

"He said 'the Originator'?" Sefton inquired as he leaned forward. "You're sure that's what he said?"

"Yes. Does it mean something to you?"

"Maybe," said Sefton. "I've heard whispers. If they're true, they point to the incubation facility."

Bowie's eyebrows rose but he said nothing.

"A great rottenness," said Sefton musingly. "And 'the Originator.' Whatever they are, we're getting close, brother. I can feel it. Close to finding the truth. Think you'll be here to see it?"

"I hope so," said Bowie, pulling one of the trackers from his jacket and pushing it across the table. "This will help me find you when I return."

"We need to coordinate carefully."

"Dates, times, places," said Bowie, holding up a slip of paper. "If you can keep to this schedule, I'll see you again."

"If not?"

"Then we should say our goodbyes now."

The gravity of the remark caught Sefton off guard. His face clouded with thoughtfulness, then he stood slowly and extended his hand across the table.

"Forever and forever farewell, Bowie," he intoned, pulling once more from Mrs. Dunn's collection of quotations. "If we shall meet again, we'll smile. If not, this parting was well made."

Bowie found himself at a loss for words. He clasped his brother's hand firmly and shook it once. He turned in silence for the door, thinking about how to get back to Washington's bike as quickly and inconspicuously as possible, but as he reached the door he recalled the last time he had been here and he paused.

"I remember Mrs. Alsace," he said, his head hung.

"What?" asked Sefton who was still somber, processing all that Bowie had told him.

"The curry lady," said Bowie. "That's what we called her. I do remember her. Always have."

Sefton considered him and the two men exchanged sad, thoughtful smiles loaded with things they would never say.

"Yeah," said Sefton sadly. "That woman could really cook."

There was no one around, and the woods were eerily quiet, save for the occasional shriek of a screech owl in the night.

Rossi focused on the little tracker Bowie had given her, its simple red light indicating the direction of the parked bike. She hadn't thought she would need it, but in the dark the forest felt wholly unfamiliar and impossible to navigate. At times she was sure she was turned around or—worse—had not been in this place before, but she trusted the little device because she had no choice not to, and when her instincts told her she was lost, she ignored them and shuffled on through the fallen leaves and pine needles. Her greatest panic came as she reached the bike itself—according to the tracker—but couldn't see either the bike or Bowie until the big man shone a light in her face.

"Thought you weren't coming back," he said.

"I was fast!" she replied.

"Not what I meant," he said.

She let that go and unveiled the atlas like someone presenting a prize, but Bowie was all business.

"This was the most detail you could find?" he remarked, scanning the pages.

"For Louisiana? In a library in Massachusetts? Yeah, this is the best I could find. And what have you been doing all this time? Sitting on your ass making sure no one stole the bike?"

Something flashed through his face and he looked away.

"What?" she demanded. "Did something happen? Did you go somewhere? I swear to God, Bowie . . . !"

"Shh!" he hissed, turning suddenly.

"If you're still keeping secrets from me after all I've done . . ."

Bowie held up a hand, his eyes urgent and his voice low.

"There's someone coming!"

Rossi dropped to her knees, head cocked.

Voices. On the road some fifty yards to her left. Men. One of them chuckling softly at something. She closed her eyes to listen.

"Nah . . . Parilli can't get it done. We saw that!" said one voice.

"You wait till we play at home," said another, a higher, younger voice. "Get a Fenway crowd behind him. He'll show ya."

The next remark was indistinct but then she heard the laugh again, quieter now, as the men walked on by. She realized that Bowie was staring at her intently, waiting—it seemed—for a translation.

"It's fine," she said. "Just a couple of guys talking about the Patriots."

"A political group?" said Bowie, still earnest.

"A football team. That, for some reason, is playing in a baseball stadium," she answered.

Bowie just shrugged.

"No football?" Rossi pushed. "Any sports? Nothing? Wow."

Bowie seemed annoyed by the questions. He looked tired too, preoccupied, and again she wondered what he had done in her absence.

"We should give them at least ten minutes to get off the road before we fire up the bike," he said. "I don't want them reporting back."

Rossi said nothing, but settled down and, on impulse, lay on her back, gazing up through the trees to where she could just make out the glimmerings of stars, while Bowie studied the maps and tapped at the guidance system on the bike. He said he thought he had figured out how to derive coordinates from the previously used data points, which would tell them exactly where and when Washington had been, but it looked like there were only a few preexisting coordinates in the system.

He frowned.

"You didn't bring back anything to eat," said Bowie, glancing at her bag.

"Nope," she said, watching the sky.

"Getting hungry," Bowie remarked.

"Don't be a baby."

"I'm just saying that we haven't eaten for a while. I have some protein packs, but we should ration them. Operatives need to keep their strength up. If you go hungry you get weak, slow . . ."

"A, I'm not an operative," Rossi shot back, "and B, if you want to eat, you'll want to wait till we get to New Orleans."

"Why's that?" he asked.

"Trust me," she said.

Relay Station Twenty-Seven controlled the power grid for the entire west side of the city. It was laboring now, struggling to route electricity from the stations that hadn't been hit by the resistance's coordinated sabotage. Rolling blackouts had been instituted across the whole region, but if they could just knock this one relay out of action,

Sefton knew the impact would be massive. Take out relay twenty-seven and they would kill the power, not just to the government center, but to the security buildings that surrounded it, and the so-called research facilities, including the incubation labs. It would cripple the Design for hours, maybe days.

Which wasn't enough. Sefton knew that. Even a blow like this, right at the heart of the Design, tangible though it was, was less a revolutionary act than it was a gesture of defiance. But it was all part of the plan.

His brother's plan. Sefton was not just risking a lot on Bowie's plan. He was risking everything.

"They think we're bugs biting an elephant," he muttered aloud.

"What?"

Greta, his deputy, was giving him a baffled look.

"They think we aren't worth their attention," he said, "tiny pests who can't hurt them."

"They'll learn," said Greta.

She sounded calm, certain. Sefton wished he felt the same way.

This uprising was already as successful as they had ever been. He was dealing the Design a humiliating blow that would send shock waves through its system, even if they had the power grid back up and running by the end of the week. It wasn't enough, but it would do what he needed for now.

We are risking everything, he thought again. *People will die. All because of the crazy story his brother had told him. His brother who was now somewhere back in time.*

It wasn't that he didn't believe him. He just wished he had seen with his own eyes all that Bowie had reported. Whatever else he was, Sefton was a laborer, a man used to dealing with tangible things, cables and stone, tools and obstacles. It was hard to get his mind around time travel and ancient evils buried in the past whose consequences shaped his world to this day. It sounded like the ramblings of a lunatic, and if he had been told about it by anyone else . . .

But it was Bowie, and though they had lived separate lives for many years, what bound them together sang in their blood in ways no lab-grown Alpha could ever understand. It might seem like they were no more than insects to the massive creature that was the Design, but there was a wider, deeper purpose to their buzzing. He believed that. He had to.

"Sefton?" Greta prompted.

"Final surveillance report?" Sefton said, falling back on protocol.

"All clear, apart from the guards on the gate. But won't be for much longer."

There was the merest hint not of reprimand but of concern in the deputy's voice and Sefton understood why. The Design would be reinforcing the station any moment. Armored personnel carriers had been reported in the streets below the central towers. Targeting skimmers would be circling overhead . . .

"Then we move," he said. "And Greta?"

"Sir?" said the deputy, surprised by Sefton's use of her first name.

"Thanks," said Sefton clasping her hand and squeezing it once. "You've done good work today. So has the whole team. Make sure they know."

The deputy's face flushed with pride, then clouded as she picked up on Sefton's mood. There was something about his tone that felt somehow loaded, final. Before she could say anything further, Sefton swung around one of the weapons confiscated from the guard station back at the farm and nodded.

"Go," he said.

He didn't wait for a response, but led the way, breaking from cover and dashing twenty yards to the foot of the steps outside the relay station before opening fire.

CHAPTER SIXTEEN

The bike roared out of the time vortex and onto a lonely highway connecting Chalmette National Historical Park—the site of the 1815 Battle of New Orleans—with the city center to the west, some six miles away. It was sunset, and the road out of the preserve was flanked by bayou and overhung with live oaks trailing Spanish moss. The air was damp, warm, and redolent of the swamp, which threatened to overcome the cemeteries and monuments of the land with every heavy rain. Bowie, unaccustomed to humidity, fussed with the fasteners of his jacket until it flapped open.

"You know where you are going?" yelled Rossi as soon as the strange nausea of the time shift had subsided.

"I think so," he said.

It was a hot July evening and he could feel the sweat breaking out all over him already. What was this place? Within a minute or two of arriving the air had come to feel stifling, thick and wet, and he found himself sniffing warily and scanning the side of the highway for roadkill. In Naushon he had tasted the sea on the breeze, but here the air was dead calm, sluggish, and charged with the sweet-and-sour aromas of a life and death so intense, so physical, that he almost gagged. It was as far from his sterile, climate-controlled home as he could imagine.

The deserted highway quickly gave way to a housing development which, to him, looked like cabins, mostly wood and sitting on little weedy lots surrounded by chain-link fence. There were as many boats in the driveways as there were cars. In places there were lights on, flat fluorescents, faintly greenish, and softer amber glows that might have been lanterns lit by an open flame. For a moment he wondered if he had input the coordinates wrong, that they had leaped back fifty years instead of a mere couple of months.

Such feelings slid away as they skirted the slick brown worm that was the Mississippi and entered the city proper. It didn't feel remotely like the modernity of Dallas, the buildings timber and brick with ornate balconies and railings twisted out of wrought iron, but it was clearly a town, and there were the cars and neon that marked it as mid-twentieth century. The smells got a little less earthy and a little more industrial, but then they would suddenly complicate and blossom into something fragrant that made his mouth water. While the swampy woods had been empty, the streets were busy at noon, people coming and going, some of them with bottles and glasses in their hands, raucous voices and music dribbling out from the doorways and windows as they rode past. Bowie turned in bewilderment and found Rossi was—improbably—grinning.

"Oh yeah," she muttered vaguely. "Now we're talking."

They found a low-rent motel, considered the rooms and opted for something a little more upscale on Julia Street, parking the bike in the darkest corner of the open lot. Bowie paid cash in advance, laying out the bills cautiously, unsure of when he had presented enough.

"Two rooms," said Rossi pointedly.

The clerk, a weaselly white man with a pot belly and skinny arms, gave Bowie a wicked grin and said conspiratorially, "Seem like you gonna have t'look elsewheres if you gonna pass a good time in N'awlins. Fortunately, I figure we got ya covered." Bowie gave him a blank stare and the man's impish grin faltered. "Just sayin'," the clerk added, hands raised. Bowie let the man count another two dollars from his stack.

"That'll do nicely," the clerk concluded, handing them their keys and shooting Rossi a wink.

"You got a spare sheet or tarp?" asked Bowie. "Want to cover my bike."

The clerk frowned but got busy as soon as Bowie laid down another dollar.

"Don't throw your money around, big spender," said Rossi as they walked to their rooms.

"I have more."

"Not my point," she replied, jingling her key. "We are trying to be inconspicuous, right? This is a town which spots tourists fast, especially if they are flashing a lot of money. We don't want any trouble."

Bowie took the point.

"Paper money," he said. "It's weird."

"That right there is the point," she said, turning on him. "Every time you get your wallet out, you look like you just flew in from Kathmandu."

"Where is . . . ?"

"Somewhere far away," she replied, waving the question away with a local map she'd swiped in the lobby. "I mean you look lost, foreign. It's obvious. Try to be more casual, and don't hand out money like it's just paper you have no use for."

"OK," he said. "When do we eat?"

"Gimme ten minutes," she said. "I'll find a restaurant; you come up with a plan."

The restaurant was little more than a hole in the wall off Royal Street in the heart of the French Quarter, but the food was spectacular. Bowie, who was ravenous, ate a massive amount: an oyster po'boy with shrimp and grits, a cup of gumbo, and half of Rossi's crawfish étouffée. By her second glass of wine, she was watching him with a kind of horrified amusement.

"I take it there's not much Cajun food in the future," she observed.

"That's what this is?" he replied, his mouth full and barely looking up from his plate. "No."

"My sister—Veronica—loves Cajun and Creole food," she said. "I mean loves it! The spicier the better. One time we made a spicy gumbo at home and my father—big tough guy, but not so great with the spicy food—was in so much pain! He tried milk, orange juice, water . . . but nothing worked! I don't think he's eaten gumbo since!"

She laughed at the memory.

"I didn't know you had a sister," said Bowie, still shoveling food into his face.

"Well, with all the time traveling and shooting, we haven't had much time for small talk." He nodded, chewing, so she went on. "We're pretty close. Or were when we were in the same time period. She'll be getting married soon. In 1964, I mean. That's the plan at least. After that, who knows. Brian—that's her fiancé—is nice enough but . . ."

She ended lamely and shrugged.

"What?" Bowie asked.

"I don't know," she replied. "He's kind of controlling. I think so, at least. He's already said he doesn't want Veronica to continue working after they get married. She's good at what she does, too. She's a realtor. Do you still have those? Anyway, I tried to get her to push back a little, but she doesn't want to spoil things with Brian. I said that if you can't even talk about your own career with your fiancé then there's something wrong but . . ." She nearly ended up by rolling her eyes and saying "you know Veronica," but of course he didn't, never would, and probably didn't care. She watched him eat, wondering briefly what had compelled her to share so much, until he realized she'd stopped talking and looked up.

"Go on," he said. "Veronica. It's interesting."

She laughed at that and waved the conversation away. He gave her a puzzled look, then paused, apparently considering the music playing through the restaurant's speakers.

"There's that sound again," he observed vaguely.

"More jazz," she said. "Not quite the same, though. This is more Dixieland."

He nodded dreamily, as if he knew what that meant.

"You don't have music either, huh?" she said, but this time her amusement was tempered with something like pity.

He heard the tone and met her eyes briefly.

"Not like this," he said, and went back to his food.

"OK," she said. "I found the grub. Now you tell me what we're doing here, other than eating our body weight in shrimp."

"This food is unbelievable," Bowie muttered.

"The plan," she insisted.

"Right. We are now several months before the assassination, and could remove Oswald from the game board, but that only prevents the assassination if he is, as you say, a lone wolf. If he is part of an organization, which is beginning to look more likely . . ."

"They would have time to replace him with another gunman before JFK comes to Dallas."

"So we keep it simple," he said. "We know Oswald is here. We find him. Observe him from a distance. See who he is dealing with. We do not engage. But we see who he meets, talks to, spends time with, and whether we think those people are really the ones behind assassinating the president. If we decide he's on his own, we act against him."

"By bringing hard evidence to the authorities that doesn't rely on newspapers from the future."

"Or we kill him," said Bowie simply. "What?"

She had been nodding and smiling through their conversation thus far, but suddenly she was wary of him again, as if he had been wearing a mask which had slipped.

"Nothing," she said, shaking her head and avoiding his eyes. "I guess I forget who you really are sometimes."

"Meaning?" he replied. She didn't respond so he prompted her. "Who am I, Sandra?"

She looked up at his unusual use of her name and for a moment she looked flustered, but then her face hardened.

"A soldier sent from the future to kill people," she said. "If your own people hadn't turned against you, you might have killed me like you tried to kill Jimmy."

"I was just—"

"Following orders," she said. "Yeah, I know. But it's probably good for me to remember that while you are now trying to protect the president from an assassin, not long ago you were trying to do the opposite."

"I didn't know that Oswald was going to . . ."

"Yeah, yeah," she said. "I know. You didn't have all the facts. And they have your brother. I remember that too. But will you act to save my society if it means destroying your own?"

He held her gaze, then said, "You can trust me."

"Yeah?" she said, challenging and tough as granite. "I hope so."

He just nodded, as if that was as much as he could hope for, then said, "While you were getting the atlas I found a way to reverse display the bike's coordinates."

"Meaning what?"

"Meaning that if we have to go farther back in time I will at least know where and *when* we are when we get there."

"OK," she said. For a moment she watched him, almost sure there had been something evasive about that "while you were getting the atlas" remark. He was still holding something back, and it was tied to what he had done on the island in her absence. She would wait on that. If he continued to evade, to lie, she would reassess her options. For now, she'd let it lie. "Let's concentrate on the present," she went on. "And I have a way to start," she concluded, wiping her mouth and becoming businesslike, all her previous hostility gone. She could feel Bowie taking a second to catch up, as if her shifts in tone left him off balance.

Good, she thought. *I can use that.*

"Oswald was—*is*—supposedly working for a pro-Cuba group," she said. "I took a quick look at the local paper and phone book. I think our best bet is to start here." She unfolded the local map and indicated a spot with a jab of her fingertip. "Seems like several of these organizations are based in the same area. It's maybe a twenty-minute walk from here."

Bowie, his mind apparently still lingering on their previous conversation about his loyalties, just looked at her.

"Are you listening?" she asked.

"Yes. We can walk over there tonight if you like."

"When you've finished eating," she agreed. "Assuming that happens at some point."

It would have happened sooner, but Bowie spotted their waiter flaming a brandy-soaked bananas Foster at a neighboring table.

"As soon as I've had one of whatever that is," he said.

The streets were, if anything, even busier when they came out of the restaurant. Although it was close to ten o'clock at night, it seemed like everyone was out and talking at once. Rossi seemed to bask in the sound, pointing out the peculiarities of the local dialect with a kind of delighted wonder. Bowie wasn't sure he could hear all the details as she did, and he didn't understand when she compared the accents to versions of New York and the Deep South simultaneously, but he could tell the place was unique.

"I wish I had my camera," he said, half to himself.

"You're a photographer?" Rossi replied, clearly amazed. "Wow, I did not see that coming."

"What do you mean?" he replied, sensing something like mockery in her manner.

"You don't seem like an artist."

"I'm not," he said quickly, as if she had insulted him. "I just like the way the camera helps me see things."

"Sounds like an artist to me."

"Still no," he said. His photography had always made him self-conscious, as if the interest exposed him as somehow suspect. Deviant. Still, he considered his surroundings as if composing an image in his view finder.

The area was equal parts vibrant and seedy, with a higher density of bars, clubs, and restaurants than Bowie had ever imagined possible. Drunken laughter seemed to follow them from one street to the next, and at one house a pair of scantily dressed women called to Bowie from the balcony.

“Are you blushing?” asked Rossi, amazed.

“My world is not like this,” he replied.

“Any of it? You don’t have strip clubs and hookers in your perfect society?”

“No,” he said, and there was a ferocity to his response that held her attention.

“What’s that, feminism, or puritanism?” she asked.

“Both,” he said. “And neither. Your society’s interest in sex is foreign to us.”

“Is that so?” she said, teasingly, watching the way his eyes lingered on the women in their corsets and stockings.

“Yes,” he said flatly, snapping his eyes front. “We think such things decadent. Animal.”

Rossi raised her eyebrows, clearly taken aback by his palpable discomfort, but she wouldn’t let the matter go.

“Some artist you are,” she said.

“I told you,” he began, but she waved his protests away, and came back to her point. “So sex is just for married people?” she said.

“No,” he said again. “We have evolved beyond such things. The Alphas and Betas, at least.”

“Wait,” she said, stopping in her tracks so that an elderly man in a pristine suit had to weave around her. “You don’t have sex at all? Any of you? How do you have children?”

“There are procedures,” said Bowie stiffly turning to face her. “Programs. Incubation facilities. You wouldn’t understand.”

“You mean that children are genetically engineered and then gestate in labs?”

“So you do understand. Most of them, yes.”

“OK, but don’t people still experience lust, desire?”

"They are bred not to," said Bowie, his discomfort swelling. "Genetically. And they receive hormone treatments through their food supply."

"But you are not one of these Alphas."

"What difference does it make to you?" he said walking away, unsure why he was being defensive.

"I'm just curious," she replied as she caught up, clearly amused by his uneasiness. "So your people reproduce without physical interaction and the embryos develop in some kind of laboratory?"

"That is the mechanism of it, yes," he replied, not bothering to go near that "your people."

"And you say we are barbaric," she sneered.

"We moved away from the obsessions of the flesh which so consumed previous societies."

"You were pretty consumed by fleshly obsessions when you were putting away three pounds of shrimp a minute ago."

"I said you wouldn't understand."

"You're right," she said. "I don't. Do you?"

"Do I what?"

"Do you buy all this stuff about your sexless world? You say it's about the Alphas, but you aren't one of them. In fact, if I've got this right, they are the ones trying to kill you. Yet you still parrot their ideas like you agree with them."

Bowie looked away, unsure how to respond.

"They are the ideas I was raised with," he said at last.

"Even though they don't apply to you?"

"There is only one way to think in the Design. If you deviate from those ideas, you are exactly that: deviant. Outcast."

"So you have internalized the beliefs and rules of a system that oppresses you," she observed, "to such an extent that even when you are cut free from the oppressors you can't quite shelve their beliefs. Interesting."

"Don't analyze me," Bowie replied, his irritation mounting.

"I'm just saying that it's fascinating," she persisted, smiling. "It's the ultimate form of control, right? Getting the victims of oppression to believe that the conditions of their servitude is natural."

"I told you not to analyze me," Bowie snarled through gritted teeth.

"I'm just saying," she replied, "I feel sorry for you, but you have to admit it is a little bit funny, especially here . . ."

"Stop," said Bowie turning on her.

"Don't be so sensitive! Rossi retorted. "I was only teasing . . ."

"No," Bowie insisted, his voice low as he caught her by the arm. "Behind me. Look."

She did, and there in the middle of the intersection between Camp and Common Streets, wearing a crisp white short-sleeved shirt and a dark necktie, his hair carefully brushed back, was Lee Harvey Oswald. He was approaching passersby in front of a building announcing itself as the International Trade Mart and handing out single sheet leaflets. Surrounded by the mostly dismissive people enjoying a night out, he looked out of place: small, fussy, and unremarkable. Rossi stared at him in something like fascinated horror until Bowie tugged her toward the patio of a streetside bar. Her body moved first, leaning in the direction he was going, her feet coming to life a second later, even as her eyes lingered on Oswald.

"Move," Bowie insisted.

"Table for two?" asked a waiter.

"Yes," said Bowie. "Just there, please." He nodded to an elegant little round table on the patio, barely largely enough to accommodate the two of them.

"I can't believe it's him," Rossi breathed as he steered her onto a high stool. "We should do something. We should stop him . . ."

"We talked about this," said Bowie, leaning across the table. "We watch. We do not engage."

"But he's right there!" Rossi said through clenched jaws.

"I know. Just . . . breathe."

Bowie stared at Rossi and the surprise in his face meant that there were tears in her eyes. When one ran down her cheek, she seized a napkin off the table and furiously wiped it away, holding it to her face for a moment, then mashing it over her mouth and giving a strangled cry. Bowie's eyes widened in alarm and, clearly unsure of what else to do, he snatched her free hand and squeezed it. At last, she took the napkin away, and spread it carefully on the tabletop, carefully ironing it flat with the palm of her hand.

"I'm sorry," she said. "It's just so . . . *frustrating.*"

It was more than that, and Bowie could probably tell, but he just nodded and smiled with something like understanding.

"I know," he said.

"Can you hear him?" she said, cocking her head fractionally in Oswald's direction. "What he's saying to people?"

Bowie shook his head.

"We should get closer," she said.

"He'll see."

"He doesn't know us."

"He will the next time he sees us. I saved his life," said Bowie sourly. "Or I will."

"He didn't see me," she replied. "The night you saved him, the night you shot Jimmy, I was still in the driveway."

"He knew you were there. He would have heard you."

"I don't think he saw my face. Let me just . . ." and she got to her feet.

"Wait," said Bowie, "no," but when he reached for her arm again, she twisted away, moving quickly out into the street. Bowie half rose to go after her but sat down again with a sigh of resignation as she walked briskly away. She kept her head bent low as she moved to where Oswald was offering one of his flyers to a man who glanced at it and shook his head, spreading his hands and walking away. Oswald watched him go, then turned to her.

"Good evening, Miss," he said. "Something you might want to read. Fair Play for Cuba."

Rossi hesitated, her eyes still down, then—very slowly—she took the paper from him like it was fragile and—equally slowly—looked into his face.

"Thank you," she said, holding his eyes for what seemed like an eternity. "I'll be sure to read it."

And then she walked on past him and down the street, slowing as she got some distance from the man who would kill the president.

"What the hell was that?" Bowie demanded when he caught up to her.

"Ah, slang!" she said crisply. "You must be serious."

"You could make things worse!"

"How?" she said. "In a few months that man will precipitate a national disaster of massive proportions! How can his seeing me make it worse?"

"He might kill you too," said Bowie.

As soon as he had spoken the words, he looked as surprised by them as she was, like he wanted to take them back. Rossi gaped at him, all her studied nonchalance and disdain swept away by his remark.

"What do you mean?" she asked, genuinely uncertain.

Bowie hesitated, then took a blustering, casual tone that was not convincing.

"If he realizes—now or later—that he is being watched, and if he is part of some kind of conspiracy, he's going to take steps. He might look harmless, but that doesn't mean he's someone you want to cross."

Rossi met his eyes and started to open her mouth, as if to say that that wasn't what she meant but then changed her mind and simply nodded. She held up the flyer. In bold type it read "Hands off Cuba," and in the smaller print it advertised a free lecture at 544 Camp Street. It was stamped "L.H. Oswald."

"Tomorrow," she said.

It was a statement of purpose and Bowie knew it.

CHAPTER SEVENTEEN

Bowie dreamed of the Great Conflagration, the smoke and noise and terror of those days in the ruins of old Des Moines—out of ration packs, out of ammunition, out of time and out of hope—when the remote tanks had come through, targeting by infrared with clinical precision, blowing holes through his bots one by one in the darkness until only he was left. He had taken cover in the shattered wreckage of a twenty-first-century convenience store, long empty. He remembered studying the faded advertisements for products he couldn't identify, the improbable faces smiling through the graffiti, the stained unfathomable logos: the remnants of a world which had ended forty years before the dissidents rose up to halt the advance of the Design. His blaster was as dead as his team. He had nothing left but a pressure mine and a near-useless sidearm with enough energy for three shots, not that even ten of them would penetrate the armor of the rollers.

He smelled oil and bitter rain.

The tank came through the wall and obliterated a rack of shelves. The bots were conserving ammo too, or else they would have vaporized the husk of the store the moment they picked up his heat signature. He had moved, rolling to his right as the building exploded in gunfire. He kept moving anyway, not even sure if he was hit or not, driven by something weary and relentless, something beyond rage. He clambered up the side of the tank and onto its rear deck, jamming the mine under the overhang of the turret, and rolling away again before its guns could find him.

The tank spun on its tracks, guns blazing indiscriminately, close enough for Bowie to hear the whir of its servos as it calculated his presence. He weaved between the empty aisles, and the tank came after him, plowing over and through what he had to go around, until he was out in the open with nowhere to go. The turret spun and he saw its auto lens tighten as it sighted on him, and then he heard the snap of the mine as its pressure trigger came free of the turret. There was a white, phosphoric flash, a wall of sound heavy as concrete, then fire and debris.

He remembered coming to, deaf from the concussion, and blinded by the smoke, feeling the skin of his hands burn as parts of the vanquished tank rained down around him, hissing in the rain. The first noise he heard was something strange which faded in through the fog of the battle, something so unexpected that it took him several seconds to realize that what he was hearing was the sound of his own laughing sobs.

He woke suddenly, trembling from head to foot, and remembered where he was. New Orleans. 1963. The Great Conflagration was over. They had won.

Except not really.

It rained overnight. A storm had blown in, seemingly from nowhere, dumping torrents of water on the hotel, rattling the shutters and making its old timbers creak and groan, so that Bowie—used only to the silent climate-controlled state of his bedroom at home—lay awake for the rest of the night, eyes open and listening. He spent several minutes standing at the window, wondering at the splashing, swirling chaos of water in the street outside, the sudden force of it all, the volume. It was astounding.

The following day the locals did a little sweeping and tidying where leaves had been caught up and dumped, blocking drains and such, but for the most part they just got on with their day as if nothing had happened, and that was astounding too. In Bowie's world, rain like that was a once-a-year event at most.

They had beignets and coffee for breakfast at a café off Magazine Street, sitting under a tree with vivid green leaves the size of his hands, waxy and beaded with rainwater. It was pleasantly warm, the air freshened by the storm, but the day promised to be hot, and Bowie found himself wishing vaguely and uncharacteristically that they could forget everything they were there to do and just sit in this moment, enjoying the fragrances of coffee and food amid the bustle of the waking city . . .

Freeze time, in other words, he thought, realizing the irony.

Rossi, by contrast, was all about the mission.

"I don't know where Oswald is living," she said, "but if we can spot him close to the place where this lecture will take place, we can follow him, find out who he deals with, what he's up to. This handing out flyers business makes no sense to me by itself. If he's a few months from killing Kennedy, there has to be more to it. I've reached out to someone I know at *The Times-Picayune* . . ."

"You did what?" said Bowie, startled out of his reverie.

"It's the local newspaper."

"I gathered that much. You called someone there?" he demanded.

"Standard procedure when a journalist visits a new city," she said with a nonchalant shrug. "Particularly if you're working a local story."

"You're not! Do I have to remind you what would happen if people found out that—"

"No, you don't," she said briskly. "I didn't mention Oswald by name. Or the president."

"So what did you tell them?"

"That I was researching a piece on US attitudes to Cuba, specifically to the Castro regime."

It was a smart play and, recognizing it as such, Bowie relaxed.

"And?" he prompted.

"Well, it's weird," she said. "The address on those flyers for the Fair Play for Cuba committee isn't an office, and apart from the fact that people—mostly Oswald, from the sound of things—have been handing out leaflets, the organization doesn't seem to have any presence or even a membership in the city. Not officially, at least. That Fair Play for Cuba chapter might just be him. Which is weird, right?"

"If it's an unpopular political organization, it might make sense that they keep their activities quiet," said Bowie.

"I thought so too," Rossi agreed, "but, like my sister always says: 'Location, location, location.' So I looked into it. It's on Camp Street, right? The five-hundred block? That puts Oswald's group—a *pro*-Castro group, remember, in some very odd company. Why? Because that block is the heart of the *anti*-Castro activity in the city. Some of that activity is driven by Cuban emigres, like you'd expect. But I'm told there are also heavy ties to US intelligence services, and *their* agenda is about as far from the Marxism Oswald claims to espouse as you can get. And, this might be the strangest part: there's at least one ex-FBI guy, up to his eyes in anti-Cuba stuff, who operates out of the very same address that's on Oswald's pro-Cuba flyer."

Bowie put his beignet down and leaned forward.

"You have names?" he asked.

"I'm a journalist," she said, popping the last piece of beignet into her mouth with a self-satisfied grin, "of course I have names."

"OK," he said, "so where do we go first?"

"*I* go to see the anti-communist I mentioned: a Mister Guy Bannister. *You* stay here and enjoy your café au lait."

"What? Why?"

"Because you stand out like a vegetarian at a Texas barbecue and because Oswald got a good look at you—or he will—so, according to your rules, you should stay off his radar."

"He saw you last night."

"As a moderately attractive stranger who might plausibly be interested in his activities."

Bowie considered the way she smiled.

"You intend to exploit their sexual urges," he observed.

"I may use a few feminine wiles to make them more talkative," she corrected. She showed him the address on the flyer. "If I'm not back in an hour, come find me." She thought for a moment and amended the statement. "Make that two hours. I need to buy some clean clothes."

The Camp Street address on the flyer was part of what was called the Newman building, a three-story affair featuring a rustic, French stone front, and a simpler, unadorned side which ran along Lafayette Street. A second entrance on that side brought Rossi to the office of Guy Bannister, private investigator. Rossi hesitated at the door, running her story through her head, tapped on the frosted glass and opened it.

There were two men inside. Neither was Oswald. One of them, perhaps sixty, solid, white, with a graying widow's peak and a face like clotted cream, she took for the former FBI agent, Guy Bannister. The other, a smaller, stranger man entirely, half turned to look at her and she froze in the doorway, aghast.

Washington?

It couldn't be. But the pallor was the same, the stature, and—most unsettling—the hair was the same reddish wig. The same artificial stuff had been shaped into eyebrows, and he glared at her from under them.

"I'm sorry," she stammered. "Wrong office."

A second later she was back out on the street, eyes wide and heart hammering.

What have I done? she thought, horrified. The time rider didn't know her, not here, not now, but he would know her a few months from now when he met her in the bar of the Adolphus in Dallas. *And then what?*

Would time collapse in on itself? Would she accidentally alter history? He would recognize her, and then what? Suddenly she saw it all clear in her head as if it had already happened . . .

Do I know you . . . ?

Then the memory of her blundering into his New Orleans plans would dawn on Washington and he would bolt, knowing something was wrong, leaving the hotel before he could die in a barroom brawl, and then she would never see *The New York Times* he had brought from the future. Bowie would not come. This version of the present would fold over and over until it winked out of reality as never having come into being, and she would . . . what? Vanish? Just cease to exist? Or would her consciousness go back to the woman who had sat with Jimmy in the Adolphus booth dreaming of their first big scoops and frustrated that they were assigned to cover the empty ceremonial politenesses of the presidential visit?

For a wild moment that seemed almost as bad as disappearing from the world.

She needed to speak to Bowie. So she fled from Guy Bannister's office, not bothering to conceal her panicked haste, so that the inhabitants of the Big Easy watched her breeze past with interest and amusement.

Bowie was exactly where she had left him.

"Washington!" she gasped. "He's here!"

Bowie's brows knotted then cleared.

"He can't be," he said. "The coordinates would be in his bike's nav system."

"Then it's another time rider!" she said.

"Wait," he said, holding up a hand. "Did you see him or not?"

"I saw . . . someone like him," she confessed, trying to make sense of it in her own head. "Short. Pale. Bald but with that weird fake wig. Fake eyebrows too."

Bowie frowned at that detail.

"You never said Washington wore fake eyebrows."

"He didn't!" she said. "At least, I don't think he did. I'm not sure."

"But you thought this was him?"

She sat down heavily and put her face in her hands.

"I did . . . but now that I think of it," she admitted, "maybe it was just the shock of seeing someone so like him. Freaked me out. That hair . . ."

"OK," said Bowie, his voice soothing now. "So it probably wasn't him, but it's possible that it was another time rider. That changes things. We can't risk . . ."

"But I already did!" she exclaimed miserably. "He looked right at me. He'll know who I am."

"Not necessarily. Even if he came from the future, we don't know what part of the future. He might have left there before I did, in which case, he may know nothing about me, about us."

"What are we going to do?" she gasped. She hadn't felt this agitated since the morning Jimmy had been shot. Even on the bike, as they were being shot at, she had kept a cool head. Now she was unraveling, terrified that she had made a bad situation infinitely worse.

"We're still here," Bowie said. "Still alive."

"We should get out of this place, this time."

"Maybe," said Bowie. "But first I want to see this man."

"Bowie, no!"

"I need to know what we are up against. If we are going to leave, I want the visit to have been productive. Every time we make a jump, we're taking a risk: a lot of things can go wrong. I need to know we got something out of being here. Other than the food, of course."

He smiled faintly and she calmed a little, appreciating his attempt to lighten the mood.

"OK," she said.

"You don't need to come."

"I will. And we should have our things with us. And the bike, in case . . ."

"The bike is too conspicuous, too unusual. If this man is a time rider, he'll recognize it immediately."

She nodded fervently and looked down, thinking.

"What's Stockholm syndrome?" Bowie asked out of the blue.

She looked up and shrugged.

"No idea," she said. "Why?"

He looked away, suddenly distant.

"Just something I heard," he said.

She waited for him to elaborate, but when he didn't, decided to get on with her task.

"OK," she said, "let me drop in on my friend at *The Times-Picayune* first. You can go over there, stake the place out.

I'll see what else there is to learn about this Guy Bannister and if there's anyone connected to him who might fit the description of the wig man I saw. Even if he's not one of yours, he's distinctive enough looking that if he has a record or has made the news in any way, they'll know him at the newspaper."

They stowed their few belongings in a compartment on the side of the bike and Bowie took it—and the sheet he was using as a tarp (for which he left another dollar on the nightstand)—and parked it in a side alley, tucked behind a dumpster. As Rossi headed over to the newspaper offices on Saint Charles Avenue, Bowie made his way to Camp Street, a newspaper under his arm and a fresh cup of coffee in hand. Trying to look as natural as a time-traveling soldier from 2157 could possibly look in 1963.

Justine Simmons was a year younger than Rossi. She had been at what she thought of as the *T-P* since graduating from Tulane, working her way slowly up from editorial assistant on the society pages, to reporter on the local beat, covering everything from bar brawls and road closings to town council meetings and school board elections. She had met Sandra Rossi at a women reporters networking conference in Houston three years before, and they had hit it off over shared gripes about work conditions, discriminatory practices, and the general slog to be taken seriously by colleagues and witnesses alike. Justine had liked that Sandra had a tough, no-nonsense approach to getting what she wanted, but could also mute her ruthlessness under fluttering eyelashes, bashful smiles, and elongated southern vowels when she needed to turn on the charm to disarm someone.

"You let them think you're some clueless girl and they'll tell you anything, especially if they think they might get up your skirt," Rossi had said. "And then you take whatever they gave you and you nail them with it."

Justine had applied the strategy, not always expertly, and never when her male colleagues were around, and had found that it was true: sometimes you killed more wasps with honey than with vinegar.

They pecked each other affectionately on the cheek and made small talk as they settled and Justine lit a cigarette. Justine had her own desk—no small achievement in itself—and they sat on either side of it, catching up and smoking like chimneys, though she could see that Rossi was not herself. She seemed flustered, rushed, and for all the apparent casualness of this visit, she recognized a woman on a scent.

"So this Cuba thing you are onto," she said. "What else do you need?"

Rossi seemed relieved to get down to business. She relaxed visibly, then leaned forward, face and voice earnest.

"I'm looking into that Guy Bannister character you mentioned, particularly his associates."

"A real charmer," she said with apparent distaste. "Bully, brute, racist, fascist. All the fun of the fair. Very involved with the anti-Castro set. Weapons stockpiler and gun runner involved in the Bay of Pigs fiasco, if you can believe that."

Sandra nodded but seemed less excited by that last piece of information than Justine had expected.

"I'm trying to get a handle on the people he works with," said Sandra. "Particularly a weird looking guy with fake hair and eyebrows. He seems to work with Bannister in some capacity but . . ."

"That's David Ferrie," said Justine without a moment's thought. "He's in tight with Bannister. Pilot, *formerly* with Eastern Airlines, possible intelligence connections, and yeah, a very weird guy. Real off the wall, you know? Mixes in some very strange company. All kinds: from society types to mobsters, homosexuals, pimps, politicos, military, even priests. You name it, he's connected."

"How do you know all this?" Sandra asked, impressed as well as surprised.

"Well, like you said, he's odd. Definitely stands out. But he's also come across our blotter several times in the last few years."

"Oh yeah?"

Justine flicked the ash from her cigarette and started to tick the charges off on her fingers.

"Implicated with Bannister in the raid on Houma where their munitions were cached: rifles, machine guns, grenades—you name it, they had it; got some ink when he said publicly that the president should be shot over the Bay of Pigs; involved in legal action over his dismissal from Eastern on morality charges. I suspect the list is much longer but that's all I know for sure."

"So he's been here a while?" said Rossi.

"At least ten, fifteen years," said Justine, puzzled by the question. "I have an address for him here: 3330 Louisiana Parkway. Why?"

"Just trying to build a picture."

"Speaking of which," said Justine. "Hold on. There's something you should see." She took a long drag of her cigarette which reduced its length by a quarter, then set it in an ashtray carefully while she went to hunt through a filing cabinet on the wall opposite the windows. "Goddamn it, Harry!" she yelled without looking around. "Didn't your mama tell you to put things back where you found 'em?"

"Yeah, yeah," grumbled a heavyset white reporter whose desk was squeezed into the corner of the room, shaded by an immense potted plant that made him look like he was trying to hide.

Justine slammed the cabinet drawer shut pointedly, opened another and, after a moment of rummaging, produced a manila folder with a shout that was a mixture of triumph and defiance. She waved it pointedly as she returned to her desk, and the reporter behind the plant gave another unimpressed "Yeah, yeah."

"You're gonna like this," she said, sitting down and seizing the cigarette before flicking through the folder. "Here we go," she said, satisfied, sliding a glossy black and white across the desk. "Meet Mr. David Ferrie."

The image showed the strange looking man with the artificial hair and eyebrows looking regal in heavy, formal robes and a chain of office. There was a hint of lace at the cuffs but the fabric of the surplice was glossy and dark, with some bright inlaid pattern and an ornamental cross in the center.

These aren't robes, Sandra realized, astonished. *They're vestments!*

"He's a priest?" she said.

"Better than that; a bishop!"

"In what church?"

"Best as any of us could find out, one he pretty much made up. A version of some old Catholic ideas and institutions, cobbled together but without any actual church building, parishioners, or clergy other than him. It's basically dress up. But he was actually ordained or consecrated or whatever by an archbishop. It's here in his file, someone who calls himself Archbishop Christopher Maria. There's a network of these guys with occult leanings, but what they actually do as bishops, if they have, you know, parishes, church buildings, and worshippers or are they just in it for the funny hats and dresses, we haven't found out. Might be a story there, though, if you can find enough of them."

"This is so weird."

"Right?" She let the word linger for a moment as Sandra continued to stare at the picture as if entranced. "So, why are you really interested in this guy?" Justine asked. Sandra looked up quickly and a couple of different emotions flashed through her eyes. Embarrassment, maybe. But something else too. Something darker and closer to fear. "I mean, I get that he's the walking proof of truth being stranger than fiction," Justine continued as if she hadn't seen the look, "but what's your angle?"

Sandra hesitated. Stalled, more like, and before she could say anything which would almost certainly be less than the truth, Justine cut her off.

"This isn't about Cuba, is it?"

Sandra took a breath and gave her a tight smile.

"Honestly, I'm not sure," she said. "It's just some stuff that I'm trying to make sense of." Justine waited, saying nothing, and eventually her friend continued. "You ever look at the stars at night and try to find the constellations? You can see the clusters, and you remember seeing them connected in old charts, and you're like 'OK, that's Orion. That's the Great Bear.' But then you look at those super-clear photographs of the night sky, the ones taken on a really long exposure, and suddenly, instead of there being just a few dozen stars grouped together in separate patterns, there's, like, thousands. Millions. All the constellations you thought you could see so clearly vanish in this chaos of points of light. And you think, OK, so maybe I could find Aries or Capricorn, but now I see all these other stars just as clearly, so I could draw lines between any of them, and each line I draw would make a new picture, a new constellation that would be just as valid as the ones people have drawn for centuries. I mean, they're all stars, right? And each star is a point that could be connected to any other point, and each connection builds something, creates a kind of meaning, but you never know if the meaning being created is just your own creation, just randomness, or if it adds up to something true, something real."

Justine cocked her head on one side.

"That's what you are doing," she said, peering through the cigarette smoke, "drawing new constellations."

"Maybe," said Rossi. "Honestly, I'm not sure. One thing for sure, saying it out loud doesn't make it any clearer!"

They laughed at that.

"And now, I'm afraid, I have to make tracks. But thank you for all of this information. It's more than I could have hoped for."

Justine watched her leave with something like puzzled amusement, but in the course of the day her mind kept straying back to their conversation. She wasn't sure why, but it changed in her mind, as if she had—to use her friend's rich analogy—begun connecting different stars until the picture shifted into something quite different. She couldn't say what it looked like, but it stirred something, something deep down that made her anxious for Sandra Rossi, something very much like dread.

THE ART OF
TIME
RIDER

Record
Captures Flying Saucer
in Roswell Region

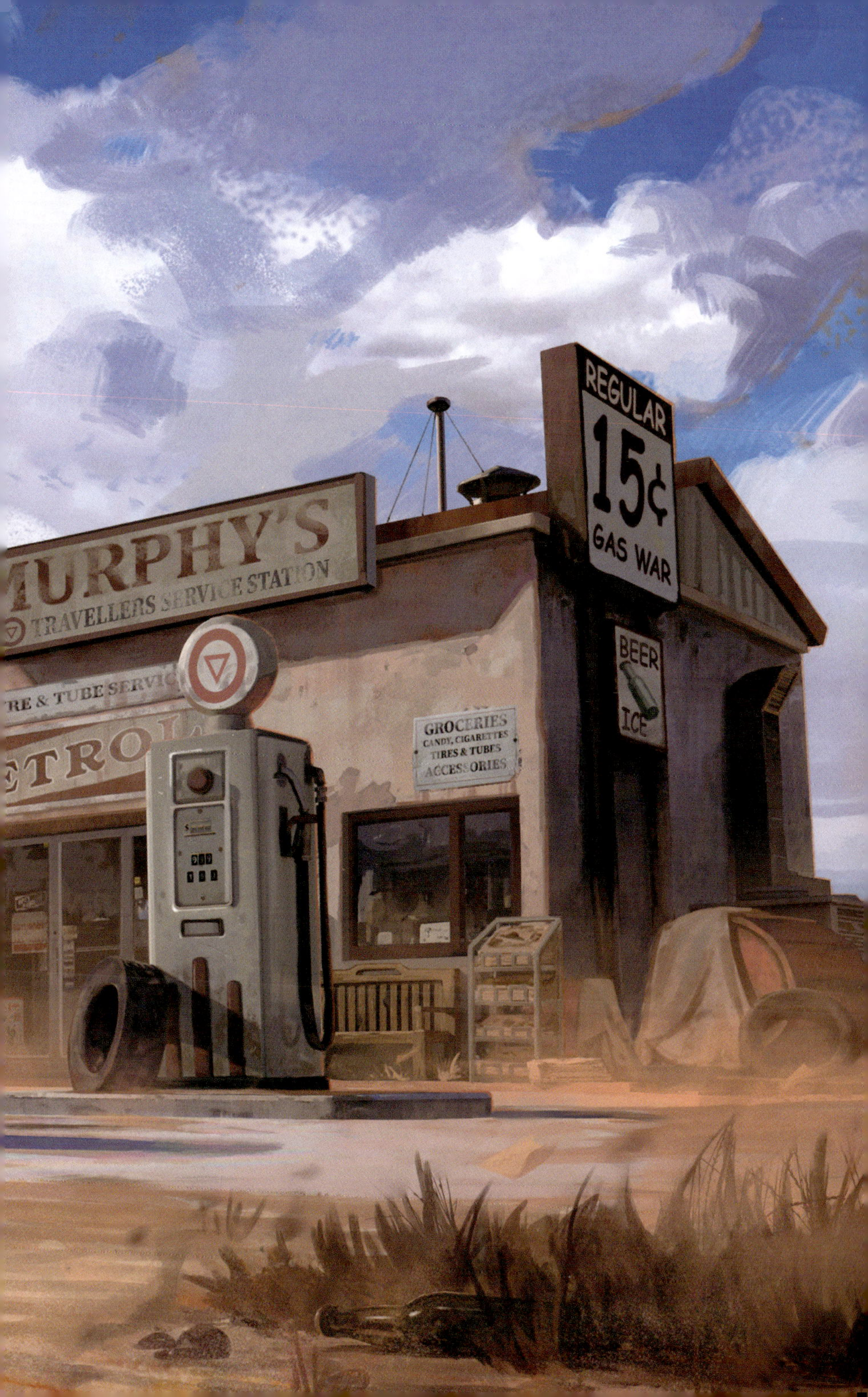
MURPHY'S
TRAVELLERS SERVICE STATION
REGULAR
15¢
GAS WAR
BEER
ICE
GROCERIES
CANDY, CIGARETTES
TIRES & TUBES
ACCESSORIES

GET IN!

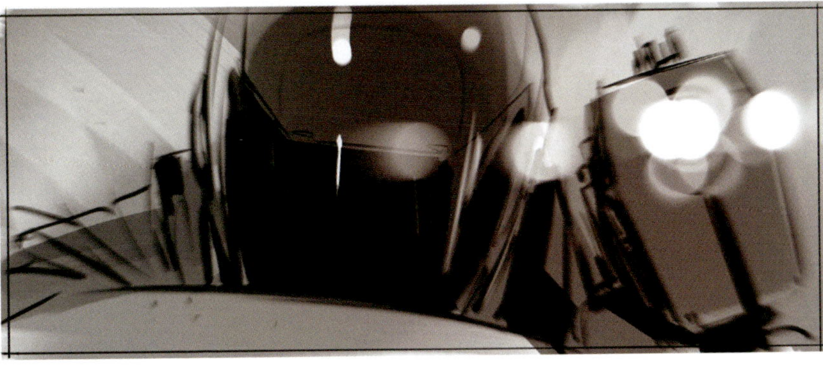

CHAPTER EIGHTEEN

"I saw him," said Bowie as soon as Rossi rejoined him. "Your Washington look-alike. It's not him, but I see what you mean. If he is a time rider, or an Alpha for that matter, he's not one I recognize."

"If he is one, he's in deep," Rossi replied. "Been here years. Is that a thing your people might do? Bring an agent back in time and keep him on site for a decade or more?"

"I don't think so, but I honestly couldn't say," said Bowie.

It was humiliating, how little he knew, how much of what he had been fed was lies. They had implied he was the first to come back in time like this, but they wouldn't have needed to send him if Washington hadn't already failed. Could they have put agents in place and left them for years? If so, maybe they had ultimately failed as well. Or not. He simply did not know. He couldn't imagine why they might do such a thing, but he couldn't say for sure that they didn't.

"Is he still in there?" Rossi asked.

Bowie shook his head.

"Left about a half hour ago. I was going to follow him on foot, but he had a car, a big thing with wood on the side."

"A station wagon."

"I don't know where he went. I couldn't be seen so—"

"I have an address," Rossi interrupted. "Might not be where he is right now, but he'll be there at some point."

"Walking distance?"

Rossi showed him on her map.

"Best part of an hour on foot," she said. "Ten minutes on the bike."

Her tone made her preference clear and, for once, he didn't feel like arguing.

"Then we ride," he said. When she raised her eyebrows in surprise he shrugged. "In the last hour I have been offered a lot of things, most of which I did not understand. I would like a break from being a pedestrian."

She grinned and reached in her shoulder bag for her cigarettes, then caught herself as she saw his expression change.

"What?" she asked.

"Nothing," he replied.

"You don't like me smoking."

Bowie hesitated, but only for a second.

"It's unpleasant," he said. "The smell. It gets into your clothes. I have no idea what it does to your lungs but it can't be good."

She gaped back at him as if he had slapped her and then, unexpectedly, started to laugh. Bowie, who had been bracing himself for the worst of her vitriol stared, bewildered.

"You're right," she said. "Though I can't believe you said it. I've actually been planning to quit."

"Why don't you?" he replied, opting to pursue his advantage, even if he didn't understand how he had gotten it.

"I only smoke when I'm stressed," she said. "And, from the moment you entered my life, things have been much more fucking stressful." Bowie winced at this but couldn't argue the point. "So until things calm down, I'm a smoker. But I appreciate your concern, and I will try to limit them to as-needed therapeutic uses only," she said with a grin.

Five minutes later they were heading west on Thalia, the bike's great thrumming engine turning heads as it cruised along New Orleans' uneven pavement. Bowie could smell the cigarette she was smoking, but he could also feel Rossi's head pressed hard against his shoulder blade, one arm tight around his waist. He could smell her hair as well as the smoke. It was different today. Fresh and fragrant. She must have washed it. He considered saying so, but not understanding the protocol of such things, decided against it.

Still, the closeness of her . . .

As they rode, Bowie considered what they would do when they arrived, and he came to a decision. This low-risk espionage approach wasn't producing quickly enough. When they reached the house, he was going in, one way or another. If he had to throw his weight around to get answers, that's what he would do. This Ferrie character had already seen Rossi, and that hadn't sent the timeline into free fall, so they should use the comparative safety of the moment to find out what was really going on.

That the man with the strange hair might be a time rider on a long-term assignment was alarming. It suggested a carefully planned operation with deep roots, very different from the impromptu terrorist counter measure Merrick and the professor had sold Bowie. An alternative possibility was that this Ferrie character was somehow stranded here, like Bowie had been before he got hold of Washington's bike. But then why hadn't the Alphas sent a team to rescue or eliminate him as they had Bowie?

Someone is going to tell me something today, Bowie resolved grimly.

They parked on Toledano Street under the shade of heavy and ancient trees, and Bowie draped the sheet over the bike and knotted it under the frame: it wouldn't deter the truly curious, but it would have to do. When they reached the house, Bowie led Rossi around the back, then drew his revolver and checked the cylinder.

"You have that little automatic?" he asked.

She patted her shoulder bag but looked troubled.

"I told you," she said, "I despise guns and I don't know how to shoot one. What happened to just watching for fear of derailing the basic structure of reality or whatever?"

"I am not good at waiting," he said. "Not when people are being killed and our lives upended. Not when they can't offer me a single grain of truth about what I am supposed to be doing here. Not when I don't know what else to do. I am going in. You can wait here. But when I come out, I'm going to have a plan based on information that I think is accurate."

He spoke evenly, matter-of-factly, his voice low and without inflection, but there was something in the set of his jaw, a flinty quality in his eyes that spoke of a simmering rage.

"I've got your back," she said. He opened his mouth to ask her what the phrase meant, but she said, "Just go."

As if to make the point, she reached past him, grabbed the handle on the screen door and pulled it open, revealing the backdoor proper: wooden bottom half, divided glass panels above.

From his tactical jacket he drew a disk the size of a small plate. It had a sliding piece which rotated around the edge. At the backdoor, he pressed the disk against the glass in the upper half, and turned the sliding piece twice. A circle of glass popped cleanly out, and he was able to reach in and unlock the door. He turned to give Rossi a steadying look, laying a finger on his lips as he eased the door open. She rolled her eyes, but under the cynical bravado he thought she looked frightened.

Probably smart to be, he thought.

They emerged in a kind of galley kitchen, squalid and cramped, the sink full of dirty dishes, but before he had a chance to fully determine that the room and the hallway beyond it were unoccupied, he became aware of music. Not jazz. Not like anything he had heard before: a droning sound, long low notes turning up a tone or two at the end of the line, then reverting to the same repeated pitch.

It was a voice, but whether you could call it a song, he wasn't sure. It was barely music at all, but there were, he realized, words in it, though no matter how hard he strained to listen, he could make no sense of them.

Rossi nudged him and he gave her a sharp look.

She had produced her notepad. On the facing page she had scribbled with a stub of pencil "*Latin???*"

Bowie shrugged fractionally, and inched closer to the sound. It was coming from upstairs. He moved cautiously over the carpeted floor, but as he was about to mount the first step the sound changed. In place of the droning single voice, there was suddenly a rumble of other voices answering with a singsong tone: three syllables, the first two the same note, the third a tone higher:

"Amen."

Rossi grabbed his arm and squeezed it. She leaned into his ear and whispered.

"There are people up there. A service. Maybe a mass."

Bowie nodded then whispered back, "Good thing I brought my gun."

She gaped, but he took the first step, then the second. He was halfway up the stairs before he sensed her coming up behind him. He kept moving carefully up, testing each stair for creaking before putting his full weight on it. The third one from the top whined softly under his foot so he lifted it away, keeping very still, until the droning voice assured him no one had heard the noise. There was no landing at the top, just a narrow hallway with doors on either side, three closed, one open. The open one was clearly a bathroom. The sound was coming from the door at the far end of the hall which was, if Bowie's sense of the architectural layout was right, probably the largest. It also should have been the brightest because he had seen large windows from the street, and they should have brought the midday light streaming in, but while there was a crack of daylight under the other doors, this room was dark.

He inched along the hall—carpeted with a narrow runner—and leaned close to the door. The droning voice continued, and while it was clearer here, he could make no more sense of it. As he closed his eyes and focused on the sound, his hand rested gently against the door just above the handle, as if the vibrations from within might tell him something. Suddenly his brain registered what his fingers had found, and he dropped quietly to his knee. There was a metal oval a couple of inches over the handle, and in the center, a hole. Specifically, an old-fashioned keyhole. He pressed his eye to it.

As he had thought, the room beyond was dim. Some kind of blackout blind had been pulled down over the three large windows which ran down the left side. The chamber was long, and chairs had been arranged on each side in three rows facing the far end, and with a narrow aisle running between them. The door was in the center so he could see between the chairs to the opposite end of the room where there was a table.

No, thought Bowie, remembering a different word. *Not a table. An altar.*

There were candles in tall brass candlesticks positioned on each end of the altar and by their light he could just make out some kind of gold-colored cup.

A chalice.

There were six men in the room, all with their backs toward the door. One of them, sitting by himself, was almost certainly Oswald. The others, he didn't know.

The droning voice came from the man at the altar who was leading the ceremony. He too had his back to his congregation, but Bowie knew that odd thatch of auburn hair: David Ferrie. He was wearing a stiff and shiny vestment, blood red, and trimmed with gold thread. On the back was a vaguely cruciform pattern which framed a complex design of circles and a hooked line traced in black and gold. Bowie's mouth fell open with astonishment. Of all the things he had imagined he might see in that room, that familiar pattern of symbols had never occurred to him as even a remote possibility. It made no sense. When Rossi pushed him aside so she could look, he moved in a kind of daze.

How was this possible? What could it mean?

Rossi squinted through the keyhole, and, for a moment, she wondered if this was what it felt like to be a time traveler, to look in on something utterly alien, something clearly of the past but not precisely of *your* past. Half an hour earlier she had been in bustling contemporary New Orleans, city of music and light, fun and adventure. She knew of its mysterious African undertones, the voodoo, the Haitian witchcraft and swamp magic, but this was none of that. This was medieval, but refashioned somehow, and though she was not Catholic, she'd seen enough to know that this felt different from that, darker and stranger. The form of the ritual was of the cathedral, but there was something grimy and sinister here. If she were in the room, instead of spying on it through the door, she felt sure she would smell blood literally and—and this was somehow worse—metaphorically. It was as if the people in there—she recognized Oswald and Bannister but not the others—who were murmuring along to whatever the false priest Ferrie was saying, were steeped in it. It was not just a ritual of blood; it was a religion of blood. Blood and death.

It wasn't just Ferrie's vestments that were scarlet. The room was hung with swaths of crimson fabric, in places cinched with black cord. There was a strange and complex insignia above the altar, the same insignia that adorned Ferrie's priestly garb. Thought, time, and money had gone into this. The rest of the house was innocuous, ramshackle, dirty, and poorly maintained, but this room looked like a temple, uncluttered, pristine and balanced, with everything in its place oozing significance and purpose. In the flickering glow of the candles, she felt a power she had never associated with religion, something imminent and threatening that made her hair stand on end, something like static or stink which her senses were picking up like an ancient alarm and telling her to run.

She realized she was holding her breath; afraid her breathing would give them away, or terrified that she might inhale something of the unholy mass's fetid air? She thought of the churches she had grown up around in Texas: great, bright barns full of white folks in their Sunday best suits and dresses. She had grown wary of them as she had become a woman, found they were too often on the wrong side of the issues she cared about, if they were willing to think about them at all. At times she had decided that there had been no God in those churches. But this was something else entirely, and it had no interest in any God she had ever learned about. This was a church of dark corners, of secret practices and dangerous beliefs, but while the power of the churches of her youth had been in its people, their capacity to vote or to otherwise shape the culture in which she lived, the power here was different, otherworldly, but real. She wasn't sure why she thought that, but she felt it in her bones like you felt the eyes of a predator in a dark alley. She had gotten a hint of it off the man who called himself Washington, though the strangeness of the man and the confusion around what had happened to him had kept the feeling in check. It came back to her now, as she watched the peculiar man in the preposterous wig raise his hands over the altar in incantation.

Magic, she thought. *Blood, death, and magical power bent on shaping her world.*

Bowie felt lightheaded and had to steady himself against the wall, his mind racing. He barely noticed when Rossi stood up, took him by the arm, and gave it an insistent tug. She wanted to talk, and that meant getting away from the door. He followed, unresisting, barely thinking as he fought to maintain some kind of mental equilibrium.

This makes no sense, he thought.

"We can't go in there," Rossi breathed. "There's too many of them. We should wait until we can get Ferrie on his own. If we . . ." She stopped, considering his face. "What's wrong with you?"

"The design on his priest robes," Bowie said at last, his voice low and cracked. "The emblem, the hooked line and circles."

"Yeah, I don't know it. Looks occult. Maybe some ancient Egyptian sigil or something."

Bowie shook his head emphatically.

"No," he said, louder than he had intended, so that Rossi shot an anxious glance back toward the door. "It's from my world! It's the symbol of the Design. It was our battle flag in the war and became the emblem of our society. Either my people have come back for something much more involved than just assassinating your president . . ."

"Or?"

"Or they were always here."

Rossi looked at him, seemingly baffled or unsure what to say, and before they could exchange another word they heard a familiar rumble from the street, one that cut through all the other traffic noise.

Motorcycles. From the future. Bowie's time-traveling hunters had found them again.

CHAPTER NINETEEN

Rossi didn't need to be told that the long odds of dealing with the men in the secret mass had now become unthinkable. She bolted down the stairs with Bowie at her heels, and though the noise of the bikes outside might have been enough to drown out the sound of her descent, she didn't give the question a thought. They had to get out of that house, now.

At the foot of the stairs she hesitated, the front door was closer, but it was also the door the time riders would likely use. She made a left and was just entering the kitchen when she heard the click of the latch behind her. She rounded the jamb of the kitchen entry and flattened herself against the wall to its right. Bowie did the same on the other side. Their eyes met across the gap, and he gave her the smallest of nods and raised the revolver in one crooked arm until its muzzle pointed to the ceiling. She considered her shoulder bag, which contained the automatic she didn't really know how to use, but popping its catch open was more noise than she dare risk.

She heard the front door open, heard the steps in the hallway.

Two of them?

She raised two fingers and Bowie nodded again. She had expected them to enter at a run, weapons held out in front of them, but their gait sounded casual, and they were talking as the door opened, though she couldn't catch what they said. One of them, a man—the one dressed as a cop?—laughed derisively at whatever the other had said, and then she heard a woman say "Upstairs." Rossi wondered if the woman was carrying the bright red helmet. As they clumped slowly up the stairs another idea went through her head: *they don't know we're here.*

They were too casual, too slow. That meant that while they were surely hunting for her and Bowie, they didn't expect them to be here. They had come to see someone upstairs. Ferrie? Bannister? Oswald?

Bowie seemed to have come to the same conclusion. They could only be halfway up the stairs but already he was moving softly and swiftly toward the backdoor. As he carefully turned the handle and pulled the door open, he motioned to Rossi to go first. She did, moving backward through the kitchen, unwilling to take her eyes off the foot of the stairs. When she edged close enough, he caught her with his free hand and pulled her to him. There was a moment when they were close and she could feel the warmth of his body, of his breath, and she felt something shared between them even if it was just adrenaline, tense and humming like electrical cable. Then she was squeezing past him, pushing the screen porch door wide and stepping carefully out into the humid New Orleans afternoon.

He followed, leaving the door open, but she realized too late that he wasn't used to screen doors. The spring mechanism snapped it shut, and though he reached for it hopelessly as it brushed by his shoulder, it slammed into the door frame, rattling through the house.

"Run!" Bowie shouted.

He caught the sound of heavy feet on the upper floor before he was clear of the path, and when he risked a look back, he saw faces at one of the windows. Rossi must have seen more than he did because she shoved him into a hedge as a single cracking sound, flat and unimpressive came from the house.

The bullet pocked the concrete curb of the sidewalk not five feet away.

"The bike!" said Bowie, hoping that their pursuers hadn't already found and disabled it.

But then they would have come into the house knowing they were there, right? he thought desperately. *Right?*

He would have to hope so. Rossi was right. There were too many of them to fight, especially since an ugly truth was now clear. He had been sent to do an errand, but the suggestion that he had been the Alphas' first choice now looked like a bitter joke. He was an errand boy whose military experience had been entirely about stalking bots and remote tanks. The team he was up against now were the true elite agents and they were trained in hunting people.

There was no sign of the time agents' bikes, though he had heard them close to the house. Hopefully they had parked them on the west side.

Doing a lot of hoping here, Bowie, he thought, in Rossi's wry tone.

"All I have," he muttered aloud in response.

He made a left onto a street lined with trees, checking that Rossi was with him, then turned into an alley and peered down it. Just visible at the other end, shrouded in the wind-tugged sheet, was the bike.

"Get the cover off it," he said, taking cover by a brick gate post, pistol at the ready.

"What about you?" she exclaimed.

"I'll cover you," he said. "Just get it ready."

She ran, and he turned his attention back toward their pursuers. The one in the police uniform was the first to round the corner. Bowie bided his time, staying out of sight, until the man got clear of cover then he fired two of his precious rounds, low, hoping—there was that word again—to catch him below his body armor.

The "cop" spun at the sound of the first shot, and crumpled at the second, clutching his thigh. The blond woman emerged from behind a tree, aiming an automatic rifle, as Bannister came walking around the corner brandishing a massive pistol. He walked like he owned the place, slow, almost casual, out in the open but apparently unconcerned, and firing with each step.

Bowie managed one more shot, but then the woman opened up on full auto and he could do nothing but duck and run. He heard Bannister shouting instructions and knew that the rest—Oswald, Ferrie, and who knew how many others—would be looking to head them off. They had seconds at most.

He reached the bike after a hard dash. Rossi had got the sheet off and was astride the pillion, gazing back at him desperately. He leaped on and jammed the key into the ignition. The engine caught just as the first shot rang out.

"Go!" Rossi yelled, as if that option might not have occurred to him.

He gave it full throttle and shot out into the street, half sliding into the center of the road to make the first left. In that instant he caught a blur of red—impossibly bright—in the corner of his eye: Ferrie, still in his bizarre priestly garb, a shot gun in his hands, was blasting away. Bowie twisted the handlebars so violently that the bike kicked, and he felt all the weight of the machine shudder into the steering column as the back end started to slide. He held on, gripping with all his strength and forcing the bike into a tight circle. By the time Ferrie fired again, they were going in the opposite direction, accelerating fast.

"You OK?" he yelled over his shoulder.

"Where are we going?" Rossi replied.

"Away from here," he replied.

"Good plan," said Rossi. He felt the shudder of her body against his back. It took him a second to realize that she was laughing: a low chuckle at the absurdity and danger of their predicament which was just this side of hysterical weeping. While still watching for gunmen and listening for the inevitable sound of bikes in pursuit, Bowie tried to calm her nerves.

"I don't think they can track us in time," he shouted over the engine. "Not easily or quickly, at least. They didn't know we were here and they never came for us on the island."

"So we do another time leap?" she asked, apparently getting a grip on herself. "To where? Or when?"

He cursed to himself. He should have studied the map and programmed coordinates in when they had the luxury of time. Rossi seemed to be thinking along the same lines.

"Another preset?" she suggested.

It made sense. Use the same coordinates Washington had used before. It had worked for them at Ruth Forbes's house . . .

"OK," he said. "But I won't know where or *when* it will take us till we get there."

On cue they heard the whine of a large motorcycle at high speed behind them.

"Do it!" shouted Rossi.

The pops and bangs behind them didn't sound like engine noise. Bowie checked the speedometer just as it hit eighty miles an hour, an insane speed to be racing through these little neighborhood intersections. But it wasn't enough.

"We need a faster road," he shot back.

"So find one!"

She was looking backward. He checked his mirrors. Both bikes—the cop and the woman in the red helmet—

were on their tail, eighty yards, back, maybe a hundred. Easily in range of their weapons. He started to make the bike weave, but he knew that if they slowed or—God forbid—had to stop, they were dead. He turned the throttle and the bike surged forward.

The next sound he heard was the flat pop of Rossi's automatic. She was shooting back. He heard the automatic return a burst and swerved as a streetlamp ahead of them burst.

Need to go faster, he thought.

Without looking down he found the coordinate panel and started to scroll back through Washington's destinations until he got to the one prior to Naushon, his fingers working on automatic as they had in the dark forest of the island. It was like stripping down his weapon in pitch blackness, something he had done routinely in the war . . .

He glanced down to check that the coordinate lights were on, then increased the bike's speed.

Ninety.

One hundred.

"Bowie . . . ?"

Rossi was gripping him tight but leaning around to look ahead.

They were streaking toward another intersection, but this one was blocked. A massive 18-wheeler was sprawled across it, stuck in furious traffic. Bowie gritted his teeth. There was a gap in front of the truck's cab. Maybe four feet wide.

They could get through. Just. So long as the truck didn't . . .

It rolled forward, closing the gap.

"Bowie!" yelled Rossi, desperate now. He glanced down, eyeing the booster button.

They were seconds from slamming into the side of the truck.

He couldn't wait any longer. He punched the boosters which catapulted them forward with a deafening bang, maxing the speedometer as he stabbed blindly at the temporal launch control. The bike leaped for the energy stream, and Bowie felt himself yanked back by the thrust, momentarily weightless.

A half second before smashing into the truck, the vortex opened for them, seizing them in its swirling maelstrom and hurling them through blue-white chaos and into . . .

Darkness.

Merrick raged.

"How can you not know where he is?" he demanded for the umpteenth time. "He's using your system! If it wasn't for one of your agents getting shot *by Bowie* and returning for medical aid, we wouldn't even know he was in this . . . this *New Orleans*."

He said the name of the city as if it was something bizarre and unpleasant. Something foreign. The lights, which had flickered back on a minute or so earlier, went out again. Merrick slammed his desk in frustration. He still had only fragmentary reports as to what was going on with the power supply, and though troops were being deployed—enough troops to comfortably wipe out the handful of insurgents who had orchestrated the sabotage—the attack had caught them unawares. It was insufferable. And it was the last thing he wanted to be dealing with when he needed to prioritize why Reissen and the agents that they had sent back to fix their growing problems in the timeline were being so completely ineffective.

"We have deployed another agent to take his place in the search," Reissen was saying, "but the ranks of agents who are both loyal and sufficiently well trained are, as you know, limited."

"If we'd sent Four Nine, Bowie would be dead by now."

"If you remember, Director," said Reissen with exaggerated patience, "you recalled Jäger Zero Four Nine. When he was re-inserted it had to be to a different temporal point."

"You should recall Four Nine and send him . . ."

"We need to keep him available," Reissen protested, "in case Bowie can find his way to the moments of either the assassination or the bombing."

"How? He is in an earlier period. How could he return to November 22?"

"By waiting!" Reissen exclaimed. "We now know he was in Louisiana three months before the assassination. All he has to do to be a threat to the operation once again is to stay alive and get to Dallas by November."

"But you said that when he escaped your agents," Merrick returned, "he went farther back in time!"

"Yes," Reissen conceded. "But—and respectfully, Director, they are *our* agents, not mine—he could have gone back years or only a few days. He could easily get back to Dallas in time to interfere with the operation."

Merrick fell back on a familiar sense of frustration and outrage.

"I still don't see why you couldn't devise a way for your agents to keep track of each other's locations."

"There is no way to send locator data back and forth through time," said Professor Reissen. "The time vortex has to be open for anything to go through. Our operatives can open it briefly, but they have no way of knowing where a target is in space or time."

"You've said all this!" snapped Merrick, unimpressed. "What you are not saying is why. Communication between agents is a basic element of field work . . ."

The word stung Reissen and his steely calm broke like a flooded levy.

"Basic?" he fired back, infuriated.

"Yes! If the target is using our tech, then the hunting team should know at all times where that target is! I call that basic."

"*At all times*?" Reissen barked, trembling with exasperated rage as his face flushed. "They are in a different time! That's the point! They can't say 'let's check where he is now' because their now isn't his now! Why is that so hard to grasp? The only thing which is basic about this is your understanding of the mechanics of time!"

Even in his rage, the professor knew he had gone too far, and in that instant, Merrick became very still. It was like watching the torrent of a waterfall freeze suddenly, all its rivulets and gushers turning to pointed shards of ice. Reissen took a deep breath and hung his head.

"Apologies, Director," he said. "I overstepped."

"I'm not interested in your apologies," said Merrick coolly. "In case you hadn't noticed, we are under attack in both the present and the past. I want Bowie's head, and if you don't give it to me, I'll take yours and every agent who works for you. Do I make myself absolutely clear?"

Something of Reissen's former anger stirred again, prompting him to rouse himself like a wild horse, bucking and kicking at his undignified servility, but he knew Merrick too well. The director had not risen to his position by allowing anyone to question his decisions. That was not how the Design worked from the Designer down. The merest flicker of weakness would be pounced upon and eradicated. Even if it had not been in Merrick's nature, his place in the higher order would demand that he punish anyone who defied him.

And it was very much in his nature. Reissen considered Merrick's ice-blue eyes and wondered how long it would take for him to learn officially of the extent of the director's displeasure, and what consequences he would have to face. The list of possibilities was long and humiliating, possibly even painful. He remembered their society's watchwords: Design Through Strength.

He had always known the many small evils such words obscured. Now he was likely to learn about them firsthand.

"Recall your agents," said Merrick. "Be very clear to them, Reissen, that failure to find and eliminate that *Beta* will be treated with the utmost dissatisfaction. And that extends to everyone involved. Do you understand what you are being told, Professor?"

Reissen shrunk a little under the weight of what that meant.

"Yes, sir," he said.

"I want your personal guarantee that this activity will not jeopardize either mission," he said. "Both are essential."

"Yes, sir," Reissen said again. "I will see to it."

"I want all of your agents involved. No exceptions. Bowie must be eliminated and both 1963 temporal alterations must be completed."

"I understand."

As he spoke, the door opened and an officer in the black-and-silver uniform of the security forces leaned in.

"What is it?" snapped Merrick.

"The terrorists have attacked Relay Station Twenty-Seven," the officer reported. "An armored platoon was in transit through that district and was able to deploy immediately."

"And?" said Merrick.

"We have them surrounded."

"Finally, some good news."

"Also, sir," said the officer. "The leader of the power farm insurgents?"

Merrick's face lit with sudden realization. He raised a hand.

"Let me guess," he said, sitting back as if savoring the moment. "A man known as Sefton."

CHAPTER TWENTY

Bowie killed the engine and braked hard, sending the bike into an angled slide. The front wheel bucked on the uneven ground, but the headlight was off and the world was black. Something flashed past, inches to their left, and then another, and another. Trees. He twisted the handlebars as hard as he dared and the bike kicked a couple of feet to the right, slid another few yards, and came to a juddering halt.

Without releasing his grip on the handlebars, he took a long, ragged breath, checked that Rossi was still with him, then tipped his head back and looked up, simply glad to be in one piece. The world was black. He had never known darkness like it, and though it was risky, he snapped the headlight on in the same way as he had sucked in the air, as if he needed the light to stay alive.

The first thing he saw did nothing for his state of mind or the nausea triggered by the time vortex. They were in a forest bisected by a single rutted trail, but while he had seen forest in both Naushon and Louisiana, they had been tangles of life, chaoses of a thousand different plants—shrubs, bushes, vines, moss, trees of countless varied types—coming together to form a jumbled screen of greenery. Where they were now was so utterly unlike that that, for a second, he wondered if they were still in the same world. It was a forest, but here the trees were all the same: firs of roughly the same height and thickness, pyramidal, and evenly spaced. They looked like the columns of some ancient, living temple. The forest floor was a carpet of brownish pine needles, also even and improbably neat. He twisted the bike's front wheel and the headlamp flashed across the tree trunks, so that they leaped suddenly into view, the tree trunks pale and bright everywhere he looked. They seemed uniform and, in the brilliant glare of the headlight, surreal, an impression heightened by the silence. The other woods had seemed to be alive with birdsong, with the rattle of leaves and branches touched by the wind, by the natural movement of a living forest. In stark contrast, this place was still, so still in fact, that for a moment Bowie wondered if something had gone wrong with the passage through the vortex and they were in some kind of temporal pocket, a frozen moment where time did not exist. He leaned impetuously forward and thrust his wristwatch into the light, staring at it until he was sure he could see the seconds tick by. Even then, as he looked up and about him, the place felt uncanny. It was much cooler than New Orleans had been, but there was more than that behind the shiver which ran through him. More than anywhere he had been so far on this mission, Bowie felt out of his element, like he did not belong.

"Where are we?"

Rossi hadn't vomited this time, but she sounded dazed. He blinked, forcing himself to focus, and went through the reverse sequencing process he had figured out in Naushon until a series of numbers came up. He recited them to Rossi, who pulled out the atlas and moved it into the light where she riffled through pages until she found the coordinates. She triangulated with the forefingers of each hand, sliding one from the bottom of the page, one from the side until they met in the middle and she leaned closer to study the resultant spot.

"Maine," she announced. She looked up at the blank, empty woods. "What are we doing in Maine?"

Bowie shrugged and climbed off the bike.

"Got me," he said. "What were we doing in Naushon? What were we doing in New Orleans?"

"Fair point," she said. "What month is it?"

Bowie checked the display.

"June," he said, adding without thinking, "1953."

Rossi spun around to face him.

"What?" she demanded. "You're joking."

She looked, for some reason both horrified and furious. He shook his head, puzzled.

"No," he said. "Why would I joke about when it is?"

"You moved us ten years?" she shouted, shoving him squarely in the chest. "A decade? Without telling me?"

"I didn't know where we would finish up! How could I? I told you that. You told me to go. You said that exactly: 'Do it,' you said."

"I didn't know I was about to lose a decade of my life!" she protested.

"Actually, you got an extra decade," he said, opting for reasonable. "You can relive everything up to November 1963 . . ."

"But I'm not ten years younger, am I?" she interrupted, clearly beside herself. "I'm the same age as when you showed up! So I get to live through the fifties all over again but when I get back to where I started, I'll be ten years older! What about my family? I can't show up at my sister's place a decade older than the last time she saw me!"

Bowie wasn't sure why she was so upset, but he guessed that saying so wouldn't help.

"We needn't stay here," he offered.

"But you can't move us forward in time, remember? So all we can do is go farther and farther back, aging by decades each time till I die in my own past, years before I was born. I had a life!"

There were tears in her eyes now.

"That's not how this works," he said.

"Just . . . ." She went quiet, holding up her hands. "Just stop talking for a minute."

So saying, she walked a few steps into the trees on their right and stood there, hands on her hips, her head bowed, statuesque as the strangely uniform trees.

Not knowing what else to do, Bowie returned to the bike's digital display. He didn't know why Washington had come to this patch of woodland, desolate as it was. Perhaps he had merely used this as a safe entry point to the general location, before traveling somewhere else? He nudged the controls to scroll through the related data points and deduced that though the time rider had arrived in this spot, he had left from a point a few miles away, a point which was—if his map reading was to be trusted—closer to the coast and a couple of miles south of a place called Camden. He checked his compass and oriented himself, deducing that they needed to turn the bike around and follow their tracks back up the path and then out toward the coast. He also noted that there was only one more data entry for Washington's previous time jumps. If this place didn't yield what they were looking for, the bike would only offer one more possibility. Then they were on their own.

"It doesn't bother you," said Rossi without warning. "This wandering into other periods, leaving your life behind, knowing you are stranded, alone."

It did, in fact, but not as much as it clearly bothered her.

"I am used to being alone," he said.

"Really?" she said, walking back to the bike slowly. "No friends in the future?"

"Not for me," he said simply, feeling the words chime in the empty woods like a bell, resonant and loaded with meaning. "I told you; where I come from, I am . . . unusual. An oddity. Not someone others want to associate with. I work for the ruling elite—or I did—but I am not one of them, and Gammas—the lower orders who I deal with as part of my job—do not trust me."

"But you have your brother."

He wondered for a moment if he still did, but nodded, then picked his words carefully.

"My brother works in a Gamma camp. I see him occasionally, because of work, but we do not socialize. We were raised in a kind of orphanage, then were separated by the war. We see each other now but our lives diverged a long time ago," he hesitated, "It sounds easy, *socialize with your brother*, but in my world nothing was easy. I should have found a way, and I'm trying to reconnect with him now that I see . . ." He stopped, not wanting to give too much away about the pincer mission he had enlisted Sefton to help him carry out against the Design. He shrugged and went back to her question. "But, no. No friends. No socializing. And yes, I suppose that makes the prospect of living out my days in another world easier." He considered that, and added, "I am sorry you have been dragged into this."

She smiled tightly at that.

"Yeah," she said. "Me too. But I'm pretty much by myself too. Never been very good at making connections with people. Not *real* ones. Apart from Veronica."

"What about your friend? Spear."

"The one you shot?" she said, grinning. "Poor Jimmy! A colleague. Mostly a friend, but also, sometimes, a bit of a competitor, if I'm honest."

"Not a lover," said Bowie, trying out the word.

"Jimmy? God, no. I'm not his type and he's not mine."

Bowie didn't know what to say to that and just nodded.

"Anyway, yeah," she concluded. "Never been much of a social butterfly." She smiled, suddenly self-conscious and glanced around the woods. "And I've always liked the idea of New England, so it's not all bad, even if I don't relish being in my mid-thirties by the time I meet you for the first time."

"Yeah?"

"Yeah. I think I'd rather be in Boston than Maine though."

“Is Boston nice?” he asked.

He knew the question sounded odd, unlike him, and he wondered why he had asked. Was he picking up the gift of small talk? Or was it something about her, an impulse to please her. That was odd. Or maybe he actually cared what she thought about things, no matter how trivial. That was even odder.

“I don’t know, to be honest,” she replied. “Never been. Always wanted to. I’ve heard they have good museums, art galleries. A bit European in feel, whatever that means, and some cutting-edge institutions.”

“Like what?” he was fishing now, though he wasn’t sure why. Perhaps he just found her uncharacteristic openness pleasant.

“Harvard, Tufts, MIT,” she offered. “They’re universities. And they have world-class hospitals. I read a piece about a surgeon at Mass General who reattached someone’s arm last year. Not last year. 1962. His whole arm!”

“That’s impressive,” Bowie agreed.

“Don’t make fun, it is!”

“Not making fun,” Bowie said.

“In your super advanced world that’s probably not a big deal,” she said.

He considered that. He couldn’t imagine most of the pampered, desk-bound Alphas ever being in a situation where they might lose an arm. If it happened to a Gamma, they would be left to die.

“Was he an important person?”

“The surgeon?”

“No, the man who lost his arm.”

"It was a kid! Some twelve-year-old who was fooling around in the freight yards, hanging onto the side of a train when it went under a bridge. Took his arm right off."

"A child?" said Bowie, amazed. "And they went to these lengths to save his arm?"

"Yeah," said Rossi, clearly catching something in his face that puzzled her.

"Yes," he said. "It is a big deal."

She nodded, apparently satisfied, then took the thought further.

"Hell of a thing to do, reattaching an arm. I just write words, and tomorrow they are in the trash. So, I thought maybe now I was finally being given the chance to do something remarkable, you know? Make a real difference in the world."

"By saving the president."

She nodded.

"But now that seems unlikely," she said. "The farther back we go, the less chance we have to derail the assassination."

"Don't you at least want to know why it will happen, who is behind it?"

She thought for a moment, then shrugged miserably.

"I guess," she said. "But if it's going to happen anyway, no matter what we do, what's the point?"

He didn't know what to say to that. That flash of her personality—all her guards down—was gone. She suddenly seemed spent, lost and unengaged.

"So it's 1953," she said miserably. "I've just started high school a couple of thousand miles away. My family . . ." But she couldn't finish the thought and looked down as tears filled her eyes.

Bowie didn't know what to say. Suddenly, for reasons he couldn't quite place, he wanted to go back to talking about Sefton, wanted to tell her how he had gone back and seen his brother and what they were planning to do. He didn't know why he had kept it from her and now he couldn't think of how to explain away the deception.

Just tell her now. Show her you aren't holding things back. It will make her feel better.

But she was still staring at the ground and may as well have been ten years and two thousand miles away.

"Washington didn't stay here," he said at last. "He rode that way. We should too."

Rossi just stood there, as if she hadn't heard him, a vague look on her face, her eyes wandering into the woods but focusing on nothing. Eventually she drifted toward him, but she moved resignedly, as if simply drawn by the pull of the bike or Bowie himself, though she didn't seem to care one way or the other.

She has lost interest, he thought, a slang phrase he had heard thrown around casually, but which seemed to him loaded with something like despair. When she got onto the bike behind him, he had to lace her hands together around his waist to keep her from falling off.

As they rode carefully down the path, the trees became less uniform, weaving hardwoods into the mix, but the woods did not fully lose their claustrophobic strangeness. Maybe it was just being in the dark, the sense of uninhabited emptiness. Bowie wasn't sure.

He kept on course for where Washington had left the area and, without warning, the forest opened up and became pasture. With the trees gone and the sky above suddenly clear, Bowie was surprised to see the moon, bright and perfectly full, riding high overhead. The moonlight gave a silver cast to everything in sight beyond the tree line and, nestled in a hollow served by a private road, he could see a large house with attendant outbuildings. He brought the bike to a stop, turned off the headlight, then killed the engine.

"Washington left from down there," he remarked.

Rossi said nothing.

There was an incline running down toward the structures. Without restarting the engine, he released the brake and lifted his feet off the ground. The bike rolled forward under its own weight, slowly at first, but then it picked up speed, and within fifty yards or so, he was having to reapply the brakes to keep it under control. Between them and the house was a pond shining bright in the moonlight, and to one side was a grove of young trees with shiny, coppery leaves. It offered the only real cover in the area, and Bowie coasted toward it, slowing further as they reached its uneven rim, allowing the bike to push through the outer thicket of brambles and penetrate the tiny wood. In the center, he stopped, dismounted and nudged the still lethargic Rossi to do the same, before carefully laying the bike down on its side. He moved to the furthest edge of the trees to get a better look at the house.

It was imposing and gloomy, with steeply gabled roofs sprouting tall chimneys. Ivy crawled up the walls and under the eaves. There was a second-floor veranda on one end, and a round window like an oversized porthole on the other. Two of the windows had lights in them, but the place still felt desolate, and other windows seemed to have been overgrown by the stifling ivy shroud. From this side he couldn't see where any vehicles might be parked. There were a pair of ramshackle sheds, and two larger structures that might have been barns. One of which sat between the grove and the house.

A good place from which to watch, he thought, thumbing on the digital lens. He wasn't sure it was worth saying so to Rossi, who still seemed apathetic, disconnected. He looked through the scope which made the view bright as day. As he considered the strangely shrouded house, another light came on, and then a side door opened. The lens adjusted and refocused, revealing someone navigating a series of steps before picking their way along a path toward them.

Bowie shrank down a little, then moved his finger to increase the magnification of his scope. It was a man. White, middle aged. He was carrying a box, which accounted for the slight awkwardness of his movement, but he was definitely heading in their direction. Without taking his eyes off the stranger, Bowie reached vaguely for Rossi to get her attention in case they needed to move. She jumped at his touch but said nothing.

The man with the box made a sudden turn and vanished into the shade of the barn. He was gone for several minutes, and though Bowie strained to hear, he could make out no sound of what the man might be doing. Gradually a soft, golden glow became visible through one of the roof vents, and a moment after that, the man reemerged without the box and made his way back to the house. The light in the barn stayed on.

"Come on," Bowie whispered as he stowed his scope. "I want to see what's going on in there." Even as he said it his ears picked up the distant rumble of a familiar engine.

Washington.

Bowie kept very still, turning carefully to look back the way they had come as a single headlamp meandered down the forest trail and into the pasture. Bowie's mind suddenly conjured the dreadful possibility that their bike—actually Washington's—might have left a trail which would lead the time rider right to them. He hadn't checked. The ground had been hard, baked by the summer heat, but an experienced tracker might still see plenty that would give them away. He reached for his pistol.

But the bike rolled past the grove and on down toward the house, coming to a halt under the veranda. The uncanny silence of the night as the engine shut down was startling. The rider had parked just out of view, blocked by an ivy-covered wall. But the sound of his knocking was easily heard and someone—perhaps the man who had been carrying the box, but then again, perhaps not—admitted him into the house.

"Quick," said Bowie. "To the barn." Rossi didn't move at once, and he turned to find her still looking lost and strange. Young, somehow. "We're here," he said firmly. "Let's find out why."

She gave a kind of nod that was at least half a shrug and got slowly to her feet. Bowie took her hand and gave her a gentle, encouraging pull. Together they loped toward the back wall of the barn, flattening themselves up against it and inching around toward the door. The foundation was stone, but the structure itself was timber and smelled of pine and something related but stronger which—for Bowie—were almost as overwhelming as the aromas of the swamps and kitchens of New Orleans. His world, for the most part, did not smell. Everywhere here was an assault on his senses which made his head swim.

"Creosote," Rossi whispered off his wrinkled nose. "A kind of preservative for wood."

He gave her a grateful nod, then they slipped quickly around the front, eyeing the house for signs of anyone else coming out. Finding the barn door was not just unlocked but propped open, they slipped inside.

"Whoa," said Rossi, the first sound of emotional engagement she had made in ages. Bowie spun around to face her.

"What?" he said.

"I thought it would be just a barn," she said.

The word meant little to Bowie.

"It's not?" he asked.

"Not a lot of barns have furniture and wooden floors," she said, gazing around her.

The interior was lit by a wrought iron chandelier, a great iron wheel hanging from chains in the center of the barn roof and sprouting nine oil lamps. That number seemed intentional, as below it, evenly spaced, were nine chairs arranged in a circle on the swept wooden floor, stiff, high-backed affairs, ornately carved of heavy, dark wood.

Between them all there was a red rug, also circular, trimmed with black and gold, and in its center, half covered by a wooden crate which looked to be the one the man had been carrying . . .

"That design!" Rossi gasped pointing at the insignia of circles and a hooked line on the rug. "That was what Ferrie had on his vestments."

"The symbol of the Awakening," Bowie agreed. "Of the Design."

"What is going on here?" she asked, clearly perplexed, even upset, but Bowie heard that tone with relief. She was invested again. "This is not set up for the kind of mass that we saw in New Orleans. Not sitting in a circle like this."

"Something is about to happen here," Bowie agreed. "And it involves Washington. We need to see what it is."

He offered the thought to her and waited.

Finally, she nodded. "Yes, we do."

CHAPTER TWENTY-ONE

Bowie's eyes left the lighted circle and peered into the shadows where the origins of the place as a bona fide barn were still clear. Rusty farm implements hanging on the walls, some kind of stall for animals . . .

"There's a hay loft," said Rossi, pointing.

Bowie followed her gaze. At the far end, just out of the light of the lamps, was a rough-hewn ladder up to a kind of balcony. A good tactical vantage point, but without alternate exits. Rossi was already inspecting the rungs of the ladder, hauling herself carefully up. Bowie turned quickly: voices coming from the house. He took three long strides and joined her on the ladder.

More aromas awaited him at the top, this time the sweet, grassy fragrance of fresh cut hay, recently baled and stacked in the loft. He inhaled it deeply, momentarily forgetting their peril as the rich, intoxicating scent of meadows surrounded him. Rossi had already moved softly to a point where she could see down into the barn proper between neat blocks of hay bound with baling wire. As the voices outside got louder, he quickly crossed over to where she had nestled and squeezed down low beside her.

The dialogue below was confused, several different conversations going on separately and simultaneously, men's and women's voices blended but talking about different things.

"Which is the problem of the superconscious," said one.

"I spoke to him about that," said another. "He said that the Feds had been on it since Roswell."

Bowie shifted, feeling the prickle of the hay against his arm as he tried to get a better look. There were more of them than he had realized, more than had been in David Ferrie's makeshift chapel in New Orleans. He peered through the bales. Ten of them. Six men and four women. They each carried some kind of oil lamp which they placed by their chairs as they took their seats so that the circle on the floor seemed to glow, though the corners of the barn—and, fortunately, the hayloft—remained plunged in shadow.

They were short one chair, but one in the group moved into the center of the circle and sat cross legged on the rug marked with the logo of the Design. This man was darker than the others, and unlike them—who were dressed in the elegant fashions of the day—he wore a long white smock with a saffron colored drape arranged diagonally across one shoulder and carried a string of ceremonial beads. Beside him he set a statuette of a humanoid figure with the face of an ape, and on his lap he placed a copper plate. As he settled, the space grew uncannily quiet, and Bowie felt the air of anticipation, all eyes on the man in the center.

At last, he closed his eyes, took a long breath and said, "I am Doctor D.G. Vinod and I will mediate this meeting of the Nine. Please introduce yourselves."

And they did, going around the circle, giving their names. Bowie felt like they knew each other already. The naming was less social than it was ritual.

"Doctor Andrija Puharich," said the first, who Bowie instinctively took to be the leader.

"Henry Jackson," said the next.

"Georgia Jackson."

"Alice Bouverie."

"Marcella du Pont."

"Carl Betz."

"Vonnie Beck."

"Arthur Young."

"Ruth Forbes Young."

The last two Bowie had seen at the big house on Naushon Island welcoming the woman who had lived with Lee Harvey Oswald, the woman who had arranged for his job at the Texas School Book Depository.

And the one calling himself Vonnie Beck was the man Bowie knew as the time rider Washington.

Rossi's mind reeled. The Forbes Youngs she had seen before, but now they were in the company of a du Pont (of DuPont chemicals) and—in Alice Bouverie—an Astor, some of the richest and most powerful of America's high society. These people were more than moneyed. They had deep roots in

America's oldest and most profitable institutions, while gliding above the muck of it all like the proverbial swans, all elegance and good breeding. The wealth and influence sitting in that circle boggled the mind. What was going on here?

It was certainly no mass. The arrangement of the chairs made the place look like Stonehenge, but Vinod, the man in the center, seemed to be Indian, and she thought the statue beside him looked Hindu, though she could not recall the monkey god's name. But what unfolded was no Hindu ceremony. In fact, she thought, with a thrill of bewildered exhilaration, it looked more like a séance.

Suddenly, Vinod sat bolt upright and intoned, "M, calling. We are nine principles and forces working in harmony to promote the positive and teleological aspects of existence. We have determined to bring you peace, which is more than the absence of war, through the natural enrichment of personality, as a means to utilize you in the fulfillment of evolution. Tonight, we will create Brahmins in this world, engineering a world order which will work toward the elevation of your species."

Your species?

Rossi tried to process what she was hearing. Making Brahmins? Half the room were Brahmins already, at least in social and financial terms, so Vinod—or the character of M who was supposedly speaking through him—apparently meant something else. She frowned at Bowie, and as she looked back she saw a momentary flash in the center of the circle, and when it went away there was a mound of what seemed to be fine cords: nine of them, as it turned out, since Vinod handed one to each of the assembly and instructed them to wear it as a sash running from shoulder to waist. There had been an audible gasp at this seemingly supernatural appearance, but in the afterglow of the flash, Rossi saw the now familiar swirling blue-white trails of a time vortex.

The cords had come from the future!

She stared at the man she knew as Washington, the wigged stranger who was destined to die in the bar of the Adolphus Hotel in Dallas some ten years later, and she knew that whatever the others thought about what was going on, he knew the truth.

"These cords are the Yadnyopavita," Vinod proclaimed, "the sacred threads consecrating your rebirth as Brahmins this full moon."

As Rossi puzzled over that, Vinod's focus shifted and abstracted in a long and peculiar monologue. He was talking about alchemy, the process of transmuting base metals into gold and of generating an elixir of life. Rossi had read of such pseudoscience in her European history class, and a part of her wanted to laugh out loud that it was being laid out in all seriousness here.

Perhaps he means it metaphorically, she wondered, *a transformation of people into some higher form of themselves?* But then he concluded with more nonsense:

"Of course 'Al' means God, and 'Kem' means Egypt, so Alchemy was God of Egypt and the God of Egypt was this."

It was lunacy. And yet here they all were—smart people, powerful people—drinking it all in, initiates in some occult mysticism which she would shrug off as farcical, except that she knew where it pointed, where this strange intersection of people seemed to lead. She had, after all, seen the future.

KENNEDY IS KILLED BY SNIPER AS HE RIDES IN CAR IN DALLAS

That was what the headline would say. Was this part of it? Spiritualist self-congratulation and magic tricks from the future leading to a murder which would change the world? Was that possible? If so, how and why?

Now Vinod was talking about Buddha, about transcending death and decay, and it made no more sense to her than did his alchemy. It was madness. She turned to convey as much with her face to Bowie and found him huddled back, surely unable to see what was going on below, his face red and eyes streaming, hands clasped over his mouth as if in pain.

What the hell?

He gave her a desperate look, but when she leaned in close enough for him to whisper, he shook his head violently and clamped his hands tighter over his mouth. He wasn't in emotional distress. The tears, the redness, they were physiological. Dimly, as Vinod droned on below about magic and science and consciousness, she took in the baled hay and put the pieces together.

"You have allergies?" she breathed.

He gave her a wide-eyed—red eyed—look and shrugged expansively. He didn't know. Why would he? From what he had said about his home world, barns full of mown grass hadn't played much of a part in his life.

It was almost funny. But he was clearly fighting to suppress the kind of sneeze that would alert the entire building to their presence. She thought fast, unsnapped her shoulder bag as quietly as she could and searched. There was a foil package with lint stuck to it. Her hay fever had been quiet this season and she had barely touched it.

"Take these," she mouthed, offering him two. She glanced around and nodded to the back of the loft where there were no bales. "Over there."

He took the pills and crawled over slowly, though whether that was about his discomfort or a desire to be silent, she wasn't sure. For several minutes he sat with his head bowed into his knees, unmoving, finally raising his head to give her a nod and a weak smile which said "Better. Thank you."

She grinned back, all the fear and strangeness of what they were doing momentarily lost in the sight of him, the time agent and soldier, looking like a sick child . . .

It was over. Vinod had conducted his séance, oscillating between science, philosophy and religion, sometimes dwelling on occult mysticism drawing on half a dozen different cultural histories, sometimes talking relativity and quantum mechanics, sometimes dealing in feel-good platitudes about harmony and being one with each other and the universe. For Bowie, little of it was comprehensible and he had no firm handle on what any ordinary rational person from this period, or any period, would think of it.

"I mean," said Rossi after, "some of it was genuinely profound, some of it was merely empty, and some of it was bare-ass crazy. What it all added up to, if anything, I really have no idea."

In the end, the Nine had held hands to celebrate their communion with M—the astral intelligence which Vinod claimed to be channeling, and then they had gathered their regalia and totems, their beads and their statues, and they had blown out the candles and filed back to the house under the light of the full moon. By then it was two in the morning, and though Bowie's allergic response to the hay had subsided under Rossi's ministrations, he was glad to descend the ladder and get out of the barn.

They went back to the grove of trees where they had stowed the bike, moving stealthily in an easy silence which belied the strangeness of their evening. He had grown accustomed to her and, against all the odds, she seemed to have grown accustomed to him as well. Maybe it was more than that, for him at least. He didn't have the experience to know.

"Did that feel like it was about JFK?" Rossi asked doubtfully.

Bowie had been thinking along the same lines.

"No," he said. "I have to assume it was related but it makes me wonder."

"What?"

"Whether what is going on is about more than just a single assassination."

She scowled, clearly unhappy about the idea that the event she thought of as the core of their mission might only be one part of it. He thought of his brother, about the idea that what they were doing was tied across history.

But what could "the Nine" be about if it wasn't just the murder of an American president?

"Where do we go next?" she asked. Maybe she was changing the subject or trying to pull it back to something she could contain, something that gave her things to do. Bowie thought for a moment, trying to find a way of leading into what he wanted to say.

"I told you I had figured out how to go back through the bike's destination coordinates," he said. "And that I could track where Washington had been."

"And?"

"I didn't tell you there was only one destination left."

She gave him an inquiring look, her face pinched and earnest.

"What does that mean?" she asked as they picked their way through the undergrowth.

"It means that we have been following in Washington's footsteps in the hope of making sense of all this," he said, "but we're down to our last clue, and I don't think you're going to like it. Before this, he went to New Mexico."

They reached the bike and as he busied himself with its controls, she settled onto a fallen tree on which a pale fungus grew like soft plates embedded in the bark.

"OK," she said, not getting it. "Gets us closer to Dallas than here . . ."

"In 1947," said Bowie.

She sat back at that, nodding slowly in silence, but he saw her face fall.

"Five more years," she said.

"We can go there," Bowie continued. "I mean, I intend to. But I can't get you back to 1963 without returning to my own world first which is . . ." he shook his head. "Too dangerous."

"So, what are you saying?"

"I think I should go by myself. Leave you here. Let you just . . . stay. Live your life. Eventually return to Dallas, but not till there's no danger of you meeting your past self."

"So like, the day of the assassination," she said bleakly.

"I don't think you can stop it by other means, so yes," he agreed. "If you were somehow able to get Oswald killed or arrested beforehand, they'd find a new trigger man. So you go to the book depository on the morning of November 22. Not a moment before. Stop Oswald before he can shoot the president."

"How?"

Bowie looked down, then shrugged.

"You have a decade to figure that out," he said.

"And in the meantime?" she demanded, her eyes swimming. "Be alone for ten years? Doing what?

"Whatever you want," he replied. "Start fresh. I have money that should last you for a few years. I was told that a few thousand dollars would go a long way in 1963. It might go even farther in 1953. You can get back to being a journalist. Hell," he said, experimenting with the colloquialism, "you might even make a name for yourself scooping events you know are going to happen before anyone else finds out about them."

She grinned briefly at that but still looked upset.

"Like the assassination of a president," she said sadly.

"Anything but that," he said. "You can't let anyone know what you have seen, what you know will happen. You can't alert the Design that you know what is going on and you can't trust the local authorities . . ."

"You think they already know?" she asked. "That they are involved?"

"Not all of them," he said. "It may only be a few well-placed people, individuals like the ones we just saw in the barn. But you say they have a lot of power. So there is a network of connected people, wealthy and influential people, whose goals are unclear to me but which somehow involve the world I came from. From your distant future. Which brings me to the other thing."

He waited, watching her wariness deepen, then spoke in a soft, even voice.

"I went back. To my own time, I mean. While you were getting the atlas."

"You left?"

"There was something I had to do."

"You said going back was too risky."

"It was."

"Then you could have been killed or got stuck there. Either way I would have come back to the island and you would have been gone. I would never have seen you again!"

Her tone was accusatory, but there was something under her anger, a hurt that touched him.

"I know," he said. "I'm sorry. But I felt I had no choice."

"You saw your brother," she said. It wasn't a question.

"I did."

"But he wouldn't come with you."

"No." He said it sadly, but he held her eyes and rallied. "Sefton has purposes of his own. And for once, or at least for the first time in a very long time, we found ourselves . . . in agreement."

She took a second to process that then nodded thoughtfully.

"So you and he are working together," she said with that quick wittedness which always surprised and pleased him. "Him in the future, you in the past."

Despite everything, he laughed.

"Exactly," he said. "Which means that after I go to 1947, I will have to go back to 2157 to help him, maybe even get him out."

"Before returning to 1963."

She said it solemnly, as if she understood the gravity of what he was going to attempt without him saying anything further. He said it anyway.

"Which will be dangerous."

She gave him a wan smile at the understatement.

"So you might not make it back to the day of the assassination," she said. "I might never see you again."

"I will," he said, adamant. "You will."

"You can't know that. Don't promise what you can't deliver. Two hundred years and men still haven't learned that?"

It was almost a joke but there were tears in her eyes.

"I will do everything in my power to honor my promise," he said.

She gave a little gasping sob that was almost a laugh, and she nodded.

"So stopping Oswald . . ." she began.

"May come down to you, yes," he said. He was done being less than truthful with her. "If I can possibly be there, I swear I will. Count on it. And Sandra?"

"What?" she asked, wiping her eyes.

"Stay alive," he said. "If I come back and you're not there . . ."

He didn't know how to finish the sentence, and for the first time that possibility filled him with a deep sense of horror and something else that felt, unaccountably, of loss and sorrow.

"If you don't come back," she remarked, more wan amusement flicking through her face even as a tear shook out of her eyelashes, "I'll find you and kick your ass. I don't care where or when you are."

"Understood," he said.

She hung her head and more tears fell.

"It feels wrong," she said, without looking up, "not going with you."

The moonlight filtering through the boughs of the trees gave her a silvery cast that made her ethereal, other worldly. On impulse, Bowie reached for her and drew her to him. His hands cupped her face and, with his thumbs, he gently smoothed away her tears.

"No," he said. "I've taken too many years from you already."

She kissed him then, a sudden, upward surge of conviction, of passion, that he met halfway. His hands moved to her waist, pulling her into him, and he felt her strain to reach him, welcoming, hungry. His mind was far away or shut down, overwhelmed by the certainty, the rightness of the thing, and then there was only the sensation of her lips on his, ravenous and tender at the same instant, and then he was almost falling, all he had been finally crumbling into dust and nothingness like the ending of the world, all fire, and leaping blood, and the long, glorious darkness of oblivion.

CHAPTER TWENTY-TWO

The intercom light on Merrick's clutter-less desk lit up yellow and an electronic bell tolled. He swatted at it irritably.

"Merrick," he said.

"The Gamma insurgent assault on relay twenty-seven has been nullified, Director."

"And the leader?"

"We have him in custody."

"Excellent. Bring him to me."

"One other thing, sir."

"What is it?" snapped Merrick, alert to the note of concern in the security chief's voice.

"The power disruptions have affected systems in the incubation facility."

Merrick stood with a surge of something close to panic and glared down at the speaker on his desk.

"How badly?" he demanded.

"Reports aren't in yet. The structure has been sealed even to the security forces."

Of course it had. That was built into the emergency response protocol. The incubation labs required the highest possible security clearance; the smallest ripple in the usually placid and predictable life of the Design would put them on absolute lockdown.

"Meet me there. Development Unit Four, Alpha wing. I'll enter your authorization code into the system."

"Yes, sir. And the insurgents?"

"Put them in holding cells until this matter is resolved. I'll send interrogation teams later."

"Yes, sir."

"Ten minutes."

"It may take us rather longer than that to get over there. The outages have impacted the transit matrixes . . ."

"Ten minutes," said Merrick, and snapped the intercom off.

Merrick brought the docupad which contained his encrypted mission logs and took the internal monorail four buildings over to the main elevator shafts and then went down three levels. At each junction he was met by a guard who escorted him to the next stage of the journey. He did not speak to any of them, and when one of them had the audacity to make eye contact with him, he gave him a laser glare which turned the man's face pink. Merrick said nothing, but he made note of the man's service number and had tapped out a disciplinary memo to the guard's commander by the time he was off the elevator. He rode the moving walkway to the next security checkpoint and showed his credentials, not that they didn't know him on sight. He felt the flicker of fearful recognition as soon as they saw him. And surprise. He wasn't exactly a regular visitor to the development wing.

They waved him through the security sensors, detectors, and other scanners, checking his biometrics as politely as they could manage, and Merrick felt their anxiety at his presence, that they might say or do the wrong thing in ways that could jeopardize their careers or worse. He was shown into the Alpha wing of unit four by guards who he knew were considered among the highest-rated operatives of the Design's vast military and intelligence department, but at the final doors they hesitated.

"Sorry sir," said one. "Without the commandant's direct approval, the innermost security lockouts cannot be breached."

"Read the badge," Merrick snapped. "My clearance outweighs hers. This is an emergency situation. Override the locks." They weren't happy about it, and they took rather longer than he would have liked to verify that he was who he claimed to be, but at last the flashing red bars over the doors turned green. "Keep them open till I tell you otherwise," he said. "We may need to evacuate a lot of material."

"And personnel?" asked the guard.

"That's a secondary priority," said Merrick. "Out of my way."

He went through the heavy doors and into the primary lab, but his welcome was frosty.

"Director," said the unit commandant, a hard-faced woman who Merrick knew had commanded the elite Valkyrie unit during the Great Conflagration before being moved into scientific security, "I must protest this unannounced intrusion. The sensitivity of our work cannot be jeopardized by random visits from the intelligence services."

"My operational seniority extends to your facility, Commandant," Merrick replied evenly. "Let us not waste time with idle posturing."

"You have the authority to visit any time," the commandant agreed, "and are most welcome to do so. But some advance warning would be appreciated in the future."

"Given the impact on your systems from the power outages, it was necessary that I be apprised of the situation immediately. Frankly, I am surprised that you did not alert me yourself."

The commandant's brow puckered.

"Impact on our systems?" she said. "I was aware of power disruptions within the city but I have not heard anything to suggest that our operational capacity here has been in any way impacted."

She turned to one of the guards who shook his head in confirmation.

"What do you mean?" asked Merrick, momentarily adrift.

"All systems here are normal," she replied. "Our backup generators adjusted to the loss of external power."

"I was told you were in lockdown."

The commandant moved to a display panel and entered a few commands pulling up several digital displays. She shook her head.

"Our security is as tight as ever," she said, a note of perplexity in her voice. "As you can see, all systems here are working at optimum levels."

She glanced pointedly around.

The chamber was vast, and though the temperature was probably no different from the rest of the facility, it felt cold. Everything in sight was fashioned from bright steel trimmed with white, and the light was harsh and tinged blue. Most of that light came from the countless glass-fronted storage units, both horizontal and vertical, which were arranged around the room as far as Merrick could see. They had various dimensions, some upright and man-sized, like old-fashioned refrigerators, some half that size or less, and some mere cases of compartments each holding dozens or hundreds of miniaturized versions of the same glass containers, these no larger than test tubes. Banks of monitors, all policed by techs in white lab coats, generated constant digital readouts, and each unit—no matter its size—was connected by wires and hoses to an array of computers and fluid tanks.

"I understand that you may be at pains to conceal any disruption in your operations," said Merrick flatly, "but I am acting on the Designer's direct orders. If the running of this facility has been compromised in any way, however briefly—"

"It has not," said the commandant, standing her ground. "Director, the security of these facilities is our utmost priority. We have multiple redundancies designed to ensure we are invulnerable to something as trivial as a failure in the city's power supply. Whatever information you were given was, respectfully, incorrect."

Merrick stood there. For all his delight in small cruelties, his reveling in the powerlessness of others, he thought of himself as a good public servant driven by patriotism and a dedication to the ideals of his society. His eyes flashed over the incubation chambers, the genetic processing units, the sterile efficiency of the whole operation and what it stood for. This place, more than anything in his purview, was the heart of the Design, and he usually felt a rush of pride as he looked upon it.

He felt something else now. There was an anxiety at the edge of his consciousness, a dull but swelling awareness like a sound on the edge of hearing or an unfamiliar odor, and with it came unease. Something wasn't right.

And then it registered. He heard again in his head the voice of the security chief telling him what he had expected—wanted—to hear: that the terrorists had failed. That their leader had been taken.

But that had been a lie. He glanced behind him to the great security doors which—on his orders—gaped wide. The commandant's gaze followed his and her eyes widened with the same horrified realization.

"Lock down the building!" he ordered. "Seal all doors!"

Even as he said it, he heard the burst of weapons fire from beyond the great hall. The attack wasn't over. The sabotage of the power systems hadn't been an end but a means, maybe even a diversion. The insurgents' true target was this building, and he had handed them the keys . . .

A series of pulsing flashes came from the corridor. One of the guards ran to the door but was cut down before he could get a shot off. Others took cover and returned a stream of shimmering blasts, but they were scattered and unprepared. One by one they dropped, and a horrified hush descended on the chamber as slowly, cautiously, their weapons raised and ready, five insurgents entered one of the Design's most secure facilities. One of them was wheeling a heavy-looking steel case of the kind issued to special military units, though what it contained, Merrick could only imagine.

Leading them was the Gamma called Sefton. He was ragged, and dirty, as was to be expected, but he also had one eye swollen shut, and his face and hands were streaked with blood. His long unkempt hair fell onto his shoulders in sweaty rat tails, and even at this distance Merrick thought he could smell him. But the man had an air of command and he moved with confident economy. He had one of the compact energy weapons they called juicers cradled in both hands. Merrick didn't doubt the man knew how to use it.

The commandant's face tightened with disdain and loathing, but she raised her hands in surrender. The techs followed her lead. One of the insurgents checked on the fallen guards, kicking their weapons away in case any of them were still alive.

"You are not authorized to be here," Merrick stated flatly. He had not raised his hands and his tone was cold and haughty. "Your presence in the facility is known. You cannot hope to walk out through those doors again."

Sefton glanced at his men and the corner of his mouth twisted in an insolent smirk which made Merrick's blood boil.

"Walked in through them, didn't we?"

One of the insurgents with him—a lean black woman —chuckled.

"How dare you . . . ?" the commandant began, but the grinning terrorist just raised her weapon purposefully, and she fell silent.

"What do you want here?" Merrick demanded.

"Answers," said Sefton simply.

"This is a classified facility," snapped the commandant. "Beyond top secret. The idea that we would share our work with anyone, let alone *Gammas* . . ." The contempt she injected into the last word meant that she didn't need to finish the sentence.

The leader took a slow, idle step toward Merrick.

"I believe you know my brother," he said.

At the word "brother," he saw the commandant's face tighten with confused interest. The techs looked stunned, appalled. Their eyes flashed toward Merrick.

"His name is Bowie," said Sefton. "He works for you, but I'm guessing you've come to wish he didn't."

Merrick's face went hard as he fought to control his feelings.

"Tell them," said Sefton, nudging Merrick in the belly with the muzzle of his blaster.

Merrick thought for a moment, then shrugged.

"That's right," he said to the room in general. "He has a brother. Equally degenerate and disruptive. It must run in their family."

He said that last word with arch disdain then, reading the bewilderment in the faces around him added, "Yes, a family. Which is, of course, impossible. How could such a thing happen in a place like this?"

The Gamma gave him an amused look but said nothing.

"I'll tell you how," said Merrick, enjoying himself. "He has a brother, because he has parents!"

He presented that last word like a magician pulling something strange and repulsive from a place it could not possibly have been, and this time he heard the gasps of the lab techs around him.

"Director, I must protest!" interjected the commandant, caught between amazement at what she thought violated the secrecy of the facility and sheer revulsion.

"I understand," Merrick said, turning his calming gesture on her, but still smiling his cold, crocodile smile. "It is shocking to hear of such a thing. But it does not do to ignore corruption, to turn away from a thing merely because it is distasteful to look upon. Mr. Sefton, here, like his *brother*, is a throwback, albeit an improbable one. Blood, as they used to say, will out. Degenerates generate degenerates," he added, amused at the phrase. "Despite the best efforts of the Design, some still have urges we cannot suppress, and the result is children born outside the sanitary and moral confines of respectable society. So there are orphanages. A few shameful halls where these half humans are raised until they can be given a purpose and integrated into society."

"In the work camps," said Sefton, his tone indignant. "Among the Gammas you breed to be your slaves."

"And where is your gratitude?" Merrick exclaimed. "At least the Gammas were built for what they do. You aren't even worthy of that. We should have cast you into the fire, stamped you out the moment we found you and those like you, but in our mercy we gave you a place in the Design!"

The room was thick with silent tension. Merrick turned to the techs who looked amazed and repulsed by what they had heard.

"See how they reward us for our kindness? Challenging their betters, subverting, destroying. It is all they know how to do. We should round them all up, every puppy from this mongrel litter, and put them to sleep in the interests of social purity."

Sefton half turned away then rammed the butt of his juicer into Merrick's midriff. The director doubled over, the air momentarily knocked out of his body, but when he straightened up, he was laughing softly.

"Is that it?" he pressed, gasping the words. "You fought your way in here, risking your life and the lives of your misguided reprobate followers for an admission that you were born outside the system? Congratulations: your shame is confirmed. Was it worth it?"

"Not quite yet," said Sefton coolly. Despite the flare of anger which had led to the blow, he seemed to have reclaimed his composure with surprising speed. "Why don't you tell me exactly what you do here?"

"Classified!" barked the commandant. "How dare you even ask . . . ?"

"It is no matter," said Merrick, calming her with a glance. "These are dying men and women. They may not look like it, but they are breathing their final moments. What they hear, what they learn . . . It is no more than dressing a corpse for burial."

Sefton smiled at the phrase, cocking his head on one side in a kind of shrug.

"OK," he said. "Then talk."

"This facility," Merrick went on, "is, as you know, how we reproduce our species. By *we* I mean the true citizens of the Design. We are raised clinically, precisely, Designed—so to speak—to be the perfect fit for what our world needs of us, and to be the optimal manifestation of our society, our values. This is the way it has been in our world for almost a hundred years, since long before your kind tried to disrupt it in the Great Conflagration. You did not come from here. Neither did your *brother*, Bowie. You are outliers, the spawn of some debased, carnal union of man and woman in the tradition of apes and monkeys. I had—in my misguided and over-generous optimism—thought there might be a use for you in our world, a way to overcome your barbaric origins, but you are not and cannot be civilized."

"You like hearing yourself talk, don't you?" said Sefton. "But is that all you have to say, recycled propaganda and petty malice? No, Mr. Merrick. Not nearly good enough. I want to know," and here he leaned in close and slowed the pace of his speech so that each word came out like the tolling of a distant bell. "What is in vat zero, zero, one?"

This time Merrick couldn't contain his horrified amazement. His already pale face went bloodlessly white and his mouth gaped open. Out of the corner of his eye he saw the commandant staring, equally stunned, her hand coming up to cover her mouth. She knew what they were talking about. The techs didn't, but they picked up on the pregnant silence and their terror deepened.

Merrick picked his words carefully.

"VAT-001 is a Gamma myth," he said. "It does not exist."

"Then you won't mind opening security door 6-B and taking me to the vault," said Sefton evenly.

Again, the commandant's look gave her away before Merrick could frame his strategic bafflement. Sefton shot her a look and grinned wolfishly.

"For someone who works in a top-secret facility," he observed, "you are terrible at keeping secrets. You wanna know what I think we'll find?" Merrick's lips were clamped shut. Sefton grinned and nudged him in the chest with the barrel of the juicer. "I think we're gonna find the Originator."

The commandant gasped audibly.

"Who gave you this information?" she demanded, her face hot, her voice unsteady with outrage.

"You think you have everyone in your pocket," said Sefton with a knowing shake of his head. "The Design. The elite. The Alphas. The Great Awakening. You parrot these things and because you don't *hear* the dissent you think there is none. But you are wrong. We are here. Under your noses. And not all of us are orphans or Gammas. Some of us are Betas. Some are even *Alphas*."

"Lies!" shrieked the commandant, taking a step forward and raising a hand as if to slap the arrogance from his face. The black, female insurgent stepped in front of her, weapon raised. The commandant fell silent, and Sefton gave a satisfied nod.

"Better," he said. "Now that we're all a little calmer, security door 6-B."

The bike hardly bucked at all as it emerged from the time vortex and hit Highway 285 arrowing north through the New Mexican desert some fifty miles north of Roswell. Bowie sat back, allowing the bike to slow a little as he assessed the situation and any immediate danger. There was none. The road was broad, straight and empty. It was dark, but to his right the coming dawn was visible as a softening of the blackness and in a matter of minutes it would turn the sky to the red-gold fires of sunrise. Bowie found himself anticipating the moment.

It was a strange sensation. But then he had had a lot of those in the last few hours. He thought of Sandra Rossi and felt first the heady exhilaration of the time they had spent before parting, and then a wholly unexpected sense of loss and despair at when—or if—he would see her again. The joy of what-had-been sat alongside the emptiness like the disorienting chaos of the time vortex in which you felt somehow upside down and right way up simultaneously, as if mind and body were in multiple places at the same time, as you were stretched into a being of ether, everywhere and nowhere all at once. He didn't know what to call it, but the ache inside him was so acute, so powerful and strange, that it felt like the first true sensation he had ever had. It felt . . .

Human.

The word bubbled to the surface of his mind, improbable, baffling, but feeling as clearly and deeply right as Sandra's first kiss had been. But then if this was what it felt like to be human, what had he been before? His world had defined itself against both the insurgents, who were considered subhuman, and the machines, definitely inhuman, through which both sides had waged war. Those two entities were everything the Design had stood against, though Bowie found himself wondering what it was about either that they had particularly despised. They had fought, they said, against threats to their very humanity, and though he had been an agent of that fight Bowie no longer understood what it was they had been defending.

The Awakening had brought the Design, but what version of humanity had come with it? Bowie thought of Gammas and outcasts like Sefton in their camps, laboring for the good of a society they would never be a part of, and of the Alphas, cool-headed and separate, comfortable and . . . And what? What did they feel? Distaste, for sure, particularly for the Gammas and whatever else they did not value or saw as inferior. Patriotism, of a sort, mostly judgmental: a way of marking out who was in and who was not, who was acceptable and who was not, what they valued and what they did not. They felt anger too. Also, resentment. Jealousy. But, joy?

No.

They felt amusement and some kinds of satisfaction, but in Bowie's experience both were tainted by an underlying meanness.

Desire? Appetite? The blissful elation of hearing a moving piece of music, eating a wonderful meal, or feeling the stirrings of sex?

No.

There was art in the Design, but it was ideological. Anything else was decadent, even something as innocuous as his guarded still life photos which were all about light and texture. There was music in the Design, but it was mathematical. Elegant in its way, but designed to demonstrate control, to manifest the superiority of the player, the artist, even the audience. It was not emotional. It did not dip into pain or grief, it did not swell in the blood or sing in rapturous delight. It was music such as might be laid out with a calculator and a slide rule: measured, predictable, soulless.

Soulless.

The word turned over and over in Bowie's mind as he rode on through the desert's pink dawn, and he wondered why he had never thought it before. Had Sefton? Probably. All those times that Sefton had tried to remind Bowie of what it meant to taste, to feel, to really be alive, Bowie had shut him down, hiding behind the walls that the Design had built to separate him from such things. On the heels of these thoughts came the last absence, the final thing the Design was set on destroying, which he had not understood until now.

Love.

The coldness of the Alphas, their dispassionate separateness even from each other, was their highest virtue. They did not invest in others as they did in the abstractions of their world. They had no families. They were raised in isolation, lived their lives unencumbered by the personal ties of friendship, of camaraderie, and they did not love. Indeed, they defined the values of their world against it. Love was softness, weakness, a mark of something base and un-evolved. Love could not exist within the Design.

And yet here was Bowie, riding it across the vast emptiness of the New Mexican landscape as surely as he was riding the bike.

He had driven Rossi down the coast road to the railway station in Portland, from there she could go wherever she wanted. Along the way she had nestled against his back, her hands around him as they had been several times before, but feeling different now, a difference he basked in like the warmth of a fire. It reminded him vaguely of something long forgotten, but he couldn't place it, and despite the frenzied intimacy they had shared in the Maine woods, what he felt now was something calmer and more secure. It was as if he had spent his life at sea, battling the great gray waves he had glimpsed from the shores of Naushon and the rocky outcrops of the Maine coast, but was now guided by the reliable pulsing glow of a lighthouse. Yes, he thought, it was like coming into port after a long voyage, looking ahead to warmth and good food, a fire in the hearth, and the ground solid and unmoving beneath his feet.

For someone who had never been to sea, it was a curious thought, but it felt right, as did the strangeness of the allusion. Nothing from his own world, from his true home, seemed to fit.

He had given her money and kissed her goodbye, and promised to see her again in Dallas, though that was years away, at least for her. He had plans of his own but their precise shape was still uncertain. Watching her walk into the station, into the next stage of her life, without him, had left him with an overwhelming sense of emptiness which cut as sharp and deep as a sword. The power of it was staggering. It was hard to remember that mere days before he would have found such feelings unimaginable, incomprehensible, even contemptible.

Now, for all the hurt, he reveled silently in what he felt. And he grasped just how dangerous it would be to the Design for the people of his world to experience this for themselves.

As if to punctuate the thought, Bowie's wing mirrors flashed blue-white as a time vortex opened up behind him. And then another. And another. Two more. Then a sixth. Each one brought a time rider. They materialized in an orderly line front to back, led by the woman in the red helmet. He was out in the open on a deserted road, with nowhere to go but onward, and massively outgunned. As they adjusted their positions to fill the road, Bowie leaned hard on the throttle in an attempt to put some distance between himself and his pursuers.

It wasn't enough, he realized, as the controls on his handlebar display flashed a message he had never seen before:

CORE DATA SYNCING . . .

Somehow the bikes behind him were trying to do what no computers had been permitted to do since the Great Conflagration: they were attempting to create a network. Which meant what? That his pursuers would be able to take control of his bike, turn off the engine, drive him off the road?

"No, no, no," said Bowie, feeling the panic rising in him in ways matching the escalating whine of his accelerating bike. He risked another look down and pushed at a couple of keys whose purpose he hadn't deduced.

The controls prompted:

DISCONTINUE CORE SYNC?

"Hell yes," said Bowie, repeating his stab of the relevant key. For a second nothing happened, then the message vanished and was replaced by something new:

CORE SYNC DISCONTINUED. CONNECTION LOST.

And then, just as he was breathing out a sigh of relief, a new possibility:

GEO-TEMPORAL COORDINATE LIBRARY UPDATED.

Before he could fathom what that suggested, he saw the first flash of their weapons behind him. Their opening volley exploded around him, but he did not shoot back or even swerve to make himself harder to hit. Instead, he steeled himself, fixed his eyes on the road ahead and pushed his bike even harder. The pitch of the engine wound up and he sped forward like one of the shots heading his way. He leaned low over the headlight, flattening his body, the morning air tearing through his hair.

Faster.

He gritted his teeth, feeling the flesh of his cheeks ripple as he accelerated, pushing the bike farther and harder with each yard. He could not fight six of them. He could not dodge and weave without losing speed. But he could outrace them. Or so he hoped.

He hit the bike's booster and felt its explosive leap forward.

This motorcycle had become part of him now. What had first felt foreign, when he had considered it Washington's bike, was now his. He knew the feel of every ridge and rivet. He knew its sounds, felt its moods. It was only a machine, but it felt animal to him, always had, and he'd developed an affinity for it. That would have once been shameful to him, something he would have buried deep and denied because it made him less than his handlers, but now he embraced it, relished it.

"Run," he whispered to the bike. "Show them what you can do."

He felt the impossible rapture of the machine as it accelerated into a long sweeping curve, creeping ever closer to its maximum speed.

He saw the truck coming toward him as he came out of the bend, but he adjusted fractionally, and it streaked past. Even over the roar of his engine he heard the impact as one of the riders behind him met the truck head on. He caught the moment the rider was thrown like he had been upended by a furious bull.

Five left. They were matching his speed and there was still nowhere for him to go.

Unless . . .

He glanced down again. The readout was still in place:

GEO-TEMPORAL COORDINATE LIBRARY UPDATED.

He had exhausted Washington's trip database. But if the computer had new data on places and periods his pursuers had visited before . . . He could indeed race them, and not just in space. He could race them through time.

He pushed a button, pulling up a list: coordinates by longitude, latitude, date and time.

He chose one at random.

The vortex streamed into being ahead of him and as he shot through it, the world went white.

It stayed so, though it was night now, and Bowie gasped as the frigid air hit him in the face, driving the breath from his body. He was streaking along an empty highway several lanes wide which ran along a frozen riverbank flanked with fir trees weighed down by snow. He checked his mirrors as the vortex folded back in on itself and showed only the road behind him through the frosted woods.

He remembered to breathe, then laughed and let the bike slow a fraction. The road surface was laminated with blue-white ice sheets that sparkled under a full and ghostly moon. He turned in the saddle and caught a curious play of green iridescence rippling in the sky to his left. It shifted like waves on a seashore, as the energy moved from emerald to ultramarine and a profound, loaded purple. It was mesmerizing.

The Northern Lights, he thought. He had never seen them before. He wondered what year he was in, but before he could look down, his mirrors flashed.

The vortex behind him was open again. They were coming.

Sefton checked the number of each security door as they passed through the great fortified laboratory, Merrick leading the way at gunpoint. The commandant and techs were herded behind them in stiff silence, guarded by the insurgents, one of whom towed the wheeled storage case. Though the facility was huge, it had been largely evacuated when the fighting got close, and the skeleton staff remaining had been confined to a central operations room where they monitored the data stream from hundreds of incubation units. Merrick seemed resigned to doing as he was told, but Sefton didn't trust him, so he double-checked their route stage by stage against the data they had obtained in the weeks leading up to their attack. One of his team was wearing a headset with a camera. Their discovery would be documented and shared with the world. All those years of careful social engineering—the biological structure on which the Design was based—segregation and slavery, built molecule by molecule . . . Today he would show it to the world, and with that core corruption exposed, the Design's great tower would collapse as surely as if they had detonated a thousand bombs.

"Security door 6-B," Merrick announced at last. "But I can't open it. We are locked down and even my security code can't override it. I don't know what you thought you were going to find but—"

"Out of my way," said Sefton, pushing past him to the heavily shielded metal portal. On the wall to the right were access panels and something that could have been a retinal scanner, but he knew they weren't getting in that way. "I don't need your keys. I have this."

He nodded to the team with the wheeled case which they had already laid flat by the door. Merrick watched as they opened the latch, revealing another piece of equipment they should not have been able to access.

"A thermal lance," said Sefton. "It will take a minute, but we're going through."

Merrick blanched but then half turned toward a distant popping noise. It was muffled and seemed to reverberate through the floor as if originating on a lower level, but Sefton recognized it as weapons' fire.

"Better hurry," said Merrick, and something of his cool amusement was back. "I don't think you have much time."

CHAPTER TWENTY-THREE

Bowie mashed the display screen so clumsily that he wasn't sure which location he hit. Not that it mattered. He was still doing something close to two hundred miles an hour, as were the five time agents chasing him.

Again the vortex, the seething, weightless chaos and confusion of the transition and then . . .

A broad, long and flat avenue, imposing skyscrapers on the right, trees on the left and beyond them a vast expanse of water: the ocean or the largest lake Bowie had ever seen. It felt like early morning, the light low and slanted on the windows of the shops and offices, but the streetlights were still on and they, like the buildings, had a warm, analog glow. Bowie took in the few rickety cars with their thin, spoked wheels trundling along the street as he zipped by and knew he had fallen farther into the past. At one corner shop where someone paused to gape at him, he saw a horse-drawn cart. There were people too, shabbily, almost uniformly dressed:

workers en route to factories, perhaps. They turned to point and stare at Bowie, alarmed at how clearly he did not belong. He immediately punched another button.

The vortex spiraled around him and he appeared on a long, thin road. He slammed his brakes hard as he processed the stagnant line of ancient vehicles: a convoy of primitive tanks, horse-drawn artillery pieces, and soldiers bundled up against the cold. It was day, and the land was trenched mud, speckled with the remains of trees whose tops had been blasted away. Bowie slowed further, braking hard to avoid what might have been an ambulance, focused on staying out of the pond-like ruts and away from the antique military hardware which lumbered along at something close to walking pace.

As the bike skidded and lurched to a halt, his mind raced. He had reached the earliest limits of the twentieth century and further jumps would take him deeper into the past where he would be even more conspicuous, even further out of his element. He had to get back to New Mexico in 1947, but that meant going forward in time, something the bike wouldn't let him do unless he first returned to 2157.

He cursed, exploring every colorful phrase he had learned from Rossi, until a dirty and wounded soldier began barking at him in a language he didn't understand. Bowie held up his hands and murmured apologies in English, which only deepened the consternation on the officer's face. He barked an order, and a pair of men in rain ponchos and spiked helmets began unshouldering their heavy-looking rifles.

Bowie revved the engine and sped forward, but even as he did so he felt, rather than saw, the electric surge of the vortex opening behind him. He glanced over his shoulder and saw the five time riders appearing in silhouette, coming right for him.

The soldiers responded with panic, raising their weapons and shooting wildly. One of the tanks began to turn its little riveted, trash can of a turret as its machine gun began to flash fire and fury. The time riders returned fire, streaks of purple laser laying cover for a micro missile that found one of the tanks and blew it to fragments.

Bowie didn't have time to bring the bike up to speed. He hit the boosters and held on for dear life as the bike bolted from a near standstill. Pulses of laser fire sliced through the smoke of the battle around him. Bowie steered toward the only opening he saw, shooting the gap between two tanks and missing them by inches.

The trailing time rider was not as fortunate, his bike exploding in a ball of fire as it slammed into one of the tanks. Bowie focused on the space ahead of him and triggered another vortex.

Once more the coordinates were chosen at random, but he knew he was barreling back through time, moving in the exact opposite direction from where he needed to be.

He glanced at the bike's display as soon as his wheels touched down, but the numbers meant nothing to him. His pursuers had lost at least one more of their team, but if more of them had fallen to the bewildered soldiers, he had no way of knowing. He had to keep moving.

But where and when he was, he couldn't say.

It was high noon over a desert plain pocked with boulders and the kinds of wizened shrubs that survived even the harshest of weather conditions. A dust cloud, tightly formed but vast, moved off to his right, and as he watched he saw animals, a great herd of heavy, cow-like beasts with massive shoulders and curled horns. Pursuing them were bare chested men on horses armed with bows and spears . . .

Bam! Another vortex behind him and there they were, four riders still on his tail.

Bowie was stumbling backward through time, racing beyond all he had ever thought was civilization.

He reached to hit another button, then hesitated. Behind him, he heard the blast of a weapon and flinched as an energy bolt shot past his shoulder and turned a rocky crag to dust and powder.

Think . . .

The farther back in time he went, the harder it would be to find anything like a viable road. Risk was one thing, the increasing probability of materializing at a couple of hundred miles an hour in a landscape of boulders and trees was something entirely different. And even if he survived the transition he was straying farther and farther from where he needed to be. The only way out of the cycle was to return to his own time. Again. This time they would be waiting for him. It would be suicide.

Maybe not. Maybe they won't anticipate such a ludicrous strategy . . .

He could do as he had before, when he had returned for his meeting with Sefton with a new sense of what was going on and what they could do about it. He had returned to the future, but bounced off his starting point before the professor and his staff could figure out what was going on, skipping back and away to the labor camp where his brother worked. Perhaps he could do something like that again, punch in a new set of temporal coordinates before he came to rest at the launch site.

It was riskier this time. They had seen him do it before. Who knew what counter measures they may have employed to trap him if he tried it again . . .

Only one way to find out, he thought.

His hand reached for the home button and hovered above it while he scanned the data list which had populated from the incomplete sync with his pursuers. He chose, then hit the home button.

The vortex was different this time, folding out around him rather than appearing as a portal in front of him, but even as it started to collapse and the reality of 2157 flickered into place, he hit another set of coordinates.

The universe seemed to stutter. For a moment he was nowhere and everywhere at once, and then the world resolved, a new portal opened, and Bowie shot through it into a world he recognized only too well.

There were tanks here too, but there was no one operating them. He took in the shattered wastes of the Ohio battlefields, the scattering of ruined buildings, and the burned out husks of the machines. He was back in the dark days of the Great Conflagration, which meant . . .

He had leaped back to 2157 but spun off to a point no more than a decade or so before. He had survived the return to his own time and—more to the point—now had the entirety of history in front of him, including a direct route back to 1947.

He threw his head back and crowed with triumphal delight. He had found a way. He had beaten the system . . .

He saw the flash of the vortex behind him in his mirrors. They were still on his tail. His elation vanished like the closing time portal, which was all light and fury and then gone as if it had never been.

They have the same location data that you do, he thought. *They know where you are going.*

Which meant he had to deviate from the geo-temporal list he had downloaded, input new coordinates which would be harder to track.

Too risky, he thought, as he shot past the burned out husk of an armored personnel carrier. Any deviation from the list introduced too many variables to be safe. He might appear inside a newly constructed building or in a diverted river.

So limit the deviation. Nudge the coordinates by a few minutes. Same location, just a fractionally different moment.

A volley of weapons fire from behind shot overhead. One of the battle-ruined hulks to his right burst like a firework, showering metal down around him.

Gotta get out of here . . .

He picked a set of coordinates, then thumbed the dial on the time index, moving it one, then two, then three seconds from the designated spot. What difference that would make, he couldn't say. It could set him free or it could cost him everything.

He checked his mirror and saw the flash and smoke plume of a rocket heading for him. The bright red spot on its nose said it was laser sighted.

He hit the temporal launch button and the vortex opened in front of him. With the missile closing on his tail, he shot through the portal, his breath held.

He appeared on a crowded nocturnal highway in early twenty-first-century New York City, hitting the asphalt perfectly, but right in front of a yellow cab which blared its horn. He fought to decelerate, while weaving around an endless stream of cars and trucks, still doing well over a hundred miles an hour. Buildings flicked by, crowded with neon, the towers of glass and stone going by too fast to process.

He braked harder and his rear tire skidded and slid so that his nose was suddenly full of the bitter smell of burned rubber. More horns sounded.

"The fuck did you come from?" someone roared.

He leaned and the bike arced around a postal delivery van, slipping along the lane divider so that startled drivers swerved and cursed.

He checked his six. No pursuers. The risk had paid off, but it had been tight. He took a breath and slowed some more, trying to match his speed to the traffic around him, though it felt unbearably slow after blasting through space and time.

His stomach dropped as a series of vortices flashed sequentially behind him—farther back, because of the time delay—but still there all the same. He counted all four and knew that their arrival would be safer than his had been since they were using the preset coordinates. He cursed himself for having slowed down so much.

He assessed the highway and sped up, nipping across one lane, then another, hitting the hard shoulder and accelerating even as he reached for the temporal coordinates. He made a selection, adjusted it by five seconds this time, and sped up. A pair of cars was parked in front of him. One of them had strobing blue lights on top.

Police.

No matter. He shot past it like a javelin, measuring the gap between the parked cars and the traffic to the right perfectly. As he swerved back onto the shoulder, he hit the boosters and reached for the vortex control.

Bam!

There was the disorienting brilliance of the portal, then the fight to soak up the details of his location—a long multi-lane suspension bridge in the dim light of dawn in some unfamiliar nation, the broad water below him black and glinting. Japan, according to the readout. Over on his left the ornamental tower of some shrine or temple rose up from a tiny island . . .

Bam!

A logging route through dense rain forest, the air thick, the bike bouncing savagely on the rutted ground, Bowie using all his strength to keep it upright, his headlamp flashing on the tree trunks as he threaded through . . .

Bam!

A bright mountain ridge, all stony angles, steep slopes and long drops. The stretch he landed on was the only straight section, and he had to slow to almost nothing to navigate the first hairpin turn.

Bam!

The paved, deserted top of a fortified wall, dotted with towers so old that Bowie had to check that he hadn't gone back too far in time. He slowed, checking his mirrors but he had, at the very least, bought himself a minute or two without his pursuers. By now they would know what he was doing and would take chances of their own to ensure he didn't get too far ahead of them. Bowie made another adjustment to the coordinates and prepared to make two consecutive jumps. The second would take him back to the deserts of New Mexico in 1947. The first was riskier . . .

Bam!

Rush hour in Milan, 1987. His front wheel bucked in a pothole and Bowie felt the whole bike kick out from under him. As if in slow motion he saw the massive wheels of the trash truck beside him as the time cycle became suddenly weightless, even as he noted the pop of other vortices opening around him. He leaned, gripped the handlebars with all his might, and as gravity seemed to return, fought to hold on as the bike stuttered and pulled out from under the truck. He felt the wind of it, and then he was shooting past, dodging and weaving.

There was the clang of a collision behind him and in his mirror he saw one of his pursuers thrown clear as his bike hit the truck.

He didn't slow down, streaking through the traffic as he opened the portal to his final destination.

Bam!

New Mexico, the bright, impossibly wide, blue sky, the orange and pink of the desert all around. Nothing else. The road was empty.

Now it would just be him and however many of them had survived. He saw the flare of the vortices opening behind him. One. Two, then, a second later, a third.

More than he had hoped.

He increased his speed. The bikes behind him had lost their tight formation, and as Bowie pushed his machine to the limits of its capacity, he felt the uncertainty of all but the red-helmeted leader. She matched him yard for yard, even as the others wavered, unwilling to risk the kinds of speed he was reaching.

Two hundred and ten miles an hour, now, and rising. It took all his focus to assess the road ahead. A single rock no bigger than his fist could spell disaster.

There was no cover in this flat strap of land, and Bowie felt like he could see for miles. And be seen. With no bends, no hills, no buildings or trees, speed was his only friend.

Faster and faster he went, feeling the grit of the road pock his face like splinters of glass. He had his eyes as close to shut as he dared, but they streamed with tears as they had back in the barn. Even as the morning bloomed pale around him he felt like he was rocketing through a tunnel, that he could see nothing beyond the road ahead, and that even the most momentary shift in his concentration would kill him as surely as an oncoming truck.

He checked his mirrors. One of the three riders was well back, but the other two were still with him, and the woman in the red helmet had closed the gap by some fifty yards. Even in that momentary glimpse, he saw the way she rode, low and streamlined, guiding the bike with feather-like adjustments which kept her streaking after him with mathematical precision. As the road curved slightly she leaned just a fraction, hugging the inside of the bend so that she lost not so much as an inch.

Instinct or training?

Either way, she was good, which was bad, and determined—a believer—which was worse.

He heard a dull thud and caught a glimpse of a tight little cloud of smoke from the third bike, realizing with horror what had caused the time rider to lag behind only as something arced overhead and exploded.

Grenade launcher.

Bowie swerved wildly, losing both stability and momentum. He fought to keep the bike upright as the shell burst overhead. For the merest fraction of a second the sky went blindingly white. Then came the noise, the smoke, the shrapnel.

The bike pulled hard to the right, onto the rough shoulder. Bowie leaned to the left, using all his strength to yank it back onto the road, but he overcorrected, so that it crossed both lanes, and went over the opposite shoulder, hitting dirt and rock. It slid, and he had no choice but to brake firmly or risk totally losing control.

The motorcycle, which had been sleek and dolphin-like moments before—a creature of speed and elegance—became a lumbering, unwieldy monstrosity—a half-blind rhino or some archaic steam-driven locomotive, and in that agonizing moment of slowness, Bowie turned to see the other riders bearing down on him.

Speed alone had failed him, so he abandoned it. He rolled from the saddle, drawing his revolver. There was a boulder ten yards from where the bike had come to a groaning, wheel-juddering halt, almost as tall as him on one edge, and looking like a broken tooth rising out of the desert floor. He made a dash for it, his ears full of the sound of the other bikes. He flung himself into the rock's meager shadow and turned to find one of the bikes—the one with the agent still dressed as a cop—reach the edge of the road and keep racing toward him at full speed. It dipped slightly and then soared as it rose up out of a depression. Bowie jerked back behind the boulder that shuddered him from the impact of the airborne bike, which tumbled overhead before crunching to the ground, its mangled rider pinned beneath as it slid hard under its own terrible weight and momentum.

The other two had taken a less direct approach. He could hear that their bikes had slowed to an idling purr, but without sticking his head out from behind the boulder, he couldn't be sure their riders were still on them. He released the strap on the automatic holstered to his hip. The revolver's six shots weren't going to do it this time.

He was thinking what to do and listening fiercely, when he caught the distinctive thunk of another grenade being chambered. He huddled as low and tight as he could, squeezing his eyes shut and covering one ear with his left hand. Even so the impact of the grenade on the rock blew him backward in a chaos of light, stone fragments, and a roar of sound so disorienting that for a moment he didn't know which way was up.

He sprawled back, stunned, and in his mind he saw the ruins of an ancient convenience store and a robotank pushing its implacable way through the walls, its gun barrel swinging right and left like a search light, looking for him.

But this time he had no mine to wedge under the turret overhang. He had two handguns. He readied them both and—his ears still ringing and his vision blurred—he did the one thing they would not expect.

He came out shooting.

In fact he rolled out, landing prone on his stomach, sighting and firing both guns in one motion. He could see little beyond the bright red helmet so he aimed there first, just as she was snapping her assault rifle around to find him. He hit her twice and she collapsed. Then he sprang upright, catching the other rider as he switched between the heavy barreled grenade launcher and his machine pistol. The agent went down as his weapon spat bullets aimlessly into the sky, and then it was quiet.

Bowie sank onto his butt, breathing hard and wiping the sweat and blood from his face as he waited for his hearing to return to normal. He had no idea how many shots he had fired and had to check both weapons. The revolver was empty. He had probably snapped through several empty chambers obliviously. He had only two rounds left in the automatic.

But his pursuers were dead.

He took the red helmet off the blond woman, thinking that though he couldn't use its interface, at least it would keep the dust and grit out of his eyes . . .

And then she lunged for him, a triangular knuckle blade sweeping for his jugular. He swatted the edge aside but was too taken aback to disarm her.

Body armor, he remembered, too late.

He had her knife arm in his left hand, wrestling for control of the blade. She jabbed her left hand at his throat, but he was just alert enough to turn the worst of the hit, and then he had that hand too, and she was pinned with one arm across her body. She had a bullet wound in her right shoulder, and as he pressed her arm down across the soft flesh below her chin, he realized that at least one of his bullets had hit her somewhere vital, and that this last-ditch attack was the final act of a dying woman. Strength was ebbing out of her like blood.

"How many more of you are there?" Bowie demanded, releasing the pressure on her throat.

She blinked, and the ineffectual rage in her eyes became something else, something like amusement.

"Enough," she said in a low voice. When she spoke he saw there was blood in her mouth.

"How many?"

She smiled then, even as a rivulet of the blood ran from the corner of her mouth and down her right cheek.

"Forty-nine," she said.

He gaped at her and she laughed, a dark, liquid chuckle which brought up more blood.

"You stink of them," she managed. "The Deltas. You are a disgrace to . . ."

And then the light went out of her cold eyes and she became still. As close to her as he was, he felt the moment her heart and breath stopped, and a strange opaque cast came over her skin.

Forty-nine?

That wasn't good, though he didn't believe the Alphas could furnish that many agents and bikes. She had been amused by the statement, as if she was making a joke, a smug, confident joke at his expense. But why forty-nine?

He didn't know. She had said he stank of the "Deltas." One step below the loathed Gammas. Did she mean the humans of this period, or people like him and Sefton, men and women born outside the Design's precious incubation labs?

Same difference.

He considered her face. Even in death it was hard, but Bowie felt a ripple of something uneasily close to pity. She had given him no choice, but in a way she was almost as much a victim as he was.

No, he decided. She had chosen this. If she was a victim, she was a willing one.

A believer, he thought again.

But a believer in what exactly? The agents who had come after him were not the robotanks he had fought in the Great Conflagration, and not just because they were muscle and bone instead of motors and steel. They had minds, hearts, even if—according to his new way of thinking—they did not have souls. They were people as he was, or at least as he had been. But they had forgotten how to be human. Or they had been forced to forget it. They had become the thing they had once fought against: automatons, electro-chemical machines driven by a purpose that was not their own, a mission they did not understand, driven by scorn and contempt.

"I'll beat you all," he said aloud to the desert. It was a decision, and a promise.

The light from the thermal lance was blinding. The operator was wearing smoked goggles but everyone else had half turned away as soon as it began to slice into the reinforced steel of the security door. Smoking, liquid metal was pooling on the floor, filling Sefton's nose with its hot and acrid tang. But it was slow going, and the sound of weapons fire was getting closer. Sefton sensed it as much in Merrick's recovering composure as in the noise itself.

"Cover the hallway," he ordered one of his men. "Make sure they know who we have. We need more time."

He doubted that their hostages would provide the bargaining chip they needed. Sefton knew the Design. They would sacrifice their own rather than risk their deepest secrets being revealed. His men were almost through the security door, but the vault itself would probably be as close to impenetrable as possible. He had no intel on the vault. They knew it was in there, but anything more than that was rumor and speculation.

Did Merrick know what was in VAT-001? Sefton couldn't say for sure.

There was a loud bang from somewhere back along the hall, probably the stairwell. A grenade. One of the techs began to weep. Sefton exchanged a glance with Greta.

"Cover the stairs," he said. "Set your explosives on the supporting pillars."

"You would dare to destroy this, the cornerstone of the Design!" snapped the commandant with furious indignation. "Animals!"

Sefton ignored her.

"That's your top priority," he said to Greta. "You understand what I'm saying?"

His deputy held his gaze, then nodded.

"And you," Sefton said to one of his men as he pointed at the scared techs, "get them out of here."

Doubt flashed through the soldier's face.

"They won't do us any good," Sefton said, "and we don't have the personnel to guard them. Take her, too," he said, indicating the commandant.

She stared at him, surprised that a creature like him could be . . . what? Merciful? Pragmatic? She assumed both were beyond him. The thought did not soften her features and she looked like she wanted to spit in his face before being marched away.

That left only Merrick. He exchanged a look with the commandant as she left, then turned back to Sefton.

"You can't possibly escape, you know," he said conversationally. "Stop now and I may be able to limit the scale of your punishment."

Sefton gave a snort of amused derision and turned his attention back to the security door as the cut was completed, and the team kicked the panel free. It clanged to the floor, its edges still smoking.

Sefton was first through the hole. The chamber beyond was small, and though its walls were lined with controls and displays, it contained only one thing, a metal container the size of a sarcophagus, upright and featureless, save for a transparent panel at roughly head height. Sefton approached it and peered in, but the vat was full of a milky liquid and he could not make out the face of whoever was entombed within.

The Originator.

As he looked, the fluid seemed to swirl and agitate as if stirred by some eddy, though what caused it he couldn't see.

He also couldn't see any conventional locks, though the casing was clearly hinged and designed to open.

"Get the lance on these joints," he ordered, but even as he did so he heard a burst of energy blasts and a cry.

"I think," said Merrick, "that you are out of time."

CHAPTER TWENTY-FOUR

Bowie dragged the bikes and the bodies of their riders into a shallow gully which was invisible from the road, pausing for breath as cars and trucks went by, though they were few and far between. He didn't take the time to bury the corpses, but he went through their store of weapons and other equipment, and took what he thought he could use, including the red helmet. He hesitated before he put it on, uncomfortable with the way it might savor of its previous rider, the woman he had killed. Rossi had smelled faintly of cigarette smoke, floral soap and a mildly spiced perfume, and—after New Orleans—of the slight, earthy tang of sweat and—after Maine—sex. He forced the helmet on warily—it was snugger than he'd like—but it smelled only of some kind of cleaning agent, as if the time rider had wiped it down before taking her final ride. Even so, he didn't like wearing it and decided to switch it with the one worn by the cop who he had never really seen. He took it off him, careful not to look too closely at the dead man's face.

Just another machine, he thought, as he returned to his vehicle.

Bowie wasn't sure what he was doing in New Mexico, but he could deduce—as he had before—that the agent who called himself Washington—and, apparently, Vonnie Beck—had entered the period at one spot and left from another. The entry point was a matter of safety, both in terms of his not being seen and his physical health: the almost empty desert highway had been well chosen for that purpose. But he had left from what looked to be an even more remote location some thirty miles to the northwest. That gave Bowie a target. But was it the right one? He checked the bike's chronometer. July 9, 1947. What had Washington been doing here? Mixing with what Rossi had called the New England blue bloods in Maine and Massachusetts had made a kind of sense. These were people who could shape their society from within, who could alter the future with promises and payments which changed laws and policies. It seemed unlikely that he would find such people out here in the barren wilds of the west.

Bowie felt more at home in the desert than in any of the places he had been since coming to this century. Its empty, sun-bleached expanse was closer to the planet as he knew it, especially to the solar farms where Sefton worked. But there was still life here, stark and rugged though it was. He saw bursts of color in the shrunken bushes which dotted the landscape, little points of pink and orange and yellow, bright as fire in the morning light. Great hawks and vultures soared overhead and once he saw a dog-like creature padding carelessly along the edge of the road. A wolf?

Coyote, he thought, though he wasn't sure where the word came from. Some ancient picture book he had seen as a child, perhaps, when such animals were no more than the exotic denizens of a dead past. It half turned to watch him ride past, and for the briefest of moments he met its yellow, feral eyes.

A half hour later he stopped for fuel, not because he needed it, but because it was the only gas station he had seen since arriving and he thought he should top up the tank to be safe. He went into the ramshackle store to pay, remembering how strange it had been to do this when he first arrived in Texas, how much his sense of the world and himself had shifted since, and found an elderly man stocking shelves. He was as tall and as brown as Bowie, and his face had striking, strong lines as if carved from the desert buttes, and an aquiline nose. He gave Bowie a nod but kept on with his work. There was a radio playing by the register, and Bowie found himself listening, first to the music then, after a series of beeps, to what appeared to be some kind of news bulletin.

"The Army has announced that a flying disk has been found and is now in their possession," said the radio. Bowie stopped what he was doing and turned to it. "Army officers say that the disk, found sometime last week, has been inspected at Roswell, New Mexico, and sent to Wright Field, Ohio, for further inspection."

Bowie found the gas station proprietor watching him.

"That's here," Bowie said.

"So they say," said the other man, his tone unreadable. "Read all about it right here." He nodded at a stack of newspapers in a wire rack. Bowie picked one up. The header identified the paper as the *Roswell Daily Record*. It was dated the previous day, and the front-page story was titled:

RAAF CAPTURES FLYING SAUCER
ON RANCH IN ROSWELL REGION

"Five cents," said the tall man, considering Bowie's cut and battered face frankly. "Plus the gas."

"You know anything about this?" Bowie asked as he got his money out.

"No," said the man, "but we see a lot of strange things in the sky out here."

"That right?" Bowie replied, trying to lead the man into further confidences.

"It's what I said, ain't it?" the other replied, taking the money and returning to his work. "You ride safe now."

"When did this happen?" said Bowie, tapping the paper. "The object, spaceship or whatever. When did it actually come down?"

"A week ago, maybe two," said the stone-faced man.

So why, Bowie thought, *did Washington arrive only now?*

Maybe his arrival here was nothing to do with the alleged crash.

Or maybe it was specifically about the aftermath?

"You know where this ranch is? Where this . . ." Bowie checked the paper, "Mack Brazel lives?"

The big man got up, turned slowly, and with the deliberation of a man who wastes neither words nor actions, he approached Bowie until he stood no more than twelve inches in front of him.

"Funny," he said, mirthlessly. "You don't look like a government man."

"Government?" said Bowie, feeling suddenly uncomfortable.

"Fed. Air Force. Cops of assorted flavors. They all come through here. But you don't look like any of them. Or a reporter. So what are you, mister, and why are you taking up my time asking about things which don't concern you?"

The frigid politeness didn't bother to conceal the threat of violence, and Bowie found himself quickly assessing how hard it would be to put the stone-faced man down if he had no other choice. He could do it, he concluded, but it wouldn't be easy.

He raised his hands in mock surrender and smiled.

"Just curious," he said. "No offense intended."

Stone Face said nothing but neither did he relax nor step away. Bowie was finding his closeness unnerving. A possibility occurred to him.

"Someone else came here recently," he said. "Small man. Pale. Weird hair, or bald if he wasn't wearing his wig. Riding a motorcycle like mine."

"Very like," said Stone Face quietly, his hard eyes fixed unblinking on Bowie's.

"He was . . . rude," said Bowie, trying to recall what Rossi had said about how Washington had conducted himself in the moments before his death. "Condescending."

"I did not beat him," said Stone Face, slowly, musingly, as if recalling an intriguing conundrum. "But I considered it."

"I'm sure you did."

"I'm not sure I made the right decision."

"For the record, I wouldn't blame you if you had," said Bowie. "In fact, I may do it for you. He's a prick."

Stone Face considered that, then laughed suddenly and took a step back.

"The ranch you're looking for is a ways down the highway. You give yourself a good turn of speed," he observed, "you might catch up with him."

Bowie nodded, relieved that he didn't have to fight the big man.

"Will give it my best shot," he said.

"Ride safe," said the big man. "Gonna be storms later."

He glanced at the sky outside, but Bowie could see nothing that suggested a shift in the weather. He thanked him anyway and headed out, exhilarated to know Washington wasn't far ahead.

Still, flying saucers?

What was that about? He thought of the bizarre séance in Maine with its elite, powerbroker membership and tried to remember what he had learned about the people in it. Arthur Young was involved in military aircraft development, right? Helicopters. Was that a link to unidentified flying objects?

Possibly, he thought, as he kicked the bike into action and turned onto the open road, *but I'll need more evidence to make the link, and that still doesn't connect us back to Kennedy.*

He thought of the emblem of the Design, the hooked line and circles he had seen on David Ferrie's priestly vestments in New Orleans, and on the rug where the mystic Vinod had spoken as M, voice of the nine principles and forces that promised to reshape the world. What had Rossi said about why someone might kill Kennedy? He was mad about space, about going to the moon and maybe about a partnership with the Russians on that front. That was another instance of him being, as some said, "soft on communism," too liberal, too progressive.

He thought about that last word. It suggested a forward movement, a leaving behind of old ideas and prejudices. But *progressive* made it sound inevitable. The opposite was *conservative*, the impulse to conserve a version of old values, to conduct the present according to the terms of the past. Both positions tacitly acknowledge that the natural movement forward in time was a shift away from what people once held to be true and good toward the acceptance of new ideas and people who thought differently. But Bowie had come from the future and he knew the world as it would become. It was not progressive. It was segregated along lines of race and class. Like most people who lived there, particularly those who lived in comfort, power, and security, he had grown used to it, which was unsurprising given how thoroughly the Design had eliminated any kind of historical awareness from its people. He was from the future, he thought, puzzling out the paradox, but the values of his world were of the past, and not Kennedy's liberal version of the past. Where had Bowie's world—the Designed society—come from really?

He rode on, thinking about flying disks and mystic séances and the promise of a president who wanted to build a coalition of Earth powers to get into space, all cut off by a rifle bullet.

Sefton's instincts had been right. Threatening to kill the director had made no difference to the determined advance of the security forces. They had kept coming no matter what his men threw at them, and within two minutes of them breaching the vault, the insurgents had been overwhelmed. In that time they had cut one of the hinges on the great sarcophagus, but they would have to cut three more to pry it open. The strange milky liquid which swirled in the small window never cleared. Sefton had taken over the use of the thermal lance so his men could focus on protecting the stairs, and he had continued to work with total focus, directing the needle-like jet onto the metal hasps, becoming so still and consumed by what he was doing that he didn't even notice the moment that the last of his men were killed or taken.

Merrick shut the lance off, and only then did Sefton turn to face his captors who regarded him the way his ancient progenitors may once have faced a wild boar cornered by the hunt. Even then he turned back to the sarcophagus, threw himself on it, trying to work his fingertips into the seam of the lid as if he could tear it free by brute strength alone . . .

They subdued him with a rain of blows which crumpled him to the floor, and the last thing he remembered was Merrick stooping low, his face a mask of amusement and genuine confusion as he said, "You didn't really think you could beat us, did you?"

It was looking more and more likely that Washington's departure point was at, or very near, Mack Brazel's ranch. So the closer Bowie got, the more alert he became. It was imperative that Washington didn't see him, and there was no way of approaching his target inconspicuously out here: no woodland, darkness, or winding roads. Out here in the desert, Washington could see—and hear—him coming from miles away. He was going to have to hide his bike and walk, and he would also have to hope that he could get the information he needed without getting close enough to give himself away.

After riding as close as he dared, he started to look for the kind of cover where he could hide the bike but still be able to reach it quickly. A mile or so on he saw an abandoned farmhouse with an old silo tower and barn, all half-collapsed timber. He rode the time cycle cautiously down the rutted driveway, threading it through desertscrub and cactus, inhaling wild herbs and the increasingly dry, hot air. The barn looked precarious—tinder-dry boards warped and buckled, great holes in the sagging, crow-haunted roof—but it would, he assumed, stand at least a little longer yet. He left the bike there, the black helmet hooked over its handlebar grip, took as much as he could reasonably carry, and returned to the road, pausing only when a great, heavy-bodied snake gaped at him and rattled its tail.

He picked his footsteps more carefully after that, and it cost him some pace, but at last he reached the perimeter fence of the ranch, which was—he believed—his final destination. He clambered over the wire, noting that fibers clung to it all along its length.

Wool? He wasn't sure. People from this period still used animal hair to make clothing but, like so much of the history of this world, he had been taught nothing about it.

That barbarous past rejected by the Design, banished from their books and classrooms in case it tainted their precious version of the present.

He stayed clear of the road, trying to keep to the shadows provided by the occasional small tree or rock formation, following a shallow ridgeline toward what he hoped would be the main house. A few hundred yards in, he came over a rise made up of what seemed to be huge slabs of stone layered on top of each other and rounded by the elements, and saw both the house and, some hundred and fifty yards away, parked in a level clearing by the long drive, Washington's unmistakable bike. Standing motionless beside it, was the man himself.

He was facing the drive, as if waiting for something. Bowie dropped into a crouch, then lay down on his belly and pulled his scope out from his tactical jacket. He checked the position of the sun to make sure Washington wouldn't be alerted to his presence by any reflection off the lens, and focused. The man was perfectly still, like the snake had been before he disturbed it, as if he was conserving energy.

His posture radiated control, but his face was invisible. He had removed his helmet, and even at this distance the wig looked wrong. Bowie explored another pocket and came up with a sonic sensor, which he snapped onto the side of the lens. He slipped on an earpiece, aimed the scope again, thumbing the adjuster wheel for range, and focused his attention, but there was nothing to hear. He settled down to wait.

The sun got higher and hotter, but for twenty minutes, nothing much happened. A pair of brown skinned ranch hands loading an open-back truck with a coil of fencing wire paused to consider Washington who was so pointedly doing nothing, but he ignored them, and they went about their business. Bowie trained the listening device on them, but he couldn't understand the few words they exchanged. It wasn't just a dialect issue. They were speaking a different language.

Again he cursed his lack of preparation. He couldn't have learned another language in a few weeks, of course, but it annoyed him that no one in the Design had even considered that he wouldn't be able to get by with English alone.

A few minutes later another vehicle arrived, throwing up a long plume of dust as it came down the drive from the road.

The rancher, perhaps.

But as soon as he could see the car properly, Bowie decided that wasn't right. It was wrong for a ranch, too shiny, too much of a city vehicle, long and sleek and trimmed with chrome. It was black as jet and sparkled in the sun, despite the dust cloud, and though Bowie couldn't read the culture of the moment with any great accuracy, he felt sure the car had an air of officialdom about it. It pulled over beside Washington's bike as if according to some prior arrangement. Bowie trained his scope on the car but couldn't see the driver through the sun-spangled window glass. The passenger door opened and without a moment's hesitation or a word of greeting, Washington got in. The car started off again, rolling slowly toward the house, and the two ranch hands gave it a long, curious look.

Bowie got to his feet and began to run, staying below the crest of the ridge so he wouldn't be silhouetted against the sky if anyone looked over. He should have positioned himself closer to the house in the first place. Now there was a chance he might miss whatever Washington had come to do.

He picked up his pace, feeling the heat on his back and thinking about what he would do when he got to the house.

The building was a low, single-story wooden affair with a wraparound porch and a huddle of outbuildings. By the time it came into view, the black car was already parked, and the two men who had been in it were standing at the front door. Washington had shed whatever outer wear he had been wearing on the bike and appeared dressed in a black suit, very much of the period, and identical to that worn by the man next to him. Bowie could only see their backs. He got low and trained his lens on them again, adjusting the sound meter for distance as the front door opened and a heavyset white man, pink with sunburn, opened the door, but in the same instant he winced away from the noise in his earpiece. At first he thought it was another time rider bike, the engine had that same guttural snarl, but as he snatched the scope from his eye he saw the tractor only thirty yards from the house. It was a big, rusting skeletal thing, small wheels at the front, massive wheels with huge, ridged tires at the back, and it was the center of three men's mechanical attention. One was in the saddle, the other two were considering the engine critically, a battered red toolbox at their feet.

Bowie could hear nothing that was being said on the porch, and he saw the rancher—if that was who the white man in the house was—shoot the laborers a look. He seemed to consider telling them to go away, but thought better of it, merely opening the door wider and leading his visitors inside where they could talk undisturbed. And, to Bowie's displeasure, unheard.

He needed to get closer. He put one of his pistols in the waist band of his trousers, then shrugged out of the tactical jacket, and left it where it fell, then rubbed his hands in the dry earth. He smeared his face and shirt with the dirt, then headed down toward the house, still unsure of what he was going to do when he got there. Just before reaching where the sleek black car was parked—hood still ticking as it cooled—he picked up a well-used pickax, hefting it over one shoulder for the look of the thing, though he knew it might prove a serviceable weapon if it came to that. He ambled over to the tractor, watching critically as if he knew what he was doing, though he kept a hand up to his forehead as if shading his eyes.

The rancher was already inside the house, Washington with him. The third man, the one who had driven the car and was wearing a fedora pulled low on his brows, went in last, and as he half turned to close the door behind him, Bowie saw him properly and looked quickly away. He had first seen that heavy, clotted cream face at his private investigations office in New Orleans, the same office from which he had run anti-communist operations and where Bowie had also seen "Bishop" David Ferrie. Then he had seen him again at Ferrie's peculiar mass which had ended in gunfire . . .

It was the ex-FBI man, Guy Bannister.

CHAPTER TWENTY-FIVE

Bannister didn't seem to notice him, but Bowie kept his head down anyway, coming to a loitering halt with his eyes on the tractor, his back to the windows of the house, and his mind on the men inside. He had thought that the only connection between this place, the séance, New Orleans, and the assassination in Dallas, had been Washington, but Bannister provided a new through line. They were all connected.

I have to hear what they are talking about, he thought.

But he also couldn't be seen, not by Washington or Bannister. Neither would know him yet, but recognizing him the next time they saw him would be catastrophic. And now that he thought about it, could he be sure Washington didn't know him already? The time rider might have been briefed by Merrick and the professor, given a list of the other agents who might be sent after him. Either way, Bowie needed to stay invisible.

The noise of the tractor's engine shifted up a few tones, became smoother, and when the men working on it began nodding and smiling with satisfaction, he met their eyes and joined in, though he did not understand the words they said. They showed no sign of surprise that he was there, which was good. Perhaps the ranch was large enough to employ occasional laborers and they did not all know each other. He used the moment of the mechanics' apparent success to walk along the side of the house, still holding the haft of the pick, trying to look busy as he scanned the house for an open window. There was one on the side, but standing there in full view of the tractor crew was bound to get him noticed, so he kept walking around the back and found two more windows with their sashes cracked.

The tractor engine was still running, playing havoc with his listening device, even as he positioned it on the windowsill and aimed it into the house. It couldn't separate the relevant from the irrelevant noise, so he could make out muffled voices, but not what they were saying. They seemed to be in a room at the front of the house. The window he was at looked into an empty bed chamber, starkly furnished in wood. Bowie glanced around, then raised the sash gingerly. It stuck a little, but moved under his touch, and—with a little careful wiggling of the frame—slid up, wide enough for him to fit through. He checked his surroundings again and, leaving the pick propped against the wall, hitched himself up and through.

He moved softly around the bed to the door, which was slightly ajar, and nudged it open a little farther with the back of his hand. Abandoning the listening device entirely, he pocketed the scope and strained to hear.

"Didn't look like that," said a voice, presumably the rancher.

"I think you will find that it did," said another. That was Washington. Bowie recognized the superior tone, the clipped enunciation. It reminded him of Merrick.

"I know what I saw," the rancher replied, surly.

"Seems like you don't," said a third voice: Bannister. Bowie had heard voices like that in New Orleans, the strange mix of sounds that Rossi had said sounded like the Deep South and New York at the same time. "You think a balloon is like what kids buy at the fair, but it ain't necessarily, not when it's specially designed for monitoring the weather. Important matter for a rancher like you, right? The weather? I'd expect you to have more respect for the means used by your government to track it."

"I don't know about that," said the rancher, holding on to his defiance, but just barely. He sounded badgered and overwhelmed.

"Clearly," said Washington. "But what you know doesn't amount to very much now, does it?"

"Let's talk about the symbol you say you saw on the side," said Bannister.

"I already told you," said the rancher. "It was weird. A straight line with kind of a hook and four little circles over the top."

"No," said Bannister. "No, that wasn't it at all."

"You think I'm simple?"

"I think you are misremembering," said Bannister. It might have been conciliatory, but the remark had a jagged edge. "I think what you saw looked like this."

There was a momentary silence as the rancher was presented with something.

"No," said the rancher. "It was nothing like that. And this has words on it. American Meteorological Society. I would have seen that. This is totally different. It was a line and circles. Like, a symbol or something. No words."

"It was the logo of the American Meteorological Society," said Bannister evenly. "You are misremembering. Or maybe you are just lying. To officials of the US government. How do you think that's gonna go for you?"

The rancher's resentment turned into something harder and more certain.

"I'd like you gentlemen to get the hell off my property right now," he said.

"And we will," said Bannister, "once we have assurances from you that you understand your predicament."

"I don't have to talk to you," the rancher replied, though the uncertainty was back in his voice.

"As a representative of the FBI," said Bannister, "I beg to differ."

"The Air Force already came through," said the rancher. "Why do I have to go through all this again?"

"Separate investigations as ordered by the Bureau's director himself," said Bannister. "Would you care to take the matter up with Mr. Hoover?"

There was a leaden silence and Bowie heard the floor creak, as if the rancher was shifting from foot to foot.

"No," he said quietly.

"Well now, he'll be mighty glad to hear that," said Bannister. Bowie could hear the smile in his voice. "And you know what else he'll hear?"

"What's that?"

"Every goddamned word out of your mouth for the next ten years." The smile was gone now. The voice was low and stacked with menace. "So, you get your story straight—the right story, mind, the one you have recalled in light of our little chat today—and you stick to it. Got it?"

"Yes, sir. I got it," said the rancher, quiet now, the fire out.

"And that goes for everyone who works here," said Washington. "Friends. Family. All those brown people working out there for you."

"Most of them don't speak English anyway," said the rancher.

"Then they shouldn't be a problem," Bannister said.

"But remember," Washington cut in, adding his own thinly veiled threat, "your friends. Your family." The words friends and family came out with increasing disdain, as if it were contemptible even to utter them.

"Yes, sir," said the rancher, wary and fearful.

"Then we will be on our way," Bannister concluded. "But remember: every goddamned word."

There was a rumble of footsteps and Bowie used the sound to cover his own retreat, crossing the room and climbing out of the window in a matter of seconds, his heart thudding. He dropped to the ground, checked he had not been seen, and then took the pick and, head bowed, moved back toward the front of the house.

The tractor was still running, but the men working on it were turned toward the porch and, as if in response to some signal, the driver shut it off. Bowie moved around the far side of the machine and, feigning interest in the rear axle, dropped to a crouch, hands on one of the massive wheels. He heard one of the men offer a practiced "No English" and, through the pipes and cylinders of the tractor's mechanisms, saw Bannister wave the men away as Washington smirked into the distance.

"Ignore them," he said. "They aren't even Deltas. I may have to invent a new category. Thetas? Omicrons?"

Washington looked at the laborers as they walked away and grinned.

"Goddamned Mexicans are everywhere round here," Bannister muttered. "Blacks and Indians too. I swear, we would have been better joining forces with Hitler against the commies. Now we have this shit to deal with."

"Such things will be resolved," said Washington, serenely unconcerned. "In time." He added those last words with another smirk, as if laughing at a private joke.

"First Maury Island, now this," said Bannister. "I hope you people know what you're doing."

"I would have thought that was self-evident," said Washington, then checked his watch. "I must go," he said. "But we will meet again."

"You bet," said Bannister, extending his hand.

Washington did not shake it. He looked at it for a moment, smiled his private smile, and turned to the car.

"A ride to my vehicle, if you please," he said.

"I thought you said it smelled in there."

"It does, but I would rather endure that than walk around like some kind of ape."

Bowie watched Bannister shrug, then spit in the dust. The two men were allies, but they did not like each other. The FBI man looked up at a wall of approaching storm clouds.

"You're gonna get rained on," he said, clearly pleased by the idea.

"Only for a moment," said Washington.

As they got into the car and drove away, Bowie realized that the rancher was watching them from the porch. The man stood there, humbled and uncertain, until the sound of Washington's bike firing up reached him, then he turned to go back inside, closing the door behind him.

Bowie stood up, forcing himself to walk slowly, casually, the pick still over his shoulder until he reached the edge of the drive, then cut up and right toward the ridge. The sky had darkened just as the big man at the gas station had said it would, great purple clouds rolling in like something solid, pushing the light away. It was a massive storm front moving fast, and—now that Bowie looked up and studied it—flickering with pockets of lightning trailed by long rumbles of thunder. He was still in sight of the house when the first rain drops came.

He collected the tactical jacket from where he had left it and cut across the fields, climbing over the barbed-wire fence, and making for the abandoned homestead where he had left the bike, the conversation he had overheard turning around and around in his head.

Weather balloons?

He needed Rossi to translate.

The rain was coming down hard now, the pocked ground collecting pools of it faster than he would have thought possible. The ridge ran with rivulets of water and the thunder shifted from distant drum rolls to great deafening barks so loud that he winced away from them. The lightning which rippled the clouds now forked the air, driving to the ground in ragged, stabbing lines of blue-white power. Bowie looked around for shelter, but there was nothing. He would have to wait until he got to the derelict farmhouse before he could get out of the downpour and, already soaked, he kicked himself again for not parking closer to the ranch.

He walked through the rain for ten more minutes before he caught a whiff of smoke on the damp wind. It was blowing directly in his rain-streaked face which meant . . .

It's coming from the farmhouse!

He paused at the horrible possibility, then picked up his pace, breaking into a ragged, splashing jog. Five more minutes and he came through a clump of thin and stunted trees, emerging onto a spot of high ground which—despite the low light—gave him a view of the vast emptiness of the desert. There in the center, like a beacon, was the farmhouse, though the building was no more than a frame which gave shape to the fire. It roared up into the storm in defiance of the rain, belching dense gray smoke which was lit by the flames below. As Bowie watched, the tumbledown barn blew apart, scattering timber fragments and sparks, as something within it exploded.

The bike.

He was stuck.

Helplessly he stood and watched it all burn as the rain hissed down on the wreckage. That wreckage, he reminded himself, included not only his method of travel through space and time, but the weapons cache he had taken from the dead time riders. Now all he had was his twentieth-century revolver.

He thought fast and remembered the riders who had come after him. The fake cop. The blond woman. He had left their bodies by the road some twenty-five miles away. With them were a couple of automatics, a shotgun, and at least one serviceable bike.

How long would it take to reach them? The rest of the day and most of the night, probably.

Bowie sighed and, with a vengeful look at the storm overhead, began to walk.

It was quiet in the great incubator facility. The gunfire had stopped. The dead and wounded cleared out. The captives removed. The director had gone back to his office and his security forces were completing their sweep of the structure. A sweep that was thorough, but not complete. For, unnoticed in a storage cabinet on the third floor, knees drawn up to her chest, breath slow and silent, ears focused and listening—as she had been for the past several hours—was Sefton's most trusted deputy.

She had been given a mission before her leader had been killed or taken, and the deputy—whose name, insofar as it mattered to anyone but her and Sefton, was Greta Cole—had not abandoned it. The acid strips had been laid on VAT-001, Sefton's last-ditch attempt to access the inner vault he hadn't had time to breach in person, and the charges had been set. They may be cleared by the security forces' bomb squad eventually, but right now they were in place, fastened to structural supports throughout the building, ready to play their part. Greta stirred fractionally, raising her hands so she could see what she was doing in the almost total darkness of the cabinet. In them, held as carefully as if she were cradling a newborn baby, was the detonator.

But blowing the facility sky high was only one of her tasks, and—if at all possible—she wasn't to do that until her other job was complete. Sefton had been clear on that, and she intended to honor his wishes. The trust between them ran deep.

More than trust, she thought now, with a pang of sadness and regret.

She consulted a device and its tiny screen. It was linked to a server long forgotten by the net-phobic Design and was streaming the view from a single camera which Sefton had set discreetly into the ceiling above the half-opened vat. Its edges, already partly cut by the heat lance, smoldered as the acid did its work.

Sweating, Greta set the upload relay to search for a signal and checked her watch.

"Come on," she whispered. "Come on."

Bowie walked through the rain, until the thunderhead passed, and then he walked through the cool, clean air of the desert—twelve miles or more, he guessed—until it was too dark to orient himself, and he lay down on a patch of bare earth using his tactical jacket as a pillow. The heavens above were clear and spectacular, a million stars in clusters and swirls that he gazed at, mesmerized. At home it was rarely clear and dark enough to see the stars. Looking up at them now Bowie felt infinitesimally small, humbled by the scale of the universe but also—surprisingly—content. He wasn't sure why. He thought of Rossi looking up and seeing the same stars from wherever she was in 1953. Even if their timelines had diverged, even if he never saw her again, the starlight reaching them would be the same.

Was that true? He wasn't sure. He had been careful not to disrupt the timelines for fear of triggering some kind of collapse or paradox in the future, but he didn't really understand it, and he was starting to wonder if Merrick and the professor did either. They had told him that his venture into the past had been triggered by some kind of terrorist activity from their own period, but that had been a lie. One of many. It was certainly true that Bowie was not the first, or last, to be sent back to the twentieth century, but how that all played out in future time, he couldn't say. Was he functioning in a single timeline, jeopardizing whether he would ever actually be sent back, or even exist at all, in ways that could cause the whole escapade to vanish in a puff of temporal logic? Or were the time agents creating new lines with everything they did? Was time in flux, its outcomes uncertain but singular, or were their actions in the past effectively creating new universes as numerous as the stars overhead? He had no idea, and the possibilities made his head spin.

He thought back to the conversation he had overheard between Bannister and Washington, all that stuff about the Mexicans and his belief that the US should have sided with the Nazis against the Soviets. Rossi had confirmed Bannister's racist leanings in New Orleans, suggested that was part of his hostility toward Kennedy who they thought was dangerously progressive on such matters. But what did that have to do with alleged flying saucers? He tried to recall what Rossi had said about the president.

He's obsessed with space and has talked about some kind of partnership with the Soviets . . .

Could that be the link? It didn't tell him who or what was responsible for these saucers, though the fact that Bannister and Washington were telling people they were weather balloons suggested there was something more sinister going on, something they didn't want being circulated, presumably because it would upset their plans.

Which are what?

Well, among other things, the purification of their society, and the establishment of the kind of those absolute categories of people which Bowie had grown up taking for granted. Alphas, Betas, Gammas, all classified and compartmentalized in ways that determined their role, the opportunities open to them, their level of comfort and security and, ultimately, their value. That was surely what Washington had meant when he told Bannister not to fret over the presence of the non-white people.

"Such things will be resolved," Washington had said. "In time."

Bowie knew that time. He came from it. But there had to be more to their plan than simply a racial re-engineering of society like that attempted by the Nazis. Whatever had come down on that ranch clearly bore the same insignia that Bowie had seen at the séance and at David Ferrie's "mass," the symbol of the Design. So the crashed saucer was like Bowie's bike, an envoy of some sort from the future? Or was it from somewhere else entirely, and the appearance of that symbol here was the beginning of something that would eventually become the Designed world into which Bowie had been born? Washington had said something about an Originator, and this was the earliest point in his bike's temporal coordinates. Was this where it started?

Bowie didn't know, but the possibility worried him in ways he couldn't fully explain.

He slept fitfully on the hard ground, waking to find a large black scorpion inches from his hand. He sat up quickly, and did not try to go back to sleep. It was unexpectedly cold, and he sat with his hands tucked under his armpits, then ate a protein bar, which had been stowed in a pocket of his tactical jacket. He drank fresh rainwater that had puddled in the hollow of a rock, cursed himself for not having a means of carrying water with him, and then forced himself to drink even more.

He opted to start walking even though the sun wasn't up yet. Washington was as good as gone, but it was better to cover as much ground as he could before the heat got too intense. So he gathered his meager belongings, oriented himself, and began a steady trudge across the desert floor. Within the hour, the sun rose, which made navigating the uneven ground easier, and he picked up the pace a little. Two hours on, however, he felt no nearer, and he was becoming alarmed by the lack of familiar scenery. He told himself it was just the uniformity of the desert, and the fact that—stupidly—he hadn't been paying enough attention as he shot by this region at sixty miles an hour, but it worried him nonetheless. From time to time he'd see a rock formation which he thought he knew, only for it to be replaced by another that was almost identical. He climbed and descended; he crossed lengthy flats, which might once have been lakes; hiked over solid rock where the only growing things were the lichens that clung to them and the thin, spiky weeds which emerged from cracks in the stone; and he pushed his way through areas of sudden abundance: shrubs, bushes, flowers, even small trees. He saw a pair of long-eared galumphing rabbits and a tortoise with an intricately decorated shell, and he felt the eyes of circling vultures watching him from the endless blue of the sky. He kept his distance from the road, but made a point of keeping it in sight, so that even when he felt most lost he could point to it and prove to himself that he had to be going the right way.

After a few more miles like this he decided to get closer to the road, weighing the risk of being seen by the occasional traffic against the danger of missing the spot where he had wheeled the bikes down into the hollow, which ran this side of the asphalt. At least he could generally see the few cars and trucks that came along long before they might see him, and he got into the habit of dropping low until it was safe. It broke up the monotony of the walk and took his mind off his mounting thirst.

Two hours after noon, when the sun was blazing down from directly overhead, when he had begun counting his steps to convince himself that he was making progress, he finally found the bikes and the bodies of their riders, unburned, and showing no signs they had been touched by anyone since he'd left them. A couple of scraggy vultures flapped off their carcasses as he approached, but settled again a few yards away, watching and waiting.

Bowie rampaged through their stores, sucking one canteen dry in a single, desperate draft, drinking a quarter of another slowly, and saving one more unopened. He sat for a while, composing himself, eating again, then went through the weapons he had not bothered to take before, selected a fully charged juicer among other things, and chose a bike.

Since the others were too damaged, it had to be the one ridden by the female agent, and he took her helmet too, though he did not study her face this time. He liberated a few straps and cables from the rest of the gear and made some modifications to the bike, adjusting the saddle for his height. It was different from the two he had ridden so far, sleeker, and was equipped with a visual readout screen which seemed to work independent of the helmet.

Might be useful.

He gave one last glance to the bodies of the time riders whose names he did not know and wondered briefly about the forty-nine agents he had been taunted to expect, then fired up the bike. The engine was smoother than he had grown used to, a tone or two higher in pitch, and when he twisted the throttle experimentally the power surge was instantaneous and massive. No wonder he hadn't been able to stay ahead of her.

How much faster could a bike go? He wondered with excitement and just a hint of trepidation.

He guided the bike back to the road, performing one last check of its gauges and readouts, familiarizing himself with the controls before mounting it and pulling out onto the blacktop. As he did so, the two vultures eagerly returned to the corpses he had left behind. Bowie gave them a long look, then rode away. He headed north on 285, though it didn't much matter. He wouldn't be on it for long.

He thought of Rossi, hoping she would forgive him for what he was about to do. He had made a promise, and he intended to keep it, but before he did so, there was something else he had to take care of.

He pictured his brother, laughing about Mrs. Alsace's curry, and despite everything he had been taught, he thought of Rossi saying simply "family, though," and the rightness of what he was doing crystalized in his head and in his heart. Sandra would do more than forgive him. She would understand. She would urge him on.

He gave the engine more gas and leaned into the wind as the bike accelerated, eating up the road with a ravenous appetite like that which had driven him to drain that first canteen of water. It wanted to run. That was its nature. He got that. He felt something similar.

Eighty, one hundred, one twenty. It felt like the bike would accelerate forever, shooting missile-like to two hundred, three hundred, a thousand miles an hour. He didn't need anything like that, of course, but he liked the hunger of the thing, the passion. He thought of the dry, cerebral Washington dismissing the people around him as

Thetas, Omicrons, and he thought of New Orleans étouffée and Dixieland jazz, and the feel of Rossi's body against his, and—as the speedometer moved to one hundred and sixty miles an hour—he hit the bike's booster. The spike was easy this time, still loud, still heart-stoppingly charged, but almost smooth, familiar, as if he and the bike had reached some kind of agreement. He savored the moment, then reached for the one button which was programmed to return him to where it had all begun.

2157

The trip might well kill him, but there was a fire in him now of a kind his Alpha masters had never seen.

Well, they would see it now.

The portal opened before him, the swirling chaos of light and dark like the lightning in the storm the night before. He took a breath, gritted his teeth and sped toward it with a strange and savage joy.

Bowie was going home.

CHAPTER TWENTY-SIX

Bowie had given Sefton a timeline, but given the nature of what Bowie had charged him to do, it was even money as to whether Sefton would still be alive, and if he was, Bowie fully expected to find him in dire straits. He could be anywhere, and though the tracker Bowie had given him would solve that problem the moment he got into the right time frame, there was no way to guess where he would be in advance.

Have to be alert, Bowie told himself. Have to be ready. Have to get him out.

It really was that simple.

As Sefton had said, the Design depended on two major structures: the incubation facility and the security headquarters which housed the temporal launch site and its associated technology. Everything else—the governmental buildings and presidential palace included—were window dressing. The birthing labs were what produced the Design's segregated citizenry, and the security forces enforced the social structure, including—Bowie now knew—reverse engineering the past.

The incubation facility and the security headquarters: those were their targets. Sefton's insurgents had targeted the first, Bowie would target the second. But before he got to that, he had an appointment to keep.

He had programmed the bike's navigation system to lock onto Sefton's tracker the moment he reached the designated temporal coordinates, but how physically close he would be able to get the time cycle, he couldn't say. At least the geographical data of 2157 was reliably locked into the system, unlike in the past where the Design's information was cursory and incomplete. He thought that he could adjust the coordinates as he came through the portal, but he would have only a few seconds and knew he would be disoriented. As the time vortex opened, and the bike's boosters fired, Bowie hoped a few seconds would be enough.

The bike kicked like a stung mule as its navigation system picked up the tracker and tried to adjust mid-jump. Bowie felt a tide of nausea and bewilderment rush through him but forced himself to keep his focus on the display that swam before his eyes. As the light swirled around him, he tried to make sense of what he was seeing.

Sefton—or at least the tracker Sefton had been carrying—was on a street a mile west of the security quarter. And he was moving.

That was all Bowie could absorb before committing to the re-entry site. Fumblingly, feeling like he was concussed and adrift in space, he punched the screen a hundred yards from where the tracker flashed.

The bike kicked again, slewing to the right in a gut emptying slide like a plane suddenly dropping a thousand feet. Bowie could hear himself crying out as the spiral of color shifted, blurred, and resolved onto a wide, empty street at night.

The bike's entry was the smoothest he had experienced so far, which—given the fog in his head—was just as well. Bowie blew out the tension and forced himself to look, to absorb his surroundings, and to think.

There was the familiar austere regularity of the Design's buildings, the muted lights, the aura of restraint, of control, and there, directly in front of him and speeding toward the detention facility, was an armored truck. It was black and marked with the now ominous logo of the Design.

So they did have Sefton. Or at least his body.

Bowie pushed the second thought away. It was unhelpful. He would act as if his brother—his comrade in arms—was alive. There was no other choice. So he lowered his head like he was digging in, bracing himself to face a wave of C-bots, and his mind cleared.

The truck ahead was maintaining its course. Bowie could see no escort, no armed outriders.

Strange.

The time cycle was loud, and the vortex put out a lot of energy, yet the truck continued to drive ahead of him as if it hadn't seen him appear.

Not possible. So, what? They think you're with them? Or they just don't have another option?

It occurred to Bowie that if Sefton were dead, they wouldn't bother with an armed escort, but again he thrust the idea down.

Maybe the security forces were stretched too thin to worry unduly about a capture they had already made? Maybe Sefton's men had achieved more than Bowie could have hoped?

Let's go with that, he thought, twisting the throttle until the bike's engine bellowed and thrust him toward the transport. He aimed the shotgun, loaded with solid metal slugs, at the rear driver's side wheel.

The kick of the shot nearly tore the weapon from his hand, but it found its mark. The tire flapped wide and the truck swerved as the heavy vehicle unbalanced. It might have been still drivable, but it was going too fast, and the sudden swerve toward the median rail had caught the driver off guard. He overcorrected, and the truck flipped, crashing onto its side, and sliding along the road in a shower of sparks.

Bowie slowed, stowing the shotgun and drawing his sidearm as he brought the bike into the cover of the truck's rear corner, and dismounted. He leaned around the corner, one of the truck's wheels still spinning idly beside his head, eyes on the cab to see if the driver was climbing out, but as he did so, the rear door cannoned open. It caught Bowie just above the ear and sent him tumbling to the ground. He rolled, braced for the fatal shot, but it didn't come.

As he fought to get his pistol trained on the darkness in the back of the truck, he saw a guard in full tactical gear, juicer raised but waving erratically, still disoriented from the crash. Bowie fired twice, and the man dropped, but before he could look inside he heard the driver's door open.

Bowie pulled back into cover, and moments later a stream of energy flashed through the air and pocked the road. The driver was firing blind, but it was the right strategy and kept Bowie pinned down. He still hadn't dared to look into the back of the truck, afraid of what he might see.

"So this is your version of a rescue?" said Sefton's deadpan voice from the dark interior.

Though Bowie's heart had been racing it now leaped with something other than adrenaline.

"Are you free?" he asked, giving nothing away.

"Cuffed to a rail. That clown has the key."

The clown in question was the man Bowie had shot, but the sound of movement from up front suggested that the driver was climbing out and heading his way. Bowie took a breath, dropped low, lower than his enemy would expect, and leaned out, gun blazing.

The driver was halfway out of the door and clambering onto the truck's side, which meant he was slow to get his weapon aimed, and his first shot was high and wide. He didn't get a second.

Bowie seized the keys from the belt of the downed guard and clambered into the back of the truck. Sefton was half hanging by his wrists from a metal rail bolted to the truck's frame.

"Didn't think you'd make it," he said, as Bowie freed him.

"Said I would," Bowie said flatly. "Family, right?" He felt embarrassed by saying it and, sensing Sefton's surprise, moved quickly past it. "How did you hide the tracker?"

"Believe me when I say you don't want to know."

"Fair enough," said Bowie. "Come on. They'll be coming."

And they were. Even as Bowie struggled back out of the truck and onto his bike, he saw the distinctive pop of light far down the highway.

"A time rider," he said, dismayed. "Get on!"

"One second," said Sefton, moving to the front of the truck and hoisting himself up.

"Now, Seff!" Bowie yelled, as he fired up the engine.

He looked back to check the distance to the time rider and realized it wasn't one rider, but two. They were astride a single bike, one driving, the other leaning around from the back and aiming a weapon. There was a crack, and a burst of energy punctured the wrecked truck, blowing neat holes through its armor.

Bowie winced, but Sefton emerged unscathed holding a black synthetic pouch which he belted on as Bowie rolled the bike toward him.

"Had to retrieve my personal effects!"

"Seriously?" yelled Bowie.

Another arc of weapons' fire zipped over Bowie's shoulder and into the sky. Somewhere something exploded and a siren began to ring out.

The moment his brother threw his leg over and slipped one hand around his waist, Bowie released the brake and the bike lurched forward. "Hold on," he yelled over the time cycle's accelerating roar. "This is going to be rough."

"Where are we going?" Sefton shouted back as they roared down the street. "Or do I mean when?"

"Just hold on," said Bowie with a quiet certainty that was almost meditative, as he punched the boosters and aimed at the opening portal.

"Whoa," Sefton breathed over his shoulder.

"Yeah," Bowie agreed, his eyes fixed on the maelstrom of color, as they shot toward it and into the past.

CHAPTER TWENTY-SEVEN

November 22, 1963

It hadn't been easy for Sandra Rossi to find work as a woman without papers or qualifications in 1953. For a while that hadn't mattered so much. She had plenty of money, thanks to Bowie, but after a string of dead-end secretarial positions in Boston she decided it was time to return to the career she had loved. Using her reporter instincts she connected with a minor figure in the Irish mob who, for a few of Bowie's dollars, fixed her up with a new name, a degree from Mount Holyoke, and a Social Security number. For the next decade she was Kelly O'Malley, a deliberately androgynous name which helped her get interviews and story credit without declaring her sex. That only got her so far, however. She plied the local beat for a series of minor New England papers over the next couple of years but was never given the opportunity to break the big stories, or tackle anything of national or international significance—even when she "remembered" the story before it broke.

So much for knowing the period before it happened, she thought.

Her break came when she decided that the best way to make a name for herself was to go after the stories the men didn't want, and the perfect example of that was in popular music, something most of the serious papers dismissed as a baffling and ephemeral fad. In late 1955 she took a trip to Memphis and saw her ticket onto the staff of *The Boston Globe* in the person of Elvis Presley, a largely unknown performer who was yet to release his first album. By the time that came out, the following year, Rossi was perfectly positioned to champion the singer as the star she knew he would be. And so began her career at the frontline of the emerging field of pop music journalism as rock and roll vied for the top spots with the likes of Bing Crosby, Johnny Mathis, and Frank Sinatra. Rossi—or rather O'Malley—was quickest off the mark, and she soon became known in press circles as something of a pop music tastemaker, and although she was always careful not to change the general course of history, it was still exciting work. She was currently writing a column on four boys from Liverpool whose first UK single, "Love Me Do," hinted at something special in the making.

She had kept clear of Dallas and, indeed, of anywhere close to where she, that is Sandra Rossi, might be at the same time. It was strange, knowing that there was another version of herself out in the world, and occasionally she would seek out copies of *The Dallas Morning News* to look for her name in the byline on pieces she remembered writing. Twice, after a couple too many drinks, she picked up the phone to call Veronica. Once she even dialed but hung up as soon as she heard her sister's voice, then sat by the phone sobbing.

In many ways, it was a very long ten years.

She had been mostly solitary throughout that period, focusing on the work, and socializing primarily with musicians, record producers, and fellow journalists, never letting any of them close. She had friends, mostly women, but none of them knew who she really was. She had quickly learned that the best way not to get caught in a lie about her past was to keep it to herself. She volunteered little about herself, true or false, and this had created a reputation, she knew, for being cool and standoffish. It was odd, in a way, but the person she had been before she met Bowie hadn't been all that different to this new one. Back then, she'd naturally kept most people, not including her sister of course, at a safe distance. But now that she had to do it, had to keep so much of herself hidden, it suddenly felt forced and unnatural. And it made her yearn for someone she could talk to openly and honestly.

Other than the work for which she got paid, she had also continued to investigate the people and events from Dallas, New Orleans, Naushon, and Maine. Always quietly and discreetly, looking for connections, logics, and agendas. She had built a massive dossier on the president himself, his personal life as well as his administration-to-be's priorities and political leanings, but while it sometimes seemed that she had found the golden thread which linked everything and everybody, it always broke when she tugged on it hard, or it led to other threads which took her in different directions. A decade since Bowie had left her, she had a lot more data, and several hunches, but no hard answers. She wondered if he had learned more from Roswell in '47, something that would give her the hard, simple answer she had been seeking. She wondered also if he was out there somewhere, living slowly—as she thought it—like her, easing back into 1963 one day at a time. He would be older. She had been only twenty-five when she first met him. Now she was thirty-five—practically an old maid in the parlance of the day—and he would be, what? Forty-three? Forty-four? Something like that. She hadn't known how old he was when they met, but he probably had a good five years on her then. Of course, since he planned to go back to his own time for his brother after Roswell, he might only be days older than when she had seen him last.

Or he might be dead. Given his plans, and what he was up against, he probably was.

She knew this was true but she didn't like to think of it. She had known him only a few days but he had altered the very fabric of her life.

He was why she was still single. At first, she was ashamed to admit it, even to herself. Thought it made her sound like a schoolgirl. So she had dated for a while, went through a period of trying to forget, even trying to move on with someone else, but it was an act, and she finally found strength in her conviction. So it was, that ten years on, she still loved a man she had known only for a matter of days.

As she entered Dealey Plaza on a day she knew would go down in history, the president, who had just addressed a mostly Republican crowd in the grand ballroom of the Hotel Texas in Fort Worth, was en route to Carswell Air Force Base. She had arrived in Dallas the night before, staying in a motel on the north side of the city in an area she had never visited before. It was the first time in a decade that she had set foot in the town she had—in a former life—called home. Her old self would be gone by now, whistling through the past on the back of a giant motorcycle. It was an uncanny feeling, and it brought with it an added sense of responsibility, as if she now had to do both versions of herself proud. She had tried to calculate the precise moment her old self left, wondering if she would somehow feel the departure in the moment, but she felt nothing. One instant there were two of her in Texas, and then there was one. The world continued as if nothing had happened, and no one knew the disaster that was coming.

She had considered, of course, sending her materials to every law enforcement agency she could think of, naming Oswald and his alter ego, Hidell, but she had nothing a rational person would consider evidence, and her diagrams of intersections and probabilities looked, she knew, like the ravings of a lunatic. More to the point, she had come to realize a very hard truth; Bowie had been right. Her best chance to save the president was to do nothing that would alter Oswald's plans, or those of the people controlling him, in the present or the future. The moment she derailed their operation, they would change it. A new assassin would be selected and he—or, she supposed, she—would intercept Kennedy at some time or place she could not possibly anticipate. It could happen during any visit to any state in the union, or right there in the halls of the White House. It could happen at any time of day, in any month of any year.

No, her best option was to let things play out exactly as she remembered, stepping in at the last possible second when Oswald was exactly where he was supposed to be, on the sixth floor of the book depository with his rifle.

But that meant that she had to be ready. So for ten years she prepared, and that meant putting aside some of the person she had been before. She took self-defense classes. She studied judo and aikido wherever she could find teachers who would take her, and she exercised with a regularity and intensity which—when her coworkers glimpsed it—seemed to verge on mania.

Most radically for the person Bowie had known, Sandra Rossi decided to change her relationship with firearms. That was a tougher adjustment, one that demanded she separate the guns themselves from their cultural baggage, their associations, and the million misuses she had seen as a citizen and a reporter.

They are tools, she told herself, that first day she forced herself to enter a gun shop. She refused the pearl handled automatic the store owner suggested because it looked like a toy or—worse—an accessory and pointed to a purposeful looking revolver with a six inch barrel. What she thought of as a cowboy gun.

"Big gun for a little lady," said the man behind the counter with a smug look.

It was, too, she realized, as soon as he handed it to her and led her to the range in the back. The first shot almost blew it out of her hand, and it took three more to even hit the target. Maybe she could build her strength up, learn to master the kick of the thing but it was, she thought—annoyed with herself as much as with the I-told-you-so look on the shopkeeper's face—too much.

"Wanna try that .25 auto now?" he asked, grinning.

"You have something like this," she said, nodding to the revolver, "with similar stopping power but less weight." Her use of the term "stopping power" quashed his smile and something like concern flashed across his face. "I need to know that it will work reliably if I need it," she said, giving him a level look and speaking in measured tones. "So that if I have to use it, it will do what I need it to do, the first time."

He nodded then, as if understanding multiple things at once, and considered his display wall.

"The .38 comes in a four-inch and a two-inch barrel," he said. "That reduces the weight and makes it easier to carry. You lose a little velocity and accuracy with the two but—"

"Let's try the four," she said.

"It's still a lot of gun," he warned.

She felt the heft of it, then nodded.

"It has to be," she said, her voice seeming to come from a long way away.

She frequented shooting ranges in every place she lived from then on. She favored her revolver, but she trained with an array of firearms: handguns, shotguns, and rifles. She took classes with law enforcement officers to improve her technique and sense of safety. She hated every step of the process, but she'd be damned if she was going to let that stop her.

For ten years she prepared to do what needed to be done on the sixth floor of that building in Dallas on November 22, 1963. Whatever happened that day, she would be ready to do her part, whether Bowie showed or not. Given his mission and the odds against him, she had steeled herself for the very real possibility that when the moment came, she would face Oswald alone.

So she loaded, and aimed, and fired, over and over and over again. When that moment finally came, she would be ready.

Now as she bought herself a cup of tea and sat for a moment in sight of the Texas School Book Depository, where Oswald was—presumably—already at work, she felt like an army of one, up against unseen forces that at that very moment were moving to assassinate the president of the United States of America. It sounded insane. No less so today than when she had started on this mission a decade ago. But she knew it to be true. She *knew* it.

She found herself looking for Bowie. She always did, never sure where and when he might appear, but as the years had rolled on the endless peripheral searching had cooled until it became background noise, more a general awareness than a specific action. The frantic, conscious scanning for him was back now, however, and had been since she crossed the Texas border.

He said he would be here, she thought. *He said he would meet me.*

But there was no sign of him, and Rossi—in her head she was Sandra again, though she realized she could never revert to that name, even if she were to survive the day—suspected that stopping Oswald would fall to her alone.

If so, she thought, *I'm ready.*

She had two Smith & Wesson Model 10 revolvers, .38s with four-inch barrels, concealed in shoulder holsters under her jacket. One of them had been the first firearm she had bought, and it was still her favorite. They were big guns, heavy but reliable, and she had shot them so often that they felt like extensions of her arms. There was a simplicity to them which was a kind of elegance. As the minutes ticked on, she found herself slipping a hand inside her jacket, gripping a gun for comfort against her growing dread, not that she'd be the one to have to shoot the assassin Oswald, but that Bowie's absence meant that all her worst fears for him had come true.

She checked her watch. If all was on schedule, Air Force One would be in the air by now, more than halfway through its short fifteen-minute flight from Fort Worth.

Kennedy would be dead in an hour.

The enormity of it all hit her like a bullet and she had to set her tea down. She felt suddenly unsteady, overwhelmed by the scale of what was about to happen, and she found herself rethinking the plans she had built over the last obsessive decade. Perhaps she should just run through the gathering crowds shouting that she saw a man with a rifle entering the book depository. Surely, someone would listen? Maybe they would cordon off the area? Change the motorcade route?

And maybe they'll just arrest you as a nut or whisk you away so their friends can do the job they came to.

She couldn't trust anyone, including the men in uniform. She had learned that much.

If Bowie doesn't show, it is up to you.

She forced herself to take a series of long breaths, then finished her tea and collected her things, moving with a studied slowness not to attract attention. She went to the bathroom and, once she was in the stall with the door locked, checked the pistols, six rounds in each cylinder and a dozen more in the pockets of her jacket.

More than enough for the job at hand.

Until the crucial moment came, of course, she would use every art of charm and misdirection that her time as a journalist concealing her identity had taught her. She dabbed a little cold water on her face, then touched up her makeup, settled up at the register, and walked calmly along the street toward the great brick building on the corner. She had her press pass in hand in case anyone stopped her, but no one did. She circled the building and tried a back-door beside a loading dock. It opened, and she ducked quickly inside.

She had considered pulling blueprints for the building from the county records office but decided against it, being overly cautious not to do anything that might attract attention or create even the slightest deviation in Oswald's plans. Now as she entered the main floor, she felt a sudden anxiety that her ignorance of the place would attract attention, but everyone was either working or gathering at the street-facing windows in anticipation. She moved quickly, located a stairwell and began to climb, counting the flights carefully in her head until she reached the sixth floor. There she waited, taking out a packet of cigarettes as if she had just stepped off the main floor for a surreptitious smoke. She hadn't, of course, and she didn't take a cigarette from the pack. It had taken her the best part of a year, but she had quit. She no longer even missed it.

Unbidden the image of Bowie wrinkling his nose at the smell of her jacket came into her mind and almost made her smile.

Almost.

She could hear the noise from the street below as the crowd grew, but there was nothing to suggest that there was anyone up here but her. Ten minutes she waited, and it felt like hours. Still nothing, and no sign of Bowie.

He's not coming.

It was a crushing thought, and though she had been bracing herself for the possibility for years, the looming truth of it was devastating.

OK, she thought, focusing. *Then it's up to me.*

Five more minutes, and then she cracked the door and peered in.

It was a long, open floor, without separate rooms, so it looked like a warehouse. Windows ran the length of the floor, their frames set within shallow arches that were almost elegant. The rest was mostly gray and brown, functional and untended, the brick walls covered unevenly in whitewash. The wooden floor was cluttered with cardboard boxes and crates that were stacked haphazardly, some of them stamped with a logo, but the central aisle was clear, and she could see all the way down through a series of square supporting columns. There she could make out a pile of boxes which seemed a little less random than the rest. It screened the last window on the right, the one overlooking the plaza. It looked like a bunker or nest.

He's in there, she thought. *Oswald, with his rifle*.

It flashed through her mind that in all her time at the range she had never shot at a target who might fire back.

Breathe. Be calm. You can do this.

She checked her watch. Twelve twenty. Ten minutes to the moment which was stamped in her head from the newspaper reports she had read a decade ago.

KENNEDY IS KILLED BY SNIPER AS HE RIDES IN CAR IN DALLAS

Silently, Rossi slipped off her shoes, drew one of the revolvers from its holster, and pushed the door wider. It opened soundlessly, and she took her first faltering step onto the floor. She studied the door, feeling its weight in her hand, making sure it would not swing back by itself, then let go. She walked precisely forward with the pistol at her side, heel toe, heel toe, feeling the dusty wooden planks under her feet. She expected to be sweating, her heart racing so fast and loud that the sniper might hear it, but she was quite calm. She had a job to do and she was trained and ready to do it.

Two more steps and then she had to step sideways around an empty cardboard box, stamped with the word "Books" and the slogan "Building for Today, Pioneering for Tomorrow." Given the circumstances, the phrase felt ominous. She wondered vaguely if Bowie had ever found out what the agent called Washington had meant by "the Originator."

Doesn't matter now.

She moved around the box toward one of the concrete support pillars. She raised her left hand in case she needed to steady herself, but didn't, and kept her eyes locked on the barricade that Oswald had built at the far end of the room.

Two more quiet steps, and now she raised the revolver in her right hand, training it on the stack of boxes screening the far window. Suddenly she heard the distinct sound of a man clearing his throat, followed by a shift of movement. She froze, listening, her breath held, and for a second it felt like she would never be able to move again.

And then a strange light flickered around the long room, white and blue and aquamarine like a brilliant search light, slashing up from the bottom of a swimming pool, but swirling and flecked with deeper shards of color. Then came the sound, dopplering in from far away, the thundering roar of a motorcycle . . .

Bowie!

She turned as the bike and its two riders burst through the flickering portal of light on the far wall, hitting the wooden floor perfectly, and decelerating in a rapid, chaotic slide which scattered boxes and filled the air with the scent of burning rubber. Rossi stepped quickly aside as the bike slipped past her, its wheels locked, and she saw a face leaning out of the sniper's nest.

Oswald.

His mouth was set but his face was bland, and though his eyes locked onto Bowie's bike, he showed no amazement, no dismay.

He expected it, she thought as she raised her pistol. *Which is weird . . .*

Oswald turned to her but had no weapon she could see, and Rossi hesitated. He looked not so much afraid as confused, and when he spoke his tone was more warning than alarm.

"You shouldn't be here," he said.

Even in her terror, Rossi felt the sudden ache of confusion and uncertainty. Something was wrong. She turned quickly, desperately, to Bowie, but the men on the motorcycle had pulled off their helmets.

Neither was Bowie.

The first rider was a bald man with a hard face and piercing blue eyes who she had never seen before. She stared at him, open mouthed, as he calmly brought up a strange looking device and fired it at her.

CHAPTER TWENTY-EIGHT

Bowie felt his brother's hands tighten around his waist as they hit the portal, heard his gasp of astonishment, and then they were hitting the floor of the book depository, and he was fighting to make sense of what was happening, even as he tried to stop the bike.

There were two other time riders, seemingly the same ones they'd just left in 2157. Somehow, they had managed to arrive before Bowie and Sefton, and their juicers were already flashing.

But not at them.

Someone else was there. Bowie saw her dive behind a concrete pillar.

Her.

The word broke through his mind like the tip of a nail hammered through his temple.

Sandra.

Bowie spilled from his seat before the bike had stopped moving, blasting with the shotgun over and over until it was empty. He flung it aside and drew the juicer, moving for cover as the long room flashed, and the air crackled, with bolts of purple energy. By their uneven light, Bowie saw who was shooting at them, and though he didn't know the bald Alpha agent in the black leather jacket, he recognized the tall, athletic one as the legendary Jäger Zero Four Nine.

Forty-nine, thought Bowie, finally realizing what the time agent in the red helmet had meant. *They sent Zero Four Nine after me.*

The bald agent was moving laterally, deft and precise, targeting Sefton who had taken up position behind a pillar on the opposite side and who leaned out and fired four quick shots in return.

Bowie ignored them all, including Oswald, who had looked back to see what was happening then returned to the window, presumably to take his shot at the motorcade. All Bowie's attention was on Rossi. She was crouching behind a concrete post, a large revolver gripped steadily in her hand, and for a moment she looked like someone he had never seen before. Even as he watched, she leaned around the pillar, fired twice and withdrew to cover with the composed efficiency of a soldier.

More energy blasts tore through the building.

Bowie leaned out with his juicer and fired a burst that punched holes in the wall beyond the sniper's nest, causing one of the boxes to explode in a burst of paper confetti. In that instant he processed the strangeness of the tableau this revealed: Oswald, recoiling from the shots, shock and terror on his face, but with no rifle in his hand. Next to him was the bald time rider.

“Hey, that’s my gun,” said Oswald blankly, gazing at the agent like a man sleepwalking. “What are you doing? Where’s Washington?”

The time rider pushed Oswald aside and crouched down by the window. He fired his juicer at Bowie who ducked back, trying to make sense of what he was seeing.

Oswald isn’t the assassin! All this time we’ve been chasing the wrong man!

But how could the real hitman be a time agent? That kind of direct action surely violated every temporal principle . . .

Bowie fought to get to his feet, but Four Nine was still shooting, providing cover for his partner with a constant stream of energy that lit up the long chamber like fireworks and kept Bowie from getting off a clear shot at the bald assassin. But even half glimpsed from heavy cover, the scene felt wrong. The assassin was crouched by the open window, the rifle down at his hip, his attention seemed to be more on the battle in the room than the approaching motorcade on the street below. Bowie looked to where Oswald had barricaded himself, trapped behind a concrete column.

Trapped! Because he’s not the killer. Oswald was never the killer! He’s just here to take the fall!

Bowie felt a wave of frustrated impotence rise in him.

All this time, all this effort, for nothing.

He thought of the newspaper picked up by Washington days after the assassination. Bowie had assumed that meant the shooting had originally taken place in history *without any interference from the time riders*. But the assassination was happening now *because the time riders were going to make it happen.* Bowie hadn't been sent back to preserve history. He'd been sent back as part of an operation to change it.

And he, Sefton, and Sandra would probably die in the process. Four Nine fired again and Bowie shrank back as more energy bolts slammed into the nearby concrete, scattering chips of debris and puffs of bitter smoke. Four Nine shifted to get a better angle, and Sefton caught him with a blast to the thigh that sent him tumbling heavily to the ground. As he went down, finger still wrapped around the trigger, his weapon sprayed wildly.

Bowie ducked down, but heard his brother cry out.

"Sefton!" Bowie yelled.

"Hit," came the reply, low and weak. Followed by the chuckle of the time agent.

"You can't stop us," said Four Nine. "I'm amazed you thought it possible. The likes of you mongrels against the Design's elite?"

"Hit," muttered Sefton. "Not dead."

And he rolled out shooting. Agent Four Nine held his ground, aimed, and fired again. Sefton cried out and slumped to the ground, facing the ceiling. Blood ran out from under him, and he grew still, though Bowie could hear his desperate, uneven breathing. Then came the first rifle shot. It rang out, hard and flat and loaded with significance.

Four Nine leaned out to finish Sefton, but ducked back as Rossi opened fire, two quick shots that spat chunks of concrete from the post.

Bowie moved toward the sniper nest. The bald agent had the rifle pointed out the window, but he seemed more focused on his wristwatch than on the motorcade down below. As Bowie tried to get a clean shot, the man fired a second time, quickly chambered another round, and fired again. Never once bringing his eye to the scope.

Sandra fired twice: precise, level shots which tore out the sniper's throat and dropped him where he stood.

But the third shot had been fired which meant . . . Kennedy was dead or dying? But how? There was no way those shots, fired from Oswald's rifle, had found their mark. But it didn't matter. Oswald didn't matter. None of this mattered.

After all they had been through . . . this was what? A distraction? Misdirection?

Bowie couldn't get his mind around it. It was too much to process. And in that moment, he realized he had taken his eyes off Four Nine.

He spun to find the agent coming up behind him. Something thumped hard into the underside of his chin and Bowie's head rocked back, his eyes sightless long enough that he didn't see the second blow coming. Four Nine crashed the butt of his juicer into Bowie's face and he felt the bone in his cheek shatter. He went down, powerless to break his fall, his gun skittering away across the floor and then there was Agent Four Nine, smirking over him, raising his weapon to fire.

But not at him. He was sighting along the gallery to where Sandra was sheltering. Her attention was still on the carnage in the sniper's nest. Bowie tried to cry out a warning but managed only a rasping gasp. Then Four Nine unleashed a quick trio of energy blasts. The first two grazed the right side of Sandra's ribs. The third cut a hole through her left shoulder and all but blew her arm off. She half rose from the impact, then collapsed in silence.

"No!" Bowie cried.

Four Nine grinned again and aimed his weapon at Bowie.

"You were never going to win," said the agent, looking from him to the motionless Sefton and back. "You degenerates. What did you possibly think you could achieve?"

His finger tightened on the trigger.

Three sharp bangs rang out and Bowie shrank away, his eyes shutting reflexively. When he opened them again he saw Four Nine, his eyes wide and his mouth open. Blood trickled from it, then belched out suddenly in a thick, dark river which ran down his front, blurring with the holes in his chest. He started to look down at his wounds but collapsed to the floor.

Bowie snatched the fallen agent's juicer, then rolled wildly over and saw Sandra, lying where she had fallen. Her gun was extended in her one good arm, its barrel smoking. He scrambled to his feet and limped to her.

She was pale and gaunt, her eyes wide with shock, but she was still sighting down the barrel of her .38 to Four Nine's body. There were two shallow holes in the right side of her chest, and a large one up by her shoulder. The wounds were black-edged and smoking. She was bleeding heavily. The one near her shoulder was deep and wide enough to show the terrible paleness of bone, and her upper arm was too far from her shoulder.

"Sandra," he whispered. "Stay with me."

Her head rolled back and something like focus came into her eyes.

"I didn't get him," she managed, her eyes full of fury and grief. "Oswald. All this time . . . I didn't get him."

"It's OK," Bowie soothed, his eyes flashing over to where Oswald was standing in a daze. "This was never about him."

He tore a sleeve from his shirt and lashed it tight around her shoulder, binding the all but severed arm into place, in a feeble attempt to slow the bleeding. She cried out, eyes widening at the pain. The shock of it seemed to bring her back to reality.

"Bowie?"

"Yes."

"You came back," she said, smiling despite everything.

"Of course I did," he said, kissing her forehead.

"Go," said Sefton. "Get her to a hospital."

Bowie turned in disbelief. He had thought his brother was dead. Joy leaped in him, but as soon as he saw Sefton's condition he knew it was only a matter of time.

"How?" he replied with more bitterness than he meant. "It's chaos out there. And the police will be here any minute."

Oswald looked at the bodies of the fallen time riders, and his gaze drifted out the open window and down. He looked stunned, like a man waking from a deep sleep.

"This isn't right," he stammered. "Where's Washington? He said he'd be here . . ."

He backed quickly away, arms half raised. Bowie brought up his weapon, but his brother's command—the voice of an officer giving orders to his men—stopped him.

"Leave him!" he instructed. "Take her on the bike!"

"What about you?" Bowie fired back.

Sefton looked down at the wound in his belly and managed a pained smile as he shook his head.

"I'm done," he said.

Bowie's mind raced for things to say, things to do.

"It wasn't supposed to go this way," said Oswald, staring at his rifle as if in a daze. "They'll blame me!" he murmured, as if the realization was just dawning on him. "They'll take me in like some patsy. I gotta get out of here."

He broke into a ragged, uneven run for the stairs, and as Oswald reached the door to the stairwell, Bowie forgot about him and his eyes slid back to Rossi. Maybe if he could use his bike to get her to a medical facility, she might have a chance. But Sefton . . .

As if reading his look, his brother put a bloody hand on his shoulder and hauled himself painfully up.

"Go," he said. "This is as good a time to die as any. But I'll stand as long as I can."

Bowie wasn't sure why he said that, why he insisted on getting up on his feet and balancing carefully, his legs splayed. Sefton grimaced as he took the stance, his fists clenched, ignoring the blood that trickled from him and pattered at his feet like rain.

"Seff," said Bowie. "I'm so sorry."

His brother shook his head.

"No, don't be," he said, speaking slowly, dredging the words up from somewhere deep. "This is my part, I'm ready for it. Today will prove to be a good day." He nodded again, as if confirming a decision, then said, "You'll get her somewhere, then you'll go back? To our time?"

Bowie glanced to where Rossi lay, then his face clouded and hardened.

"Yes," he said.

"Take this," said Sefton, fumbling in his pouch and producing a slim, rectangular device about five inches long. A small blue light pulsed on one edge. "Kind of a receiver. Old tech. I mean," he qualified with a grin that showed the blood in his teeth, "not as old as this place. Keep it on when you go back."

"Why? What does it do?"

"Just do it," Sefton managed, wincing in pain as he held it out. His eyes closed briefly, but then he forced them open again and they went to Four Nine's bike. "That agent wasn't planning to stop here."

Bowie followed his gaze and frowned. The bike had a suitcase-sized device with a digital display strapped to the frame. He knew immediately what it was.

A bomb. Low shrapnel count but high blast area. He had seen the type used during the war. An M-72 or 85. It was an indiscriminate weapon.

He moved quickly to it and unbuckled the explosive device from Four Nine's bike. As he did so, his gaze fell on the handlebar display which was different from any of the other bikes he had seen. They included a map with a set of coordinates already programmed ready for a quick jump.

"Washington DC," he said aloud.

So not just JFK. There was to be a second strike at the US government . . .

"They planned to take out much more than a president," said Sefton, his eyes moving back to Rossi. "You need to go."

Sefton smiled again vaguely. He was close to losing consciousness. Bowie felt an agony unlike anything he had ever experienced, as if one of those blasters had sliced right through his heart.

"We didn't change the future the way we wanted," Sefton said, still standing, but wavering like one of the drunks Bowie had seen in New Orleans.

"Not yet," Bowie agreed, "but we will. We'll take down the Design."

"You will," said Sefton. "I knew you'd get here eventually."

Bowie looked away to hide his tears, then moved toward his bike. The professor had said the cycles needed sixty feet of open road. He assessed the length of the gallery. There would be no room for error. He got Rossi upright, then lifted her over to the saddle, and sat her in front of him on the bike. She was silent now, unconscious. He had to stretch out his arms as far as they would go to reach the handlebar grips and then lean around her to see where he was headed.

"And Bowie?" said Sefton.

"Yes?"

"Find our mother."

Bowie turned to face him.

"Our mother?" he repeated, stunned.

"Like you said," Sefton breathed, "Family, right? Find her."

Bowie was staring at him when he was startled by the sudden roar of a time cycle starting up and he spun around to see Four Nine's bike coming to glowing, smoking life over by Oswald's sniper nest. As he had been focusing on the bomb and then Rossi, Four Nine had dragged himself back into its saddle.

No! Bowie thought. *He was dead! I saw him die.*

But he hadn't. He had seen him hit, had seen him bleeding, but he should have used one more shot to put him down for good.

Now Four Nine's bike was already rolling into position. Bowie reached wildly for one of the weapons he had stowed, but with Rossi in front of him, he couldn't get to them in time.

Four Nine, bloody and clumsy, managed to give him a look, and then his bike was moving faster, picking up speed as it ran at the far wall. Bowie could do nothing but watch as, with the last of his strength, Sefton launched himself at the time rider. He bellowed with the pain of motion, flung his arms wide, and seized Four Nine around the chest as he sped past. As the boosters flashed and the bike tore away like a hawk chasing prey, Bowie saw his brother hanging on to the surprised agent.

Bowie shouted something, but the vortex was already open and swallowing them up.

And then, before Bowie could say all the things he wanted to say to his dying brother, they were gone and there was nothing for him to do but what he had promised.

Bowie held onto Rossi's limp body and fired up his bike's engine. A moment later he raced toward the wall as if he was going to punch a hole through the universe.

Sefton clung to Four Nine knowing he had only moments to live, even if he managed to stay on the bike. He stretched forward, feeling the agony of his wounds as they opened farther, and mashed at the bike's glowing map with his bloodied hand.

"What are you doing?" roared the agent, taking one hand from the handlebars to pull at Sefton's outstretched arm.

Too late, thought Sefton with grim satisfaction, as he swiped the map from the green and gray of the Washington DC area out to the endless blue of the Atlantic and punched it.

The world leaped and swam as the delirium of pain meshed with the swirling light of the portal and Sefton was outside of himself and fading. He heard the time rider's shout of denial and panic as they cleared the vortex and fell through the air like a stone.

They dropped from six stories high into a spot two hundred miles out into the dark waters of the ocean. As Four Nine cried out his furious and impotent defiance, Sefton let go and fell free from the bike, the wind whistling past him. He thought of Greta, and of Mrs. Alsace's curry being greeted by joyous children, and he thought of his brother. Another of Mrs. Dunn's quotes floated to the surface of his dying mind.

"His heart burst smilingly . . ." he whispered.

The bike shattered on impact, and as the cold, implacable water closed over its doomed rider, the remains sank into the depths.

Bowie's bike materialized on Fruit Street on the east bank of the Charles River in Boston, three hours before the assassination that would change the future of the United

States. He parked, ignoring the braying horns and outraged shouts, and carried Rossi's limp, bleeding body into the main entrance of Massachusetts General Hospital. She had lost consciousness before they left Dallas. He could find no pulse, and her breathing had shallowed to nothing.

"Her arm," he managed, as a man in scrubs rushed to him. "It might be too late but . . ."

"What happened?" the doctor demanded.

"She was shot. A weapon," said Bowie flatly. "I don't know what kind."

The doctor's forehead tightened, and horror mixed with the confusion in his eyes as he considered the state of her shoulder. He shouted for a gurney and orderly assistance, then for blood and saline and a host of other things that Bowie didn't recognize, and then they were wheeling her away.

"We'll take it from here," said a nurse. "Are you a family member? A spouse? The nurse at the desk over there can take her details . . ."

But Bowie was already walking away, no longer hearing, barely seeing anything between himself and the bike.

He had not saved the president, he might not have saved Rossi, but he had one last mission and nothing would stop him from completing it.

Director Merrick's eyes went to the wall display where an orange illuminated sign read:

MISSIONS IN PROCESS: 2. STATUS PENDING.

The latter phrase flashed slowly. Merrick gave the professor his beadiest stare.

"They should be done by now," he said. "You are certain they made the initial time jump successfully?"

"Yes, sir."

"And you sent them when I gave the order, not several hours later according to some whim of your own?"

Reissen's face went rigid but he managed to incline his head fractionally and say, "The moment you gave the order."

Given everything that had happened, the attacks on the power grid, the raid on the incubation facility, and the director's own rumored brush with death at the hands of the terrorist ringleader, Reissen wasn't about to contradict him.

"And you trust these agents to complete their assigned tasks?" Merrick inquired icily.

"Absolutely."

Merrick frowned and blew out a long sigh.

"Then something has gone wrong," he concluded. "You have their last temporal coordinates?"

"Yes, but they may not be there anymore. Without sending more agents back we have no way of knowing and we have no more time cycles or agents . . ."

"Yes, yes," Merrick, snapped, his eyes returning to the display panels with their unsatisfactory message. "I know."

He stared at the display. Both missions were still in process, which was just another word for incomplete . . .

The room went still as everyone followed his gaze. For all the petty bickering, the air throbbed with anticipation. In one corner, three Betas clad in the white coats of the science team waited with achievement medals specially created to mark the occasion. They were carefully covered in a sterile white sheet. If there was nothing to celebrate, they would melt quietly away.

The medals had been Merrick's idea. This mission would prove the potential of shaping the past to create a better future. It would show that they could pre-emptively remove dissention, avert wars, and ensure that the Design was able to be realized in its purest form.

Assuming things went to plan . . .

As if he had willed it, the sign changed.

MISSION 1: COMPLETE.

A great, satisfied cheer went up from the assembled crowd. Merrick gave a nod indicating that the covering sheet was to be removed, revealing the medals in all their glory.

This was a good day. As the moments passed, the display wall filled up with further confirmation of their achievement: historical accounts and images of the president's death at the hands of a Dallas sniper. Merrick gave his usual, twisted little smile as his eyes met Reissen's. He hadn't decided how long he would keep the man in his present position, but he had—surprisingly—completed the task assigned to him, albeit somewhat messily.

The first part of it, anyway. The second mission—the bombing of the US Capitol Building, an act which, on the heels of JFK's death, would bring the government crashing down—was still showing on the display as incomplete.

Give it time . . . he told himself.

There was a rumble somewhere far off and a tremor ran through the building. It was followed by a nervous hush which cut through the celebratory chatter as if sucking it out of the air.

"What was that?" demanded Merrick.

"Felt like an explosion," said Reissen.

"Can't have been," sputtered Merrick. "The terrorists were contained. Defeated. Their mission failed!"

And, he thought, the alteration of the past would be rippling through to the present, perfecting the Design, making the very idea of insurgents inconceivable . . .

And yet . . .

"Perhaps there was some time-delayed device or . . ."

"Get someone to the incubation facility!" Merrick ordered. "I want a full status report." He took a steadying breath. It would be all right. They had achieved the impossible! They had changed their own history. His eyes went back to the board and the status of mission two.

Even as he looked, it went from orange to red.

MISSION FAILED.

No!

Merrick gaped. How was that possible? The agents had been in place. They had the explosives with them. The Kennedy operation was a success. By comparison, with all eyes on the chaos in Dallas, entering the Capitol with their bombs should have been child's play.

It made no sense.

In seconds the mood in the room had inverted. Suddenly everyone looked wary, anxious. Some gasped audibly as they saw the updated mission status. Others quietly looked for the exits. Unless ordered otherwise, they wanted to be elsewhere when Merrick processed the scale of this disaster. Some of them wanted to be somewhere with windows. They hadn't liked that noise or the tremor which followed it and wanted to be able to see what was going on in the city.

"This can't be happening," he muttered.

"It can and it is!" snapped Reissen. "And it's your fault!"

Merrick stared at the professor whose face was pink with fury and defiance.

"What did you say?" he demanded in his most dangerous voice.

"You heard me," said Reissen, taking two bold steps toward him. "This is your fault. You had to meddle with time! Insulating the present, you said, by refining the past. And I told you it was dangerous, that you could unravel the entire fabric of our reality, but you did it anyway!"

"How dare you speak to me like this!" Merrick exclaimed, genuinely amazed at the man's audacity.

"Because it's true!" roared Reissen, so that everyone in the room turned to stare at them with horror and embarrassment.

"The insurgents were a growing threat to the Design!" Merrick shot back. "We missed our chance to wipe them out completely in the war, so we had to tackle the problem in the past. Seed the Design earlier and more completely, secure a totalized revolution which would make our present perfect, all detractors assimilated or annihilated. It was a perfect solution!"

"But you couldn't know what your fiddling with time would produce!" Reissen barked, undaunted, "and now it's all unraveling. The very thing you were trying to prevent. How dare I speak to you like this? How dare you risk our lives, our world over a delusional, megalomaniacal obsession!"

For once in his life, Merrick was lost for words, but the sudden silence was torn apart by the buzzing of the comm on Reissen's desk. The professor snatched it up.

"Yes?" he demanded, his face still hot, his eyes on Merrick.

He hesitated, his face clouding.

"What is it?" Merrick demanded.

Reissen set down the comm somberly and spoke, looking the director squarely in the face.

"There has been a series of explosions at the incubation facility," he said.

"What?" Merrick said again, quieter this time, as if in disbelief. He caught himself and managed to add, "Status?"

"The structure is partially collapsed," said the professor, his face hard. "And burning."

Merrick stared at him, as if he didn't understand the words. He waited for more invective from the professor but he just looked at him, as if this proved everything he had been saying, that this was all Merrick's fault.

Taking refuge in activity, Merrick glanced at the tech who was monitoring a bank of controls to the left of the sealed tunnel mouth.

"Recall the agents," he said. "The past will have to wait."

The stunned tech pulled herself together and nodded.

"Entering order now," she said, tapping keys.

"Let me know the moment any of them—" Merrick began, but the tech cut him off.

"Excuse me, sir," she said, her brow furrowed. "It seems that one of them is already returning."

Merrick still looked dazed by the news of the explosion but managed a grim nod.

"At least some of our people know how to follow orders after all," he observed bitterly.

But even as he said it, he saw the confusion in the tech's face, the way she shook her head fractionally, and he knew the recall could not have been processed that quickly. He opened his mouth to object, but in that instance the tunnel opened with a blue-white flash that came rippling along its walls, making the shadows in the hangar leap and rearrange themselves. The professor shaded his eyes against the glare, then put his hands to his ears as the great motorcycle roared down the steel tube, braking hard so that its tires skidded and smoked.

It was Vrubel. Even without her identification code on the monitor he knew her bike, her crimson helmet. She had rigged the handlebars of her cycle with what looked like a series of long tubes, and as the bike came to a full stop, she twisted them around and one of them coughed, belching a flash of flame and smoke.

And then the room exploded.

Bowie didn't bother to reload the grenade launcher. He slid from the saddle without removing the red helmet, and strode through the smoke like a nemesis, his shotgun raised. He fired once, then again, as the guards leaped into action, but he had halved their number before they realized they were even under attack. Now they dropped behind monitors and stanchions, drawing their weapons and firing, half blinded by the smoke and the concussive force of the blast. Bowie pivoted, reloading, and cut another down. A tech, unarmed, made a desperate run at him but he swung the heel of the shotgun butt into his face hard and he crumpled without a sound. Not missing a beat, he turned, re-chambered the shotgun, and fired again, then discarded the weapon and drew Four Nine's juicer.

He moved with the thoughtless economy of a trained soldier, his mind switched to a mode of operation that made him as close to the machines he had once fought as he could become. It was easier that way. His enemy had been off guard, never dreaming something like this might happen, but they were moving into the same mode now, their training kicking in and taking over. Bowie made a crouching run to a bank of computer terminals, rounded it and fired once, catching one of the guards in the throat. He went over in a fine spray of blood, just as the terminal Bowie was behind exploded, hit by a rapid fusillade from across the room.

Bowie slid behind a kiosk and returned a quick burst of his own that took down another one of the guards. A second burst scattered three more who were trying to improve their positions, clipping one of them. He knew just how devastating even a graze from one of these energy weapons could be. He had seen it. An image of Sandra Rossi lying on the floor of the Texas School Book Depository flashed into his mind, and he fired again, a long stream of furious and devastating brilliance which cut down another guard and blew the lights out of the mission status display.

A stream of compact directional energy came back at him, cutting a line in the wall behind him, like a dozen lightning strikes arcing through the air. The juicers made no more than a ratcheting series of clicks, but the pulses burned holes through the wallboard and dug deep into the concrete behind. They also showed exactly where the shooter was hiding. Bowie pulled a flap on his tactical jacket and removed a black metal cylinder not much larger than a D cell battery. He pulled the pin from the top and rolled it across the room like a bowling ball. It popped with a white flash, and as the guard burst out, one arm of his tunic aflame, Bowie put him down with his juicer.

There was only one guard left. He was crouched behind an exhaust manifold beyond the bike's launch pad. There would be techs, and he had seen Professor Reissen dive for cover, but they wouldn't be armed and would only be a threat if they tried to be heroes. Bowie checked the power display on the side of his juicer. It was down to its indicator light: maybe three sustained seconds of fire. He had four rounds left in the revolver. The automatic holstered on his thigh would give him another ten shots, but he was in enemy territory now, and he had to assume an alarm had been raised. More guards would be arriving soon.

He tugged the helmet from his head and dropped it.

The final guard peered around the manifold and squeezed off a stream of lightning bolts from his juicer. Something behind Bowie burst and a shower of white-hot fragments rained down around him. He knew he was safe for the moment where he was, but time was not on his side. He let the juicer hang from its strap around his neck and drew his revolver. He rolled to the right toward the heavy storage cabinets which housed some of the period equipment, and as he got into the open, he fired once. His target ducked back behind the manifold, and as soon as he did so, Bowie halted and backtracked as silently as he could. He waited, one, two, three seconds, then rolled out to the left. The guard had moved clear of the manifold and was aiming at the cabinets where he assumed Bowie was hiding.

One bullet was all it took.

There was a sudden silence in the hangar.

"Show yourself, Professor," said Bowie. "Come on. I'm not going to wait all day."

Slowly, hands above his head, Professor Reissen stood up. His face was blanched and blotchy, his eyes wild, and his mouth was opening and closing, babbling.

"I'm unarmed. I never meant . . . I was just following orders. You can go. I can help you get out of here . . ."

Bowie sighted along the barrel of his pistol.

"How does it work?" he demanded.

"What . . . ? I don't understand . . ."

"How do you open the portal?" Bowie said.

The professor gaped, baffled, head shaking.

"That's what you want to know?" he stammered.

"Yes. How does it work?"

"You wouldn't understand," Reissen replied.

"So you said before," said Bowie. "Don't underestimate me."

"Well, the portal is triggered by the device embedded in the controls of the time rider vehicles . . ."

"How?"

"It's a quantum singularity which disrupts the space-time continuum."

"How exactly, and made by who?"

"What?" said Reissen. He was fidgeting now, his fingers fluttering, eyes flashing around like a cornered animal as his discomfort increased.

"Who devised it?"

"Our scientists have long been working on a device, which—"

"You said terrorists built it first. That we were just fixing what they had created."

"Right," said the professor, remembering. "Yes, well, they must have gotten access to our research and—"

"You're lying," said Bowie, cocking the revolver.

"All right! Don't shoot!" Reissen exclaimed. "There are no temporal terrorists. We created the problems ourselves when we tried to change the past to perfect the future."

"Still lying!" said Bowie, louder this time.

"It's true!"

"Who built the device? The first one?"

"Well, I . . . I worked with several colleagues, other people, but . . . I made the first one."

"Then tell me how it works!" Bowie demanded.

"I told you, there's a quantum singularity which—" Bowie fired the penultimate round in his revolver inches over Reissen's head. The man shrunk into a crouch, whimpering. "All right!" he exclaimed. "I don't know how it works! We didn't build it. It came from— "

Bowie recognized the anticlimactic popping sound only after the hole appeared in Reissen's head. There was a spray of red matter, and he dropped lifeless to the floor. Bowie turned to see Director Merrick swinging the guard's juicer from the dead professor to him.

"You are even more short-sighted and simple-minded than I could have predicted," said Merrick, that familiar smile of dry amusement crinkling the corner of his mouth. "I wondered where you were. It never occurred to me that, after all you have witnessed, you would do anything as asinine as coming back here to die. I thought for sure you would stay in the past with the other Gamma animals."

"You know nothing," Bowie replied. "Your arrogance blinds you. That's why you don't understand the past. You and your Design have forgotten everything before the war. On purpose. You turned your back on what the world was, and now you are trying to change it, but you don't even know from what, what that past looked like, how it felt, what the people were like."

"Why would we care about such things?" Merrick replied. "The present and the future of the Design is all that counts."

"Whose present? Whose future?"

"What?"

"Who is giving you the orders?" Bowie pressed. "Who is really in charge, Merrick?"

"Why don't your ask your brother," said Merrick, and he fired again.

Bowie ducked easily, but knew he had only moments before deadly reinforcements arrived.

"Why kill Kennedy?" he demanded.

"It was necessary to accelerate the Design."

"People will know it wasn't just Oswald," said Bowie. "They'll catch him and they'll know he couldn't have pulled it off by himself, and they'll ask questions, connect the dots . . ."

"Leading to time travelers from the future?" Merrick scoffed. "We have ensured they have something better suited to their limited worldview. I assume your lady friend also perished?" He grinned, that same soulless grin that said who he was and what he valued.

Bowie gritted his teeth.

"How sad this all must be for you!" Merrick concluded. "All you have done is delay the inevitable and increase the body count."

"How did your attack on their capital go?" asked Bowie.

"We'll find another way," said Merrick, but Bowie could see the rage beneath the mask. "The Design lives on. Praise to the Design."

And again Merrick fired.

Bowie ducked back behind a terminal but, on impulse, kept moving, emerging on the other side. Merrick didn't realize he was there until Bowie had him in his sights, and as the director spun and tried to drag the deadly stream of his juicer over to him, Bowie held his ground and fired once, neatly, precisely.

Merrick's head kicked back, and a great change came over his face as the life left him.

Bowie stood up and checked the doors. The place would be swarming with guards in seconds. He didn't have much time, none to savor his victory over Merrick. Fortunately, Zero Four Nine had primed the explosives for him. He set the cumbersome charges on the launch pad and gave himself twenty seconds. As his bike roared to life, he felt the ping of Sefton's receiver in his pocket but ignored it, focusing his attention on the portal.

As the time vortex opened and Bowie leaned down over the fuel tank, the bike rocketing forward and backward through time, he caught the momentary flash and the ripple of the shock wave behind him, as the security facility, hub of the Design's iron grip on the world, tore apart behind him.

It was about time.

CHAPTER TWENTY-NINE

1963

A week later, Bowie sat, half dozing, beside Rossi's bed at Massachusetts General Hospital. She was strapped and bandaged, hooked up to various drips and drugs, but she was alive. Her almost severed arm had been reattached, a procedure first performed, as she had once told him, at that very hospital the previous year. They had survived the firefight in Dallas, and she had survived the surgery. Now there was only the future.

Kennedy had been pronounced dead while she was in the operating room, and by two o'clock, as the president's body was being airlifted back to DC, Oswald was caught and arrested, charged first with the shooting of a police officer he had encountered near the rooming house where Bowie had first seen him, and then with the assassination of John F. Kennedy. Thirty-six hours later, while being transferred from the basement of Dallas police headquarters, and live on national television, Oswald was himself assassinated by local nightclub owner, Jack Ruby.

Clean up, thought Bowie, *albeit ham-fisted, and the kind of solution that raised as many questions as it answered.*

But it was done, that part of it at least. Kennedy was dead, the future had changed course, and the responsibility had been dumped on a strange, nondescript young man with some confused political principles and delusions of grandeur who got in with the wrong people at the wrong time. Perhaps if the world knew the truth something of their dire future might be averted, but even if they knew the truth, how could anyone prove what had really happened?

The papers said nothing of the time agent whose body had been left in the battle-worn sixth floor warehouse of the book depository. Whether he had vanished in some kind of temporal paradox, was spirited away by whomever had fired the actual shots that killed the president, had been collected by other time agents, or some combination of all of those, Bowie couldn't say, and no one else knew enough to be asking the right questions. Oswald had been little more than theater, a sacrificial lamb. Bowie doubted anyone would ever know what had really happened, and in that at least, Merrick had been right. Time agents roaring through history on supercharged motorcycles? It was absurd.

But the attack on the Capitol in Washington DC had not happened. For days, Bowie had monitored the newspapers and the television, but there was nothing. He took some comfort from that. They had failed to protect the president, but they had prevented what would have been another, equally massive event. It felt like an achievement, though there would never be any record of it. Could you call it an achievement if it meant something *didn't* happen? He gave an inward shrug. He had learned from the war that you took your victories where you could find them.

And this is another war . . .

He thought of his brother riding to certain death clinging to a wounded time agent and wondered what had happened next. Perhaps Four Nine had survived, escaped, and might return with a vengeance and a new mission from the Design.

No, he thought, with absolute certainty. *Sefton would not allow that to happen.*

He was, after all, a soldier.

And Bowie had destroyed the temporal launch facility and the security complex in which it sat. The Design had lost a technology it didn't know how to recreate unaided, along with all the people and materials they would need to even attempt a rebuild.

Another victory. A big one.

Rossi had been in and out of consciousness over the last few days. When she heard confirmation that the president had indeed died, she had wept silently. She hadn't been alone in that. Bowie was unprepared for the scale of the mourning from ordinary people. He had chosen Boston because he remembered what Rossi had said about the hospital, but he had been taken off guard by how much the city would be devastated by the death of the president. People cried openly in the street. Parents clung to their children, and the whole area seemed to shut down. Doubtless there were people who had despised Kennedy for his politics or personality, but at least here those voices were silent. Boston felt devastated and, from where Bowie was sitting, so did much of the world, as if on some barely understood level, they felt a sense of connection, of community.

Family though . . .

It was humbling and, in a way he had never considered, humanizing. The president had been a figurehead, a political icon, and a lightning rod for public opinion. Now he seemed at once both more and less than that. Now he seemed like a man, and Bowie, who had barely known anything about him, felt that even he had been touched by the man's death. It was as if grief could be caught from other people, contagious, like a disease.

When he talked to Rossi about it, she smiled sadly and patted his hand, as if he was in the hospital bed, not her.

"Look at that," she remarked, smiling softly, "the robot has a soul."

He smiled too, but the word rolled around in his head like a loose bearing.

Soul.

He still wasn't sure what it meant, having heard it used in a variety of ways. It suggested both feeling and spirit, the deepest and most real part of a person, but also something somehow distinct from mind and heart. It was what made people who they were, and what survived them after death.

Bowie wasn't sure he believed in it, but it bothered him that he had never thought about it until he met her, and the more he wrestled with it, the more he came back to the idea that had wormed its way into his mind as he hiked through the deserts of New Mexico in 1947: the world he had come from had no soul. The Alphas had no soul. He puzzled over the phrase, still unsure what, if anything he was saying by it, but certain that somehow, in some way he could not properly comprehend, it was true, and that it was central to all they had been through.

"Find our mother," Sefton had said.

Why had he said that, and why did the memory come to him now as he thought about souls? He didn't know, but he felt the tug of connection, the yearning for family. He looked out the window at the scores of people milling about, living their lives, persisting despite everything, and he wondered vaguely about buying a camera. Who knew how long he would be here? It might be interesting to capture faces rather than buildings.

He started at Sandra's touch. *Kelly's touch*. He was going to have to get used to that. The Sandra Rossi that this world knew had disappeared from Dallas. And this one, ten years older and lying in a hospital bed in Boston, was awake and considering him thoughtfully. Though her arm was still heavily strapped, some of the color was back in her cheeks and her eyes were alert.

"It isn't over, is it?" she said. "Like you said, it was never about Oswald. There's more, lots more, that we don't know."

"No," he said, wondering how she would respond. "It's not over. The president was only part of a plan that will unfold and refold over the next two hundred years and there is much we have to do to derail it."

Some people would have blanched at that, panicked or just backed away, weary and afraid. Not Kelly O'Malley.

"OK," she said. "What do we have to do?" Bowie stared at her, unsure how to answer, and in the silence she reframed the question. "What are we fighting for?"

He wondered about that, and for a moment he thought of the robotank searching for him in the ruins of an ancient convenience store, and of the Design which resembled them: implacable, relentless, and empty. He looked out the window to the city, the hubbub of ordinary people all carrying their own hopes and fears, dreams and anxieties . . .

"Everything," he said. "The future of humanity. Mind. Body." He hesitated, then added, "Soul."

She watched him in silence for a few seconds, then reached with her good arm and took his hand.

"So we should probably get on that," she said.

He reached in his pocket and withdrew an unopened carton he'd bought at the gift store.

"Cigarette?" he offered.

She smiled but shook her head.

"I quit," she replied.

Bowie nodded.

"Thank heaven for small mercies," he said.

EPILOGUE

In 2157, the incubation facility burned. Fire crews fought to contain the blaze, but their dispatch had been hampered by a breakdown in communications as the Director of Security was focused on a separate concurrent incident in the bowels of Central Headquarters. The firefighters were further hampered by the commandant of the facility who insisted on limiting access to only those with top ranking security clearances. By the time the various political disputes over who could enter the engulfed building had been resolved, it was too far gone, and efforts shifted from an attempt to save the structure to one of limiting damage to surrounding buildings.

The cause of the fire was ultimately unknown. The official report cited electrical problems rooted in recent failures of the power grid and called for closer monitoring of the Gamma-run electricity farms where the fault had first appeared. Rumors of spent ammunition found in the structure, of explosive residue, and of the removal of bodies of both Gamma laborers and Alpha armed forces, were dismissed as insurgent propaganda.

Officially, the Design had suffered the kind of unfortunate disappointments which were natural in a society which relied on a sub-optimal class of workers who could not look after themselves and had proved incapable of adhering to safety protocol. The tragic loss of certain Alpha personnel, some of whom were of significant rank, would be memorialized in a televised ceremony celebrating the heroism of men and women who had sacrificed themselves in the service of the state and the preservation of both its people and its values. The Designer himself vowed there would be a prompt rebuilding and cautioned the state against the dangers of complacency.

In the heart of the ruins, specially erected walls were guarded around the clock by a team of the Design's most elite security guards. They screened from prying eyes a single fractured container, metallic and upright, large enough to hold an adult human.

The walls protected the container from the cleanup personnel that were working around it at the damaged site, but they did not shield it from the tiny camera mounted in the ceiling above, which still peered down on VAT-001. It was connected to an ancient network of servers, recently brought back online by Sefton's band of Gamma insurgents, Greta in particular, through which it was transmitting its live feed of the container. When Bowie had returned to 2157, he was unaware that Sefton's receiver device—still powered on as promised—had connected to that server and downloaded the feed.

But Bowie was aware of it now, his eyes fixed on its tiny screen as he sat in Sandra's hospital room in 1963. He saw smoke, and as it cleared he saw the vault marked VAT-001.

The Originator.

The vault was heavily damaged, its barely connected door hanging at an odd angle, and there was a body inside, but Bowie had no way of knowing whether it had perished in the fire or before. Either way, it appeared to have also been damaged by the fire, but the heat and flames alone could not account for the strange condition of the corpse. It was thin, and small, save for the head which was disproportionately large. Its skin was a pale and silvery gray. The facial features were minimal, barely discernible, though the eyes were large, glossy, and black. Whether it was male or female was impossible to tell from the footage. Nor was its age.

Bowie stared as he watched the contents of VAT-001 being carefully lifted out of the vault and placed in a new container by what he assumed were Alpha personnel in protective suits. Then they shifted out of frame.

Bowie could guess the rest. A new lab would be constructed, if one hadn't been already, and that body, the Originator, would be relocated there. It had, after all, shaped humanity's past. There was no reason to assume that being dead meant it could not continue to shape their future.

Bowie would see about that.

THE END